"THROWIN' BRICKS AT THE PENITENT...

Chapter One

"Da Pick Up"

No one eva told me hustlin' dose streets was like throwin' bricks at da penitentiary,which unfortunately could land a bitch of my standards damn near a life sentence. Well I'm Queenie Miles living da fabulous ecstasy life of a Kingpin only difference was between me and 'em,I had female runnin' threw my bloodline. Who would have eva thought drugs would be my life,my choice of hustlin'? Now as a child Queenie wondered how she could become rich befo' she turned 18 years old Da girl had plenty of ideas an 'er entrepreneur skills were one an expertise. To be wut chu would think of as, a sweet innocent kid of only 15 years of age.

Hot summer of 89' when all da kids at Queenie's age were out jumpin' double dutch,ridin' bikes,runnin' 'round playin' catch-a-girl kiss-a-girl or bein' hot in da ass,Queenie had utter shit on 'er mind an a millionaire status goal to accomplish. Instead of chasin' behind a nigga to get his attention,when da time presented itself Queenie knew how it would play out. Only one nigga had an could hold 'er attention. Level, but to Queenie it seemed like he didn't have interest in 'er. Which only made Queenie think harder. "Okay Level its not how hard chu work, its how smart chu work at wut chu do." Queenie thought to 'er self. "Aiight I ain't sweatin' dat kid he will see me." She said to no one particular. Queenie knew to a certain extent, Level was no where on dat horizontal plane,wit da height she had,but it was cool fo' 'em to be a normal kid especially if Queenie's plan would work out to 'er advantage.

Queenie some one yelled makin' 'er snap back out of 'er day dreamin' stage dat she was havin' 'bout Level. "Yo' wutsup?" A yell hit 'er attention again comin' from downstairs. "Girl wut chu doin'?" Someone was takin' two steps at a time to reach 'er it was 'er cousin Tez it was time fo' 'em to ride out. "Damn nigga hold da fuck on I gotta get my loot." Queenie exclaimed. Prepared fo' da day Queenie placed 10 stacks in 'er pocket as pocket change. Exchangin' eye contact wit Tez. She asked. "Nigga wut we ridin' in? Yo' ol' school Chevy drop or my new school SE5600 Benz?"Wit a grin on'er face."Yo' shit, Queenie chu went an copped dat shit?" Tez asked wit his fist bald to his mouth,hurry up I need to see dat shit. Cuz dat shits out back,tossin' 'em da keys. Afta' she finish placin' $30,000 in a red and black Nike duffel bag. Queenie jetted down da stairs yellin' yo' ma I'm out. Reachin' fo' da back door knob,she saw 'er mother at da kitchen sink. 'Er mother turned 'round dryin' 'er hands off asked; Wut time will chu be back? I'm not actually sho',but don't worry I will make it to school in da mornin' on time. Queenie was takin' an accountin' class ova da summer, on top of hustlin' and bein' da star point guard in da summer basketball tournaments."I know I ain't gotta worry 'bout chu makin' it to school 'cus chu tryin' to floss dat new fly ass ride chu jus' got." Ma do I detect a slight hint of jealousy? Queenie asked. Befo' Liz could respond, Queenie told 'er ma don't sweat da small happy meal. Jus' let me handle my biz' an I'll get chu dat new joint chu want next Saturday. And chu to will have a fresh joint in front of yo' house. Queenie was an only child 'er moms and pops were split up afta' she turned 2 years old. 'Er pops was ghost, dude neva looked back,dis made Liz fend on 'er own fo' da 2. Liz neva sold drugs she may have done a few in 'er days,but far as distributin' neva. Liz was always a hard workin' parent, always holdin' down at least 2 jobs to make ends meet fo' Queenie and 'er self. Queenie respected and admired 'er moms fo' dat reason alone.

Knowin' dat she could always depend on 'er moms fo' wut eva,but was neva da one to put pressure on Liz jus' to keep da stress off 'er moms, was of course one reason Queenie turned to da street life. Turnin' 'er back diggin' in 'er pocket,Queenie came at 'er moms wit a stack,kissin' 'er on da forehead. "Dis is fo' chu go buy yo' self somethin' nice today its hot out,treat yo'self I'll be back late." Tryin' to get out da door befo' da questions started up again or Liz tried to give da money back. "Queenie baby be safe,chu all I got." Without turnin' 'round,Queenie responded. "Aiight ma." Hearin' da sincere in 'er moms voice. "I'm out." Closin' da door behind Queenie,Liz said a silent prayer fo' 'er only child to be protected,befo' she went back to doin' 'er befo' Queenie entered da room.

"Nigga why da fuck chu blastin' my sub woofers chu tryin' to have my moms noisy ass neighbors call da po-po's?" Queenie shouted. Nah fam',but I didn't eva think chu was gone bring yo' crazy ass out da damn house. Tez said;askin' all in one breath girl wut da fuck took yo' ass so long? "Yo' nigga I had to make sho' my ol' g was straight. Hell did chu do da same befo' chu left da crib?"Queenie asked. "Tez I told chu 'bout dat shit dude,dese is da only ma'fuckas we got and we all dey got. We both got no good ass sperm donors,so as hard as dey bust their asses to take care of us nigga stop bein' cheap an take care of yo' moms. Damn chu da fuckin' nigga, chu would think dat would be yo' first priority,yo' moms. Man dude I don't want to have dis press conference wit chu again cuz. Look no disrespect we family cuz, chu older dan me." Queenie retorted continuin' 'er statement she spoke; "Listen I look up to chu like a big brother an even doe chu got a girl in yo' life right now, dat woman inside dat house an auntie are da only 2 women in our lives dat mean us any good an when dey are gone,we will be lost. Jus' as well,if we departed from 'em do to dese streets 'ere dat will be a heart breaker fo' 'em. So cuz step up and do da right thing. Queenie told 'em listen I ain't tryin' to tell chu how to run or manage yo' money,but I'm tellin' chu how to treat my auntie fam' dat's all. Now lets get outta 'ere, I'm guessin' yo' ass decided wut whip we pushin' huh? "Wit out a doubt." Queenie said wit a smile on 'er face. Tez bobbin' his head to "Da D.O.C tape NO ONE CAN DO IT BETTER." Yo' Ueenie pull dat shit out we runnin' behind schedule. Imma pull in yo' spot 'til we get back,I don't want my shit left on da street. Queenie felt like da Queen she was,wit da mind of da most intelligent person dere lived. Da best dressed to out dress da most classy an soon to be da richest bitch sittin' on top of a Kingpins throne. Parkin' in da middle of da street,openin' da drivers door leavin' it wide open Queenie walked 'round to da passenger side of da car,getting in. Tez hopped in also askin'; “Yo' cuz chu ready adjustin' da seat to fit his persona. Queenie said yeah,but chu know wut chu gotta do befo' we leave right?” Nigga yeah,Ueenie I know we finna stop by moms crib first. Tez replied.Yo' girl chu better be glad chu my lil' cuz an as close a nuff to be my lil' sister 'cus utter wise dat shit chu be lettin' fly outta ya mouth sideways,puttin' chu in yo' place wouldn't be a problem. Tez told 'er. “Nigga yeah,but chu know I ain't no docile lil' bitch. Imma keep it real wit chu fam'. Once dey dropped off $1500 to Tez moms,their next stop was East St. Boogie. Befo' turnin' off da Clark exist Queenie reached ova fo' da remote to change da music,searchin' fo' MC LYTE tape, Queenie stated; Yo' Tez hit dat Krystal's ova dere,my stomach touchin' my back fam'.Yo' ya can call dude while we eat. Let his ass know we 'ere. An come to think of it nigga why we make it to dis ma'fucka right on time? When from da time we left both of us already knew dat time wasn't our friend. Tez smiled an dropped his head wit out 'em sayin' a word. Queenie said; nigga how fast da fuck was chu goin'? Listen fam' damn, I jus' got dis joint let me blow da motor in dis bitch first cuz. Queenie said. Be glad I was sleep 'cus if chu woulda hit dat shit while my eyes were open,I woulda made it my biz' to connect wit yo' jaw cuz. “Tez replied; yo' Queenie Imma let chu have dat lil' girl.

Lil' girl was wut he called Queenie when she crossed da line wit 'em. Away of lettin' 'er know to chill da fuck out 'cus she's ova steppin' 'er boundries. Knowin' jus' how far to take it wit Tez ,in acceptable she did have a line to cross back ova. Queenie changed da subject back to business . So wutsup wit yo' nigga Cortez' is he ready to see us or wut? Queenie asked. Stuffin' his mouth wit chicken rings,Tez said yeah he wants us to meet 'em at da college. He'll be parked in lot c,row 5,spot

120.Washin' his food down wit a orange soda, he said he'll be dere in 30 minutes. Aiight,Queenie said dat gives us 'bout 15 minutes to finish up 'ere. Listen cuz, Queenie retorted. "I don't mean to be seemin' like I'm disrespectin' chu an shit 'cus dat car don't mean shit to me nigga, I can buy a nutter one an better,but chu know where my head is an wut I'm really tryin' to do out 'ere. Yeah nigga I know I am only 15,but I thought we were on da same level,da same page? Tez I've heard all of yo' concerns 'bout me bein' in da game specially 'cus of da fact I am a female. Trust and believe I respect chu cuz,but chu also gotta respect my decision fo' bein' out in 'em streets. I won't let no nigga stop me from reachin' my goal of becomin' a millionaire by time I turn 18,now chu know I got much love fo' chu Tez. I'll neva cut chu off,but I'll damn sho' cut chu loss fam'. Now chu either gone be wit me or ya goin' against me,Queenie exclaimed. Tez raised his brow like he wanted to say somethin' utter dan wut he said. Puttin' a fist across da table fo' Queenie to meet wit 'er own fist;chu know chu my nigga 'til da day we die. Chu my lil' nigga Ueenie its ride and die baby,anyway chu know I would have to leave dis earth to, if auntie found out I let anything happen to ya. Now lets go,so we can get outta East St. Boogie we got moves to make. Standin' to his feet Tez hugged Queenie tight. I love chu cuz on da real chu my lil' nigga. Tez whispered in ear shot. "Love ya to fam'." Queenie shot back,now lets be up,we got 20 minutes to get where we need to be. Meetin' Cortez' right on time as dey pulled in next to 'em he was jus' turnin' his ignition off,dey all got out da cars grabbin' duffel bags and back packs da 3 of 'em walkin' into da college like some students dat belonged dere makin' their scene as natural as possible dey all broke out into laughter at da seriousness,Queenie had on 'er face afta' Cortez' said; "Damn Queenie if I didn't know any better I would think chu was tryin' to be da richest young bitch walkin' Chicago streets. "Queenie retorted nigga I am."

Only thing was it was all a joke to Cortez',but da utter 2 knew better , Tez and Queenie knew

"THROWIN' BRICKS AT THE PENITENTIARY"

Cortez' would become a enfeeble King to Queenie's, Queen 'cus she's 'bout to be big as da world wide web. "Yo' nigga why chu got jokes? Lets handle da biz' at hand jokes ova." Curiously, Cortez' nudged Tez. "Yo' peoples how old again?" Tez replied she's 15 nigga why? "Damn dude if chu wasn't my homeboy an biz'ness associate I would get at dat fo' sho'." Look bein' cut off by Tez dats my lil' cuz she's like a fuckin' sister to me mo' dan anything I'm 'er protector in many ways fo' many reason 'cus she's still a kid in age,but as yo' ass can see in body,mind and game status she's mo' woman dan chu know. Yo' dude shameless as it sounds I really don't think ya on 'er scale. I know who and how Queenie gets down,so jus' a fair warnin' bein' blunt wit chu 'cus we boys. If and when chu come at 'er no matter wut dude, don't disrespect 'er in anyway,'cus I will be at yo' ass homeboy. Cortez' thought 'bout it an said aiight. I gotta hit da lil' boys room (bathroom) a que fo' Tez to follow 'em an Queenie to go find a table in da cafeteria closet to da doorway leadin to da hallway.

Once da guys were in da bathroom an da stalls were checked makin' sho' da coast was clear dey locked da door behind 'em. Cortez' went straight into biz'ness mode. I brought 60 bricks wit dat said wut chu lookin' to get he asked. 25 Tez replied. "So I take it beautiful wants 25 also? "Queenie may want da extra 10,but I ain't in 'er pockets so really can't tell ya 'bout dat fam'". Lets jus' handle dis an she can come an talk to chu 'bout wut moves she gone make. Tez replied. Fam' don't be in 'ere pushin' up on Queenie like dat 'cus right now she all 'bout biz'ness,so if chu ain't tryin' to get shitted on jus' stick to da biz' at hand. "I got chu, send 'er in Cortez' spat." Queenie looked ova 'er shoulder befo' enterin' da men's bathroom. Givin' one tap Cortez' opened da door and locked it back afta' she walked in. "Wutsup?" It took y'all a minute to conduct biz',thought cuz might have got nauseous at da price chu fed 'em. Queenie stated. "Nah, we boys chu know how dat shit goes,I got 'em regardless." Queenie had a thought; yeah nigga I got chu she made a mental note fo' later to get at cuz 'bout his friend. "So wutsup shawty? Wut chu tryin' to spend?" Queenie cut 'em off in mid-sentence nigga look wut chu got wit chu? She asked. "Already know wut I asked fo',so I know my meal ticket an I'm hip to da fact dat chu brought mo' wit chu so wutsup?" Queenie said nigga my time is money an right now yo' ass wasted a nuff of it. "I'm tryin' to get da fuck up outta East St. Boogie,so I can touch my streets of Chi-Town baby boy." Well look I got yo' 25 an 10 extra so ya tell me wut chu wanta do. Queenie calculated a second, she knew wut was in 'er pocket an wut appeared inside da duffel bag which made 'er $3000 short of getting all 35 bricks,so she had to think quick on 'er toes, to see if dis nigga would trust 'er." One thing fo' sho' she knew she wanted all 35 an two was fo' certain either way it went she was leavin' up outta dat stall wit all 35 of 'em. "Aiight, Queenie asked so if I get all of 'em wuts my ticket fam'? "Queenie is da only 15 years old I eva seen wit so much heart. She feared nothin' or no one,she was very mischievous,manipulative an when da time presented itself she knew how to put down a mean flirtatious game." Look Imma jus' be blunt wit chu. No need fo' stunts 'cus I can't do da fake shit. She stated; $35,000 wuts on me so dat leave $8000 in da balance, chu can either trust me to fed ex yo' paper ova night or chu could hook me up wit a flat thousand fo' each an my word is bond I'll be back Friday fo' 45 bricks. "Befo' Cortez' could say a word, Queenie said nigga I'm good fo' it, wut chu need a cosigner or some shit?" Battin' dose sexy hazel brown eyes,placin' a smile on 'er face showin' off 'er dimples. "Nah shawty I know chu good. Cortez' told 'er;shit I jus' wish we had met on a different compound. "Why is dat?" Queenie asked. Playin' da game wit 'em dat he thought he had down all to well. Keepin' it real wit chu Queenie chu is a Queen,so yeah yo' name fits in all da right places shawty. Chu are a dime piece an truth be told chu have no reason in my point of view; chu shouldn't be hustlin' in da streets. Da venturesome dat yo' ass takin' wit yo' life,is of wut value to chu shawty? Cortez' asked. I'm not finna preach to chu 'cus dat's not a vendetta I want wit chu. Jus' sayin' shawty be careful out 'ere prison don't discriminate 'cus chu a female. “Man dey lockin' ma'fuckas up, niggas and bitches an Queenie yo' name out 'ere ringin' bells. “I'm ringin'?” Shawty right now chu “THROWIN' BRICKS AT THE PENITENTIARY” fam'. I won't front I like chu shawty in mo' ways dan one,so it's all part of da game dat I give chu heads up. “Listen on good measure shawty Imma roll wit yo' proposition of a thousand flat,I like yo' professionalism an chu kill 'em wit dat pretty ass smile.” Aiight cool Queenie replied. Switchin' da money from 'er bag to Cortez' an da dope to 'ers. Queenie said on da way out to da car, I'll get dat $8000 from Tez to give to chu 'cus I don't like bein' in debt to anyone specially when it comes to biz'ness.

“I won't fritter wit chu 'cus I know it's neva nothin' personal jus' biz'ness,I'm da same way he exclaimed to Queenie.” At da car Queenie put a bug in Tez's ear 'bout da $8000,which was no problem. Tez pulled da money off da extra $9000 he had brought wit 'em. Jus' in case bread. Tez was always predictable when Queenie was up under 'em like she was attached to his hip. “Queenie made a nutter mental note to break 'er cousin of dat 'cus it was a very bad habit of his. When niggas and bitches knew yo' every move,yo' where 'bouts and wuts in yo' left pocket befo' ya knew it could be dangerous. Tez was a tickin' bomb waitin' to happen,Queenie thought;she be damned if she let 'em be caught slippin'. Yo' Cortez', Queenie said as she walked ova to his car,reachin' fo' da door handle,Queenie sat down in his big body Chevy Classic Capri wit all white plush leather seats. In da head rest was embroider Chief Cortez' in red letterin'. Yo' dis is fly, I guess chu do got taste Queenie stated,as she handed 'em da money. “Shawty I gotta have some type of taste if I gotta an eye fo' chu wouldn't chu say?” He asked. “Still gamin' huh? She asked. Not a game shawty _well listen. Bein' cut off by Queenie;if yo' game is as legit as ya tryin' to press it to be,den when da time is right chu jus' may get yo' chance.

"THROWIN' BRICKS AT THE PENITENTIARY"

"Queenie I'm serious I need chu as my Queen,sittin' next to my Kings throne." Hell only thing was Cortez' didn't know wit or wit out 'em,Queenie had a plan in motion to sit on top of da Kings throne.

"I see chu next week." Queenie produced a smile an dat beautiful trade mark of a dimple appeared. Hoppin' into 'er Benz. Yo' switch seats I'll push it back. Cool, Tez replied. "Yo' Ueenie chu feelin' soft fo' dat nigga Cortez'?" He turned wit a raised brow in da passenger seat tryin' to read his lil'cuz. "Nah nigga chu know how I do it's all biz'ness wit me I ain't thinkin' 'bout no nigga right now, but to keep it raw wit chu, yo' boy is feelin' me. Yeah he is he told me how he felt,so I knew he would try his hand ,but I also forewarned his ass dis was not da right time 'cus chu kept biz'ness away from personal." "Yo' its all good cuz it worked out good in our favor."

"Wut chu mean Queenie?" Tez looked at his lil' cousin without a word Tez knew da girl had a gift of gab an at anytime she could work ova da (Pope) if need be.

"Wut chu mean, wut I mean?" She asked. "Nigga yo' ass gotta idea wut I did,we come from da same bloodline ain't no future in it if it ain't da 2 of us. "I got dat nigga to drop dat shit to a stack flat,each brick. Okay,okay I see chu cuz,wit his fist to his lips oooooh! Girl I knew chu had da ultimate gift fo' gab,but fo' chu to break Cortez' down dat low fam' chu da shit. Lets get dis shit back to da streets of Chi-Town.Tez chuckled lightly in amusement. "Yo' fam its somethin' else yo' boy spat at me wit seriousness. "Tez I need chu to find out da word on da streets fo' me fam'." Find out wut? Tez asked. Wut did he say to chu he demanded mo' dan a question. "Cortez' told me my name ringin' in da streets,its gotta be some truth to it somewhere if niggas know of me in East St. Boogie chu feel me?" Ueenie chu know I got chu, its good he put chu up on dat,so chu already know I'm all ova it. I will find out.

“THROWIN' BRICKS AT THE PENITENTIARY”

Chapter Two
“Streets Talking”

Tez made a phone call as Queenie was turnin' on to I 57 North head back to da city of Chicago.

“Hello.” “ Wuts up Lu?” Who da fuck is dis?Lu asked tryin' to catch da voice. “Yo nigga calm da fuck down,its Tez nigga. Lu was Tez best friend and right hand man,da only nigga he would give his left hand to or fo',but if no one knew better dey would think Queenie was his right hand man. Of course dere is a difference between da 2 besides of their gender. Lu was mo' like Tez solja as where Queenie was his equal. Knowin' 'er feisty ass wouldn't have it any utter way,besides 'er bein' sweet and vicious she was also a spoiled brat. “No ones fault utter dan Tez.” Queenie didn't know of 'er father,so Tez always took up da slack at Christmas time or he would step in at 'er basketball tournaments. Tez knew dat his auntie Liz, Queenie's mother was always strugglin' to jus' keep a roof ova their heads,jus' like his mom was tryin' to do fo' 'em. So once Tez stepped in da streets he vowed to take care of da most 3 important women in his life,(meaning his mother ,auntie and Queenie) no doubt. “Lu listen to me good fam',Tez stated.Fam' I need chu to put yo' ear to da streets. “Wuts good fam',chu know I got chu. But is it anything in particular I'm listen fo'?” Lu asked. I need to know if cuz name ringin' out dere in 'em streets. “Yo' fam I knew it was somethin' I needed to tell chu. Yeah Queenie name out dere bad bro. “Why da fuck chu ain't call me an tell me nigga?” Damn fam' stop screamin'_a nigga gotta hangover from last night,dat's why I hadn't called jet. Lu said I jus' heard last night. I was at da 50 Yard Line off in Harvey,dat's when I ova heard 2 bitches talkin' to 4 niggas,when Queenie's name came up. “So wut was da convo 'bout nigga,get to it Tez voice raised wit frustration from Lu actin' like he was still drunk as hell.” Yo' fam' ova da music all I could hear wit out bein' detected dat I knew 'er was dat fo' Queenie to be a kid she always papered up an how she pushin' a brand new off da showroom floor SE5600 Benz. One of da niggas said dis bitch moms ain't keepin' 'er caked up 'cus she has to work two jobs to make ends meet. Tez blood was boilin' at dis point_who was da nigga fam'? "I've neva seen dis nigga befo',he seemed to be a baller,he was draped in gold,da nigga was drivin' a black and gold Chevy Capri sittin' up on all gold datin's an a boomin' ass sound system, da works. "Did chu catch da plates at all nah,my nigga da alcohol had me consumed fam',Lu said. Aiight wut else was said,Tez asked. "Don't kill da messenger,but da nigga told da 2 girls,so da bitch thinks she's all of dat an a sack lunch huh?" Da next thing was a shocker. Well bring dat bitch to me one way or da utter she will be set down. If not by choice by force,'cus I be damn if she eats off my city wit out breakin' bread. Da girls he were talkin' to couldn't of been no older dan Queenie. 'Cus I did hear one of 'em say she played ball on da same team as Queenie. "Find out dat bitches name, Lu an get back at me fam'."

Once off da phone_ Yo' Ueenie its true,Lu said he was at da 50 last night,2 bitches and 4 niggas were havin' a discussion 'bout chu. "On wut level,Queenie asked wit venom in 'er voice." Tez told 'er some nigga Lu has neva seen befo' dat drivers a black and gold Chevy sittin' on all gold Datin's, draped in gold basically says, he wants chu out of da game,'cus its not a nuff room fo' a youngan of yo' status in Chicago. It was also a female who told da dude she was on da same basketball team as chu. "Who?" Queenie asked. Baby girl I don't know,but we will get to da bottom of it befo' tomorrow and dat's on da women I love. "Who da fuck has a vendetta wit me?" Queenie spoke out loud,further mo' I don't fuck wit bitches on any level fam' chu know dat. Yeah I know,but 'til we get all da info jus' stay cool. Afta' I get da drop of dis dude where 'bouts an I give chu ol' girls name chu can handle dat bitch yo' self an I will dispose of dude all together. Yo' ya not worried is chu? Tez asked Queenie. "Nah nigga fo' wut I'm not even in da streets like dat my biz'ness is conducted very well. I got ma'fuckas older dan both of us put together,who only fucks wit weight. Da only nigga workin' da stash house is Chaos an dat's family. Dese ma'fuckas are vets,so fo' one of 'em niggas to turn vixen on me now I couldn't see it. Queenie told Tez.

"Let me handle it Ueenie. I'll check out everyone dat works fo' chu even family." I won't rest 'til I get da answers I'm seekin',know dat baby girl. Existin' da Dan Ryan off on Taylor street headed fo' da West side_Queenie asked;so wut do chu think I need to do?" Should I hold off puttin' dis shit out or go on like I don't have a clue as to wuts goin' on? "Nah,fam' I want chu to continue to do chu,but fo' every move chu make let me know. Outside da house dat is,Tez exclaimed. "Fo' sho' fam',but as soon as chu find out dat bitch name I want to know." I gotta game at 7pm tomorrow night an if she plays ball wit me I definitely needs to know. I can't be feelin' all uncomfortable throwin' my game off an shit. Yeah I know fo' a female chu got a sweet as shot,baby girl dat's gone take chu along way away from 'ere. "So I can count on chu to be dere?" "Come on nigga ain't I always dere?"Tez replied,hell wit all dis new shit been added to da plate,word is bond nigga I'm dere front row.

"Queenie pulled to da back of 'er stash house,where dere was a big ass privacy fence dat surrounded da whole backyard all da way to da pavement of da alley. Da stash house wasn't to shabby,but not to da point it had to have a big privacy fence connected to it,but da reason fo' dis was to keep Queenie stash house safe,safe and discreet from nosy on lookers,called neighbors. Only utter person who know 'bout da safe would be Tez do to da fact he also had one in da same backyard. Dis was where dey stashed all of their dope and money. Da safes were safely built into da ground,Queenie décor da backyard, so it was very impossible to detect da safe an if chu did, dere was no way of removin' 'em or their continents dat laid inside. "Wit a safe in each corner of da yard Queenie designed Tez side wit a phony garden wit a rose vine bush goin' up long side of da wall of da privacy fence. All he had to do was touch da fifth rose an his garden started to lift in da air 'bout 4 feet high. Now Queenie's safe was designed wit voice active done only by 'er cell phone wit certain words fo' da combo. To disguise it she set a sand box next to two lawn chairs fo' loungin',once activated da safe it would rise from underneath da sand. All at da cost of $20,000,money was no object. "Yo' cuz we need to see dude Friday again. Queenie questioned do chu think yo' ass be ready fam'?" Yo' I'm on top of it,but why so soon Ueenie? Tez asked wit a suspicious look on his face(like inquiring minds wanted to know). "It's part of da stipulation/proposition on my behalf an my word is bond. Sho' chu right baby girl,I see chu have been listenin' to my teachin'. My talkin' has not jus' been in vain. "Nah nigga it hasn't. I can say I've learned from da best. "Queenie told 'er big cousin strokin' his ego. Takin' a step closer in ear shot she told Tez;but nigga step to da side cuz 'cus I am da greatest."

Breakin' out into laughter. "Oh so chu got jokes?" Tez asked;but I will not fake da funk wit in a short period I have created a beast,a sexy,sweet and sour beast,jus' don't hurt 'em cuz. "Aiight I feel chu I'll be on point. Jus' be cautious wit it at all times,even of our so call family. Tez said wit mo' seriousness in his voice;'cus I hate to put one of dese niggas underneath fo' tryin' to fuck ova chu. We to close fo' all dat I already feel responsible fo' chu under my wing,so to snatch chu from up under me is like pluckin' my feathers. Tez said dese niggas is not tryin' to see me baby girl. "Walkin' threw da back door of da stash house walkin' up da stairs,reachin' fo' da door knob dey heard Blue and Red barkin' very viciously,which dey neva did unless dey were 'bout to attack. Only utter person dat could control da dogs was Chaos. Who was in Detroit makin' a run fo' Queenie an he was not due back in town 'til tomorrow afternoon. Da dogs belong to Tez and Queenie blue and red nose pitts a girl and boy,da male name Blue an he's Queenie's baby,Red's da bitch an 'er owner would be Tez. Tez drew his gun on point as Queenie did da same from behind 'er back,puttin' a finger up to his lips Tez took da lead noticin' da dogs posted in front of da bathroom door. He figured da vic/vics were pin in da bathroom,scared to come out. Tez gave a high screechin' pitch a command da dogs would halt to. Da dogs calmed down still posted,neva lettin' their eyes leave da bathroom door, so dey had a seat. Showin' all teeth,Tez kicked in da bathroom door to find 2 pretty lil' bitches shiverin' standin' in da bathtub,scared as hell. "Queenie chu know dese bitches?" Queenie step wit in eye shot of da girls,knowin' she'd seen da short hair Red Bone somewhere befo',but couldn't quite place 'er face. "Aye where y'all bitches from?" Queenie asked. Red Bone opened 'er mouth to speak. Queenie said bitch I know chu_chu on my team. Dat's chu ain't it nudgin' Tez fo' 'em to make da call an find out da description of da bitch to see if she's da one from da club. "Hello fam' listen to me good an understand me on da first go round. Give me a yes or no when I tell chu da features of dis braud(broad) standin' in my house nigga." Aiight nigga come wit it,Lu said. "Is dis braud a red bone?" "Yeah!" "Does she have a short hair cut?" Yeah! "Is she 'bout 5'7 in height wit a nice ass?" Yup! Now if chu can remember describe da bitch dat was wit 'er dat night. "She's 'bout da same height,black bitch wit pink lips like she has been smokin' to much." "Say no mo' fam' hit chu later." Pressin' end on his phone, Queenie's trigger finger was itchy waitin' fo' da word,so it could be scratched. Tez placed his hand on top of Queenie's lowerin' 'er gun_I got chu baby girl I refuse to let chu fuck up yo' life ova dis. Tez told Queenie in ear shot promise chu get yo' chance. Turnin' his full attention back to da 2 unwanted guest of da house. First off I need to know how ya get in my spot "Bedroom window."Red Bone said wit hesitation,lookin' in Queenie's direction. "Yeah, sweetie well chu should be worried 'cus she's a beast an y'all cross da wrong side of da fence." Playin' an puttin' fear into Red Bone's heart made it all worth it. Honestly chu need to pay attention seein' how I got da nine aimed between yo' eyes. Wouldn't want my finger to slip an splat yo' brains across ya girls face now would we? Sarcastic Tez said; seein' how y'all in my shit it's obvious ya 'ere fo' one reason an dat's to get at baby girl fo' yo' own vicious vendetta correct. Now hold on think befo' chu speak. Tez cut Red Bone off quickly clickin' a bullet in da chamber of his nine. Red Bone swallowed da big lump dat formed in 'er throat,she responded yeah. "Okay y'all might be able to leave 'ere alive afta' all. Now tell me who's da nigga y'all were at da club talkin' to,but befo' chu speak let me refresh yo' memory,so chu won't have any confusion of which nigga since I can since y'all get 'round. Tez says it was a black nigga draped in gold he drives a black and gold Chevy wit all gold Datins. So wuts da niggas name dat wanta take Queenie off da map. "Lets not all speak at once." I can't hear chu Tez shouted. Wuts his name? Triple, dey call 'em Triple. "Aiight so where can I find dis Triple nigga at?"

"W_we don't know where he lives we are jus' suppose to meet 'em back at da 50 Yard Line in Harvey on Saturday night." So wut was da plan fo' yo' asses comin' 'ere? Tez asked. Queenie stood behind 'em between Blue and Red rubbin' da top of their heads fo' comfort, all three of 'em 'er self and da 2 dogs. "Red Bone spoke up da plan was to come 'ere an put da beat down on 'er, she said in a low whisper. "Excuse me ma, yo' chu gotta speak up I can't hear chu. "I said to come 'ere put a beat down on Queenie an give 'er a message to meet Triple at da 50 Saturday at 10:30pm.

Tez lowered his gun. "Aiight since chu bitches 'ere already anyway I'm gone give y'all a pass dis time. Puttin' da gun back on safety an tuckin' it back in his waist line he told Queenie to put da dogs downstairs. "Now chu bitches come out 'ere." As da 2 stepped out of da bathroom,Queenie stepped from behind Tez. Dis wut it is,y'all gone put dat plan in motion,wouldn't want y'all to be 'ere fo' nothin',feel me? It's 2 rules 1.dis will be an ol' school fist fight,2.no matter how it turns out,it will be da end of it. Utter wise y'all will see me an I shoot first,ask questions later. Befo' a response from anyone,Queenie stepped in view stuck Red Bone in da jaw an said bring it bitch. Da pink lip chic felt some type of courage 'cus she grabbed Queenie from behind holdin' 'er arms Red Bone ran up on Queenie. Queenie pushed back,so pink lips leveled against da wall jus' long a nuff fo' Queenie to jump up an boot Red Bone in da chin. Queenie brought 'er feet back to floor an head butted pink lips bustin' 'er shit wide open. Queenie turned 'round grabbin' pink lips by da neck choke slammin' 'er to da floor. While Red Bone struggled to getup on 'er feet,Queenie did a quick combo shot on pink lips face 'til she felt 'er body go limp leavin' 'er unconscious. Befo' Red Bone got 'er self together Queenie kick da ba'jesus out of 'er face sendin' blood flyin' across da room splattin' blood on to Tez Nike t-shirt. "Damn baby girl chu gonna kill 'er wit yo' bare hands. Queenie said dey came 'ere to deaden me,right? "Fam' chu made yo' point dey can't see chu ma,hell afta' dat beatin' dey won't even be able to talk 'bout it. Tez pulled Queenie up embracin' 'er was da only way to stop 'er from throwin' punches. Queenie had blacked out,she was in a world all of 'er own. Tez hugged his cousin tightly in ear shot; "Fam' come back let dat shit go." Tez faced Queenie, "Baby girl snap out of it dese bitches half dead. Queenie snapped out 'er trans. "Take 'em bitches an dump dey ass in da gutter,put dey ass out in da alley by da trash dumpster. Tell 'em count dey blessings I ain't lettin' da dogs at 'em 'cus dey would neva be found 'round dis bitch. Da stash house was sound proof so chu couldn't hear anything from outside,jus' da way Queenie had it designed. "Tez help me pull dese bitches to da alley."

"Yo' fam chu was serious huh?" Lookin' at da cold black empty space in his cousins eyes,he asked no mo' questions an did as she said. Truth be told sometimes she put a lil' fear in Tez heart when she had blackouts. Tez knew people who had blackouts were very unpredictable an Queenie was one of dose people. Dis was not 'er first episode an certainly not da last one. Tez tried to keep his lil' cousin calm an on da right track,so it would be no need fo' 'er to react like an animal. 'Cus Tez knew he created a beast in dis sexy sophisticated young teen. Tez regrets and curses 'em self fo' dat reason.

"She to young fo' dis life style." Queenie spoke up leave dose bitches,hoppin' back in da car dey headed towards Liz crib,it was about 9pm so Queenie knew 'er moms would be at home chillin'. Surprisingly Liz wasn't da house was empty. "Yo' maybe she's still shoppin' wit dat grip I gave 'er earlier." Cool Queenie stated; dat will give me time to clean myself up. Yo' nigga chu know chu got a few new fits in my closet,chu need to get up out dat shit. "Be my fuckin' luck we get pulled ova an chu all bloody,anyway chu don't want moms to come in an chu standin' in da middle of 'er floor covered." Hell nah,auntie will panic on me den da questionin' will start. "Yo' chu can hit da shower first,I'll put on my robe an I can go in afta' chu. Jus' in case moms pops up, we were out ballin'. Before Tez and Queenie left out Tez noticed a note on da table. "Yo' Ueenie 'ere a note from yo' moms:

Queenie,
Baby I left out fo' da mall to treat myself as chu suggested. Went by to pick up yo' aunt fo' lunch and a couple of drinks. I'll be back 'round 11pm.
Love, Mom

"Yo' our moms are together,so dey both safe wit one a nutter." Queenie,told Tez. Fam' lets be out. I'm good to hear moms and auntie are together it makes me eerie when she's out at night by 'er self. "Ueenie listen to chu actin' like a concerned parent an shit." "Dude it ain't like dat,but shit it is da only moms I got nigga;so yeah it'll be fucked up 'round 'ere wit 'er gone. Feel me. "Dat's my heart fam' an wit my line of work,it doesn't make me untouchable at all. "Shit we found dat out earlier nigga,so nah I ain't invisible an neither is my ol' g cuz.

"THROWIN' BRICKS AT THE PENITENTIARY"

Chapter Three
"Get 'Em Befo' Dey Get Chu"

Ring,ring Tez phone rang. "Hello.

"Yo' Tez, its Lu fam'. Where chu at nigga?" Lu asked.

"Wuts good? Tez asked. He replied,leavin' my second home nigga. Dat was code fo' Queenie's crib.

"Check dis I'm up 'ere at BP on da corner of 71st,and da same 2 niggas dat were in da club on last Saturday jus' pulled up." Yo' we on da way,Lu dis time get a plate number.

"Don't worry I got chu, I'm on point,jus' get 'ere,so we can decide wut chu wanta do wit dese niggas." Pullin' into BP parkin' lot,Tez spots Lu an backs in next to his car,bumper against da brick wall. "Where dose niggas at Queenie asked Lu as she load 'er clip back into 'er baby nine."

"Dat lite skin pretty boy standin' at da store front talkin' to shorty. Da utter nigga inside paying fo' his gas fam'." Lu said. "Queenie, Tez asked wuts on yo' mind cuz?" Nothin' family,starin' back and forth between da 2 dudes. "Queenie said;fill Lu in on wut happen tonight and wutsup Saturday night. Neva takin' 'er eyes off 'er prey,Queenie asked;y'all want anything outta 'ere? As she hopped out da car adjustin' 'er Levis and black and red Levi hoodie . Queenie was flawless she stayed dress to impress dat made niggas and bitches want da swagg she had. Queenie's was so efficient in 'er mind dere was no way in hell 'er ego could be broke. Dis was one of da reasons Queenie felt she was untouchable. "Queenie bumped passed da dude dat was payin' fo' gas on his way out purposely."

"Damn lil' mama,chu feelin' a nigga up or wut?" He asked. Queenie neva spoke she jus' returned his gaze an smiled at dude. Hidin' da cold look dat was in 'er eyes and heart. Walkin' into da store comin' out wit juice and black& mild,she didn't have a lighter. "Yo' excuse me do one of chu have a light? Yo' pretty lady I can help chu wit dat. Queenie said no doubt,yo' I didn't catch yo' name homeboy. "I'm Cashies." Queenie pulled on 'er black an said; "Well I am Queenie nigga." All in one swift motion,Queenie bitch slapped dude an pulled up burner on 'em. Yo' I'm dat bitch y'all lookin' fo'. Once Tez and Lu saw his lil' cousin put da slap down on dis nigga like he was 'er bitch,admittedly dey sprung into action wit burners pointed. Tez told Lu to handle dude at da pump an he appeared at Queenie's side. Lu put his 44 against da back dudes head an said don't move homeboy. "Yo' have a seat ma puttin' 'er gun on pretty boy (Floyd) lookin' nigga forehead. Queenie refused to let braud go 'cus she couldn't chance da fact she would go straight to Ola(police). "Yo' Tez put 'em in yo' car,Lu put dis bitch in yo' car an Imma finna jump in wit yo' homeboy at da pump. By da way wut is yo' homeboys name? She asked. " It's Char-Ko." Aiight be cool an y'all jus' might make it outta dis to fuck afta' all.

"Queenie had a smiled to die fo' she knew dere was no way any of 'em would walk away alive. Tez chu lead,I'll play monkey in da middle and Lu can pull up da rear. Yo' pull to dat side street an duck tape dey eyes and hands. Take 'em to da park I need to walk da dogs anyway, I know dey hungry afta' not eatin' all day.Tez had in mind to torture da 2 niggas an let da female go since she had nothin' to wit da situation, she was jus' in da wrong place at da right time. But Tez knew Queenie wouldn't let dat happen. "Yo' my mans, I need to know who's da nigga who put da word out fo' my peeps an where can I find his ass at?" Home address nigga Tez commanded. "Look, man da nigga don't give out numbers to where he rest his head,but he wants chu to know his name." "Triple" Triple is da niggas name. Lu gave pretty boy Floyd a one hitter quitter knockin 'em to da ground. "Nigga chu hard now? Get yo' bitch ass up." Lu said sternly. "So Char-Ko is it,Tez asked. Well lay out da plan fo' me homeboy, wut are yo' bosses intentions? "Da way I see it is he sent his flunkies at a braud is, 'cus he's a coward to step forward an be a man. Tez nostrils flared,growin' mo' irate dat da niggas dat was sent on da hunt fo' Queenie were niggas up in age wit 'em and Lu. "Y'all some bitch ass niggas lookin' fo' a baby cuz. I understand da street game,so I don't knock da hustle da game presents,but understand me homeboys dis game ain't fo' everybody. Most of us pick da game fo' da wrong reasons an some of us are let's say nine-out ten is in da wrong place at da wrong time. Tez gave da girl a look. Wit dat she since non of 'em were leavin' da park alive. "I am a man of my word, my word is always bond,but I gotta make an exception when it comes to goin' against da grain." Tez voice was vix, as he screwed a silencer on da nine da braud let out a scream."Bitch shut da fuck up, Queenie said as she punched 'er in da grill."Yo' no hard feelin's fellas,its all in da game.Y'all jus' got caught slippin'."

"Thuf, Thuf, Thuf three shots were distributed to da tri-sumes head straight dome shots. Wit playtex gloves dey removed da duck tape from all three quickly, leavin' their bodies where dey fell. No need to wipe off prints 'cus gloves were worn threw out da whole ordeal. "Queenie, Tez & Lu hopped in their cars leavin' da scene, parkin' Tez car in da backyard of da spot. Lu followed. "Queenie ditch yo' shit fo' da night an we'll jump in da car wit Lu. "Lu asked;where to fam'?" Yo' bend a few blocks I need to figure out wut jus' happen fam'. "Ueenie baby girl chu aiight, Tez turned back to look at Queenie. I'm cooler dan a fan cuz. "Queenie stated; I'm tired of ma'fuckas tryin' to get at me. I'm ready to get at dis Triple nigga. Saturday ain't comin' fast a nuff,he was lookin' fo' me now I'm lookin' fo' his old ass. Chu feel me cuz? "Lu looked at Tez an said shes right fam' I feel 'er, dis nigga who eva he is has been at 'er twice, double time. "I say fuck 'em snuff dis nigga out befo' word gets back to 'em 'bout da 2 flunkies he sent at 'er, "Cuz I don't think dis nigga is to hard to find. Queenie exclaimed. Fuck I'm sho' 'em he don't own dis fuckin' city I run dis bitch and will continue to 'til I decide to withdraw from dis ma'fucka. "I gotta goal to reach out dis bitch, and I be damn; its only two ways I leave dis ma'fuka wit out it. Queenie said dats in a blaze of glory or a bitch placed behind 'em brick walls of da penitentiary. "Mafucka wanta bring drama and chaos to my life all 'cus of wut?

Queenie asked. I wanta bring it to his bitch ass befo' da break of dawn fam! "Yo" wut time is it Queenie asked. Lu responded it's 1am Queen. "Dammit, change of plans. Tez I need to hit my moms crib, I need to make sho' she home an safe nigga aiight baby girl I got chu. Tez motioned Lu to hit Liz's crib so Queenie could check on 'er moms. Queenie had class in da mornin' an really had no reason fo' not goin', but she had no intentions of lyin' to 'er moms,it would jus' be an issue she dealt wit later. Fo' Queenie to lie to Liz it would be a cold day in hell. Queenie knew she could neva tell 'er moms of wut she jus' witness. Tez and Queenie walked into da house an found Liz in 'er bedroom right off from da living room, laid across 'er bed fast asleep wit a book laid beside 'er. Queenie put a finger up to 'er lips signaling Tez to be quiet as she took a blanket from da end of da bed an placed it ova 'er moms. As 'er and Tez tiptoed out of da room Queenie said I love you ma. Back in da car Lu was jus' getting off da phone. "Wuts good fam?" Lu asked. All good, yo' moms decent? Yeah , yeah auntie was sound asleep. Tez replied, "Cool I jus' got off da horn. I got da drop on dis nigga he lives in da 1700 block of west Hermmies. Yo' my sources don't know da exact address, but dat avenue is where he rest his head. "So wutsup we uppin' dis nigga or wut?" Lu inquired. "Baby girl its yo' call youngan, Tez stated. If chu get at dis nigga how I think chu will ain't no half steppin' chu pull it chu use it nigga, I know ya got dose hands, but dis ain't no fist fight. Tez said yo' chu in da big leagues now it's all gun play and if chu wanta get at dude chu gotta come correct, feel me? Tez told Lu to swing by his moms crib first. It was time to ammo up. Tez tossed Queenie and Lu some black latex gloves and mouth mussels which jus' covered da bottom part of yo' face below da eyes. Now headed fo' Hermmies Queenie sat in da back seat replayin' all da things she had to do along wit all da shit she had done within da last 24 hours. Evident to everything Tez had been preachin' to 'er;once in da game it was hard to get out. Meanin' once da streets had chu_chu no longer belong to yo' self.

"THROWIN' BRICKS AT THE PENITENTIARY"

Queenie was taught da game was jus' a game of chess,an every hustler on da board was tryin' to be King or Queen. Playin' fo' keeps was da name of da game,'til da next game started again. Whether chu got took out by gun play or Ola picked chu up an gave chu a new residence takin' majority of yo' life away from chu. Queenie tried to imagine how bein' a millionaire at da age of 18 would feel like. She was no stranger to money,but havin' millions she knew would set 'er an 'er moms fo' life. Queenie shook da thoughts,realizing first she had to make it to sweet 16. Breakin' 'er outta 'er thoughts she heard Tez say; "Yo' ain't dat da nigga car right dere? Yeah my nigga its da same joint dat was at da club,Lu replied. "Da streets were very narrow and tight so dey had to play it smart an park da car some where out of eye shot of anyone seein' 'em. Lu had already switched da plates in case anyone snatched da numbers." Walking back up da block da three acted normal like kids out afta' curfew. "At Triple's town home walkin' up da front steps Queenie peered threw da big picture window tryin' to locate any movement wut so eva,but seen non. Wut she did spot was a play pin sittin' off to da side,which only indicated dat children lived dere as well. Befo' she could blink Queenie seen a big ass pitt bull walkin' towards da back door of da home,den she saw da inevitable. "A light flicked on an she seen who she believe to be Triple.

"Yo' dere dat nigga is fam',he finna let da dog out da back door." Quietly Tez, Lu and Queenie crept towards da back of da house,hoping to reach it befo' he got out da door. Tez jumped out wit both guns pointed at Triple. Wit no time to react, Queenie and Lu were in da same poise as Tez.

Queenie stepped forward an Triple's pitt growled. "Such a pretty beast."Wit no expression on 'er face Thuf! Queenie sent it to doggie heaven. Swinggin' da gun back up at Triple,wut,wut nigga! Queenie asked wit venom in 'er voice? Triple finally spoke; W_wut y'all want stutterin' ova his words. Y_y_y y'all can have wut eva y'all came fo', jewelry, money. I_I_I ain't got no dope in da house.

Mistakin' da three fo' some punk ass street kids lookin' to rob 'em. Triple said jus' don't hurt my son, he's jus' a baby. Queenie heart cold as ice said; one mo' bastard fo' da world to raise. Pushin' Triple back inside da house,Tez asked is dere anyone else 'ere? "Nah jus' me and my son. When will his mother be back? "She returns in da mornin' to pick 'em up. Young bloods wut is dis all 'bout? Triple asked."Queenie commanded;Yo' let me fam' cuttin' Tez off befo' he could respond. She pulled 'er hood off an slide da mussel down underneath 'er chin. Triple eyes grew wide. "From yo' expression I take it chu know who I am? Feelin' like chu jus' signed yo' death certificate wit out even askin' my name huh?" "Ma da streets didn't lie,chu are jus' a baby."Triple told Queenie. "On da utter hand I can see da sweet and sour side of chu, yo' eyes tell it all chu a cold hearted killa who's headed fo' destruction." Queenie said miss me wit all dat chu was in da wrong biz'ness to be preachin' an we ain't da congregation. "Seein' how I ain't no saint,see chu in hell nigga Thuf,Thuf,Thuf,Thuf,Thuf click click.

Queenie unloaded 'er clip dumpin' da last five hollow points in Triple's head and torso. Tez whispered touchin' Queenie's shoulder we outta 'ere ,baby girl we gotta go now. Back at da car Tez said; "Cuz unfortunately yo' ass done da ultimate, somethin' I warned chu 'bout somethin' I neva wanted chu to be apart of. Dis part of da game dat has a hold on chu, chu'll see wut I mean by dat, now lets get outta 'ere or non of us will be on da streets to hear 'bout dis shit,so drive Lu. "Queenie stayed wit Tez at his crib. Makin' it in 'bout 3:30 am. Tez mother Heather was sleep hearin' Tez keys in da front door. Yellin' out Tez baby dat's chu?" Yeah ma it's me and Ueenie. Queenie _Yes ma'am it's me auntie. Heather looked ova at da alarm clock sittin' on da night stand to see da time.

"Queenie she called out auntie baby okay,it's kind of late fo' chu to be out so late. "Ma, Tez cut in she was wit me, we jus' got back in town, I told 'er to crash 'ere an I'll take 'er home in a few hours when auntie Liz wake up. "Aiight babies y'all get some sleep. I love chu both. We love chu to Tez and

Queenie sang in unison's. "Yo' fam' sleep won't come easy fo' ya tonight, yo' chu 'ere cuz. Tez told Queenie afta' dey got to his bedroom. "Like I was tellin' chu earlier, chu can't take back wut chu did family. I'm sho' chu know dat,besides wonderin' if anyone saw us, yo' conscience will fuck wit chu viciously. "Yo' cuz on our way 'ere I closed my eyes an visions of all fo' bodies kept flashin' in my head, even da fuckin' dog cuz. Queenie stated. "Listen Queenie dat's 'cus chu pulled da trigger fo' da first time. Da visions of da utter three chu can see clear now 'cus chu were dere when it happen an da adrenaline at da time took ova yo' body,so chu had no time to think 'bout da situation. Queenie chu can focus now 'cus da adrenaline rush is ova. Dis maybe somethin' chu'll neva get ova, and I wish I could help ya baby girl, but I can't, jus' so chu know dis was one of my fears. Chu becomin' a killa it's jus' like dat nigga Triple said befo' chu laid 'em down; "Yo' heart is cold as ice." Queenie lookin' into yo' eyes earlier when I gave chu dat fist fight an ya blacked out. Dat's da exact same look chu had tonight, only difference dis time chu pulled da trigger.

Queenie listen to every word Tez had to say took it all into marinate as she let da water from da shower hit 'er face. Closin' 'er eyes she saw Triple tellin' 'er, bitch chu will pay fo' my death da streets of Chicago will not let chu survive. Chu took me from da game, my son and family chu will pay. Queenie grasped fo' air under da runnin' water. Da vision of Triple seemed all to real, Queenie felt as doe she was drownin', she clutched 'er chest an opened 'er eyes. Queenie slipped on one of Tez t-shirts an a pair of b-ball shorts. Next mornin' afta' a few restless hours of unwanted sleep, she called 'er mother. Ring, ring, ring. "Hello, Liz said on da fourth ring." "Ma, its me, Queenie responded.

"Queenie, baby why is chu callin' me from yo' aunts house?" "We got in later dan we expected so I crashed 'ere." Chu alright? Liz asked. "Yeah ma, I'm cool,but I'm gonna miss class today. I couldn't sleep last night, so my brain ain't where it needs to be. "So wut 'bout yo' game?"

"THROWIN' BRICKS AT THE PENITENTIARY"

"It's not 'til tonight, I'll be dere wit bells on I can't miss dat ma, dat's our meal ticket up outta 'ere. Ma chu'll be dere right? "Liz said; front row and center baby chu know it." Dat's da same way Tez says it when I ask 'em. "Well Queenie chu know dat lil' nigga ain't gone miss a beat when it comes to chu. Aiight let me get ready fo' work." Queenie told Liz; I love chu ol' g, I'll be dere befo' chu leave.

"Liz was all Queenie had she respected 'er wit da up most, chu could neva find 'er disrespectin' 'er moms in anyway at all, Queenie would standup to a ten foot man when I came to 'er moms. Queenie whispered fam' chu up? Yo' Tez I gotta be out I need to see my moms befo' she goes to work cuz. "Man why so fuckin' early cuz, baby girl can chu jus' give me one mo' hour?" Queenie threw a pillow at Tez an said; "Nah nigga, chu can't we got shit to do. An it's mandatory I straighten out my moms pockets, so get yo' ass up cuz. "Aiight, aiight damn." Sittin' at da side of his bed he asked Queenie,so how chu feelin' cuz, did chu get any sleep. "Nah, fam' sleep wasn't on my side at all my nigga. Sleep didn't come easy, but I don't have any regrets 'bout it doe. Now hit up Chaos fam' see if da ma'fucka on point." Chaos picked up on da first ring.

"Yo' Tez sup my nigga?" Chaos choked den let off a cough, barely audible; "Dis some bomb ass shit, wut up fam' he asked in a very low tone?" Nigga chu smokin' havin' yo' mornin' wake up huh? Tez asked. "An yo' ass know it, gotta have my ooh wee so I can function correctly ,won't start my day wit out it my nigga. "So talk to me fam'." "Yo' Queenie needs to know if chu handled dat an wut time yo' ass touchin' Chi. "Tell lil' cuz I'm on point and I am already on da turn pike headed back wit 'er $60,000 in duffel. I should be at da stash house 'bout 11am instead of noon feel me?" "Yo' we'll be dere. Queenie lets bounce everything is done an Chaos is ahead of schedule wit his crazy ass, but on some seriousness, he'll be 'ere by 11am, he an hour ahead of time. "Cool, cool so I take it everything went smooth?" Tez nodded his head reassurin' Queenie dat Chaos had all 'er money.

"THROWIN' BRICKS AT THE PENITENTIARY"

Chaos was an old head,vet who has been dere done dat. Chaos is Liz and Heather's first cousin, which made 'em Tez and Queenie's second blood relative, who has been in and out of da penitentiary since he was a shorty growin' up in Robert Taylor homes. Chaos finished his last bid an Queenie had been in da game a short time, but Chaos was desperate afta' he touched down. Unfortunately while he was locked down he lost everything and everyone he loved except Liz and Heather, who gave 'em a place to stay. Dat was cool fo' awhile wit Queenie, but havin' Chaos livin' under da same roof made 'er watch da house to much an she had utter shit goin' on. Queenie talked it ova wit Tez 'bout givin' Chaos a job runnin' da stash house. Queenie figured dat would be da perfect way fo' 'em to get out of 'er moms crib. Chaos would have a place to lay his head, Queenie had da bedroom decorated fo' comfort at da stash house. Chaos was content wit arrangement, he told, Queenie; "Cuz I won't let chu down, I can do wut eva chu need me to do. Queenie stated; "Yo' fam' chu a grow ass man do wut chu say and mean wut chu say an we'll be cool. 'Cus I do an chu only get one chance wit me, chu fuck up an dat's yo' ass. Queenie told 'em family or not chu dead, I'll bury yo' ass literally six feet under fam'.

"Imma send chu off proper doe, no joke intended. Chaos looked at Queenie curiously an said baby girl I don't want any mishaps, we got an understandin'. "Since yo' ass cool wit it we gotta few stipulations 'bout da stash house, dere is no company wut so eva. Don't bring non of yo' side pieces through nor yo' jail house buddies. Da stash house is my safe haven my place of biz'ness, yo' job and where chu lay yo' head, so I don't need any unnecessary and unwanted attention feel me?"

"No disrespect cuz, but dis is biz'ness I don't do personal, so yo' job is to take care of Blue and Red's needs 'cus dis is their residence, so in order to take da job chu gotta be able to deal wit 'em. "Queenie dat's cool ain't no problem. "Aiight secondly we need chu to make runs from time to time, 'cus I be at school or tournaments, now most of yo' runs will be done outta town, 'cus in town I really wanta keep chu low key, but we will discuss dat a lil' later. Tez and I will take ya in 'bout an hour to get chu yo' own whip. "Chaos had no idea he signed his fate ova to Queenie, Chaos would soon find out his lil' cousin is no joke."

Chapter Four
"Game Knight"
Dreams Washed Away

"Tez and Queenie pulled up jus' as Liz made 'er way outside. "Yo' ma hold up leave da door open. Queenie jumped out da car along wit Tez." "Wutup ma?" Queenie asked as she kissed Liz on da head. "Wutup auntie? Tez hugged Liz an kissed 'er on da forehead." "Nothin' baby jus' on my way to work to make dat all might dollar. Liz was a RN at Rush Presbyterian Hospital of 13 years. Liz started workin' dere when Queenie turned 3 years old, it was manageable wit da help of 'er sister. Queenie presented to be a pretty good kid at least dat's wut Liz believed anyway, Queenie did no wrong in 'er eyes, but den wut she couldn't see she felt wouldn't hurt. She to would find out different.

Queenie said; ma come in da house fo' a sec. "Queenie baby I gotta go befo' I be late." Queenie shot back chu don't need dat job anyway, chu need to quit chu work to hard. "Baby hard work pays da bills, as long as it doesn't kill me I'm fine. Anyway I don't need any money I'm good I still got pocket change from yesterday. "Ma stop playin'." Queenie reached in 'er pocket an gave Liz $500 an put it in 'er purse. "Tez whispered auntie chu know how she is jus' take it." "Alright my babies y'all be good an I'll see y'all later on at da game, Queenie don't fo' get to lock up my house.""Yo' Ueenie it's10:30 hurry up. I wonder wut auntie left in 'ere to eat." "Don't know,but look while I change my gear real quick den we can be out." "Yo' auntie left some bacon,eggs and sausage in da oven. Chu want some?" "Yeah make me a sandwich I'll be down in two seconds." Queenie pulled on a pair of black wit gold stitchin' Levi's an a gold Levi t-shirt steppin' into a pair of fresh out da box black and gold

"THROWIN' BRICKS AT THE PENITENTIARY"

Jordan's sprayin' 'er self down wit CK ONE perfume she was almost set. Givin' 'er self da once ova in a full length mirror; "I'm sexy as hell" Queenie hit da safe up she replaced da $500 she gave 'er moms. Queenie grabbed a black Levi hoodie an nina an headed to da kitchen. "It smells good down 'ere fam'." Tez replied I jus' heated an slapped it on bread. "Yo' chu put any mayo on my bread?" Nah cuz. "Queenie said I'll meet chu at da car,let me doctor on my sandwich an I'll be out." In da car Tez said somebody finna be sweet 16 in a few days huh? So wut chu wanta do fo' it? "Queenie replied I don't know I hadn't thought 'bout it to be honest. Queenie thought to 'er self shit I gotta make it to see 16 first afta' da last 24 hours I jus' encountered. Tez had already put plans in motion fo' Queenie surprise party at a night club "Secrets." Most would have thought he was 'er nigga da way he carried on every year fo' 'er birthday. Tez threw money 'round like it was runnin' water dat a child would leave on,but it was no doubt where Queenie got it from. Dis year he had his mother and aunt Liz to handle all da arrangements fo' 'em. Fo' a private party wit jus' family an his friends, he dropped $6,000 an dat didn't include da $20,000 he gave up fo' da caterin' and decorations. Wit Tez it all had to be baller's status, he wanted nothin' but da best fo' his lil' cousin. He knew she deserved it all,'cus even doe she had issues he knew she was a good kid.

"Yo' its game night tonight baby, is chu ready to put yo' skills down? Baby girl go out dere an sho' dose ma'fuckas who stands behind #33. "Queenie was extremely talented on da court, watchin' 'er sprint up and down da court made Tez go ballistic. Queenie was a superstar on da court an a boss to da streets. Game time Queenie had a sweet 3 pointer from half court, she yelled hussle,hussle to 'er teammates. Queenie was unstoppable stealin' da ball from 'er opponent, she did a cross ova, dribbled da ball between 'er legs an stepped to da side fo' a nutter easy 3 points. "Swoosh." Da stands went wild wit all their cheers, but only voices she could hear were Liz and Tez screamin' dat's my baby. "Cuz chu da shit fam', he love to see Queenie get busy on da court 'cus da passion she had fo' it was extravagant." Da buzzer sounded off it was halve time, wit all da cheers an high fives from 'er teammates Queenie noticed death stares comin' from Red Bone. Queenie knew she needed to keep da team spirit, but unfortunately Queenie couldn't fake wut was 'bout to be. Dat joy in 'er eyes turned ice cold of a killa. Tez noticed Queenie came to a complete stand off like she was 'bout to have a show down. Queenie eyes were fixated on somethin' or someone, so he followed 'er stare 'til he made da person Queenie was focus on. "Tez wuts wrong wit Queenie? Liz asked; wut is she lookin' at, wuts wrong wit my baby. "Nothin' auntie she's cool." Not takin' his eyes off of Red Bone an Liz not takin' 'er eyes off 'er baby girl, Liz called Queenie's name breakin' 'er out of 'er stare. Queenie turned an made contact wit 'er mother, not wantin' to seem suspicious she smiled an raised 'er hands up indicatin' she was number one. Queenie saw Tez nod his head in Red Bones direction, but befo' she turned Red Bone blind sided 'er. Stumblin' out of a daze, Queenie shook it off, asked; Red Bone dis wut chu want? Red Bone charged Queenie, but was no challenge. Queenie met 'er wit a quick round house as Red Bone flew backwards dat push da crowd back. Tez knew dere would be no way in hell dat he would get Queenie to walk away from dis fight. Tez informed his aunt dat da girl had been pickin' wit Queenie fo' awhile. Liz knew dis would fuck up 'er daughter basketball career, but she decided against breakin' up da fight. Instead she stood by Tez's side an became an on looker like everyone else. Queenie gave Red Bone a double right hook, 2 shots to da eye_ Ugh! Red Bone screamed, she came right back slammin' 'er fist into Queenie's jaw. Da sounds of bones crushin',_ "Oooooh!" Were da sounds from da crowd, everyone thought it was Queenie's jaw bone breakin' an dat aggravated 'er. Red Bone den screamed out in agony from breakin' 'er fist, by dis time Queenie blacked out an lost control of 'er self. Throwin' punches left,right,left,right 'til Red Bone hit da ground, still conscious Queenie pounced on top of 'er like a beast. "Bitch chu fucked up my life, Queenie screamed out." Knowin' da shit coulda been avoided an stayed in da ghetto streets of Chicago away from da one place she had glory, Queenie knew 'er meal ticket out of da hood had jus' been snatched away. "Sirens heard from a distance, Tez yelled out Queenie's name an tried to bring 'er out of da trans she fell into. Runnin' towards his lil' cousin wantin' to get 'er up outta dere befo' Ola got to 'er, his conscience had said it was already to late an Queenie would be goin' to jail befo' she turned 16. Liz screamed out Queenie. "Tez get my baby,she gone kill 'er." At dis point Red Bone laid on da ground lifeless.

Tez realized dere was no way in hell he could carry Queenie off wit out calmin' 'er down an bringin' 'er back 'round befo' Ola got dere. His thoughts were interrupted _ Woop- Woop! "Freeze wit guns drawn on Tez and Queenie. Da situation feared Tez, he had his cousin in a bear hug 'cus he didn't want anyone to see 'er eyes. Dis would be da first time Queenie eva heard or seen 'er cousin cry. Tears rolled down his face at da same time he whispered; Queenie baby I need chu to snap out of it or we both gone die out 'ere tonight. Tez didn't care wut happened to 'em,but he couldn't let his auntie witness 'er only baby die in da streets like an animal by da hands of Ola. In ear shot Tez told Queenie; come on baby we gotta get down on da ground, Tez still tryin' to shake 'er out of da trans. Come on lil' nigga I need chu to hear me. Queenie finally said huh. "Look ma dey finna snatch chu up, I need chu to cohere wut I'm sayin' chu finna go to jail Imma need chu to be cool, say nothin' 'til yo' lawyer gets dere." Queenie finally came back fully lookin' at 'er hands all bloody. "Fuck Tez wut did I do?" He whispered befo' Ola snatched 'em both off da ground, " Chu damn near killed Red Bone.

"Ola said chu have da right to remain silent anything chu say can and will be held against chu. As dey placed da cuffs on Queenie, Tez hugged his aunt. "It's gone be aiight." Liz cried as dey put 'er baby in back of da squad car. "Tez wut happen?" "Auntie she blacked out an its not da first time an it won't be da last. I jus' wish dis shit coulda stayed in da streets, not on da courts where she felt comfortable at." I gotta a lawyer dat will bring 'er home, so let me make a call and go see 'em. "Damn it seems like da mo' I try to protect 'er da mo' someone's pullin' 'er away from me an irritates da fuck outta me." Tez kissed his aunt on da forehead waitin' fo' 'er to get in 'er car an drive away. "I'll call chu soon as I hear somethin'." "Hello Demontea and associates da receptionist answered.

"Yes may I speak wit Mr. Demotea, Tez spoke into da receiver. "Yes hold one second please."

"Demontea speakin'." "Yeah Mr. D dis is Tez Miles." "Yes Mr. Miles how can I help chu?"

"I've got a dilemma I need chu to fix." Mr. Demontea was a lil' Jewish man dat Chaos had put Tez up on while he was down on a bid, dat he could no longer afford da services of, so when Tez got into trouble Chaos put Tez up on Mr. D. Afta' Tez broke down da trouble Queenie had inquired Mr. D told Tez to meet 'em at da precinct. "Cool Mr. D. I'm on my way." Tez replied. Once at da precinct Tez didn't want to be seen comin' out of his pocket fo' Queenie's bail. Tez had his aunt Liz meet 'em dere. Once Liz got word she beat Tez to da precinct she was already posted up across da street. Tez got of out his car down da street, motionin' his aunt to get out."Mr. D. dis 'ere is my lil' cuz mother Liz_ auntie dis 'ere is my lawyer Mr. D. he will handle everything. 'Ere put dis envelope in yo' purse it's $6,000 'ere fo' Queenie's bond. I'll be right out 'ere, Mr. D. bring my lil' cuz up out dat hell hole. 'Bout 20 minutes later Queenie ran out da front door straight into Tez's arms wit Mr. D. and Liz walkin' behind 'er. "Baby girl chu good?" "No doubt cuz, Thanks cuz chu know dese ma'fuckas hit me wit a $2,000 dollar bond."

"Lil' nigga don't trip on dat shit fam' I'm jus' good to know yo' ass straight."

Mr. D. walked up an Queenie shook his hand_ "Thank chu sir." "Ya welcome Ms. Miles, I need to see chu in my office on Monday,an Tez we can talk den 'bout our arrangements. "Aiight Mr. D. we'll see ya den.” “It was nice meetin' chu Ms. Miles,I hate it was under dese circumstances doe.”

“Nice meetin' chu also Mr. Demontea an thank ya fo' yo' help, we are grateful.”Liz stated.

“Auntie I need to talk to Queenie, so if it's aiight wit chu I'll bring 'er home. We right behind chu.”

“Okay a nuff has happened fo' one night, so I'll see y'all at da house.” Tez knew his auntie was still shaky not knowin' wut actually happen to 'er daughter she would have plenty of questions. One thing fo' sho' Liz knew Queenie was in danger, headed fo' death or prison. In da car wit Tez, Queenie spoke first. “Fam' I wanta thank chu fo' keepin' my moms, I think if chu weren't dere to bring me back 'round I would be dead or facin' life fo' killin' dat bitch, an moms woulda lost 'er mind. Man I can't believe I lost control of who I am doe, out in 'em streets in front of my moms cuz an while I was in my glory_ nigga I gotta rep to up hold an chu know da name I carry is a big fuckin' part of who I am, now I'm caught up in dis dumb ass shit. “Fuck_Fuck_Fuck!” Queenie screamed. “I gotta take a break I need to get away from 'ere cuz,it's long ova due fo' a vacation. Somethin' I shoulda been done anyway.”

“Well cuz far as da get away chu gotta put on hold 'til we find out wut Mr. D. talkin' 'bout. Besides dat yo' moms is distraught ova da way she saw 'er baby change into someone else afta' I convinced 'er to not break it up. I can only imagine da questions dat are flowin' through 'er head right now. Knowin' auntie she'll neva let chu out of 'er sight 'til yo' ass turn 35 fam'.”

Tez said jus' so chu'll know, I filled 'er in on yo' blackout situation, to calm 'er nerves a lil' so be ready to explain dat off da back, but don't worry I won't leave chu to explain by yo' self.” “Yo' we got biz'ness to handle tomorrow Lu and Chaos already know wutsup.” Afta' da commotion an all da questionin' Liz actually understood wut happened, she was hurt by da fact 'er daughter got caught up at da scene an da fact she had a record now, she knew dis would mess up Queenie's career. Liz was from da hood of East St. Boogie, so she knew da consequences of growin' up in da hood , specially when chu had bitches hattin' on chu. Liz was still in da dark,soon a nuff she would find out it's not 'cus of 'er daughter looks or persona she was hatted fo'. Secretly it was 'cus she was known as da youngest "Boss Queen" of da streets of Chicago. "Early da next mornin' Tez and Queenie met up wit Mr. D., goin' ova 'er case. Mr. Demotea told 'em; dat he checked da status of Red Bone an she was goin' to pull threw, so Queenie would be jus' charged wit domestic battery in a public place. I can get dat dropped, but chu will still get probation 'cus dey feel chu dangerous. "Man dis is 'er first offense, she's neva been in trouble befo' now." Tez retorted. "I am jus' gone keep it real wit chu both, da prosecutor is a fuckin' prick an he always pushes fo' a conviction." Since he can't get 'er on a bullshit charge he will present probation to da judge. Now we are due in court on August 25th 'til den I need chu Queenie to be on yo' best behavior, dat means no mo' fightin'. I'll work on getting da least probation time fo' chu. "Queenie responded; thanks Mr. D., how much do I owe chu fo' yo' services sir?" "Handlin' my case won't be cheap,but I'm willin' to pay wut eva, I need to keep chu on my good side 'cus I know dis will not be da last time I need yo' services." "Seein' who chu family wit da great Chaos and Tez Miles, I know chu come from a stand up group of men, so from da weekend 'til today $4,000 an we'll be squared away unless somethin' else happens den utter fees will be discussed.

"Queenie pulled out 10 stacks an peeled off $4,000 dollars an handed to Mr. D.,den walked out of his office.

Chapter Five
"Wuts A Birthday Party Wit Out Da Trash"

Ring_ring. "Queenie stepped out da shower snatched 'er hitter off da sink an wiped water from 'er eyes. "Hello,Queenie said wit a lil' irritation 'cus da caller interrupted 'er shower."

"Wut up beautiful Queen?" Cortez' questioned. "Nothin' jus' finna get my day started. Wuts good homeboy, it's kinda early to be callin' ma'fuckas ain't it?" Is everything okay_ hold up nigga how chu get my number? She said in a jokin' manner. She knew she didn't give Cortez' 'er hitter.

“Yo' beautiful don't get upset, I jus' hollard at Tez he was fillin' me in on yo' situation chu got into, so I jus' wanted to holla at chu myself see if chu were good. I hear we also gotta birthday Queen in da house huh?” A smile spread across 'er face. “Yeah yo' it's my day today, ain't nothin' doe.”

“Yo' Queenie don't sweat dat shit dat happened, yo' ma I told Tez dat I'm 'ere fo' both of chu, wut eva y'all need, but listen chu know I'm diggin' yo' ass right an I ain't gone front I wanta get up wit chu yeah Tez my homeboy an we thicker dan thieves, but I need chu as my Queen.“Now on da biz'ness side doe y'all don't have to make dat trip 'ere, 'cus I got some shit to handle in yo' city Miss Queen, so when I touch down Imma give chu a call an we can meet up den. An Queenie don't worry I got chu on every aspect of da word “I got chu.” Queenie questioned Cortez' wut chu checkin' fo' me fo', why is it important I become urns? “Hold on befo' yo' ass answer I want chu to think 'bout it, maybe even sleep on it an when chu make it to my city we can talk 'bout it face to face. “Absolutely beautiful I respect yo' game an won't regret any decisions made, wit me it's wut eva yo' heart desires.” Cortez' replied.

Wut Queenie didn't know was only biz'ness Cortez' really had in Chicago was 'er birthday party Saturday night, an to give 'er a present dat would set 'er on top of a Kings pin throne befo' she turned 17.“Cortez' handsome ass was a fine brother from East St. Boogie. Cortez' had a demeanor 'bout 'em self dat required Queenie's attention. A few feelings had formed from their last conversation together at da college.” Queenie dictated back to 'er self da last thing she told Cortez' dat day befo' leavin' his car:

“If yo' game is legit as yo' ass pressin' it to be when da time right chu jus' may get yo' chance.” Word is bond. “Queenie was boss an she knew, she needed no nigga to do fo' 'er wut she could do fo' 'er self. She neva checked fo' any niggas 'cus she had biz'ness on 'er mind. She felt only way a nigga could get wit 'er, dey had to be on da same level. It wasn't 'bout their money, their mind had to be right,his personality,his swagg, his intelligence an fo' 'er to top it off his looks.

"Queenie, baby Tez is 'ere"_Liz shouted from downstairs. "Wutup auntie, wut chu got cookin' dat smells so good?" "Fixin' yo' lil' cousin some breakfast, so she can eat befo' she hits da streets, chu know she doesn't sit still to long." "Well yeah today is 'er birthday, so who knows wut she wants to do." Tez said as he kissed his aunts forehead. "So now y'all talkin' 'bout me when I'm not present huh?" Queenie chuckled lightly an stated nah, I ain't got nothin' planned. Queenie stuck a piece of bacon in 'er mouth. "I'm hungry ma wut chu got ova dere smellin' so good?" "Child jus' sit down an eat befo' chu take off, chu to Tez have a seat baby it's plenty." "Ma ain't no rush Tez 'ere to go wit us.

"Us, where we goin'?" Liz asked. "Remember Imma take chu to get dat new car today."

"Queenie, baby chu ain't gotta do dat I'm alright wit da one outside. We got utter issues on our plates, tryin' to keep chu from behind bars. Liz told Queenie besides dat it's yo' 16th birthday spend money on yo' self. "Ma miss me wit all dat, we spoke 'bout dis last week an chu knew den my birthday would be today. An try to stop worryin' 'bout dat case Mr. D. said it would be fine. I jus' turned 16 an I'm finna do me an live my life to da fullest. Tez smiled at Queenie an whispered growin' up I see. "Now lets go get yo' new ride a nigga tryin' to see wut it feel like wit 'er hair blowin' in da wind. "Alright let me clean da kitchen first." While Liz cleaned Queenie and Tez discuss wut needed to be done afta' dey returned from da dealership . "Yo' fam' let Chaos know he has to make a delivery dis afta' noon ova on da south side." "Don't stress dat he knows aiight, fam' yo' ass jus' concentrate on dat fly ass out fit chu gone step out in tonight." "Where we goin'?" "We gone meet Lu and Chaos at da 50 lil' nigga, have a few drinks fo' yo' birthday. Chu already know 'em niggas geek an how could dey fo' get dey bosses big day, dis is da hand dat feeds 'em." Tez whispered. Liz yelled out I'm ready.

"Aiight lets be out, dey jumped into Queenie's Benz SE5600. Dey stopped at three different lots befo' Liz spotted a black on black drop top Benz. "Dat's it, I like dat one." "So dat wut chu want ma?" Queenie asked. Queenie picked a young black associate to help 'er,cus she wanted da young man to receive da commission off 'er purchase. Queenie pointed out da car dey wanted so lil' dude could retrieve da keys. Queenie dropped $25,000 dollars on da table an told 'em dat should be mo' dan a nuff plus yo' commission. Queenie left 'er mother to do da paper work. She had 'er eyes on a car 'er self. Liz couldn't believe wut 'er daughter did next. She witness 'er 16 year old daughter purchase a $65,000 dollar Lexus SUV wit no hesitation, Liz damn near fainted realizin' 'er daughter jus' spend $90,000 dollars less 30 minutes. "Yo' have dat same lil' nigga draw up my paper work." She told a different sales man. When he finished he handed Queenie 2 sets of keys wit 2 alarm keys. Happy birthday Ms. Miles da associate said as he spoke ova da loud speaker, open da showroom window please. Tez head snapped 'round an noticed da fire red SUV an smiled an nodded wit approval. "Lets ride out family. Ma we'll meet chu at da crib, I gotta grab somethin' first." Queenie and Tez watched as 'er moms pulled away in 'er new ride lookin' sexy and sophisticated as she was.

"Yo' you think she's happy fam'?" Queenie asked Tez. "Hell yeah, chu know she's happy, who wouldn't be jus' receivin' a brand new $25,000 dollar car dat dey didn't have to buy 'em self? But now she has a raised brow tryin' to figure out how in hell chu can afford not one but 2 ma'fuckin' new cars dat chu paid a nice gawt fo' lil' nigga. I see chu doe doin' yo' damn thing cuz. I Know it's yo' day,but when it's ova we will talk." Queenie and Tez pulled up in front of 'er crib an seen Tez's moms was dere. Once dey walked into da house shouts of HAPPY BIRTHDAY rang out. Queenie's auntie mouth sounded like 20 people by 'er self an it was jus' 'er and Liz standin' dere. A giant ass cake set on da table wit 16 candles an it read: Happy Sweet 16 baby, Queen we love chu boss from yo' family fam'. Queenie said y'all didn't have to do dis. "Baby it was Tez,Chaos and Lu's idea. Dey brought it by early dis mornin' droppin' it off while chu were in da shower.

"Ah fam' chu shouldn't have grabbin' Tez 'round his neck embracin' 'em lettin' 'em know how much it meant to 'er." Liz and Heather handed Queenie 2 boxes a long and small, da long one contained a platinum five carat diamond bracelet an da box 'er aunt gave 'er had a matchin' pair of platinum five carat diamond earrings. "It was da small things dat completed Queenie."

"Thanks ma and auntie,I love it dey fly_I'll put it on tonight." Hold on Queenie dis box came jus' as I pulled up I had to sign fo' it, it has happy birthday written all ova it. Queenie took da box it had no name on it,so she shook it first. "Open da box fam' Tez wanted to see like he didn't already know wut da box held inside. Da box was Cortez' purpose of callin' Tez. Queenie opened da nicely wrapped box an dere laid a beautiful platinum diamond necklace wit a diamond name plate dat read:

"MY QUEEN" Tez replied; no dat nigga didn't. "Cuz looks like he did." Tez laughed as his mom and aunt admired da necklace. "Queenie, baby chu got some nigga sweet on chu?" 'Er aunt asked.

"Yes ma'am I guess, it looks dat way." "Well I hope chu know wut comes along wit dat territory." Tez jumped on da defensive side an said; don't shit comes wit dat, I'll break dat niggas neck."Boy cut it out his mom stated;chu can't stop everything dat goes on in yo' cousins life, I know chu want to protect 'er, but she is a teenager now an she will explore life soon or later, if she hasn't already."

"Queenie frown at 'er aunts statement an replied; "Nah auntie I'm still a bonafide virgin, I ain't got time fo' no niggas." "Niecy Poo chu jus' ain't made time fo' one, but soon as chu get a whiff of one dat catches yo' attention chu'll be wide open. Trust and believe wut I tell ya, auntie jus' keepin' it real, pay yo' cousin 'ere no mind we are women an Tez is a man my son, an will neva approve of any young men who steps to chu,'cus as sad as it maybe he know wuts on their minds. Ain't dat right son?"

"Ma cut dis convo' short, 'cus I ain't tryin' to hear it even if it is da truth." Queenie said thanks fo' da gifts an da talk auntie, but we need to bounce. Ma y'all help yo' selves to da cake jus' save me some.

Tez kissed his moms and aunt on da forehead an Queenie kissed 'em also an blurted I love chu an fled out da house. "Lets hit da stash house first Queenie stated; I gotta make sho' my paper is in order." Queenie asked; Tez if he was good? "Yeah fam' I'm straight." "Oh fam' we don't have to make dat trip to Boogie tomorrow, but I'm pretty sho' chu already knew dat huh?" Queenie said wit a lil' sarcasm in 'er voice. Tez smiled, "Yeah I know Ueenie." "So chu knew Cortez' was sendin' me dat joint huh?" "Yeah fam' I knew." "Well why chu get up tight?" "It wasn't 'cus he sent da necklace it's jus' how moms had to put it out dere. Hell yeah da truth hurts an I know it's reality, but am I ready to see niggas pushin' up on chu? No I'm not ready fo' it dat's all." "Blunt and simple, but chu kept it raw dat's my nigga. Now if yo' ass done havin' a bitch moment can we talk 'bout somethin' else? Yo' family on a serious note I wanta go to Las Vegas befo' I go to court in August." "When chu tryin' to leave?" Tez asked. "In da next week or so fam',I figure da fellas could use a break from Chi-Town. So wut chu think 'bout takin' a trip I know yo' ass could use a get away also."

"Damn right I can. Tez exclaimed soundin' excited. "Yo' I gotta confess, I know yo' ass always told me neva let my left hand know wut da right hand does an neva trust da next ma'fucka, but I don't think dat applies to chu,so listen bro'. "Wutsup Ueenie?" "Cuz I'm $500,000 thousand away from bein' da young richest bitch in da city of CHI-TOWN my nigga. At least da youngest I know of fam'.
An if all goes accordingly to my next move I will be $1.5 million dollars to da good, I will hit my mark befo' 18 cuz. Check dis da only reason I am tellin' chu in case anything happens to me I needed chu to know wutsup." "Ueenie chill out wit dat off da wall reality shit, man I think 'bout dat shit 'er day. Why yo' ass think I keep chu so close? 'Cus I ain't tryin' to have shit happen to chu, feel me." Tez said now cool out. "I know I can't protect yo' ass fo' eva from 'ere thing, but lil' nigga I will die tryin'.

"THROWIN' BRICKS AT THE PENITENTIARY"

In front at da stash house Tez and Queenie got out walked inside an got greeted by Blue and Red. "Chaos_Tez shouted. "Be out in a sec fam'." "Wutsup daddy Queenie asked Blue as he jumped into 'er arms_ 'em miss 'em mama?" Queenie put Blue down an rubbed Red on da head an tickled 'er stomach while she laid on 'er back like a baby. From da bedroom Chaos had jus' finished dressin'. "Wutsup family Chaos,asked; wuts good? Happy Birthday cuz, how does it feel? Yo' ass made it to sweet 16." Lookin' out da window Chaos noticed a Lexus SUV out front. "Yo' Tez dat's how chu playin' nigga chu showin' 'em off cuz." "Nah, mean it's baby girl showin' off dis time." "Big Boss Queen of da city hurtin' 'em, dey can't see ya cuz." "Chaos I preciate chu and Lu from da heart wit da cake. Yo' did da owners of da house eat today?" Queenie asked. "Oh yeah I fed 'em, we ain't been back an hour from da park. I gave both of 'em showers,so dey should be good. "Good once we leave dey should settle down." Queenie asked where da duffel bags from da delivery from da last 2 days? "Right where dey usually are, in da closet in da floor drop." Afta' Queenie retrieved da 2 bags she returned to da livin' room handed Chaos his pay of $5,000 dollars fo' da week. "We'll be right back in_she nodded fo' Tez to follow 'er. Tez grabbed da duffel bag dat contained $60,000 dollars an followed Queenie outside.

"Wutsup baby girl?" "Dat's chu fam' cuz I appreciate chu mo' dan chu know, so jus' take it an do wut chu please wit it family." "Listen Queenie chu ain't gotta kick me down lil' nigga wut I do fo' chu is jus' 'cus, no matter wut Imma always look out fo' chu Ueenie." "Man if it wasn't fo' chu non of wut I do woulda been possible. Hell if it wasn't fo' bailin' my ass out all da time where chu think I would be? Cuz don't take it as pay back, it's jus' a gift from me to chu bro' we family an family always look out fo' one a nutter. Right?" "Now stop always sentimentalizin' shit an jus' take it. If I didn't know any better I would say yo' ass getting softer da older I get homeboy." "Lil' girl watch yo' mouth befo' chu step into somethin' money can't even get yo' ass out of." Tez replied. "Back in da house Tez yelled

"THROWIN' BRICKS AT THE PENITENTIARY"

"Chaos lets roll an close all da doors, so da dogs can lay in da livin' room and kitchen only fam'."

"Tez and I have to go get dress, so afta' we leave JU-TOWN drop me off. I gotta go find some hot shit shit. Simple, but fly ass hell, y'all feel me? Dey can see me, but can't touch me."

"Queenie dress to impress 'er self, no one else, but had to be da first an only 1 rock it, when it came to 'er clothes and shoes. She was da best dress bitch who only wore gym shoes and boots. Now chu would think shoppin' at JU-TOWN she would have da exact same shit as everyone else. Not fo' Queenie she had a connect dat designed 'er outfits da way she wanted 'em jus' as well as 'er shoes. Dey to had to be exclusives it was always some type of detail dat made 'er shoes stand out from da rest. Queenie knew exactly wut she wanted to look like afta' receivin' 'er platinum necklace, so she placed a call an put in 'er order: halve and halve da front of 'er jeans were Burberry print an da back of da jeans were Black Label wit a matchin' jacket not knowin' dis would soon be a clothin' line. Queenie had 'er jacket designed wit platinum diamonds dat would neva come off. It read:

CHI-TOWN across da middle of 'er back a red shirt wit QUEEN across da chest also in platinum diamonds, dis was a one time outfit once she took it off it would jus' hang in da closet. 'Er shoes couldn't be faded, dey were all red suede wit gold stitchin' an QUEEN was embroider in black stitchin'. Queenie liked bein' different from da rest, so when she came out wit 'er own creations chu jus' had to respect it, 'cus da lil' bitch was fly. It was time to step out Queenie put on 'er jewelery 'er "MY QUEEN" plate laid nicely on 'er neck above da diamonds across 'er chest. Da bracelet and earrings complimented 'er whole persona. Queenie grabbed 10 stacks fo' 'er pocket along wit nina 'er baby nine an walked downstairs as Tez and Chaos entered da house. "Right on time family."

"Yo' cuz dat shit hot chu got on, I guess dey can see chu,but can't touch huh?" Tez questioned.

Liz walked in da room. "Wutsup auntie?" "Aye how chu feelin' cuz?" Chaos hugged Liz.

"THROWIN' BRICKS AT THE PENITENTIARY"

Liz stated; "Look at my baby, lookin' all sexy, let me get a picture of all three of chu now. I gotta remember dis day. Afta' she took a few mo' pictures da three left to pick up Lu. "Y'all be careful out dere." Liz yelled. Chaos stated; "Hell cuz we gone have to watch yo' ass extra close jus' to make sho' no one snatches chu up fo' yo' gear wit all da diamonds on it. "Nigga chu crazy, not long as I got nina behind me." "Put dat shit away Ueenie, ain't shit finna pop off an if it does Chaos,Lu and myself got chu. Yo' ass can't risk any trouble right now." Lu got in takin' da back seat wit Chaos. "Boss dis chu baby girl? Dis is sweet." Lu admired da plush leather. "Tez phone rung. He noticed it was Cortez' on da utter end he motioned 'em to quiet while he talked.

Chapter Six
"Wuts A King Wit Out A Queen"

"Hello, wutsup homeboy, wuts good?" Cortez' replied; I hit town a night early I figured wut da fuck might as well get it crackin' tonight. "Yo' chu rollin' solo?" "Nah, chu know I take my entourage eva I go cuz." "Fam' we jus' loaded up, we on da way ova to da 50 Yard Line in Harvey, chu know where dat is?" "Yeah, I'm 'bout 15 minutes away from it, I had to handle somethin' in Dalton,so dat's right on time." "Where chu stayin' at fam'?" Tez questioned makin' sho' his nigga was straight.

"Downtown I gotta presidential suite at da MARRIOT. Nigga chu know how we do, ain't no utter way. Yo' how's da birthday girl did 'er like da necklace?" "Stop da madness nigga chu know she did, chu can see fo' yo' self in jus' a few." "Yo' we pullin' up now an dis bitch is packed." "Aiight I'm 2 blocks away, hold fast befo' y'all fall up in dere." "Hell homeboy chu make 'em blocks we probably jus' be findin a parkin' spot." Yo' fam' dis too congested, so I hope y'all got ya walkin' shoes on 'cus I be damn I park my shit in 'ere. Queenie circled da lot an drove out of it, an hit da block. Dere was Cortez' and his entourage three cars deep11 niggas in big body Chevy's. "Bro' is dat chu three cars deep? Dis us comin' down da street towards chu." Okay, Cortez' let da window all da way down, so dis chu cuz? "Nah cuz dis all Queenie." Cortez' made eye contact wit Queenie an winked, Queenie touched 'er neck an mouth thank chu, wit a smile. "Yo' Tez we right 'ere, so tell yo' boy to back up." Dey parked a block away from da club, steppin' out of their cars dey headed towards da club. Queenie was boss an every nigga wit 'er knew dis, 'er swagg and sex appeal dat chu had to respect an dey knew she had zero tolerance fo' bein' misrepresentation. "Queenie was confident dat out of 14 fellas followin' behind 'er 11 of 'em were watchin' 'er sway ahead of 'em. But dere was only 1 she put on fo' of course 'er main prospect an dat was Cortez' 'em self. Cortez' pulled Tez coat tail: "Yo' cuz chu know we homeboys, so I wanta sho' chu respect outta love fo' ya homeboy, by lettin' chu know I'm tryin' to get up wit Queenie tonight fam'. Not on on bedroom shit I gotta have 'er as my woman cuz chu feel me?" I respect chu and 'er to much jus' to wanta hit it an leave. Nah, mean I'm serious 'bout dat one dere Tez, so if chu good wit it homeboy I'm tryin' to be in da family fo' real. "Fam' I respect yo' gangsta an I preciate chu checkin' wit me first, but Queenie has 'er own mind. Long as she neva comes to me sayin' yo' ass disrespected or hurt 'er in anyway we have no problems." Queenie seen Tez and Cortez' had pick their speed up as she made it closer to da door entrance. Da line was pass da currency exchange across da street. "Yo' y'all see da fuckan' line family?" Lu shouted to da utters. "Yeah, fam' we peeped dat shit, but dat ain't us. "Tez,Queenie and Cortez' walked up to da bouncer Skip. Skip was a long time homeboy of Tez and Cortez' from school. "Yo' check it Skip I came all da way from East St. Boogie tryin' to sho' my guys yo' city an kick it wit my QUEEN fo' 'er birthday, so I know yo' ass ain't finna make us wait out dis long ass line. So why don't chu take dis an let all of us in." Cortez' placed a thousand dollars in da palm of Skip's hand. Befo' anything Skip said; wutsup Queenie,so it's yo' birthday huh? Queenie and Skip already knew one a nutter,dis wasn't 'er first time at da club, matter fact Skip was da nigga who handle all of 'er fake ID's. "So baby girl how old are chu now 26 is it? Damn ma chu getting old, but chu still look beautiful and innocent doe."

Queenie was well aware dat Skip was fuckin' wit Cortez' head, so she played along wit 'em.

"Yo' family give us da whole VIP section." Queenie stated. "Lil' mama chu already know wut it is. When we got word chu was steppin' out we held it jus' fo' chu,no doubt." Queenie told Skip 'ere body 'ere strap an dey wit me, so afta' chu hit capacity come see me homeboy. Queenie turned to Cortez' an gave 'em a flirtatious wink. Once in VIP Queenie signaled fo' Lu to come ova. "Fam' go place our order. She handed Lu $3,000 dollars put it on da bar an tell 'em keep it comin'." "Aiight boss nothin', but Henney and Champagne. Lu walked away jus' as da DJ put on some new joint by R. Kelly, Queenie said; "Cuz dat's my shit nigga." Singin' wit da song Queenie stood up an met Cortez' approach. He held his hand out an said; "Can I get dis dance my QUEEN?" Queenie said nothin', but took his hand an lead 'em to da dance floor on da lower level, so all could see da sexiest fly bitch, wit da hottest thugg nigga. Da 2 clowned on dance floor, "Queenie thought to 'er self damn fo' a nigga Cortez' can dance his ass off." Queenie let it be known off da back Cortez' was not available fo' da vultures an he was already taken, even doe it hadn't been sign,sealed or delivered jet. Queenie and Cortez' headed back to VIP afta' da song. Queenie heard Cortez' mumble; "Damn lil' ma a nigga gotta make chu his QUEEN." So Queenie made it 'er biz'ness to stop on da stairs an bend ova to fix da laces on 'er shoe, Cortez' was so stunned he rammed into Queenie's ass. Feelin' his erection she turned an smiled at 'em. Cortez' catchin' 'er to help 'er balance he apologized; "Shit baby girl my bad.

"Is it?" She asked. Dey both laughed it off. "Lets get somethin' to drink ma." All da fellas were havin' a ball, Tez picked up a bottle and glass handin' it to Queenie an grabbed da same fo' 'em self.

"Yo' join me in a toast. I wish lil' cuz many mo' birthday's to come, 'eres to my baby girl, my lil' nigga, a QUEEN wit boss status, 'eres lookin' at chu lil' mama." Everyone said their own personal toast an when time fo' Cortez'to chu woulda though he propose to 'er. "Yo' Queenie listen ma I know wut Imma 'bout to say and do is gonna be new to chu it might even be corny, but to me it's not wut dese niggas think. Queenie stood by Tez wit a raised brow. "Queenie I respect everything 'bout chu ma from yo' intelligence, yo' boss status, Queenie yo' chu flawless ma an no utter bitch out 'ere can touch wut chu got goin' on. I like da way chu take care of yo' own an family is 'ere thing to chu I hear. Cortez' gently grabbed Queenie's hand an asked; "Queenie will chu ride wit a nigga? Do me da honor of bein' my QUEEN?" Queenie smiled pulled Cortez' in close in ear shot she said; "Nigga chu fuck up know dat's yo' ass." She kissed his cheek, which she considers as da kiss of death.

Tez thought to 'em self; "Queenie I hope chu know dis part of da chess game baby girl" but on da utter hand he was relieved dis was his boy, so he knew no disrespect would be shown, an if dere was homeboy or not Tez had no problem deaden his ass ova his. Queenie seen Skip walkin' up.

"Wutups Queenie, looks like I jus' missed da toast. "HAPPY BIRTHDAY again ma." Skip hugged Queenie. Skip also had a thing fo' 'er, but only Queenie knew dat 'cus he step to 'er wit it, but to only be shot down like every utter nigga dat approached 'er. It wasn't dat da niggas were ugly or didn't get money it was jus' dey weren't on Queenie's level. Dey hadn't reached 'er game level an dey were much older dan she. Queenie told Skip once she turned 16 dat she would give 'em a job. He hadn't excepted, even thought she was jokin' at da time, but now da time has presented itself tonight.

"First off she said; "Ere is a lil' somethin' fo' wut chu did at da door fo' my entourage, secondly homeboy I wanted to know are chu ready to work?" Queenie asked. "Imma lil' confused ma. Wut chu mean?" Queenie said today my birthday I jus' turned 16 do chu not remember me tellin' yo' ass when I turned 16 I would give chu a job?" Guess chu thought I was bull shittin'? Nah nigga I say wut I mean and mean wut I say, now if yo' ass ready to make some real paper meet me an da crew ova in Dalton at DUSTIE'S at 2pm. "Skip said word." "Word is bond nigga." "Aiight, Queen good lookin', I'll see chu tomorrow, Skip nodded to da fellas an went back downstairs." Queenie embraced Tez puttin' a bug in his ear 'bout da convo wit Skip. "Cool cuz now enjoy yo' self we'll handle biz'ness when dat time comes. "I love chu Tez." Queenie felt a lil' buzz from da liquor, but she knew 'er limits when in public. "It was a must fo' 'er to be alert at all times, crew or no crew she had to watch 'er back at all times an da backs of dose who were wit 'er. Queenie seen a certain gleam in Tez eyes dat seemed to change his party mood. "Fam' yo' ass aiight ?" Tez tried his best to play it off. "I'm good baby girl." It was to late Queenie had spotted Red Bone and 'er clique, to Queenie dey looked like a bunch of goof's wit da exact same thing on. "So I guess dey suppose to be 'ere fo' me?" Smilin' at Tez.

"I guess so baby girl, but let dat shit fly, we came to party ma." "Cuz yo' ass know I won't start it, but better believe I will finish it fam'." Da DJ played a song dat hyped Queenie's adrenaline up so she put on 'er swagger an signal Tez to follow 'er downstairs she grabbed Cortez' hand an went to da dance floor. Tez told Lu and Chaos wut time it was, so da entourage gather downstairs as well so dey could keep an eye out fo' their boy Cortez'. Tez, Lu and Chaos let it be known dat dey peeped Red Bone and 'er girls. On da floor Queenie was all up on Cortez' an every time she turned she saw Red Bone makin' faces and talkin' shit to 'er girls. Queenie thought; "Dis ma'fucka has not had a nuff of me beatin' dat ass, how much can one person take?" 'Er conscience took ova; "Fuck 'er up if she ain't caught on jet she has no win, beat dat bitch if she looks at chu wrong." Queenie tried to think logical; "No we can't do dat we already got a case to fight an chu don't want to kill 'er. It's obvious dat she needs some type of help, so lets try an talk to 'er." "Awe yo' ass need to take yo' ass way in da back an have a seat. "Boss Queen" wut we need to do is go fuck 'er up, don't listen to dis sweet bitch right 'ere she'll have us fucked up. Let dat bitch know who chu is. Queenie shook off 'er thoughts da fight dat went on in 'er head. Queenie and Cortez' stayed on da floor fo' one mo' song, keepin' 'er eyes on Red Bone an da flunkies she noticed scattered 'round da dance floor. Queenie pressed against Cortez' an whispered chu see dese bitches. "Yeah ma I'm peepin' it." Afta' da song ended Queenie peeped Red Bone and Pink Lips walk away from da bar, dat's when Tez approached Queenie and Cortez'; "Yo' baby girl chu ready to bounce?" "Na nigga chu know I don't run from no bitch, evidently she wanta squabble dey say da third time is a charm." "Queenie said besides we still got bottles to pop. I don't know 'bout y'all, but Imma have a good time I ain't finna let dat dusty bitch ruin shit fo' me remember it's my night." Tez said; "Dis is exactly wut I was tellin' chu ma'fuckas don't know how to keep shit in da streets." Tellin' Cortez' dat Red Bone is da same bitch dat fucked up Queenie's shit on 'er b-ball career and had 'er in court fo' some shit dat coulda been avoided. Back in VIP Queenie took a seat on da couch, Tez sat beside 'er he could hardly imagine wut was goin' on inside Queenie's head. But he did know she didn't like da situation an fo' dis lil' bitch Red Bone to be in da same place starin' 'er down would be a hard pill fo' Queenie to digest.

"My QUEEN, wuts good shawty chu aiight?" Cortez' asked. She replied wit a grimace look on 'er face not even lookin' in his direction. "Baby I'm good." "Yo' fam' let me holla at chu. Cortez touch da small of Queenie's back tellin' 'er he would be right back. Tez explained to Cortez' da situation wit da blackouts Queenie have, so when da enviable happened he would not be in da dark, 'cus Tez knew it was comin'. No one was prepared fo' Queenie's next move. Red Bone made da mistake of throwin' 'er hands up at Queenie callin' 'er out an Queenie leaped ova da rail off da second floor an when she landed on da dance floor it sounded like a pack of gorillas. Queenie squared up an asked; "Wutsup bitch chu tryin' to see me?" Red ran up on Queenie an Queenie heard a stampede of goons which only meant dat 'er crew was finna flood da club somethin' crucial. Queenie stuck Red Bone in da jaw 2 of 'er girls grabbed Queenie from behind an tried to restrain 'er, but Queenie was to strong fo' their hold. Queenie's lil' ass shocked da crowd wit 'er strength Queenie was back at Red Bone befo' anyone know it. Tez spotted Queenie as she came out of 'er jacket an slung it, fo' getting she had nina tucked in 'er back Tez knew it would be da end fo' Queenie if she pull da gun in 'er stat of mind. Da way Queenie acted he knew she was in a trans. Thoughts ran through Tez head; "Da strength dis ma'fucka has when she blacks da fuck out, she can take out an army by 'er self wit no problem."

Da club ducked when Queenie upped nina an da only reason Red Bone survived was Cortez' tackled 'er. Jus' as da 2 hit da floor Queenie let nina ride: blahhh,blahhh,blahhh,blahhh,blahhh. Tez ran up grabbed Queenie from behind an lowerin' 'er arm while Chaos pride da gun out of 'er hand. "Lu take care of da owner." "Cortez' shouted it's been handled." Tez lifted Queenie off da floor in da same position an carried 'er out da club. Chaos took Queenie's jacket an wrap da gun inside an jetted fo' da door. Cortez' had his crew to snatch up Red Bone an 'er home girls since dey were da reason fo' da commotion. "Queenie snap out of it baby girl come back fam'." Lu go get 'er ride. Tez toss 'em da keys, Lu took off runnin'. Cortez' ran to Queenie's side; "Wutsup fam' she good?" "Nah cuz she still in a trans." "Let me try,_Queenie my QUEEN come on baby he looked into 'er eyes an repeated; baby come back to us. "Tez stated; "We gotta get 'er outta 'ere." Lu pulled up an Cortez said; "I'm ridin' wit 'er I'm not leavin' 'er side homeboy. Yo' but first wut chu wanta do wit dese bitches." "Put dey asses_ put dey punk asses in da trunk if chu have to." "Fuck it Cortez' yelled Chuck drive my shit an put dis Red bitch in dere wit chu, da rest of y'all know wut to do follow us an stay close." Tez and Cortez sat in da back wit Queenie, Lu drove wit Chaos in da passenger seat. "Fam' I wanta kill dese bitches." Cortez' responded. "Cuz where to?" Lu asked. "Tez told 'em nigga chu already know da park."

"Lu stated; somethin' gotta give cuz boss got a hattin' as bitch checkin' fo' every time she walk out da house, dis shit can't continue on like dis." "Listen niggas I know how y'all feel 'bout Queenie an da situation, but chu know she won't be satisfied if we lay dis bitch down. Queenie has to much pride fo' ma'fuckas to even think she went out like a coward. Dis lil' nigga has boss status an is da Queen of Chi-Town an as much as I hate to say it I help created dis beast." Queenie was an exact replica of Tez.

"So non of us will take dat from 'er chu feel me?" Imma bring 'er out of dis trans an let 'er handle dese bitches at da park. "Tez told 'em I want 'er body to leave their guns in da cars, once we get to da park pat each one of dose hoes down an make sho' dey not strapped an Queenie can get at who eva comes fo' it. A straight old school fist fight." Dis struck a nerve wit Cortez'. "Wut nigga yo' ass finna allow dese bitches to jump on my girl, where dat fight come in fair at?" "Nigga listen fam' I ain't allowin' shit, but Queenie won't have it any utter way homeboy, so if yo' ass gone be wit 'er dis is somethin' yo' ass gotta deal wit, so get use to it 'cus she ain't gonna change 'cus chu wit 'er. Bro listen to me Queenie is not yo' average chic, she's a proud individual I've been dealin' wit 'er fo' 16 years now nigga an it's in 'er bloodline." Tez stated. Queenie came back 'round. "Wutsup fam' wut happen?" She asked noticin' Cortez' sittin' next to 'er in da back seat of 'er own ride. She couldn't remember wut went on afta' she left da dance floor wit Cortez'. "No, no cuz tell me I didn't get at dat bitch in da club." "Yup! Chu did baby girl, but hear me it ain't ova fo' wut eva reason dis Red bone bitch has a vendetta wit chu an she obviously gone stay at chu 'til one of chu dead."

"THROWIN' BRICKS AT THE PENITENTIARY"

Chapter Seven
"A Mother's Words"

"Queenie replied dis city ain't big a nuff fo' da both of us, 'cus dis bitch everywhere I am."

Da vendetta Red Bone had wit Queenie

was dat she's da mother of Triples son dat was left in da empty house afta' Queenie killed 'er sons father. "Baby chu really finna do dis, yo' ma chu finna fight 11 bitches by yo' self?"

Queenie looked at Cortez' an smiled. "Look I don't apologize fo' who I am or wut I do, dis is me yo' QUEEN as chu say, so yo' ass take all of me or non of me." Queenie told Tez lets do it cuz.

"Yo' y'all patted dose bitches?" Chaos questioned. "Yeah all good." "Bring dat Red bitch ova 'ere. I got jus' one question; "Why chu keep comin' back fo' dis beat down shawty?" Red Bone's response: "Yo' I'm da mother of dat baby she left in da house alone." Only Tez, Lu and Queenie knew wut baby she was referrin' to, da rest of da entourage look puzzled. Wit dat said Red Bone stole off on Queenie. Holdin' 'er balance Queenie retorted; "Bitch now I know wut we fightin' ova I will send yo' ass to me Triple in hell an yo' son really will be a bastard of da world. My guess da promise Queenie jus' made to Red Bone got to 'er, 'cus once again she charged Queenie, but dis time she caught a round house an fell backwards. Once she got off da ground Queenie swung wit a left an missed, but connected wit da right, again Queenie put da flu flops on Red Bone, 'er friends misunderstood dis was a fair fight an everyone was suppose to wait their turn, but of course dey saw Queenie getting da best of their home girl an felt da need to jump in an hit Queenie in da back of 'er head. Some wut in a daze Red Bone saw 'er chance dis gave 'er a lil' advantage ova Queenie. Red Bone gave 'er 4 quick blows to da right side of 'er face. Queenie let out a loud grunt, swingin' da chic 'round wit one hand slammin' 'er into Red Bone. Queenie broke 'er neck an let 'er drop to da ground, she cut off

“THROWIN' BRICKS AT THE PENITENTIARY”

Red Bone's air supply an choke slammed 'er on to a picnic table. She saw three bitches run towards 'er. Tez stoppin' Cortez', Lu and Chaos from runnin' to Queenie's aid. “She good fam' she's not in a trans at da moment, she still in 'er right mind.” “So chu really gone jus' let 'er deaden 'em huh?”Cortez' asked. “If dat's wut it takes nigga fo' dis braud to leave 'er alone so be it.” “So bro yo' ass want 'er to be a killa? I don't won't my QUEEN_Tez cut him short; “Nigga yo' ass don't want wut, yo' ass goin' soft or wut homeboy? Fam' let me keep it funky nigga yo' bitch already a killa so stop actin' like chu don't know da game.” Queenie let Red Bone neck go wit da quickness she put three bitches on their backs stompin' each one of 'em one by one. Wut seem like an eternity fo' Queenie to whoop 11bitches only took 20 minutes. “Red get up an kick 'er ass.” “Why don't chu do it ma'fucka.” Queenie was fine an some wut level headed 'til she was told by one of da brauds; “If Red would have stuck to da plan an blew up da house yo' ass would be at da morgue right now identifying yo' moms body.

Queenie snapped she went hem throwin hay makers. She threw punches ol' girl threw punches.

“Yo' Chaos call my auntie house make sho' shit straight fam'.” “Damn she jus' broke 'er back.” Each braud dat ran up on Queenie she dropped wit no hesitation. Red Bone got it together an hit Queenie in 'er spin, Queenie drop to 'er knees. “Ughhh! She screamed.” Red Bone kicked 'er in da face, but befo' she got 'er foot back on da ground Queenie grabbed it an broke it in three places. Falling to da ground in excruciating pain Queenie felt no mercy she finished Red Bone off by snappin' 'er neck.

Dat night Queenie murdered 11 bitches 'cus of a threat on 'er mother's life. “Yo' clean dis shit up fam', dump everybody out 'ere.” Tez told Cortez'; “Bro I hope chu know wut dis means I need yo' ass to hide Queenie fo' a minute. She needs to lay lo' behind dis one she won't like it, but 'til I hear da word on da streets I can't risk 'er bein' 'ere. Lu I need chu to check wit da owner of da club to see wut was said an by who. Cortez' see if chu can bring 'er back fam' while I help ditch dese bitches in da river." Cortez' carried Queenie back to da truck an kissed 'er lips softly. "Ma come on back baby, please snap out of it. Yo' moms is good baby girl, my QUEEN tell me ya my QUEEN. Cortez' pleaded. He looked in 'er eyes an Queenie said; "I'm yo' QUEEN nigga." He embraced 'er an kissed Queenie lettin' 'er know he neva wants to lose 'er. Cortez' yelled; "Yo' fam' she's back lets go."

"Baby right now we gotta hide chu fo' a minute 'til we figure out da next move aiight?" Tez told Lu to take da wheel an slid in next to Queenie, so he could talk to 'er. Cortez' stayed in da truck wit Quenie while Tez explained da entire ordeal. Queenie screamed take me to my ol' g, take me to my mama. Tez embraced his cousin shhh,shhh, Ueenie auntie good she unharmed baby girl. Fo' da first time since bein' in da streets Queenie finally broke down in Tez arms like da kid she really was. Queenie cried like a baby out of everything she been through it hurt 'er to 'er heart, da pain of thinkin' she could have easily lose 'er moms, made 'er react in away not even she could control. "Tez take me to my moms fam'." "We on our way baby girl. Queenie continued to bald 'til she was in Liz's embrace.

Tez and Cortez' knew of only one way to hide Queenie an dat was to fill 'er mother in on wut happened, wut 'er daughter had done an da seriousness of da situation. Liz was confused an knew it was serious, but hurt by Queenie's actions. Doe feelin' it's somethin' she has no control ova she still didn't want 'er baby hidin' out and on da run at da age of 16. Imma agree to dis only 'cus I want my baby alive and safe. "Queenie spoke up stayin' respectful; "Yo' listen y'all don't even know da word on da streets jet, so who says I'm bein' looked fo'? I'm not scared of dese streets, I run dis city an I ain't finna hide or be ran up outta Chi-Town. Now if y'all need me to lay lo' in da house, I'll give y'all a good 2 weeks of my time in da house, but I ain't leavin' town in less it's on my terms fam'. Queenie turned an looked at Tez only an told 'em; "Word is bond nigga." Liz knew 'er daughter was stubborn as a mule, so she stepped in an calls Queenie's name to grab 'er attention. "Listen chu my only baby an even doe, I'm da mother 'ere I won't make chu go anywhere 'cus fo' wut eva da reason chu have fo' not wantin' to go must be greater dan yo' own life. I jus' hope it's not a stupid one.”

“Queenie I'm not ready to bury yo' lil' crazy ass 'cus chu stubborn an has to much pride to let go of dat big ass ego of urns. Liz voice took an uneven tone. “If chu feel like chu'll be hidin' den jus' take a trip, go on a vacation. It's not like chu ain't got da money to do so, if chu can spend $90,000 dollars in 20 minutes chu can take yo' young ass on a vacation. Yeah don't think I don't know wut chu out dere doin' in 'em streets wit Tez,Lu and yes Chaos. Liz threw 'er hands up it was dead silences. “Don't say anything jus' let me finish, not tryin' to front chu off in front of yo' peeps, but I take it we all family in 'ere. Queenie, mama from da streets da hood of East St. Boogie da ghetto, so I know how da game is played, nah I have neva distributed or trafficked any drugs, but I know da signs when someone else is handling their biz'ness. I respect da game itself, an baby I respect yo' game, but don't think mama sleep on da reason why dese niggas walk 'round 'ere callin' chu “Boss” an has label chu as QUEEN of da city. So yes I know an I jus' want chu to be extra careful, I'm not sayin' ya scared 'cus I know its in yo' blood, but it fears me dat Ola will take chu from me. “Out of all my years on dis earth I've witness only 2 ways out of dis game of hustlers and murders,jus' 2 baby girl an dat's in a body bag or da penitentiary an den some neva see da streets again.” Everyone listened as Liz talked.

Queenie said; “Aiight when do I gotta leave?” “Cortez' said; “Where do chu wanta go we can leave tonight.” “So chu jus' gonna drop yo' biz'ness an go wit me not even knowin' where or how long I'll be gone huh?” “Yeah I not gone leave yo' side, I told chu ya my QUEEN.” Tez spoke up; “Auntie dis 'ere my homeboy Cortez' from East St. Boogie, dis da nigga who sent Queenie da necklace.

“Okay so chu my baby's secret admirer huh?” I see now. Liz told Cortez'; “I love my baby chu know dat right?” “Yes ma'am I do.” “Well I am goin' to keep it funky wit chu on da up and up, don't hurt 'er, disrespect 'er or put yo' hands on 'er at all an if I have da slightest feelin' she's hurt 'cus of chu I will be at yo' ass.” Liz asked; “We gotta understandin'?” “Yes ma'am.” Cortez' looked at Tez as to say damn man yo' aunt's crazy as 'er fuckan' daughter. “Change of plans “I wanta go to Vegas. Tez once chu find out wutsup 'bout a week chu Lu and Chaos can come out an join us.” Queenie stated; “I'll be in Vegas fo' three weeks, when y'all get dere everything is own me. We can kick it fo' 2 weeks den come back to da Chi. “Ma yo' chu gone be aiight 'ere by yo' self?” Queenie neva let anyone know why she didn't listen to reason,when it all boil down 'er moms was all she had. “Baby chu jus' go an have some fun an try to get yo' mind off all dis mess. Some where down da line chu were dealt a bad hand, but we will figure da shit out.” Cortez' made a call. “Hello wutup Chuck?” Cortez' had sent his entourage back to da hotel to clean 'em selves up. “Bro pack up we back in East St. Boogie tonight. Hit me when y'all ready. “Befo' we hit it south I need chu to meet me wit dose 2 big duffel bags, 'cus we not travelin' wit 'em family. Cortez' asked; “May I speak to chu both fo' a second in private. He took Queenie by da hand an walked to a nutter area of da house, dey walked upstairs to 'er room. “Tez said wutsup, cuz?” Cortez' said listen, Tez chu knew why I came to town, but QUEEN chu don't , but neither of chu have no clue of da surprise I have fo' Queenie. Shit got thrown off, so I'll tell chu now.

“I had 300 bricks shipped to my spot in Dalton fo' chu my QUEEN, it's a gift from me to chu, so my nigga gone meet us befo' we go. Baby girl dis is ova a million dollars worth of dope.”

“Why chu bringin' me bricks like dat?” “It's like dis I know where chu come from an hopefully I know where chu goin' wit it, an I respect dat. Dis man 'ere is my bro since we was knee high to a duck, so don't think we don't talk. I know yo' ambitions, bein' da richest female in Chi-Town an Queenie if it takes me to help chu get dat millionaire mark befo' chu turn 18 I'll do it all ova again triplin' bricks if dat's wut it takes ma. Despite of wut I feel 'bout chu bein' in da game.” “Damn fam' I had no idea it was dat deep.” Tez stated. “Yo' call yo' boy back an have 'em meet us at my stash house, I gotta see Blue befo' I leave anyway. Jus' tell 'em go towards da park he jus' left an dey'll see my truck. Queenie looked at Tez an gave 'em a devilish grin as to say nigga I told chu so.

Queenie grabbed 'er luggage from da closet an packed fo' 'er trip, Queenie had a duffel bag full of shoe wear, fo' every outfit dere was a pair of gym shoes to match. Da girl definitely had a shoe fetish.

“Excuse me fo' a sec.” Pointin' to da door. Queenie needed to change gear an retrieve 'er stash from da safe. She put a stack in each shoe she placed in da bag givin' 'er a total of $28,000. Afta' she changed into a all white Levi outfit wit “Boss Queen” airbrushed all ova it in red and black letters an of course she had da shoes airbrushed also wit crowns on top of Q's to da left. Queenie put a nutter 10 stacks in 'er pocket jus' 'cus money. Tez yelled yo' lil' nigga chu ready? Queenie responded; “Yeah come get my luggage fam'.” Tez sent Lu and Chaos to grab 'er bags, she carried da carry on to da bottom of da stairs an handed it to Tez. “Family put dat in my truck. “Chu ready baby?” Liz asked .

“Yes ma'am I am ready, Queenie pulled 10 stacks out 'er pocket an gave $4,000 to Liz. “Ere ma take dis an if chu run out befo' Tez comes to me I'll have 'em hit up again aiight. Liz took a good look at 'er daughter realizin' fo' da first time dis child has mo' authority dan any grown ass nigga who's been in da game all his life. “Thank chu now go head have fun an don't worry 'bout me I'll be fine, jus' be safe. An Cortez'. “Yes ma'am,” “Son take care of my daughter, let nothin' happen to 'er. “I will protect 'er Ms. Miles.” At da stash house Queenie and Tez went to da backyard leavin' da utters in da house. Outside Queenie split da bricks wit Tez. “Nigga I told yo' ass it would be a matter of time befo' we come up, nigga it's ride and die wit us. Nigga I come up yo' ass come up feel me.”

“Now put dat shit in yo' safe cuz.” “Queenie he gave chu dat so yo' ass could end yo' hustle early.”

“Fam' I peeped game, but yo' ass know I work on my own terms. Tez I'm feelin' Cortez' a great deal, but he not finna come in an change me or stop me from doin' me, dependin' on how far dis thing goes wit us, he jus' might be able to soften me a lil', but fo' now Imma do me nigga." Word is bond.

Afta' Queenie finished layin' out all 'er demands an request on Tez dey walk back in da house. "Oh yeah fam' we suppose to meet wit Skip tomorrow 'bout 'em getting down wit da team. He already filled da position he jus' needs to be screened. If yo' ass see da signs of any bitch in 'em fam' tell 'em to push on. He'll be at DUSTIE'S ova in Dalton at 2 o'clock 'cus of da mishap I won't be dere, so I need chu to handle it da best way chu see fit. Chu can put 'em on or he can wait 'til I get back. Cuz chu already know wut to do fo' Chaos I want all biz'ness put on hold 'til I return."

Queenie parked in da middle of da street an told Cortez' to switch seats wit 'er so he could drive. Tez embraced Queenie kissed 'er on da forehead an in ear shot he whispered "I love chu Ueenie, stay safe lil' nigga. Where is nina?" Right 'ere, she told 'em. "Yo' chu neva leave home wit out it huh cuz?" "Yo' I know I can't take it on da plane, so when we get ready to leave East St. Boogie I'll lock it in my truck an jus' park it in Cortez' garage." "Aiight baby girl stay in touch wit me, so I know wuts good wit chu." "Chu do da same, specially if yo' ass get wind of anything da streets talkin' 'bout."

Chapter Eight
"Neva Leavin' Da Past Behind"

Cortez' said; "Now dat I got chu alone, my QUEEN wuts good how is chu truly feelin'?"

"I'm good Cortez', but since we are alone tell me yo' intentions fo' us. Jus' lay it all out on da table 'cus to be honest,I hate bull shit an I don't like playin' games in less I'm callin' da shots, feel me?"

"Besides bein' beautiful I see yo' ass deadly wit a short fuse wit no tolerance fo' fake ma'fuckas at all shawty." Cortez' chuckled. "Damn ma lighten up baby ya wit me now an trust me I'm not gone steer chu wrong. It's like I said befo' I like yo' swagg baby besides dat sexy hard core shell on da outside I know deep down inside dere's a sweet intelligent woman who needs to be recognized as such an be treated like a QUEEN. An Queenie Miles if chu give me da chance chu won't regret it. Let me sho' chu wut every woman wants in life." "An wut is dat Mr. Fabs?" "Ma let me be yo' knight and shinin' armor, so will ya let me do dat Queenie?" "I do feel relaxed 'round chu,so I guess I can give yo' ass a trial run." Cortez' and Queenie were feelin' one a nutter. "Baby if chu feel chu can handle me an wut comes wit me I'll be by yo' side. It is one mo' thing I need chu to always be open wit me don't be afraid to speak wuts on yo' mind tell me wut eva." Queenie told Cortez' I'm still a virgin.

"Queenie I won't pressure chu ma, I'm not on dat it's when eva chu ready. I'm tryin' to get down wit chu, so sex is da furthest thing from my mind, I'm tryin' to grow wit chu an pressin' chu fo' da poo-nanny isn't gonna let me know who chu is. Don't get it twisted ma I'm not a thirsty ass nigga, so when ya ready we can make it happen, aiight. Cortez' placed his hand on 'er thigh an said; "It's all 'bout chu lil' mama. Baby is chu hungry 'cus we can stop at da Waffle House an get somethin' to eat."

"Yeah I could eat a lil' somethin'." "So shawty dat's how chu keep dat figure, chu don't eat an chu stay in da streets huh?" Da fellas trailed 'em an dey all pulled in da parking lot of da Waffle House. Cortez' parked got out an went 'round to open Queenie's door fo' 'er he placed his hand on da small of 'er back an dey walked into da restaurant. Cortez' and Queenie sat together in one booth an da fellas sat in seats on both sides of 'em an while dey ate talked, laughed and joked, Queenie felt security wit 'em all. Cortez' reassured 'er dat while she was wit 'em 'er money was no good.

"Yo' lets roll out Cortez' told his crew." Cortez' walked Queenie back to da truck an openin' 'er door fo' 'er once again, he den told Chuck; "Listen homeboy once we touch East St. Boogie go straight to da crib so we can have a meetin'." Queenie laid back an rest 'er eyes an let 'er thoughts take 'er somewhere else an dey did, back to age 14 showin' 'er how innocent 'er life was befo' she turned 15.

"THROWIN' BRICKS AT THE PENITENTIARY"

It's not no where as innocent now. Queenie had jus' started da summer league basketball tournament, it was 'er second year on da squad, she finished high school at da age 14 wit honors. Queenie was a straight A student, very smart dey couldn't believe she was a senior at 'er age. So Liz let 'er join da city squad, she knew Queenie had a passion fo' basketball an 'er skills were on point.

"Queenie stayed under Tez he was 'er keeper. Tez didn't mind doe 'cus it was like Queenie had 'er own mind an Tez recognized dat in 'er on top of dat she was a good kid. She neva questioned Tez 'bout wut he did or how he got his paper, she jus' watched, listen and learned, but on 'er 15th birthday life was turned upside down fo' da young teen. Tez picked 'er up to take 'er to 'er game. "So wutsup lil' nigga, happy birthday cuz afta' yo' game we gonna eat an do wut eva chu wanta do fo' it aiight. Wut auntie get chu?" Queenie replied; "Chu know moms gave me a pair of jumpers and a hunnid dollars.

"Tell me wut chu want fo' yo' birthday baby girl." "Anything cuz?" She questioned. "Yeah wut eva chu want lil' nigga, an I got chu." "I wanta slang dope like chu, I wanta get paper jus' like chu cuz." Tez knew she was serious as da game she played on da court, he neva denied Queenie anything. Dis was one of da reasons she's da way she is. "Sho' lil' nigga first time chu fuck up it's ova yo' ass out da game." Cool cuz was all she retorted an Queenie took Tez lead. Now look at 'er runnin' Chicago. Queenie was woken from 'er thoughts by Cortez'; "Baby girl we 'ere chu ready to go in?" Queenie set up checked 'er surroundings, she neva been to Cortez' house so she didn't really know wut to expect. Da block was some wut decent, but he still stayed in da hood. Cortez' home inside was lavish an his décor was tasteful Queenie felt he had a woman decorated fo' 'em. "Yo' Cortez who laid yo' crib out fo' chu?" She asked."Baby I did it why chu like it ma?" Cortez' took 'er by da hand to give 'er a full tour of his home." Chuck and da crew brought Queenie luggage in fo' 'er since Cortez' decided dey would leave 'bout noon. Dis would give 'em time to tight up a few loose ends in da early mornin'. He noticed his QUEEN need some rest befo' dey left fo' Vegas. Cortez' showed Queenie to da master bedroom wit a jacuzzi an told 'er to make 'er self at home. "Baby I need to have a meetin' wit da fellas real quick. I'll have Chuck bring yo' bags up, so chu can take a bubble bath or shower , so chu can relax 'cus we gotta a long day a head of us. Cortez' bein' a gentle man told Queenie he would let 'er sleep in da master bedroom an he would sleep in da guest room down da hall. "No, no chu not leavin' me in dis big ass room by myself." Queenie soften 'er tone an asked Cortez' will chu hold me tonight? I haven't slept peaceful in awhile now since my life has been in a up roar, so sleep has not come easy."

Cortez' walked towards Queenie grabbin' 'er 'round da waist; "Sho' lil' mama wut eva chu want, but my QUEEN ya safe 'ere. Let me handle dis an I'll be right back up." Cortez' kissed Queenie's lips an 'er knees damn near buckled. Chuck brought Queenie's bags upstairs befo' Cortez' walked out da room. "Ere yo' bags shawty." Queenie went to take a shower, enterin' da bathroom she noticed stereo sittin' in da corner wit stacks of cassette tapes: LAURYN HILL,JANET,PEARL JAM,VANILLA ICE,DRE,PUBLIC ENEMY. Queenie turned da shower on, so it could get steamy den she popped ADINA HOWARDS cassette in (T-SHIRT and PANTIES). "Awe shit dis my shit." Queenie danced 'round da bathroom stripped out of 'er clothes an stepped into da shower, lathered 'er body as she sang along wit da lyrics. Afta' she dried 'er physique an admired 'er self in da full length mirror. Fo' 16 years old she had a body of a goddess. Blowin' 'er self a kiss as she bent ova to lotion 'er body an put on a red and black lace bra and pantie set, an red wife beater. Queenie gave 'er self a once ova statin'; "Keep it tight baby girl." Queenie turned da stereo off an gathered 'er things an returned to da bedroom. Queenie climbed into da nice comfortable king size bed, fo' some well needed rest. Queenie said prayers fo' 'er mother and Tez an closed 'er eyes. She felt a presence besides 'ers in da room. Queenie clutched nina under da pillow an opened 'er eyes as she pointed 'er nine at Cortez'. "Yo' baby girl it's me." Cortez' was froze in his steps wit his hands in da air; "My QUEEN put da gun down ma." "Damn my bad, dis shit has me trippin' I feel da whole situation has knocked me off my square."

Queenie looked at Cortez' an stated; "But I refuse to go down like some punk ass bitch ain't no nigga or bitch gonna see me sweat or catch me slippin' an dat includes Ola. Cortez' eased next to Queenie, "Listen I'm 'ere an I plan on givin' chu auxiliary in every way I can. Do chu feel me? When I told yo' mother and Tez I was gone be wit chu an protect chu from any and everyone. Baby I meant dat QUEEN, so let all yo' fears go aiight." "Do chu want to talk 'bout wuts goin' on?" "Queenie said; "Thank chu." Cortez' said; "Baby let me jump in da shower, so I can smell fresh like chu I feel flithy, give me 10 minutes. "Aiight Mr. Fabs, I'll be right 'ere waitin'." Queenie had thoughts of wut Cortez' physique looked, she wondered if it would go wit his face. She doubted very seriously if he was flabby underneath, but had to see fo' 'er self, so she went to take a peek. Even doe she hadn't had sex jet it didn't mean 'er love box didn't get moist at da sight of certain niggas. Wit da bathroom door ajar Queenie stuck 'er head in to see wut Cortez' looked like in his glass shower. "Damn dis nigga got his build on." Queenie also recognized he hung 'bout a good 9 to 10' inches, wonderin' when da time presented itself will she be able to handle all of 'em. Queenie got back in bed wit a smile planted on 'er face tryin' to figure out how long she would make Cortez' wait befo' she gave up da poo-nanny.

"Baby Cortez' whispered as he walk back into da room; "Is chu still awake?" "Yeah I am." Cortez' wit nothin' on, but a pair of boxers and b-ball shorts on climbed in bed behind Queenie an asked; "So chu want me to hold chu lil' mama?" "Mmmmm yo' ass smell good baby, hold on don't tell me dat's Blue Maimbua." "How chu know." Queenie asked. Cortez' replied; "Ma chu ain't fuckin' wit no dumb low class ass nigga I know my shit. I stay up on all da latest colognes and perfumes, neva know when I might want to purchase my lady da best smellin' perfume. Cortez' kissed da nap of Queenie's neck.

“THROWIN' BRICKS AT THE PENITENTIARY”

Queenie almost exploded, she had neva been dat close damn near naked in a mans present. Queenie turned ova facin' Cortez'. He asked; “Wutsup my QUEEN embracin' 'er he could feel 'er body relax in his arms. Would chu like to talk 'bout wuts botherin' chu?” Da conversation started; “I asked fo' dis life, when I turned 15 Tez asked wut I wanted fo' my birthday, while we were on da way to my game an I told 'em; “I wanted to get paper wit 'em. He asked no questions, I don't know doubts may have crossed his mind, but he neva questioned me 'bout da reason.” “So ma chu play basketball right?” “Yeah I ball, but all dat might be ova fo' me.” “So how did a beauty as yo' self become, so rough?” “I guess from jus' bein' under Tez an his friends 24/7. I neva questioned 'em , I rode in silence when he went to handle biz'ness, hangin' 'round his boys I analyze every body an when we were alone I let 'em know who was true, who was fake and who would ride and die fo' his ass. So I guess me speakin' my mind didn't sit well wit niggas, now it's all good 'cus I run shit da way I want to.” I'm thorough wit my shit,so to even enter my circle of life I take chu through hell baby.” Cortez' wanted to lighten da mood, so he asked Queenie is dat wut chu gonna take me threw? Queenie looked at 'em an smiled out linin' da muscles on his chest she stated; “Nah should I?”

“I would hope not” “Queenie baby tell me wut chu expect outta me?” “Cortez' I expect nothin' mo' dan wut chu do an fo' yo' ass to be a man of yo' word an jus' neva make promises to me.”

“So is chu lettin' me be yo' man? Look Queenie I'm not 'ere to take anyone's place or be chief ova chu, but I do want us to conquer our shit together. I'm not tryin' to cut in on wut chu and Tez got goin' on baby I wanta be part of yo' family literally. Wut eva I got I want it to be ours an I only ask in return chu be my QUEEN, so do chu think we can make dat happen lil' mama an take dis shit to a nutter level?”

“So how long befo' chu fall in love wit me? Queenie ignored da question all together. “Hold up ma don't get defensive on me I jus' wanted to suggest dat chu let me take chu to a specialist I know, so chu can get checked out an see want causes yo' blackouts. I'll pay fo' it wut eva it cost , I jus' want chu to know wut ya dealin' wit, I'll even go wit chu fo' moral support. Queenie I won't pressure chu, but I needed to put it out dere, so chu understand I'm not on bull shit. Be leave it or not ya my main concern ma." Afta' Cortez' pillow talk Queenie sat up an straddled 'em. "Yo' do we have to leave out tomorrow? Can we spend da day in East St. Boogie, I wanta see wut yo' town has to it." She jokingly said; "Neva know I might leave Chicago an move 'ere, considerin' dis where my mother is from."

"Aiight shawty afta' I finish up my biz'ness we'll hit da city an do wut eva yo' heart desires. When do chu want me to make our flight fo'?" Cortez' questioned. "Chu can book it fo' Tuesday I'll be ready dat gives me 2 days to see East St. Boogie." Queenie laid 'er body on top of Cortez' an said; "Hold me an she finally went to sleep. Mornin' came, Queenie rolled ova to find she was in bed alone, fillin' da warm sun on 'er face, she slid out of bed an Cortez' walked in fully dress. "Baby do chu eat breakfast? Go get dress, so I can take chu out to eat." Queenie made da bed an went into da bathroom. "My QUEEN I'll be downstairs baby." "Aiight I'll be ready in a sec." Afta' Queenie showered she put on some purple fitted KROSS KOLOR jeans wit a purple and white t-shirt to match wit same color suede air force ones dat had Queenie embroider on da swoosh sign. Queenie placed 'er my QUEEN necklace on along wit bracelet and earrings a few squirts of perfume she placed 10 stacks in 'er pocket an 'er nine in da small of 'er back. Not conceited, but convinced Queenie walked wit a high strut da girl swagger was one of it's own. She walked in da room an Cortez' asked; "Chu ready ma? I'm in 'ere da sound came from a den dat held a pool table,sectional couch,big floor model tv, 2 Nintendo and stereo system. Dis was Cortez' an his entourages man cave. Cortez' and a few of da fellas were loungin'. Queenie tapped on da door. "Come in baby." "Wutsup fellas, how y'all feelin'?" Cortez' walked up to Queenie an kissed 'er on da cheek, she snatched 'er head away an clenched 'er teeth;

"Nigga don't eva kiss me on my cheek." Cortez' seemed confuse by Queenie's reaction. Queenie stated wit venom in 'er voice; "To me dat's da kiss of death an fo' yo' ass to kiss me my cheek will put us at a bad distance. Karma is a ma'fucka, but dat's a signature I've used on ma'fuckas I murk."

Cortez' pulled Queenie close an told 'er; "Ma fo' give me I didn't know, but trust it'll 'eva happen again, now I understand why chu kissed ol' girl cheek befo' chu snapped 'er neck." Cortez' searched Quenie's eyes fo' a sign dat she excepted his apology, but Queenie peeped his tactics an pulled 'em in close to 'er in ear shot. "Yo' ass fo' given, but stop tryin' to analyze me 'cus chu won't find wut chu lookin' fo' 'til I'm ready fo' chu to." She kissed 'em an said; "I am ready now." Once Queenie walked out da room, Chuck step to Cortez'. "Yo' bro yo' ass got hell on 2 feet right dere, so my nigga I hope yo' ass ready wut shawty finna hand chu family." All Cortez' could do was shake his head, he knew his boy had a point. Queenie was a beautiful beast an wit dat alone she's hell. Cortez' like da fiestiness in 'er he loved a challenge an Cortez' knew she would give 'em a run fo' dat challenge.

Chapter Nine
"One Wrong Turns Good But Goes South"

Cortez' and Queenie rode in Cortez' Chevy he stated; "I knew I would get chu back in my big body." She smiled an gave Cortez' mind fo' play wit sexual talk. Queenie flirted wit 'em. "Tell me since chu knew I'd be back in yo' big body wut did yo' mind tell chu I would be doin' in it?" "Jus' wut chu doin', ridin' wit me by my side ma." "Oh so chu jus' sho' 'bout yo' shit huh?" "Nah mean, dis 'ere baby girl was jus' a fluke a bad situation I wish woulda neva occurred, but unfortunately it did. An yeah I won't front it worked out in my favor, 'cus I was at da right place jus' at da wrong time baby girl. If I wasn't dere at dat time who knows where chu woulda gone an if I woulda eva seen chu again. Queenie started to feel like mush 'round Cortez' she questioned 'er self ova and ova. She couldn't figure it out whether it was lust,love 'cus she neva experienced it befo', but Queenie took it as she was fallin' in love.“Hold yo' thoughts fo' a sec I need to check on moms.” Da ringin' and ringin' of Liz phone really didn't bother 'er 'cus she knew Liz had to be at work by 7:30 am, but it was 10 am so Queenie tried again an Liz answered. “Hello.” “Ma it's me, wutsup?” “Aye baby how are chu likin' Vegas?” Queenie answered honest; “Not jet ma I wasn't ready to leave jus' jet. I wanted to see wut it be like in yo' hometown, but I had Cortez' to book our flight fo' Tuesday. Ma wut would chu think 'bout movin' back home to yo' original home?” Liz got a lil' excited. “So wut is chu sayin' Queenie chu ready to leave Chi-Town?” “Ma it could be a thought, it all depends on wut da place has to offer.” “So chu ready to leave Tez an all dis utter mess behind chu?” “Wut? Ma Tez is my ace chu know dat, so dere is no separation between us if I decide an when I decide Tez and yo' sister is movin' to. It's only da 4 of us, Tez and I is da only 2 y'all have so trust and believe when I give 'em da heads up on wut I wanta do, he'll be down.” “Anyway ma it was jus' a question, I really called to see how chu were an wut time chu got off.” “I get off at 7:30 pm, dey got da old lady workin' 12 hours now.” “Ma chu be workin' to hard fo' da lil' paper dat chu be receivin', but I guess chu do take pride in yo' job. Yo' ma yo' pockets good?” “Baby girl I am good I jus' need chu to be safe.” “Yeah ma I'm safe we are on da way to get some breakfast at da Waffle House an he's gonna take me 'round St. Boogie an probably hit a few stores up. Well Imma let chu get back to work, I love ya ol' g.” Queenie hung up da hitter fo' it only to ring. “Wutsup,who dis?” “Oh lil' nigga yo' ass don't know da number no mo'?” “Nigga how yo' ass gone act, me and moms jus' got done talkin' 'bout chu, but we can talk 'bout dat later.” “Yo' lil' nigga I call to tell chu da word. Everything seems to be good, but dey had an amber alert on tv fo' 2 missin' people Red Bone an Pink Lips it said dey been missin' fo' a few days now an if anyone has any info to call." "Nothin' mo' dan dat doe I also talk to da owner of da club everything straight on his end, so everything an everybody has been squared away. Oh yeah da owner said if Mr. D. needs 'em to be a witness when chu go to court 'em and Skip will be dere since dey were at da game, he said dey seen da whole thing. "Yo' fam dat's wutsup nah mean." Tez said; "Utter dan dat everybody who's anybody straight." Queenie laughed nigga yo' ass crazy cuz. "How is my baby Blue doin'? I know I don't need to ask 'bout Red 'cus dose 2 are jus' like their masters, dey gone stick together like glue so if one is cool da utter is to. Dose 2 are gonna die together." "It's rid and die baby girl."

"Word is bond fam'." "Fam I'm finna eat, so I'll hit chu back later, yo' fam' make sho' yo' ass make dat flight Tuesday." "Yo' we'll be dere an Skip dat's all on chu ma." Aiight don't trip I'll take care of it when I touch down cuz." Queenie knew from wut Tez said he had da meetin' wit Skip, but decided to wait 'til she returned home. "Tez yelled yo lil' nigga I love yo' ass." "Love chu always cuz."

"Y'all really dat close huh?" Cortez' asked. "Yeah I'm his baby girl an will always be."

"So be it, but yo' chu my QUEEN an will always be." Cortez' seem to be markin' his territory, but only if he knew he could neva break dat bond Tez and Queenie had even if he tried. "Now wut chu wanta eat ma?" "Let me get a T- bone ova easy eggs, hash browns pancakes wit a glass of OJ." Cortez' told da waitress I'll have da same thing. Afta' everyone ordered, Chuck sat behind Queenie in a booth to 'er left facin' da door saw a shawty an 'er crew he stated; "Damn shawty fine as my ma'fuckan Chevy fam'." "Nigga chu mean to tell me yo' ass gonna compare 'er to yo' car?" Dey all laughed. Cortez' said; "Bro yo' ass trippin' how chu gonna say dat shit?" Chuck said; " Excuse me QUEEN no offense or disrespect ma." "Yo' ain't non taken homeboy." "Aiight Cortez' bro all bull shit a side. Yo' ass gonna tell me dat braud jus' walked in ain't fine? Keep it one hunnid fam'"

"Listen 'ere fam' Imma man befo' anything, so don't fo' get dat. Now I didn't say shawty wasn't a looker, so to answer yo' question she aiight, but no utter woman can compare to wut I see befo' me. Secondly all I asked was how da hell yo' ass was comparin' 'er to a car nigga. Yo' I keeps it real, so don't front me nigga. Queenie sat back against da wall wit 'er leg stretched across da seat. Noticin' da girl Chuck was talkin' 'bout had sat at da counter 'er an 'bout 7 utters. Queenie saw da stares an heard da giggles figurin' dey were still new to life an wanted to be seen. When da waitress took 'er order Queenie peep da girl scribble somethin' on a napkin an handed it back to da waitress. "Excuse me sir 'ere is yo' food an dis is from da young lady at da counter. Holdin' out da napkin fo' Cortez' to take he looked pass da waitress to see who she was talkin' 'bout Queenie intercepted da note, wit out openin' it she asked; "Can I see yo' pen?" Queenie wrote; "He's good, but thank chu fo' yo' interest home girl." "Can chu give dat back to da young lady?" An said thank chu wit a smile.

"Y'all enjoy yo' meals." Chuck looked at Cortez' an exclaimed family dis can't be good. Queenie wiped 'er mouth an stated; I'm good it can only be bad fo' 1 person or all 7 if she brings 'er ass ova 'ere an get outta pocket. Feel me utter dan dat like I said I'm cool." Smart remarks and loud talkin' came from da counter. Queenie not lookin' their way could hear one of da girls gas 'er up. "Awe! Shit Chuck blurted out, someone else said shit finna go hem." Cortez sat back wiped his mouth wit a napkin. Non of dese niggas ran from anything an neither did Queenie, but afta' watchin' Queenie in action dey didn't want to see 'er like dat, so Chuck asked; "Y'all ready to bounce family?" "Cortez' responded; "All we can do is intercept, 'cus she ain't goin'." Queenie stated; I'm cool baby, but yo' if y'all wanta save dat face of 'ers chu say so fine it's up to chu." Chuck thought better of it an said fuck it an stayed seated. "Wutsup Popi?" Cortez' said; "Wutsup shawty?" "I sent chu my name and number, but I see it neva made it to yo' hand at all." "Nah, it didn't, chu got it back right? So wut did it tell chu shawty?" Queenie asked. "Better jet I'll tell chu wut it said; He's good, but thank chu fo' yo' interest."

“Oooooh shit dat's a dis if I eva heard one.” “See 'ere home girl no disrespect to yo' game chu tried to spit to my homeboy, but honestly chu interruptin' our breakfast.” Queenie told 'er in a sarcastic way; “Dis 'ere ain't even yo' level.” “Did I come ova 'ere to talk to yo' ass hell nah, so who in da fuck told chu to speak?”

“Yo' shawty Queenie threw up 'er hand up fo' Cortez' not to speak.” “Hold on lil' girl it really doesn't matter if yo' ass was da PRESIDENTS wife. Queenie stayed calm tellin' 'er self; “Don't let dis bitch test yo' gangsta 'cus she's not on yo' level. Chu came to have a good time an get away from all yo' problems.” So Queenie stood an walked away, Cortez' stood also he knew some shit was finna pop off, but Queenie surprised 'em when she asked; “Y'all ready to roll out?” Queenie heard ol' girl say hold on as she grabbed Cortez' hand. “Is dat how chu get down, chu got bitches speakin' fo' chu?”

“Shawty watch yo' self yo' dis ain't a game chu wanta play.” “Yo' so wut yo' ass to good to holla back or yo' ass scared of pussy?” Queenie turned 'round. “Did I hear 'er call me a bitch?” Chuck lied nah ma I don't think_Queenie shot 'em a look like shut da fuck up. One of da people who came in wit ol' girl jumped off da stool at da counter an told Queenie; “Yeah yo' ass heard 'er right. Queenie neva raised 'er voice, but kept it firm. “Cortez' bring dat bitch outside wit chu.” “Nah bitch he ain't gotta bring me no where 'cus I'm on my way.” 'Er crew followed an Cortez' made his way to Queenie, Chuck was already by Queenie's side pleadin' wit 'er not to do it. Queenie told Chuck; “Fam' I'm good I won't leave dis spot word is bond.” “Baby is chu good can we jus' leave?” Queenie looked in Cortez' eyes an told 'em; “Baby I'm straight word is bond.” Cortez' smiled at 'er an kissed 'er statin'; “Dat's my QUEEN.” But befo' dey got in da car Cortez', Queenie and Chuck heard da girl tell 'er associates; “Look at dis punk ma'fucka kissin' dis bitch. He got 'er ass talkin' fo' 'em, I should slap da shit outta both of 'em.” 'Er group started to laugh. “Yo' lil' girl yo' ass need to back off chu really don't wanta go down dat road wit dat mouth of urns less yo' ass can throw 'em hands. Jus' a warnin."

"Nigga I don't need no ma'fuckan fare warnin' from yo' ass." "Aiight bitch, an Chuck threw his hands in da air gave his homeboy dab an had a seat on da hood of his Chevy fo' a good view of wut was 'bout to come. "Yo' y'all heard me give 'er heads up." Queenie, Cortez' she shot back. "Nah, I won't sit back an let 'er continue to call me a bitch, I tried to let da first bitch go. Y'all heard me say I would, Chuck warned 'er mo' dan once an she still wanta be 'bout it 'bout it so Imma take it as she's testin' my gangsta now." Queenie took da burner out of 'er back damn near slammin' it into Cortez' chest. Fuck! Chuck. Befo' Chuck could get off da car Queenie blazed on ol' girl. Cortez' and Chuck told da utter six; "Don't run up stay da fuck out of it." Queenie slammed 'er head into da glass window of da restaurant once she fell to da ground Queenie kicked 'er in da head an told 'er; "When yo' ass been told to step da fuck off listen an move da fuck 'round bad ass." Queenie walked off like da boss she was. "Yo' lets ride." Cortez' had Chuck go pay fo' da meals since dey didn't get da check 'cus of da commotion. "Yo' baby pull up to da door, yo' Chuck fam' give dis to da manager I believe a thousand should be a nuff to replace dat window." "My QUEEN a nigga trippin' yo' ass didn't blackout 'cus truth be told ma dat shit scares me." "Man I don't know wut makes me have da blackouts, but when I peep ol' girl on bull shit I had to keep remindin' myself I gotta see my moms again, so I guess dat's wut kept me coherent. I don't like my buttons pushed when shit can be avoided, but I not finna jus' let yo' ass treat me an be aiight wit it. I tried to hold my composure." "Yeah baby chu did, I'll give ya dat." Cortez' said; "So do ya still wanta go shoppin'?" "Yeah I need to treat myself, bitches out 'ere got me breakin' a sweat and actin' a donkey out 'ere in all dis hot south weather." "Well in dat case let me take my baby to da mall an it's my treat wut eva ya want." Cortez' replied. Cortez' sent his entourage back to work except Chuck. Chuck was his right hand man da first to bust if anything went down.

"Cortez' told Queenie if chu want it get an shop 'til yo' heart is content." Queenie decided to take it easy on 'em da first go 'round even doe she coulda hit his pockets hard. "Yo' Cortez' baby y'all ain't got no special Taylor 'ere dat can hook up yo' own personal designs up? Fam' I don't like walkin' 'round lookin' like everybody else. I get my clothes specially designed fo' me. It's all 'bout dressin' to out impress myself." Cortez' told 'er; "Yeah, baby we can go see Mr. Wong he can hook ya up wit wut eva ya want. I don't know how long it'll actually take, but he'll get it done." "Befo' we go see 'em I want to stop in Nike World." Queenie bought 5 pair of shoes knowin' she could focus on how she wanted 'er outfits designed. Once in Mr. Wong store Cortez' introduced da 2 an Queenie and Mr. Wong went to da back of da store to discuss Queenie's preference. "Mr. Wong chu a biz'ness man an I am a biz'ness woman, so I won't waste yo' time 'cus mines is money. Now I like to be different when I dress from head to toe. Now I got 2 pair of kicks 'ere an if chu can get 'em done to match dese outfits designed I need 'em back by 10am Tuesday, I know it's short notice, but money is no object an if chu can get it done yo' ass got a customer fo' life." Queenie was talkin' Mr. Wong language $, so he smiled an shook his head. "Don't worry I'll do yo' designs myself." Queenie told 'em lets work 'round my shoes dey are green suede and leather da suede part I want to be dyed beige 'round da toe area to da middle section den add small gold crowns stitched on da inside of da swoosh sign add "Boss Queen" embroidered in black stitchin'. My outfit has to have 2 brands together so do Boss and Polo an of course in green,beige and black denim, beige khaki and black stitchin'. Now when chu design it it has to fit tight on da thighs den flair out at bottom half like a balloon, but don't fo' get dese are Capri's." Now da next outfit I'll keep it simple make me an all white baggy jeans wit back pockets on da front an front pockets in da back make 'em blue denim wit Queenie embroidered across da pockets. My shirt I jus' want blue jean denim t-shirt to match dese jumpers 'ere, can ya handle dat? Look on da top of my shoe across da top stitch Queenie in cursive white letters big as chu can make 'em now would ya like fo' me to pay ya fo' da time now or when I pick 'em up?" Mr. Wong said a $1,000 will be sufficient fo' now." "Cool 'ere a $1,000 an Mr. Wong don't fuck up my shoes." Walkin' from da back, Queenie spotted Cortez' and Chuck stayin' in da same spot she left 'em in. "Wutsup baby girl did chu get it done, was Mr. Wong able to help ya?" "Yeah it'll be ready Tuesday mornin' befo' we leave."

"Damn he finna rush dat shit ain't he?" Chuck asked. "Long as my shit right, yo' I gotta question is da entourage goin' wit us?" Cortez' asked; "Baby would it be a problem if dey did go?" "Hell nah dey family ain't dey? I like to have fun an me bein' in da presence of all y'all niggas jus' makes me look fly. Queenie told 'em; "All eyes on me baby." She told 'em in a flirty way "Niggas want me an bitches hate me jus' da way I like it." Cortez' pulled Queenie close an stated; "But ya my QUEEN ma." "Aiight lets shop." "Yo' chu buyin' anything baby, wut 'bout chu Chuck?" "Queenie said; "I need to stop in Victoria Secrets, so where is it I gotta keep it sexy." "Yo' ma it's downstairs, but first we gonna stop in dis jewelry store." Cortez' said. "Dat's cool wit me homeboy I need a diamond watch anyway to go wit my pieces I got goin' on." "Dey can't see ya Queenie yo' ass already hurtin' 'em baby girl." Queenie spotted da perfect watch speakin' to no one in particular; "Dis me all day long on da strength I gotta have it." May I help chu ma'am da store associate asked? He sound very sweet to Queenie in a gay way. If chu didn't look at 'em when he spoke chu coulda swore he was a female. "Yeah first off don't call me ma'am I'm only 16 dude. Secondly can ya let me try dis on dis watch 'ere?" "Mmmmm, excuse me?" "Queenie, Queenie is da name homeboy." "Okay, Ms. Queenie dis watch 'ere is $3,000."

"Hold on nigga don't get it twisted 'cus not once did I ask yo' ass fo' a price. So 'cus I told yo' ass my age now it's a problem huh." "Ma wuts da problem ova 'ere, wuts good?" Cortez walked up behind Queenie an asked. "Nah baby hold on I wanta know why dude feel he can judge me 'cus of my age?"

Queenie neva once raised 'er voice, but she sounded very harsh askin'; "Nigga did I stereotype yo' ass, I easily coulda, but nigga I didn't. I can buy an own everything in dis ma'fucka now let me try dat ma'fuckan watch on." Cortez' said baby it's a nutter jewelry store downstairs we can leave an go dere." "Queenie said nah, baby I found da perfect watch to complete my set an I want it." Queenie turned looked at Cortez' face kissed 'em an said; "Dis nigga gonna sale it to me." Da young sale associates couldn't have been any older dan Chuck or Cortez' finally placed da CARTEIR watch on Queenie's arm. Queenie pulled off $3,500 an as she placed it on da counter she told 'em; "I could be a bitch 'bout it, but I won't Imma still give yo' ass a tip. Dat's fo' da watch an wuts left fo' yo' ass." "Homeboy a bite of advise know who ya talkin' to fo' yo' ass jump da gun, an don't take dis job, so serious 'cus dat shawty right dere can make yo' ass lose it." Chuck stated. Queenie didn't want to finish shoppin' she had gotten frustrated 'bout da situation in da jewelry store. "If y'all finish baby I wanta go 'cus I'm done." Cortez' said; "We picked up our jewelry, so we good ma den lets bounce. Wut chu wanta do next?" "Lets jus' go back to da crib I need to check on my people anyway." Cortez' grab Queenie 'round da lower part of 'er back an dey walk towards da exist of da mall, but befo' makin' it out da door Cortez',Queenie and Chuck heard people loud talkin'.

Chapter Ten

"Boss In Da Streets/Virgin Gone Freak In Da Sheets"

Dere goes dat bitch right dere it sounded like a lot of commotion,so of course da three stopped to see wut it was to only see da same lil' braud from da Waffle House wit 'er crew. "Cortez' said I'm finna put a stop to dis shit 'ere an now." "Queenie wit sarcasm in 'er voice said; "Is East St. Boogie dat fuckan small ya run into da same ma'fuckas all day long? She stated, I coulda stayed in Chi-Town if I wanted to do dis shit.” Queenie took off behind Cortez' towards da girls. Chuck caught up to Queenie ma we can jus' leave an avoid all of dis remember we tryin' to catch dat plane in 2 days family. I don't want to see anything go wrong 'cus of dese stupid brauds.” Queenie looked at Chuck an told 'em; “Hold dis fam. She took off 'er watch and my QUEEN necklace. She told Chuck if she wants it Imma hand it to 'er ass.” Cortez' heard Queenie's remark an said; “Lil' mama let me handle it aiight.” “Handle it baby, jus' know if she jumps off da curb Imma put 'er ass in da gutter feel me?” Chuck and Queenie peeped 2 of da bitches wit razors in their mouths.

“Yo' ma chu peep dat shit?” “Yeah nigga I see it, I'll make 'em bitches cut their own tongues off fuckan wit me, but I got somethin' fo' dey asses.” “Yo' Cortez' baby lets ride nigga.” Queenie and Chuck wanted to lure da bitches outside, Queenie didn't want to get caught up inside of da mall. Queenie stern 'er tone wit Cortez', “Nigga lets bounce.” Out da door she told Chuck; “Pull da car up to da door an turn yo' sounds up,pop da trunk.” By time da females walked outside Chuck had already had da car at da door an Queenie was at da trunk placin' a silencer on 'er nine. “Wutsup yo' ass tryin' to see me again? I take it y'all didn't get da picture earlier huh? Well I don't know wut my nigga jus' said to y'all, but he's not me. Now since ya know I speak fo' myself wut do ya want to do?”

“Bitch yo'_Whop dat's all chu heard. Queenie pulled out nina an pistol whipped ol' girl 'til she laid in a puddle of blood. Queenie was swift no one even knew wut da hell happen. Oh shit Cortez' yelled; “My QUEEN.” Queenie swung nina 'round an pointed at da next bitch; “Try me an I'll pill yo' cap back, now pick up yo' bitch ass friend an walk da fuck off. If I eva see yo' bitch asses Imma deaden ya bitches eva chu stand. Word is bond.” Queenie got in da car she heard 'er hitter go off in an irregular breath she said; “Wutsup?” “Yo' lil' nigga wutsup wit chu, ya aiight?” “Hell nah fam' shit been ridiculous all day." Queenie broke it down fo' Tez. "Look nigga Cortez' took me to da mall we suppose to been kickin' it fo' da day. Well afta' I put some gay ass nigga in his place we walkin' out da mall an da same bitch from da Waffle House I beat down. Dese bitches carryin' razors in dey mouths wanted to jus' run up, so I handled my biz'ness." "Fam' I need chu 'ere, so yo' ass comin' or wut?"

"Baby girl yo' ya already know, so don't ask me dat shit. We on da way I'm finna grab up Lu and Chaos now as we speak, so wut chu finna do now?" We are on our way back to Cortez' crib, when y'all get 'ere I'll put y'all up in a hotel." "Dat's my homeboy he ain't gotta stay in no hotel it's plenty of rooms at da crib. Shit we all family, so jus' tell 'em I said fuck a hotel." Tez heard Cortez' in da back ground an said; "Tell 'em we on da way I'll talk to 'em when I get dere an Queenie stay put baby girl."

Cortez' put his hand on top of Queenie's an told 'er; "Baby yo' I ain't gonna let anything happen to ya, but I do understand ya feel mo' comfortable wit Tez 'round." "Imma keep it raw wit chu an don't take it da wrong way, but Tez is all I know an he knows me inside out. Dat nigga is my protector yeah he's my cuz, but to me he's mo' dan dat he's like a big bro, ya feel me?" "I guess it will take time fo' ya to loosen up to me an let me protect chu da way ya let Tez." "Baby ain't no harm an I'll neva hurt chu intentionally, but da bond Tez and I have is unbreakable da 2 of us are like Bonnie and Clyde, it's ride and die wit us. Not sayin' we won't eva have dat,but Tez will always be dere fo' me whether I do right or wrong an to tell da truth I hope we do have dat type of bond together." Cortez' smiled at Queenie an told 'er; "Ma yo' ass somethin' else ya know dat doe don't chu, but don't eva think Imma take ya away from yo' family 'cus I see wut dat means to ya. Queenie I'm jus' tryin' to fit in baby." "Aiight she whispered in his ear befo' dey got out da car to go in da house_ "I got a surprise fo' ya. Yo' chu want it now befo' Tez an da fellas get 'ere or can yo' ass wait 'til we get to Vegas?" Queenie looked at 'er watch thinkin' to 'er self if she knew Tez drivin' like she knew 'er own den he would be dere in 41/2 hours instead of 6 hours. Cortez',Queenie and Chuck walked into da house wit out a word to anyone Queenie went upstairs only to have Cortez' to follow 'er. She went straight to turn on da shower den she pushed play on da stereo “T-Shirt and Panties blasted out of da speakers. Once out of da shower she rewind da song while she oiled 'er self wit baby oil an put on sexy lace piece wit da back out dat stopped jus' at da peek of 'er apple bottom ass an straps dat covered da nipples of 'er breast.

Queenie walked back into da bedroom to find Cortez' starin' at 'er voluptuous body. “Damn ma dat lil' udig does no justices fo' dat sexy ass body.” “Well since it doesn't why don't chu take it off me, maybe chu like my birthday suit better. Cortez' hugged Queenie an asked; “Ma yo' ya sho' dis is wut chu want 'cus I told_Queenie cut Cortez' off by placin' 'er finger on his lips to silence 'em.

“Cortez' make love to me befo' I lose da nerves.” Cortez' gave Queenie everything from fo' play to oral sex. Queenie felt like she was on a water ride wit da orgasms she had, one afta' a nutter afta' a nutter. Cortez' made Queenie feel like a Super Soaker. He under dress an climbed between his QUEEN thighs playin' wit 'er clique wit da tip of his dick head. Dis made Queenie feel sexually tensed an scared of wut was to come.” Cortez' told 'er; “Baby let me know if it hurts to bad an I'll stop aiight.” “ Aiight.” She responded grippin' his shoulders. “Ma relax fo' me,chu tense right now it'll hurt less if ya relax.” She did as he asked an Cortez' started to pump slowly. “Baby am I hurtin' ya?” “Mmmmm, baby I'm ooooh shit Queenie screamed.” He stopped in mid stroke an asked; “Baby chu want me to stop?” “Nah, do ya thang, but stroke harder.” Queenie wanted to feel every stroke, callin' out Cortez' name dis was all new to 'er somethin' she neva experienced befo' Cortez' asked; “Ma ya sho' 'bout dat?” “Yeah nigga.” Was 'er response, Cortez' hit a spot dat she love da feelin' of dat gave 'er body an arch an 'er nails found their home in Cortez's back. Dat moment he bust Queenie's cherry an made 'er a woman. “Baby ya okay?” “Yeah Cortez' please don't stop.”

"THROWIN' BRICKS AT THE PENITENTIARY"

Cortez' kissed 'er so passionately, it made 'em harder and grow thicker in size. He kissed 'er breast an Queenie screamed "Cortez as she threw da pussy back at 'em. "Yo' fuck ma dis pussy is good shawty."

Cortez' pulled out flippin' Queenie ova retortin'; "Let me give it to ya doggie style ma." Queenie naive as she was wanted to ask wut was doggie style hearin' people speak of it, but didn't quiet know how it was done, but she decided to jus' go wit da flow. As Cortez' started to stick it back in he told Queenie; "Ma chu know I jus' popped yo' cherry an yo' ass felt so good." Cortez' mo' experienced dan 'er of course knew exactly wut to do to make 'er feel special. He spread Queenie's ass cheeks apart an blew 'er asshole dis made Queenie squirm wit pleasure it felt so good to 'er she could feel 'er pussy throb."Do it feel good baby?" Cortez asked. "Yeah it do, but wut is Oh,Ummmm was all she could say as she threw da pussy back. Cortez' was a freak he placed his middle finger in 'er ass while his dick was in 'er love box. Queenie entertained da feelin' by rammin' back even harder. "Mmmmm daddy." Da sound of 'er callin' 'em daddy turned 'em on, but he neva expected da next questioned she asked; "Daddy will it fit in dere?" "Fit where lil' mama?" "Will yo' dick fit in my ass?"

"Yo' ya think ya really ready fo' dat ma, I mean do ya wanta handle dat pain now?" "It can't hurt any worse can it?"Cortez' didn't actually know how it felt,but wut he did know was he didn't want Queenie to get discourage an back out, so he didn't answer he jus' pulled out of 'er tight love box an laid 'er on 'er back an oiled 'er wit baby oil. "Spread yo' legs ma an put 'em on my shoulders now tell me if I'm hurtin' ya an I'll stop baby." All doe he was hopin' dat she wouldn't stop 'em from pleasurin' his self. Queenie screamed out jus' as Cortez' put da tip of his head in he had stopped. "Ma hold on let me take it out." No she screamed I'm fine please don't stop. "Shit is it in jet?" Queenie felt a burnin' sensation. "Baby I only got da tip in." "Well baby put it all_Ugh, puttin' a pillow ova 'er face to muffle 'er loud out burst from da fellas hearin' downstairs. Cortez' did as she told 'em an da louder she screamed da mo' it turned 'em on which made his pumps a lil' stronger and forceful. "Yo' ma I'm finna come baby." Cortez' makin' all types of gruntin' noises playin' wit Queenie's clique to give 'er one last orgasm to come wit 'em.

Coretz' finally pulled out an watched his semen mixed wit blood ooze and squirt out of Queenie's ass befo' layin' next to 'er showerin' 'er wit kisses all ova 'er body. "Baby ya not hurtin' to bad is ya?" "Nah mean everything feels tingly my ass feels like it's 'bout to explode." "It's called climaxin' ma yo' body was bein' pleased, so da only way it could react was to burst into orgasms. My main thing is I didn't hurt chu 'cus I tried my best to be gentle." Cortez' not waitin' fo' a response got up an ran water in da jacuzzi tub. Back in da room he picked Queenie up off da bed he carried 'er to da bathroom an sat 'er down in da nice steamy water. "Get cleaned up baby while I jump in da shower. Shawty da purpose of takin' a bath is so it can draw out some of da soreness it'll make ya feel better."

Queenie soaked as long as Cortez' took his shower an admired his physique, but once he stepped out she lathered 'er body den got in da shower fo' 'bout 10 minutes washin' off excise soap scum.

Cortez' propped against da door frame an said; "Damn shawty ya sexy." Queenie blushed Cortez' smiled back an tapped 'er on da ass an stated; "Now get dress ma yo' family should be 'ere any minute." Queenie said; "Don't think 'cus yo' ass popped my cherry dat, dat gives yo' ass rights to start bossin' me 'round." Laughter filled da air. "Nah, ma neva dat nothin' has changed, nothin', but yo' sex status an who's it belong to. Feel me?" Queenie turned to look at Corez' an he had a big ass smile on his face. "Aiight I guess ya did put it down, but don't get cocky." Their convo was interrupted by da ringing of Cortez' hitter. "Yo', who dis?" "Wut up my nigga?" Tez questioned. "Yo' fam' we out front."

"Aye come in Chuck downstairs I'll be down in a sec." "Damn wut chu do catch a flight to dis ma'fucka yo' ass made it 'ere in 41/2 hours out of a 6 hour drive an ya still got an hour an somethin' to play wit." Tez response; "Homeboy yo' when it comes to baby girl I don't play no games. Dat's my lil' nigga an I feel she's in any danger da least lil' stress Imma be on point at all times. Word is bond fam'.

Now where she at?" "I'm right 'ere cuz." Da weather was still pretty hot out fo' it to be night time, so Queenie jus' slipped on anything a pair of black,red and white Guess Capri outfit wit matchin' air force ones dat she had designed to fit 'er taste. Speakin' to no one at da time Queenie tried to figure out where 'er my QUEEN necklace was rememberin' Chuck should have it from when she took it off at da mall. Queenie walked out da room, but not befo' she grabbed nina an placed 'er in da small of 'er back. Queenie made it downstairs wit a big smile on 'er face. "Fam' she shouted ." "Wutsup lil' nigga dis nigga got chu down 'ere clowin' wit dese Southern bitches?" Tez kissed Queenie on da forehead he glanced at his homeboy Cortez' an playfully asked; "Nigga yo' ass lettin' bitches out 'ere tryin' to see baby girl?" Everyone laughed. Chuck stated; "Dat's jus' it fam' shawty can't be touched, an I recognize and respect da heart and strength she has, on top of dat da speed she has most niggas ain't got when dey drawin' on ma'fuckas." "Yeah Chuck let me get dat necklace homeboy." "Fo' sho' ma it's right 'ere." Cortez' placed it back on 'er neck. "Listen my baby says she's hungry, so y'all niggas wanta go get somethin' to eat?" "Wutsup wit Joe's Crab Shack someone asked." "Yo' we can do dat if my baby wants to. Queenie wutsup, wut chu wanta do?" "Yo' we can go to Joe's I neva been dere befo', but I'm takin' dis won't be my last time 'ere, so really it doesn't matter if we go now or later on. Let's jus' go somewhere." Dey decided to jus' do somethin' simple so dey all ended up at Krystal, Krystal's was jus' a nutter form of White Castles somethin' Queenie and 'em were use to in Chicago.

Queenie said; "Look at dis shit 'ere cuz dis has to be da smallest town eva, I eva been in or do dese hoes jus' get 'round. Dis has to be some fuckan coincidence fam'." Tez had no idea wut da hell Queenie was talkin' 'bout, so he asked; "Wuts good cuz?" "Nigga dat bitch dere is da same braud from earlier.

Wut is it, are dese da main kickin' it spots in East St. Boogie?" "Lil' nigga we can always eat somewhere else." "Nah,nigga I jus' said I was starvin', so dis 'ere where we gonna eat fam'."

"Homeboy is she like dis all da time?" Cortez' asked curiously. "How is dat my nigga , stubborn and demandin'?" "Yo' I know yo' ass only been 'round 'er fo' 2 day now, but Cortez' don't act brand new to da game 'cus when we were 'er age we acted da same way tryin' to make our mark in da game. Only difference wit 'er she was brought up by me, so yeah she is a spoiled stubborn brat 'cus she's use to getting wut eva she wants, it ain't by bein' spoon fed, but 'cus she's seen da work dat I put in on da grind an dat makes 'er respect da game. Da way Queenie mind works tells 'er da game will respect 'er along wit ma'fuckas in it." "Yeah my nigga she is a spoiled kid wit a woman's mentality fam'." Cortez' responded. "But I groomed 'er to take shit from no one includin' me homeboy, an to say wut she mean and mean wut she say 'cus dats how ma'fuckas will take 'er serious." "Well I gotta say my baby don't back down fo' shit, but I like dat doe. She's a beast wit 'er sexy ass swagg."

Queenie told 'em; "Aiight niggas if y'all done wit y'all sermon can we go in an eat give a sista some subsistence, so I can continue to grow." Everyone laughed as dey got out da car. "Ain't shit funny niggas I'm dead serious y'all wanta do all dis talkin' an my ma'fuckan stomach touchin my back. Feed me an bitch later." Someone yelled out yo' bitch, aye yo' ass 'ere me. Yo' so now yo' ass scared , wut chu ain't got no mo' fight in ya? Da whole entourage gather 'round Queenie tellin' 'er_ "No Queenie take yo' ass inside nigga lets eat first if dat bitch wanta fight she'll be 'ere when yo' ass get done."

"But Tez did dat braud jus' call me a bitch an question if I was scared? Okay Imma go eat, but Imma kill dat ma'fucka 'cus she's tried me to many times in one day."

Chapter Eleven
"Da Beast Has Been Unleashed"

Queenie was so furious she couldn't think straight a nuff to even eat. Cortez' called Queenie's name 5 times befo' she answered. In a daze she finally said; "Yeah wutsup?" "Yo' ma why ya not eatin'?" Queenie didn't respond 'cus 'er focus was on da braud dat called 'er a bitch. Queenie had a death stare on 'er through da glass window. Tez peeped da scene an noticed da gleam in his lil' cousins eyes, tryin' to stop a situation befo' it escalade into a blood bath Tez put his arm 'round Queenie shoulder tellin' Cortez' wut to order fo' 'er. But Tez also thought better of it 'cus he knew she wouldn't eat.

"Homeboy hold up, we ain't gonna be able to eat 'ere at all fam'." Tez whispered to Cortez'; "Nigga she already in a trans an it's only 2 ways I see it goin' down at dis point 1.we let 'er loose an she does 'er thang or 2.we carry 'er out of 'ere put 'er in da car an bring 'er out of it. But it's consequences wit dat an I'm not tryin' to feel da wrath of it." Cortez' said; "Well dats a chance we'll jus' have to take man she didn't come 'ere fo' dis." "Nigga chu think I don't know dat, but if yo' ass don't know by now dis lil' nigga trigger happy fam', pull it first an ask questions later an I don't wanta risk it feel me? Tez exclaimed, I'll die fo' dis lil' nigga, but she eva pull a gun on me I'll deaden 'er, so do yo' ass feel me now. Trust I don't wanta turn 'er loose, but 9 out of 10 dat bitch word an ol' girl callin' 'er scared is playin' ova and ova in 'er head an bitch is all she focused on, so I rather have 'er in a fist fight dan see 'er fuckin wit a burner." "Damn man I ain't tryin' to see my woman out 'ere fightin' every time ya turn 'round." "Nigga once dis ova we gotta talk fo' sho' family 'cus it ain't no way in hell she can continue to live life like dis my nigga nah, mean?" Tez said; "Nigga either way yo' ass look at it dis is 'er life an I hate to say it, but baby girl already "THROWIN' BRICKS AT THE PENITENTIARY." Lets roll out y'all_Queenie wuts good baby girl, I need chu let dis bullshit go, come on lil' mama we got to many witness in 'ere trust me ya don't wanta go out like dis ma." Chuck whispered in ear shot of Cortez' and Tez both turned to look out da window to only see ol' girl 2 utter brauds an a nigga walkin' across da parkin' lot towards da door. He told Tez; "Dose da same three wit razors from earlier an Queenie swore on life she would deaden 'em if dey eva ran up again." "Thanks fam' looks like dat jus' might happen. Who dis punk ma'fucka wit 'em?" Chuck said; "Shit I don't know fam' neva seen 'em befo'."

"Lu, Chaos y'all go outside wit Chuck an see wutsup maybe dude can get dat bitch to back down." Talkin' didn't work all it did was add fuel to da fire. Tez tried to defuse da situation, but fist started swinging. Niggas fightin' bitches an vise-a-verse. "Where da fuck is Queenie." Tez yelled an dat got Cortez' attention. "Yo' she ova dere." Queenie was beatin' da girl toe to toe an from out of no where Queenie got hit across da back wit a Louisville Slugger. All could be heard was da devastatin' sound of bones crushin' an Queenie fell to da ground an both girls started to stump 'er. Tez and Cortez' didn't make it to 'er befo' da bat came down on Queenie again. "No, Queenie ma please be alive." Tez fist smashed into side of ol' girls face knockin' 'er out cold befo' she got off da third blast. Cortez' dropped to his knees checkin' to see wut condition his QUEEN was in. Tez did da same pleadin'; "Fam' tell me she ain't, God please." "Yo' Chuck call da medics she ain't movin' bro." Tez took nina out of Queenie's back an passed it to Lu. "Fam' take dis shit." Cortez' said; "She barely has a pulse, yo' y'all niggas go back to da crib." Everyone was ridin' dirty an he didn't want any mishaps wit da crew. Tez told Lu and Chaos da same. "Fam' I'll call when we get to da hospital den y'all can come." Lu seen tears run down Tez cheeks an touch his shoulder; "Family she will pull threw baby girl is tough, she's a fighter an defeat is somethin' boss won't let win ova 'er. She's a strong lil' nigga." Dey could hear sirens close an Tez wanted 'em to leave befo' dey arrived. "Get outta 'ere cuz, we'll call." "Chaos told Lu get in an yelled out at Tez fam' soon as ya get news call us." Da medics arrived, Cortez' was heated 'cus it seemed like dey took fo'eva, but someone had to keep a level head of da 2, but who dat would be was very hard to tell since dey both were ready to lose it. Afta' da medics checked Queenie's vitals a IV was started den dey put 'er on a stretcher not knowin' if anything was broken since she was unconscious. Cortez' and Tez made it clear dat dey were ridin' wit 'er to da hospital. Dey rushed Queenie into da back. “Sirs ya can't go back dere. Please sirs I need to get some info from ya so we can treat da young lady. So dey returned to da desk. “Now who are ya to 'er?” Tez ran his hand down his face. “Yo' I'm 'er first cousin an dis is 'er guy.” Cortez' mind was racin' so he couldn't think straight all he could see was visions of 'er goin' down afta' bein' hit wit da bat. “Okay when was she born, where was she born, wuts 'er mothers maiden name has she eva had a transfusion befo' an da questions went on and on. Tez answered da best he could considerin' he wasn't in a stable mind set. “Look chu need to talk to my aunt 'bout dis.” Tez dialed Liz number she picked up on da first ring. “Auntie?”

“Wutsup baby?” Liz asked. “Listen I'm at da hospital wit Queenie I need chu to answer dis lady's questions so dey can treat Queenie an I'll talk to ya when ya done. Tez passed his hitter to da nurse an afta' she finished he got back on da line_ “Hello, auntie ya still dere?” “Yeah I'm 'ere Tez tell me wuts goin' on wit my baby.” “Auntie she got into a fight wit one braud den a nutter one came from behind 'er an started beatin' 'er wit a bat den da 2 was stumpin' 'er.” Liz screamed; “Where da fuck was chu Tez? Hell were was Cortez' when dis shit happen to my baby?” “Auntie we were both out dere, hell everybody was fightin'.” “Fuck wut hospital she at?” “Yo' fam' wut hospital is dis?” Cortez' responded; “ST. Clark, so Tez repeated to his aunt. “I'm on my way.” Ova da loud speaker dey called a code blue from da surgery room. Lu, Chaos, Chuck and da rest walked in askin'; “Wut da fuck goin' on?”

Cortez' and Tez ran to da nurses desk beggin' 'er to tell 'em somethin'_ “Can ya please tell us wuts goin' on ma'am?” “Let me see wut I can find out fo' ya fellas.” “Thank ya Lu told da nurse seein' da state his 2 homeboys were in. A nutter nurse ran from da back an yelled; "We need a crash cart da entire room looked in disbelief as to wut was goin' on. "Fuck Lord don't do dis." Cortez' drop to his knees an begged "Man come on please don't take 'er from us, she's a good sweet girl jus' wit a few issues father please. I love dis girl don't take 'er ova one mistake, give 'er a nutter chance." Tez punched a hole in da wall. "Sir I'm gonna have to ask ya to leave." "Ma'am please I got 'em he's jus' upset 'cus dats his lil' cousin back dere dats his blood, so I know ya can understand he's hurtin' ma. Don't worry we can and will pay fo' da damages." Everyone was on edge waitin' on some type of reassurance dat Queenie was alright. Tez hitter went off, but he didn't answer it he had fo' got all 'bout his aunt. Next couple of seconds Lu hitter rang he also missed da call, it was Liz callin', but she got no answer. Liz picked up 'er sister Heather to ride to East St. Boogie wit 'er, Liz screamed ain't nobody answerin' da phones. Heather tried 'cus she saw 'er sister was in no condition to try any mo', so she tried Chaos hitter first. Ring! "Hello." "Chaos it's Heather baby tell me somethin', we need some news we on our way, but Liz is on a verge of an break down." Heather put 'er phone on speaker, so Liz could also hear. "Cuz no one has came out an told us anything jet, all we know is dey called a code blue a nurse ran out yellin' she needed a crash cart, but we don't know if it was fo' Queenie or not cuz." "Oh lord, Liz shouted." "Where is da nurse?" "Dey all in da back cuz ain't nobody out 'ere, but us." "Where is Tez, Cortez' and Lu?" "Right 'ere, but dey ain't in no shape to talk. We tryin' to hold dese nigga down best way we know how. Tez cryin' punchin' holes in walls an ya know dat nigga don't cry fo' shit. Cortez' cryin' he fucked up, so how far away are y'all?" "We 'bout 45 minutes away." Heather replied.

Chaos tried to enlighten da situation by makin' a joke "Damn I know Tez is yo' child, but he must of got his drivin' skills from Liz 'cus dey keep their foot to da floor when it comes to drivin'. Cuz I'll keep ya posted if we hear anything befo' y'all get 'ere, so let me get back to Tez." Heather said; "Sis I know she gone pull through wut eva it is dat's wrong. I believe dis 'cus my niece is a thoroughbred an da bloodline she carries is a die heart one, so lets not think negative." Liz said a silent pray fo' 'er baby girl as she drove. A doctor walked from behind da double doors wit scrubs on pullin' down his face mask. "Is dere family 'ere fo' Ms. Miles?" He asked da nurse. "Yo' yeah right 'ere." Tez and Cortez' led da group. "Is 'er mother 'ere?" "No sir, but she on 'er way she's 'bout 45 minutes away." "Are ya da 2 young men dat came in wit 'er?" Cortez' responded; "Yes sir." "Well let me talk wit ya ova 'ere fo' a second alone." Da three walked pass da nurses station an da doctor proceeded; "Ere's da deal she's alive,but when she got hit da force of da impact broke all of 'er ribs on da left side an dis caused a bone to puncture 'er lung,so dat's why we had to perform surgery. When code blue was called we had lost 'er, she's fine now, but dis will be along recovery fo' 'er ahead." Liz and Heather ran in screamin' where is she, tell us she's okay." Heather spotted Tez standin' wit da doctor. She grabbed Liz by da arm. "Ova 'ere sis." Tez hugged his aunt an told 'er; "She's okay, auntie dis is da doctor he was jus' explainin' to us everything dat went on." Da doctor introduced 'em self as Dr. Price an Liz did da same. "I'm Queenie's mother." "Well Ms. Miles I was jus' tellin' da fellas 'ere." An he went on to explain wut he had jus' said moments befo' da ladies ran in. "Now it will be along recovery an she might have a slight breathin' problem 'til she heals up from da bone dat was launched in 'er lung. If ya fellas didn't get 'er help when ya did she would have died fo' sho'. She's still unconscious right now, but I'm gonna run plenty of test jus' to make sho' dere are no utter damages." "When can I see 'er?" Liz asked.

Jus' den a nurse from recovery ran from back. "Doctor Price she's awake an in a lot of pain, but she's askin' fo' Tez and Cortez'." "Fellas and Ms. Miles come wit me." Rushin' to ICU da doctor stop 'em at da door. "Befo' ya go in let me get 'er some pain meds an take 'er vitals so she can be comfortable when ya see 'er. He remarked; "Queenie looks like da type of young lady dat has integrity an takes pride in 'er appearance I know dis is a devastatin' time right now but don't crush 'er ego by walkin' in takin' dat away from 'er." Afta' dey got Queenie comfortable he let 'er love ones in. Queenie tried to put on a smile, but da pain was so severe it was hard fo' 'er to do she had a machine controllin' 'er breathin', so it was very hard fo' 'er to talk. "Look at my baby, who did dis?" Liz questioned, but got no response. Cortez' stood on da opposite side of da bed holdin' Queenie's hand strokin' it softly statin'; "Ma I'm so glad ya aiightt." Queenie said; "I'm good baby dis is nothin' dey can't hold me down." Smilin', Tez told 'er; "We see lil' nigga chu a straight die heart." Queenie questioned wut happen, so Cortez' explained wut took place. "Baby ya fought ol' girl from earlier goin' round fo' round an one of 'er home girls snuck ya from behind wit a bat, but don't worry 'bout dat jus' concentrate on getting better please baby." Liz told 'er daughter; "Baby jus' rest get ya strength back an we can talk 'bout dat later." "No we will talk 'bout it now ma, don't hold anything from me now somebody tell me why I'm in excruciating pain." Queenie looked in Tez direction_ "My nigga why da fuck it feels like someone has been stabbin' me ova and ova fam'?" Uuuugh she screamed . Queenie grimace look on 'er face wit tears in da wells of 'er eyes let 'em all know she was serious . It took everything in 'er to fight da tears from fallin'. Tez stepped 'round his aunt an kissed Queenie on 'er forehead befo' he pulled up a chair to sit in eye contact wit 'er. "Yo' auntie let dis rail down, baby girl listen ya 'ere 'cus when ol' girl snuck ya she broke all of yo' ribs on yo' left side, dats why ya in so much pain. An one of yo' bones punctured yo' lung dats why ya in recovery 'cus dey had to do surgery. Ma we lost ya once dey got chu on da table, but doctor Price saved ya." Tez dropped his head tryin' to hide tears from Queenie. Queenie whispered cuz touchin' his head, Tez looked up at his lil' cousin an said; "Wutsup baby girl?" "Fam' it's cool nigga I'm 'ere an I'll be back stronger befo' ya know it cuz. We Miles an dey can't hold us down no longer dan we wanta be yo' ya feel me cuz." Cortez' was also in tears he stood at da window so Queenie couldn't see his face either. Queenie whispered in a patter breath Tez tell dat nigga Cortez' to come 'ere." "Yo' fam' Ueenie wants ya ova 'ere nigga." Cortez' ran his hand ova his face to wipe away da tears. "Wutup ma?" Cortez' put on a smile dat was not a legit one, but it was to hide da hurt he was feelin' fo' his girl, of course she shut it down fast. Queenie shook 'er head an whispered; "Baby I don't do phony so take dat fake smile off yo' face. I know ya hurt so jus' keep it funky wit me."

She grabbed 'er cousin and man by da hand an gently squeezed to get their attention to come closer in ear shot; "Listen I'm glad y'all 'ere, but ma can ya excuse us fo' a minute I need to talk to Tez and Cortez' fo' a sec?" "Yeah I'll go tell everyone else how ya doin." Queenie said; "Now dat she's out of da room be straight up wit me how long I gotta be 'ere in dis bed fam'? I need to know, I've done a lot of shit dat most could say is foul or even mischievous, but neva can a ma'fucka call me treacherous on any count. I don't start shit, but I will end it at any cost I also know dat fair exchange ain't no robbery nigga so maybe it's my fate to lay in dis bed, maybe it's my fate to die, maybe sooner dan later da inevitable will happen an it'll all be ova cuz." Tez could tell dat his lil' cousin was hurt in mo' dan one way. Queenie's pride was hurt also, it was like da doctor said 'er ego and pride was everything to 'er. Now to Tez it seemed dat his baby girl felt like da brauds had stole dat from 'er, but in Queenie's mind she pledge dat she would build it back up wit no doubts. Queenie eyes went from a hazel brown to a stone cold black as she spoke. "Tez niggas can't kill da devil shit I'm already in hell an I'm pull dose 2 bitches in wit me." Tez and Cortez' knew exactly wut she meant by 'er statement Queenie had already made 'er mind up dat once she got well she would find an seek out 'er prey an add 2 mo' bodies to 'er body count. Cortez' needed to try an to talk 'er out of doin' anything, but he was interrupted by a knock at da door. Knock knock. "Yo' can we come in?" It was Chuck,Lu,and Chaos_ "Wutup boss, how ya feelin' family?" Chaos asked. "Yo' lil' mama ya had all of us spooked out dere. Niggas didn't know wut da fuck to except." "Yo' family y'all know dey can't keep a QUEEN down, 'cus she always comes back fo' wuts rightfully 'ers. "I appreciate y'all bein' 'ere doe I know dese 2 niggas 'ere may not have held it together wit out y'all 'round."

Queenie smiled at Tez and Cortez' an got serious; "I'm glad all of ya 'ere so all bullshit to da side. We all family so I need y'all to get on da grind, I need shit moved in three days every brick." Mainly speakin' at Chuck since he was Cortez' bro. "Chuck do ya an da fellas think y'all can handle bein' down wit my family circle, wut 'bout chu baby?" Chuck looked at Cortez' as to say wutsup bro. Cortez' said; "Dats cool we all family ma." "Good now unfortunately our trip has to be postpone, but word is bond we will make it to Vegas befo' my next move." "My QUEEN wut next move is dat baby?" Cortez' asked. "Queenie responded; "Baby we'll talk 'bout dat later." Tez knew wut Queenie's later meant neva, but he thought he jus' might get lucky an she would open up to his homeboy 'bout 'er plans. "Yo' afta' dose three days is up I expect y'all to come back 'ere an plan fo' a long stay. Tez cuz yo' ass know where my package at I'll open it an ya hit me when ya got it an I'll put it back fam'. Yo' Chaos ya got 2 runs dis week 1 big delivery and 1 pick up of $200,000 thou. Since I want y'all back in three days schedule dat shit so ya can get 'er done all in one day cuz. Afta' everything is collected and accounted fo', board up da stash house take Blue and Red to my ol' g house 'til we come back fo' 'em. Now I got a question fo' ya three Tez,Lu and Chaos an be on da up and up wit me. Do anyone of ya have a problem wit me disruptin' yo' lives leavin' da big city of Chicago fo' awhile? Niggas speak now or fo' eva hold yo' tongue. I'm not sayin' it's permanent, but it'll be fo' a minute 'cus I got some shit to handle on top of recover first since I can't travel Imma have to settle in East St. Boogie, so I figure might as well have my niggas 'ere wit me, so I can be comfortable feel me?" Queenie looked 'round da room fo' any objections as she expected dere were non. Tez spoke; “Baby girl I love yo' ass, so ya already know where I stand 'cus it's ride and die lil' nigga, so I'm 'ere no questions.” “Hell boss I've been havin' thoughts 'bout relocatin' else where anyway I jus' couldn't leave my family, so dis would be da perfect opportunity.” Lu said I'm down fam'. “Cuz I work fo' ya, so plain and simple I'm 'ere fo' ya.”

Chapter Twelve
“Boss Queen”
“Relocates”

“Aiight y'all can leave tomorrow evenin' an I expect y'all back 'ere Saturday no later dan noon.” Queenie told Tez and Cortez' dat would give 'em time tonight or tomorrow mornin' to talk.

“Baby ya need to rest fo' awhile ya been talkin' fo' at least a good 30 minutes now. Cortez' kissed Queenie tellin' 'er; “Ma I need chu to get well a nuff, so I can get chu to da crib an take care of ya.”

“Ueenie when ya gone break all dis to auntie lil' nigga?” “Matter of fact befo' y'all leave Chaos, Chuck and Lu go out dere an send my moms and aunt back in fo' me preciate it fam'.” Liz and Heather entered da room, Queenie said; “Auntie wutsup?” “Dere goes my baby how auntie baby doin? I hear ya in a lot of pain? Do dey got my baby comfortable in 'ere?” Queenie was 'er only niece,so dat was 'er angel by all means she did no wrong in 'er eyes. “I'm good auntie, ya know Imma Miles baby.”

Queenie tried to laugh it off, but da pain only made 'er squeal. Ugh! Tears welled up in 'er eyes,but she couldn't fight it off any longer, Queenie had to be doped up she whispered can someone push some Morphine into me? Liz wiped Queenie's eyes wit some tissue askin' 'em if he push da button so Queenie could get a lil' relief. Mmmmm Queenie's face loosen a lil' dey could tell da medicine had started to work already. “Yo' mommy Queenie chimed like a 2 year old. “Did ya find out from da doc how long I gotta be 'ere?” “Yes baby, he said 2 weeks long as ya don't have any complications,but far as travelin' ya can't be transported to far due to da discomfort it'll cause ya." "Aiight ma I got somethin' to talk to y'all 'bout. Now we are da only 2 kids y'all got an dere is nothin' dat we wouldn't do fo' y'all. Tez and I will go to hell an back fo' either one of ya, but honestly da reason we both still stay at home is not 'cus we know we neva have to leave or 'cus we have to be dere. Our reason fo' not leavin' is 'cus we protect y'all. Yeah y'all raised us,of course an to da best of ya ability, but fo' along time now things haven't been quit da same wit me an ma I know ya noticed. How eva ya look at it or we turn out down da line from dis point remember da Miles women raised 2 of da best intelligent, enthusiastic,respectful KING and QUEEN in all of Chicago." "Queenie wut is ya talkin' 'bout child?" 'Er mother asked. "Ma, auntie it's time fo' us to leave Chi-Town fo' awhile, I can't leave or go anywhere right now, so I decided to stay 'ere an Tez,Chaos and Lu are movin' 'ere wit me."

Tez stated; "Auntie I believe it will be good fo' 'er, an ya already know dat I won't have it any utter way, but to come wit 'er." Liz questioned? "Of course chu come Lu and Chaos follows to? When is all of dis suppose to take place?" "Ma dey leave tomorrow an den will return Saturday mornin'."

"Why so soon an where will y'all live?" "Ma slow down wit da questions. I gotta catch my breath Queenie exclaimed." "I am sorry baby, but when did ya decide dis?" Queenie replied; "Since I been layin' in dis bed an I was told I can't travel to far. Ya wanta know where I'm goin' stay, well 'til I heal an get back on my feet I'll be at Cortez' crib." Liz asked Cortez' was dat okay wit 'em an his response was yes ma'am I love yo' daughter, so I have no problem wit it, I feel I need to be 'round, so I can take care of 'er. It's mo' dan a nuff room at my spot fo' everyone to stay 'til dey make da next move."

Queenie had plans on puttin' Lu and Chaos up in their own place to share, she knew Tez wouldn't let 'er get 'em one. He would purchase his own crib which was cool wit 'er long as he was dere. "Ma will ya be able to handle Blue and Red 'til we come back fo' 'em?" "Y'all still got 'em damn pups?"

Heather asked like she was surprise to hear. Tez said; "Ma ya know dose our babies dey ain't goin' no where." "If y'all want dey can stay at da house wit me since Liz work an I'm at home all day, I haven't seen Red and Blue since dey were lil' pups." "Ma if ya think ya can handle 'em 'cus dey ain't so lil' any mo'." "Well dat's fine sis on my off days and weekends I can come by an we can take 'em fo' walks." Queenie said Friday or early Saturday mornin' Chaos will bring 'em to ya auntie an Tez will give ya their paper work an he'll bring plenty of food fo' 'em. Auntie Blue is my baby an y'all know how I feel 'bout my dog, so please auntie, mommy let nothin' happen to 'em. Give me 2 months if dat an I'll send someone to reclaim 'em both." Queenie medicine kicked in an I love y'all was da last thing she said befo' driftin' off to sleep. Liz told 'em all she's asleep she needs da rest it's da only way to regain 'er strength fully. Liz turned an kissed Queenie's forehead rubbin' 'er hair den asked Tez "So she's serious 'bout y'all movin' down 'ere huh? When I talk to 'er earlier she had asked me how would I feel 'bout movin' back to my hometown, but I had no idea dat da girl was actually serious an not dis soon." "Auntie it's a lot goin' on wit Ueenie non of us know 'bout, but Imma jus' wait fo' 'er to open up to me so I can help 'er wit wut eva it is. One thing I do know is I won't deny 'er anything,so if dis is wut Ueenie wants I'll give 'er dat, don't worry doe dis is a small mishap an it's gonna be okay an Queenie will be aiight. But my question is fo' ya both, y'all gonna be okay wit out us 'round? Ain't nothin' changin', but da fact y'all won't see us everyday." Tez told his mother to tell 'em how she felt. "Look son ya my only an I love ya yo' ass 19 now an to be truly honest I didn't think ya woulda stayed home as long as chu have. Baby doe I see chu as my baby boy ya been a grown man fo' awhile now an I know I raised a damn good man son. "An I see a lot of da same ethics in my niece. Tez ya know how I feel 'bout da both of ya, but since yo' ass older, an da man it's mo' pressure on ya to take care of yo' lil' cousin baby." Tez hugged his auntie an asked wut 'bout chu auntie how ya feelin 'bout dis? "I'm good take care of my baby." Cortez' asked are chu ladies hungry, would ya like to go out an get somethin' to eat?" Cortez' said; "It's late fo' da both of ya to be on da highway, so y'all mo' dan welcome to stay at da house we got 4 bedrooms, but I want y'all to be comfortable,so I'll give up my room. Dats if 2 sistas don't mine sharin' a bed." "Baby we not tryin' to put chu out we can get a hotel fo' da night."

"No ma'am ya won't be puttin' me out,but I truly can't let my girl and homeboy mothers sleep in no hotel, but Imma stay 'ere wit my QUEEN so I can watch ova 'er myself dat way when she wakes up at least she'll see a familiar face. Well lets go get somethin' to eat den I'll take y'all back to da crib so ya ladies can rest up 'cus I know dis has been stressful." Cortez' impressed Liz and Heather wit his well manners an good hospitality. Tez stated; "Homeboy we both wait on 'er to wake up, 'cus I plan on stayin' wit 'er also." "Dats cool fam' lets go get somethin' to eat." Tez kissed Queenie's forehead 'er moms kissed da top of 'er head an 'er aunt rubbed 'er hair back an said; "I love ya niecy poo." Cortez' kissed 'er lips an whispered; "I love ya ma, I'll be back." Chuck,Chaos and Lu where still sittin' in da waitin' area while dey had sent da rest of da crew home fo' da night. "Yo' fam' how she doin'?" Cortez' replied she's in a lot of pain, but she asleep now." "Yo' we all gonna go get somethin' to eat den get moms and auntie squared away fo' da night den Cortez' and I will come back to da hospital." At da Waffle House everyone ordered their food den Chuck said out loud dis where it all started. "Yeah it is ain't it all she wanted to do was chill have a good day, but right 'ere is where all da mayhem started an now look at my girl she laid in some fuckan hospital bed." Chuck tried to make light of da situation. "Ms. Miles no disrespect ma'am ya got a beautiful daughter, but lil' mama is a beast an can very well handle 'er own an den some. I neva seen a female fight like she do, I'll put my money on Queenie any day at anytime dat she can beat da toughest nigga in da streets down."

Liz told 'em "Thank ya I'll take dat as a compliment on my daughters behalf." "I'm jus' keepin' it real yo' baby girl can hold 'er own an she's no punk or push ova. I jus' met 'er an I can honestly say I love 'er like a lil' sista she not a hood rat like ya can jus' jay down wit in da streets today. Queenie is a respected young lady, but has no problem wit puttin' ya in yo' place if ya step outta line." Tez hitter went off breakin' da convo up. "Hello." May I speak wit a Mr. Miles da nurse asked? "Dis 'em wuts wrong."

Oh Mr. Miles I apologize I didn't call to startle ya sir nothins' wrong exactly Ms. Miles woke up in some discomfort an is demandin' dat I get chu and Mr. Fabs 'ere an dis is da only number we have on file,so I hope I didn't disturb yo' sleep. "Nah I wasn't sleep so it's cool, but I thank ya fo' callin' me tell Queenie_ Ms. Miles we on da way. Look we gotta go Ueenie woke an da nurse says she demandin' fo' me and Cortez' to come to da hospital now. Dats my lil' nigga yo' fam' ya gotta respect 'er gangsta even doe she still a baby at heart." "Tez why is dat,so funny huh? Dats bein' disrespectful anyway ya look at it. It ain't nice to demand nothin' when someone is tryin' to help ya." "Auntie ya lookin' at it all wrong I jus' laughed 'cus far as I can remember only time Queenie has been in a hospital is when ya had 'er, but dat jus' brings me back to wut I jus' said ya gotta love 'er 'cus she's still a baby at heart. She's spoiled an a big baby anyway ya look at it." "Son ya had a lot to do wit dat don't fo' get,so lets go so y'all can tend to my niece's needs." His mother added. Afta' dey returned to da hospital Queenie finally settled down an was able to fall back to sleep. "Yo' fam' wuts good homeboy wit everything dats been goin' down we ain't had a chance to talk, but I guess da life style has a distance between us." Cortez' stated. "Shit look like all dat finna change doe since we movin' 'ere, but shit yo' ass know my nigga no matter wut yo' ass always my nigga homeboy I jus' been tryin' to keep Queenie leveled. But let me ask ya dis how is da streets down 'ere fam'? Shit I know our product is da same, who runs wut down 'ere in dese parts, 'cus ya know I am a man of integrity very thorough,so I work fo' no one an my circle is of few, so Imma eat no matter where I am, but I gotta make sho' where I lay my head is gonna feed me and my family. Ya feel me?"

Cortez' said; "We family ya know how we do, I got chu even if we take ova a nutter territory we always gonna eat fam'." Lookin' at Queenie, Cortez' wanted to know if she was done wit da game,so who better to ask dan da man who raised 'er. "Yo' Tez." "Wutup fam'?" "Fam' ya think she's done wit da game afta' does bricks gone, do yo' ass think she'll stop an live a normal life?"

"Fam' Imma be honest, but it's jus' my opinion I know 'er goal is to become a millionaire an wit da bricks she got fo' 'er birthday she could be dat befo' 18, but neva once did she give a number,so who's to say where 'er cut off point is, but I do know Queenie's immune to da paper. Grownin' up fo' 'er was hard an I can relate, but fo' Ueenie to do wut she's doin' makes 'er feel good to be able to help 'er moms so she doesn't have to struggle. When she puts money in 'er moms pocket it makes 'er happy 'cus she know dat she'll neva go wit out an da only reason my aunt works is 'cus she loves wut she does, but to Queenie it's not a nuff to take care of 'em both an bills. Fam' it's a great feelin' to dis lil' nigga 'ere to put a thous in my aunts hand everyday befo' she leave da house. Furthermo' outta everything she's been goin' threw she has neva asked 'er moms let alone anyone else fo' anything back. She'll do fo' anyone and everyone an all she wants or expect is to be respected fo' who she is family an dats Queenie "Boss Queen", now I wait to see how dis move plays out." "Yo' family I believe yo' lil' cuz 'ere has had thoughts of killin' da brauds dat did dis nah mean?" "Well homeboy ya can trust yo' instincts 'cus dats wuts gonna happen. Fam' if yo' ass wit 'er ya gotta be wit 'er, so anytime yo' ass got a gut feelin' 'bout anything dis lil' nigga 'ere might do, it's always a hunnid % sho' thang. Queenie neva second guesses 'er self. Da next ma'fucka might, but I can tell ya it'll be a wrong move on dey part. Fam' jus' don't eva try an change 'er she'll come 'round soon." Queenie started to wake up,wit a raspy tone in 'er voice "I hear y'all niggas talkin' 'bout me. Yo' can a nigga get somethin' to drink my mouth feels like cotton."

"Hold on ma don't try to move to much." Cortez' didn't want Queenie to hurt 'er self. "Tez help me sit up some cuz, I hate feelin' like I'm stuck. Wut time is it?" "Baby it's 4:30 am."

"So wut chu niggas talkin' 'bout? Mmmmm! Dis fuckin' Morphine got a nigga on cloud nine 'round dis bitch." Tez chuckled as he said; "It should da way yo' lil' ass 'round dis ma'fucka bein' bossy and demandin', shit dey probably gave yo' ass a double dose." Queenie smiled an retorted; "Cuz I am "Boss" shit don't stop 'cus I'm laid up in a hospital. Speakin' of dat when am I leavin' dis bitch?" "We gotta wait on yo' test an da doctor to see wutsup when he comes in today." "Can ya move yo' left arm ma?" Cortez' asked. Da grimace look on 'er face told it all, Queenie tried to cross ova to da opposite side of 'er body an screamed, Tez and Cortez' had to help'er put it back on da bed, but she refused their help. "No don't I got uuuugh I got it!" Queenie abdomen 'bout doin it on 'er own, she felt helpless a nuff said "I can do dis, dis will not defeat me cuz an Queenie slowly raised 'er arm ova 'er head, but half way into da air she let out a loud scream dat brought a tear down 'er left cheek. "Tez Tez! Nigga bring it down it's stuck fam'." 'Er voice was shaky,so da both of 'em could tell off da back dat Queenie was in a lot of pain. Cortez' held 'er hand while Tez slowly brought Queenie's arm down an Cortez' felt everyone of 'er finger nails deep in his skin, but neither of 'em could truly imagine da excruciating pain Queenie was in 'cus it had neva happened to either of 'em. Dey felt helpless an seein' Queenie lyin' dere helpless brought tears to their eyes. Queenie convinced da doctor to let 'er go home an she would do wut eva it took fo' 'er to heal properly. She knew it was to soon an could sense Dr. Price felt da same way, he gave Queenie 'er instructions of wut to do and wut not to do.

"Mrs. Miles ya need therapy three times a week 'ere at da hospital on da 4th floor." Self determination was wut Queenie had to strengthen 'er body back to da normal it only took 'er 4 months to completely heal an put 'er thoughts in play. Queenie an 'er peeps Tez, Lu and Chaos have been residin' in East St. Boogie fo' 'bout 4 months now an everything has been runnin' smoothly. She put Lu and Chaos up in their own place, dey preferred to stay in da hood of East St. Boogie, so Queenie bought 'em a 2 story house wit a basement an furnished it fo' 'em. Tez finally convinced his homeboy Cortez' to move out of da hood he lived in since Queenie was under his roof now, so while she was in 'er recovery stage Tez and Cortez' purchased 2 beautiful suburban homes dat were across da street three houses down from a nutter. Afta' Queenie fully recovered dey den would move in, but 'til den dey had to put in work. Takin' ova Martin Luther King Jr. Drive, dey shut it down an let Chaos and Lu reopen it up, of course da way Queenie wanted it ran. Queenie and Cortez' discuss da lessors on his house dey presently lived in now, so Queenie questioned wut Cortez' was gonna do wit da house?

Chapter Thirteen
"Markin' 'Er Territory"

"Baby wut are yo' thoughts 'bout dis house 'cus Imma keep it funky I wanta use it as a stash house."

"Well I had jus' thought 'bout boardin' it up, but I guess ya can use it shawty, but I thought afta' chu finished yo' ass was done? Not only dat ma who ya gonna have live 'ere 'cus I don't think ya gonna get Chaos or Lu to move out of their spot chu jus' bought 'em to run it." Queenie stated; "Baby jus' as well as I bought dat ma'fucka fo' 'em I can take dat ma'fucka away dey work fo' me. Don't trip doe I got all of dat work out already baby I jus' need chu to say yeah dat I can use it." Once Cortez' gave 'er da go ahead Queenie called ova all da fellas to come pack Cortez' crib it was movin' day an she needed to be done quickly. It was da end of da summer an she really didn't get to enjoy it 'cus she was laid up healin' it took every bit of dose 4 months fo' Queenie to gain 'er strength back an put all 'er chess pieces in motion. Queenie felt da timin' was great da fellas had put da last load on da truck to be transported to da new house an a nutter truck pulled up wit a flat bed attached to da back of it dat carried a coffee brown boxed Chevy Capri Classic wit gold flakes sittin' on 18's. "Who da fuck is dat?" Cortez',Lu,Chuck,and Chaos got on some defensive shit 'cus everyone was dumb founded to wut was happin' 'cus Queenie kept 'er game under da radar. Queenie stepped outside an threw 'er arms in da air. "Wutsup homeboy?" Cortez' jus' looked at his QUEEN. "Boss who dat?"

"My niggas dat dere is yo' newest family member of our circle." Skip jumped down out da rental an shouted wutsup lil' mama. "Awe shit dats dat nigga Skip." Skip walked up givin' Queenie 'er props first wit a hug an a wutsup boss, ya aiight lil' ma? Skip stepped back an told; "Queenie dey can't keep a good one down huh?" He looked at Tez and Cortez' given 'em an embrace statin'; "So we all back where we started at huh?" "Yeah I guess, so homeboy, but shit totally different now. Back den we were shorties wit nothin' now we are grown ass men doin' grown ass shit. Tez chimed in nigga dis game 'ere is ride and die an dis 'ere is family it's all fo' one and one fo' all ain't no venturin' off 'cus chu wit us an dis 'ere is where it at we all eat jus' da same. Everyone gets paper in dis 'ere circle an wit baby girl as yo' boss she'll make sho' yo' ass squared away."

Queenie stood dere an let da fellas drill Skip on everything she woulda said 'til she got tired of hearin' it. "Aiight I think da picture has been painted clear a nuff, we'll have a meetin' afta' y'all unload dat truck. Yo' Chuck chu an Lu come wit me Cortez' and Tez ova to da new houe,so we can get dis truck unloaded. An da rest of y'all get dis house in order an we'll bring dinner back, so we can all eat as a family den we'll have da meetin' befo' I leave town." Within Queenie's recovery time she had sent $6,000 dollars to Liz an called to let 'er know wut it was fo'. Queenie needed 'er moms to go purchase a dinette set dat would seat 20 strong, Queenie was thinkin' somethin' like da bosses of a mob family since dat's how she ran 'er entourage. "Ma I need a table fit fo' a King an I need a King size bedroom set fo' jus' one room and a livin' room furniture. Da love seat, couch and recliner an one floor model television flat screen. Ma once ya purchase it an chu got da receipt fo' proof call dis number 312-728-1414, ask fo' Skip. He's gonna rent a truck, so y'all can go pick it up, aiight." Liz asked no questions she jus' did wut was asked of 'er. Occasionally Queenie saw 'er main target in da streets while goin' fo' therapy once she convinced Tez and Cortez' she could drive 'er self. Unfortunately da motive fo' drivin' 'er self was non utter dan fo' 'er to follow 'er vics dat put 'er in da hospital. She scoped out every spot dey went to fo' three months an everyday was da same routine, so dey came predictable to Queenie. She would leave da house at da same time each day an sit jus' to see if dey would show up. Sho' nuff dey did an Queenie knew it would jus' be a matter of time befo' she made 'er next move.

"Baby wut all wanta eat?" "Some soul food would set a nigga right." Cortez' told 'er. Dats cool da rest of da fellas exclaimed. "Aiight soul food it is den." Back at da stash house Queenie laid da spread of food out on da new dinette table. Every food ya could imagine she bought: southern fried chicken, rib tips, baked beans, mac and cheese, greens, sweet hot water cornbread, red beans and rice ya name it she had it. Tez took a step back to look at da table itself. "Yo' y'all see dis ma'fuckan table? Dis 'ere is fit fo' a King." Skip responded; "Try fit fo' a QUEEN homeboy, dis 'ere Queenie's layout."

Tez, Cortez', Chuck and Lu took a good look at wut was done to da stash house to see all da new furnishings dat were setup. Tez mouthed in lip movement only chu a slick one baby girl. "Yo lets fix our plates an eat family." Everyone ate 'til their stomachs got full, Queenie cleared da table of all food wiped it back down. "Lets have a meetin' real quick I jus' need 30 minutes of yo' time. Aiight it's like I said befo' I left I gotta go back home an take care of some biz'ness, actually it's time fo' me to go face da judge, but I'll be back. Tez and Cortez' will be goin' wit me,so dat leaves y'all 'ere to hold shit down as if I was still right 'ere wit chu. Of course y'all know wut to do 'cus it's da same shit ya do everyday of yo' lives, but I got a few extra things I need all of ya to do an have done by time I return. Now dis wut I need a privacy fence 'round da back of da house 'bout 7ft. high jus' as wide as da house all da way to dat big ass tree no further. Tez knew exactly wut Queenie was doin' she was duplicatin' da stash house jus' as da one she had back home in Chicago, but he seemed to be da only one to figure dat out.

“Chaos ya know chu gotta run to Detroit fo' a delivery only cuz an in three days go back to pick up. Nah dats to much back and forth, so lets change dat up jus' put yo' self up in a hotel fo' dose three days, but stay low key an on dat third day call an meet up wit dude an be back on yo' way by noon, an somebody will give ya a call to make sho' shit went smooth. Lu dat leaves yo' ass to handle shit, yo' part 'til he returns. An fo' da rest of y'all keep doin' wut chu been doin. Yo' Skip yo' ass get da same treatment as da utters by all means, it's one hand wash da utter. Yo' I respect chu as a man an I expect yo' ass to do wut chu say an say wut chu mean, 'cus I do an yo' ass only get one chance wit me. Ya fuck up an dats yo' ass, I brought chu in dis family circle, but I'll deaden yo' ass. Imma send ya out proper doe an my word is bond.” “Now can ya handle da rules and responsibilities of da stash house? I don't care wut chu do 'ere jus' don't bring non of yo' own traffic through 'ere. Dis is where ya work an rest yo' head an in case ya don't understand dat means no bitches in my stash house. Da only niggas allowed 'ere is yo' family all dese niggas ya see befo' ya. Further mo' yo' ass handle everything dat comes through 'ere money ,packages an long as yo' ass don't fuck dat up we all good fam'.”
Skip replied; “Ya can count on me “Boss” I'm 'ere 'cus I wanta be part of da family a loyal solja lil' mama.” “Yo' one last thing I need da house sound proof, so no matter wuts said, or done in dis ma'fucka it'll stay right 'ere in dis bitch. Queenie thoughts spoke out loud befo' she knew it she said; “A ma'fucka might have to pull a double homicide in dis piece.” Cortez' looked at Tez face to see if he had

caught wut Queenie had jus' said. Tez nodded his head up and down as to say pay attention to 'er words 'cus she's on one. "Aye any questions or complaints 'cus if not our meetin' is ova an I'll see y'all when we return." Cortez', Queenie and Tez returned to da luxury homes in da suburbs endin' their night early Queenie told Tez; "Cuz we'll see ya in da mornin' baby." Embracin' 'er wit a hug an kiss to da forehead Tez replied; "I love ya baby girl, look at my lil' nigga growin' up. Aiight we out of 'ere by 10am see y'all in da mornin'." "Cool fam' holla at chu in da mornin' homeboy." Queenie needed to bring Blue and Red back, so she told Tez dey could drive 'er truck an it was cool wit 'em. "Yo' I can't wait to see my bitch." But dis wasn't da only reason Queenie needed to drive 'er Lexus back she had thoughts of tradin' it off, but she wasn't sho' 'bout wut she would do. Trade it , keep it or jus' bring both cars back dat decision would be made once she got to Chi-Town. Tez birthday was also comin' 'round August 31st to be exact Queenie wanted to go all out fo' 'er big cousin fo' somethin' she knew he would like turin' 19, but she also knew it would be hard to do 'cus he had everything, but it was one thing he didn't have dat she heard 'em speak of an dat was a motorcycle. Queenie saw a bad ass Ninja in a magazine dat said new an comin' soon, only thing was it was ova seas an no one had it jet.
It was a 1996 fully loaded turbo nitrogen XL 3500 she knew at dat moment dat was da gift fo' Tez.
He would be da first wit it befo' it even hit da market, so she called, placed an order. Queenie was told dat she could have it custom made da way she wanted it so she got it painted in Tez favorite color money green wit gold flakes through out da paint. Queenie figured wut da hell is a birthday gift if ya couldn't get it on da day of yo' birthday. Since dey were gonna be in Chi-Town on dat day dat's where da bike would be shipped to. Cortez' and Queenie walked into their new home an Queenie spun 'round and 'round shoutin' I love it baby. She jumped into Cortez' arms legs locked 'round his waist kissin' 'em all ova she whispered; "I love ya daddy." In between all da kissin' he asked;

"I take it chu happy huh?" "Hell yeah I'm happy." Queenie also knew how to get 'er nigga worked up all it took was to call 'em daddy an Cortez' got enormous bulge da word daddy made his manhood stand at attention a sensation only Queenie could fo' feel fo' 'em. "Daddy ya know we gotta bless our new home." "Where ya wanta start shawty?" He asked strippin' each utters clothes off where dey stood. "Baby where eva or how eva ya want it is aiight wit me." Cortez' picked Queenie up suckin' on 'er breast he walked into da kitchen sittin' his QUEEN on da island top in da middle of da floor. Cortez' spread Queenie like she was a smorgasbord at a private party, he kissed an nibbled 'til he made it to da inside of 'er thighs an zeroed in on 'er juicy ass love box divin' in head first he made 'er cry out. "Shit daddy, O_ooh sssss, mama's baby hungry ain't he?" Queenie squirmed an Cortez' pulled 'er back in no_no ain't no runnin' tonight baby I got chu. He stuck his tongue so deep into Queenie's pussy hittin' jus' da right spot to make 'er squirt 'er juices all ova his mouth and chin an afta' words he licked up every drop dat came from 'er love box. Quennie wanted to return da favor an make 'em feel special da way he jus' made 'er feel, but Cortez' wouldn't have it he was in a zone an didn't want his stride broken jus' jet. He picked 'er up once again an dis time he eased 'er down on his dick.
Ooooh daddy! As dey walked back towards da livin' room Queenie could feel every inch he had to offer wit every step. Squeezin' Cortez' 'round da neck tryin' 'er best to ease da pain neva da less worked 'cus he den put a firm grip on 'er ass cheeks pushin' back downward, so Queenie could feel da wrath of his rock hard dick. He laid his QUEEN on da floor, but not befo' he toss a blanket on it to cover da plush white carpet he had jus' put down. "Baby are ya okay?" "I'm good daddy."
Cortez' pulled 'er legs up to rest on his shoulders while he watched 'em self pump in and out of Queenie's creamy pussy wit a slow past askin' 'er; "Ma is it good to ya, how does it feel?"
She ignored da question Queenie was in a climax mode an was finna explode she tried hard to hold

on, but it felt so good 'er eyes rolled up in 'er head, 'er toes curled an all she could hear was Cortez' askin' 'er how did she feel an his pumps get a lil' forceful. Queenie screamed shhiiitttt daddy I'm 'bout to come. Cortez' wasn't ready jus' jet he had a lot build up an wanted his QUEEN to enjoy every inch of wut he had to give. "Oh da_daddy!" "Come on baby girl ya wanta give it den I wanta feel it baby. "Ere it come daddy, I'm comin'." "I feel dat shit ma stop holdin' back an release dat shit baby." Carryin' Queenie once again to their master bedroom Queenie in ear shot told Cortez' "Baby let me ride dat stallion. Cortez' laid across da bed an eased Queenie's sexy body down on top of his dick. "Mmmmm dat feels marvelous lil' mama." I know was 'er response. "Sshhhiiiitttt ma yo' ass know how to work it now huh?" Queenie smiled at 'em pressed 'er breast against his chest as she whispered; "So ya got jokes now huh nigga? Well saddle up daddy 'cus mama finna take ya fo' da ride of a life time." Movin' 'er hips swayin' side to side Queenie bounced up and down on Cortez' dick full force like a tunnel drop at a amusement park. Queenie teased da dick wit 'er clitoris she pumped so hard da veins in his dick started to pulsate an jus' soon as he got ready to come she pulled up slowly extractin' 'er pussy muscles to grip his dick an once she reached da top of his penis she had an orgasm an let Cortez' see all of 'er juices run down his dick. Ova and ova she played dis teasin' game wit 'em. "Ma why yo' ass keep teasin' me baby? Ooooh shiiitt, come 'ere ma flip yo' sexy ass ova, come on bend ova an let daddy see wut chu workin' wit. Bring dat ass 'ere ya ready fo' me to come?" Queenie replied; "When eva ya ready daddy." Queenie got a lot of pleasure from Cortez' suckin' every part of 'er body. He kissed 'er ass cheeks spreadin' 'em apart an meekly started to blow and lick 'er asshole which turned 'er on,but playin' wit 'er love box made da pussy drip an Cortez' loved every bit of it 'cus dis took 'er mind off of wut he was 'bout to do in 'er ass. "Yo' ya ready lil' mama?" "Shhh, yeah daddy." "Aiight tell me if ya want me to stop." Da sounds Umph O_ba_sssss, Auuuuugh den she screamed "Cortez' put it in all da way baby. Oooooh, shit." Cortez' hugged Queenie from behind tightly an pumped in and out as if he would neva get da chance to fuck 'er again in life. Pumpin' and pushin', Queenie played wit his nuts. "Yo' ya okay daddy?" "I'm good baby how 'bout chu, ya ready to come jet?" Wit his pumps a lil' mo' thrust dan befo' Queenie said; "Bring it on home baby, but don't pull out." Queenie grabbed Cortez' hand an cuffed it between 'er legs, so he could feel all of 'er pussy juices. Dey screamed in unison "Damn baby dat was some fly ass sex an it was worth da wait shawty." Cortez' pulled out an collapsed next to Queenie. "Ma I gotta question how do ya come like ya do an yo' ass can still go on?" "It's jus' how ya make me feel." Queenie replied an dey left it jus' as dat. "Cortez'." "Yeah wutsup shawty?" "I love ya nigga." "I love ya back lil' nigga." A hitter rung interruptin' their lil' love song da 2 had goin' on. Ring! "Wut up fam'?" "Damn baby girl yo' ass sound chipper dan a ma'fucka who jus' got freed from jail,ya dat eager to get back to da windy city?" Queenie said; "I don't know fam' I'm jus' happy cuz. Hell we livin' da good life, I don't have no worries I'm finna see my ol' g, I'm finna hold dat nigga Blue in my arms again. I got chu I got Cortez', we got our family circle. Shit wut mo' can I ask fo' nigga I'm "Boss Queen" and I am on top of da world baby."

Chapter Fourteen
"'Er Heart Has Been Snatched"

"Ya right lil' nigga wut mo' can we ask fo'? Laughter filled da line an Tez asked; "Baby girl y'all ready ova dere?" "Yeah cuz jus' come in da door already open 'cus I know yo' ass on da way ova." "Sho' ya right." Tez walked in an dropped his bags on da floor an yelled "Lucy I'm Home." "Wutsup homeboy?" Cortez' embraced his childhood friend . "Wut up my nigga, how ya livin' homeboy?" "Same as yo' ass family." Cortez' exclaimed. "Yo' y'all ready to rock and roll?" Tez asked. "Where's Queenie I jus' got off da hitter wit 'er." "Ere I am, I had to grab nina, but I'm ready now. Yo'

all take da front Imma hold da backseat down I need to catch a few zzzzz." Queenie couldn't figure out if Cortez' worked 'er ova or if she worked 'em ova to hard, but she felt da need to sleep it off. Befo' she closed 'er eyes she called out; "Yo' cuz while we're in da Chi let Cortez' stay wit y'all aiight. Ya know I ain't finna disrespect mom's fam'. Baby is dat cool wit chu?" "Yeah baby, I wouldn't have it no utter way, I give respect, I don't sho' disrespect." Da next time dey heard a peep out of Queenie was when dey made it to Chicago. "Ueenie_Ueenie lil' nigga we 'ere." "Aiight fam' damn feels like I jus' went to sleep." Queenie sat up an noticed da first stop was 'er aunt's house, 'cus Tez knew his aunt would be at work at least dat's wut dey thought. "Yo' ain't my moms suppose to be at work? Why is 'er car parked across da street fam'?" Dey all got out of da truck an walked towards da house neither one of their parents knew dat dey were comin' to town. Tez stuck his key into da lock, but it didn't fit.
"Damn moms changed a locks on me? A nigga gone fo' 4 months an dis how he get treated?"
Queenie felt somethin' was wrong 'cus she didn't hear da dogs barkin' an da locks were changed, didn't sit well wit 'er. "Yo' Tez somethin' ain't right fam'." Tez knocked on da door, yo' ma open up." When Heather open da door she looked like she seen a ghost. At dis time Tez went in defensive ova drive huggin' his moms he asked; "Wutsup ma, wuts wrong?" "Auntie where_Liz stepped into da kitchen befo' Queenie could finish askin' where she was. "I'm right 'ere baby girl, wut are y'all doin 'ere?" Queenie noticed 'er mother had a distraught look on 'er face an 'er eyes were super glossy like she had been cryin' fo' days. Queenie and Tez ignored da question of wut chu doin' 'ere an both asked in unison; "Wuts wrong wit y'all?" Queenie didn't wait fo' an answer she called out to Blue and Red fo' 'em to come out runnin' at da sound of 'er voice; "Come 'ere mama's baby, come 'ere Blue.
But dere was no answer it was silence. Den Tez and Queenie heard a whimperin' sound dat sounded faint an dey took off runnin' towards da sound. "Ma where are dey?" Tez yelled. "Baby in yo' run, but

we got somethin' to tell y'all first." Tez bust in da bedroom door an Liz rushed to say; "Queenie Blue has been killed baby." To only find Red underneath Tez bed beatin' half to death barely breathin'. Queenie dropped to 'er knees an screamed at da top of 'er lungs. Cortez' ran to 'er aid, but it wasn't any use Queenie jus' lost apart of 'er heart dat fast. "Who da fuck did dis?" He yelled as he flipped da bed into da wall. "Why y'all didn't call us?" Da 2 were irate, hurt and irrational from da looks dey gave their mother's were irredeemable. Liz and Heather were both cryin', Cortez' didn't know wut to do so he stood in a corner silent 'cus he knew da dogs were like kids to his girl and homeboy. "We need y'all to try an calm yo' selves long a nuff, so we can explain wut happen." Tez said man I can't even move Red." He didn't realize his own mother was shookin' up from bein' in da house when it happen. Cortez' finally was able to console Queenie embracin' 'er wit his arms 'round 'er neck. She placed 'er face in is chest an rock back and forth. He also tried to rationalize wit Tez. "Fam' calm down nigga lets find out wut happen, so we ain't gotta wonder wut to do next," Cortez' said; "Come on family lookin' down at Queenie who was cryin' out of control." But dat didn't last long Queenie did a total 360 wit nothin' mo' dan anger. "Aiight." Snifflin' she nudged Cortez' to raise up off 'er an when she looked up da pupil of 'er eyes had turned a cold black. She looked like da devil. Queenie step closer to Tez so she could hear every word 'er moms and aunt said. "Last night yo' moms and me took da dogs to da park, so dey could get some exercise since we hadn't took 'em in 2 days 'cus it was nice out. Anyway we notice a couple of young guys kept circlin' da block watchin' da pups, so since we had been dere fo' a minute we left got back 'ere Liz help me get 'em fed befo' she left an we took 'em out one last time to handle their biz'ness. Well it was afta' Liz left 'round 11pm da dogs started barkin' forcefully, so I got out of bed an den I heard a loud crash of glass breakin'. It was da same 2 guys from da park. I take it dey only came fo' da pups 'cus dey didn't harm me or take anything. Red was da first one to attact 'em an as she locked on da guys arm da utter dude must of seen Blue comin' fo 'em 'cus he kicked 'em in da chest as he jumped in da air an da made 'em whims an dat gave da guy time to pull a bat from his pants leg. He started to beat Red bad wit da bat, it was only 2 swings, but it sound like he crushed every bone in 'er body an jus' as he was bringin' it down again Blue lunged at his throat. Red dropped to da floor from bein' in so much pain I'm guessin' da pain was excruciating fo' 'er to hold on any longer. Den I heard three shots Boom, Boom, Boom afta' dat da dudes ran out. Baby's I'm so sorry. Tez hugged his mother lettin' 'er know dat he apologize fo' not hearin' 'er out first. "Yo' ma ya aiight?" He also pulled his aunt in close a kissed 'er forehead statin; "We shoulda neva put dat responsibility on y'all, but look ma I need to know did ya see dese niggas faces at all?" "Nah dey had hoodies and gloves on, but da guy dat Blue attacked called da utter one by name. He said lets go,Level Queenie ran 'er hand ova 'er face when she heard da name Level. "Yo' Tez! Red needs to be put down." "I can't find it in my heart_ an befo' he could get out da sentence dat was choked up in his throat, Queenie pulled out nina like some crazed person went into da room an pulled da trigger as she said a pray fo' Blue and Red. "No mo' pain ma tell Blue when ya get to doggy heaven his mama sent chu to be wit 'em again. It's ride and die together baby." Queenie placed a blanket ova Red an stormed out of da room, she cocked nina puttin' a nutter round in da chamber. "Now bury 'er." Queenie jumped in 'er truck tires screeched as Tez and Cortez' got outside. "Yo' auntie let me get yo' keys to da car." "Bring 'er back safe baby please!" Liz pleaded. Dey jumped in an peeled off in high tail of Queenie. "Fam' dis Level dude, does baby girl know who he is?" "Nigga dis 'ere is 'er city an she knows everything dat goes on in it an all da niggas in it. Level is a nigga dat tried to get wit Ueenie befo' she met chu, but at da time she wasn't givin' niggas play 'cus she was all 'bout 'er paper an she felt it wasn't any niggas on 'er level, so she told 'em to fall back." "Cuz ya think he tried 'er 'cus she wouldn't give 'em no play?” “Nah, fam' I think it's jus' like my ol' g said dey were jus' tryin' to come up an hit da wrong people up dis time, but trust and believe dey gonna wish dey thought better of it when dey see who at dey ass.” Fuck where she dip off to? Fuck, Fuck, Fuck, Fuck. Queenie knew Level always stood in front of da Robert Taylor Homes an dat's where she spotted 'em, wit his arm bandage an a flock of chicken heads and hood rats 'round 'em. Queenie slammed 'er truck in park leavin' it runnin' she snatched an black hoodie from 'er duffel bag along wit an extra clip. She peeped in da review to see if Tez and Cortez' were in view an jus' as she was screwin' on a silencer she spotted 'er mothers Benz on damn near 2 wheels come 'round da corner. At dat moment she jumped out leavin' da door wide open yellin' out Levels name. Wit 'er gun in hand she took off runnin' towards 'em which made everyone run fo' cover. She started to shoot Flock,Flock,Flock was all could be heard 'cus of da silencer. Cortez' jumped out of da car while it was still rollin' an jumped in Queenie's truck an pulled off behind Tez who was tryin' to get to Queenie, so he could defuse da situation befo' she did somethin' dey would all regret. Level dipped between some buildings an so did Queenie. Flock,Flock. Level felt bullets whisk pass his head as he bobbed and weaved, duckin' and dodgin' death. Queenie got close a nuff to stop an aim wit a clear shot an dat's jus' wut she did. Flock, she saw 'er victim go down, Queenie quickly calculated 'er shots realizin' she had three shots left. She ran as fast as 'er legs would carry 'er towards Level squirmin' body. “Bitch ass nigga roll ova.” Da bullet only hit 'em in upper left thigh, so Queenie stepped in his wound. “Auuuugh.” “Nigga I said turn yo' punk ass ova.” Level recognized 'er voice. “Yo' Queenie wuts good baby, wuts all dis 'bout? I thought we was good I ain't got no beefs wit chu beautiful. Queenie saw Tez out da corner of 'er eye runnin' towards 'er so she had to move quick. “Yo' ya know dat house yo' bitch ass broke into last night? Flock a bullet in his utter leg. “Nigga dat was my aunts crib.” She grabbed his bandaged arm an Level screamed out;

“THROWIN' BRICKS AT THE PENITENTIARY”

“Ouch!”Queenie slapped 'em in da face wit 'er gun. “Now nigga who was da ma'fucka wit chu dat beat my dog wit a bat?” Squeezin' his arm harder he told 'er Pooky. “Pooky is his name. Flock_ “'Er name was Red ya bitch ass nigga an my baby yo' ass killed last night his name was Blue, Flock! Queenie put a bullet in Level's head puttin' 'em to sleep fo' eva. All of Cortez' and Tez screams of no's fell on deaf ears. Queenie couldn't hear anything fo' except da clickin' of da gun from 'er still pullin' da trigger.
“Lil' nigga, lets go we gotta go ma.” Tez snatched da gun out of 'er hand bringin' 'er out of a zone. Runnin' back to da cars Tez jumped back in 'er moms car an she jumped in 'er truck wit' Cortez'.
“Fuck I hear Ola.” She stated. Cortez' followed Tez while Queenie climbed in da back an changed every top stitch of 'er clothin'. “Yo' baby I need to get rid of dis shit, call Tez hitter an tell 'em to drop da top.” Ring. “Yeah.” “Family she says drop da top she jus' stripped.” Dumpin' all da continents out a small plastic bag Queenie put all 'er clothes inside it let 'er window down an tossed da bag in da back seat. Tez let da top back up. “Nigga meet us at da stash house.” Queenie and Tez were 2 clever young ma'fuckas who refused to get caught up in dis chess game dey called life. Tez dropped da bag of clothes off at da first box dat said Salvation Army clothes fo' da needy. “Baby go 'round da back.” Queenie jumped out an unlocked da gate an Cortez' pulled in an Tez swooped in behind 'em. Queenie locked da gate back. She had replaced da clothes she had on wit a new all white sweat suit.
“Fuck ma wutchu ya do baby girl?” Cortez' asked. Tez pride da board off da back door an unlocked da back door to da stash house it was a good thing da lights were still on. Wit da house boarded up no one could see lights comin' from it. Tez said; “Baby girl ya killed dis bitch ass nigga in broad day light cuz. Fam' we came back 'cus yo' ass got court in 2 days. I'm tryin' to get chu outta trouble an lil' nigga yo' ass goin' in deeper. I feel ya on da pups baby I know dat was a big part of yo' heart I know he was yo' baby nigga, but chu mines an I don't wanta lose ya ova no stupidity. Ueenie we coulda handled

dis a better way like we usually do fam', now we don't know if yo' ass was spotted or not."

Tez looked at Queenie an saw da lil' kid dat she was befo' da vicious beast malfunctioned inside 'er. He saw da gleam in 'er eyes, so he embraced 'er an she hugged 'em back as he told 'er; "Yo' lil' nigga it's ride and die wit us an I'm wit chu all da way, but I'm not tryin' to lose ya to da penitentiary shawty." "Yo' ma I'm 'ere fo' ya also down fo' wut eva I'm right 'ere by yo' side baby how eva ya wanta move da chess pieces, but I feel my homeboy 'ere. I'm not tryin' see ya go to prison baby girl." Cortez' stated.

In a smooth firm voice. Queenie said; "Y'all hear me good when I say dis. I love both of ya Tez ya my cuz mo' like a brother dan anything to me, nigga since I can remember yo' ass been everything and everybody to me. Cuz ya stepped in when dat no good ass ma'fucka of a sperm donor disappeared out of my ol' gs life. Ya took me under yo' wing like I was yo' own an been protectin' me every since fam' we ride and die together even afta' all da shit I do an continue to do. Family ya even stick by me while I carry dis problem inside my head 'round an ya still say it's ride and die, but cuz yo' ass hasn't once stop to eva think dis maybe my fate. Afta' I killed dose 11 bitches dat night wit no remorse it was like I was da devil 'em self. I neva said I was an angel, but everyone labels me as one, but da only way I can be an angel is to be a child of God an I know I'm not. Imma child of da devil nigga." Queenie turned to Cortez' "Look I love ya, do ya still love me like ya said 'cus Imma jus' keep it raw wit chu I neva had any intentions of fallin' in love wit chu. Even doe it has been a short journey wit chu it feels right, so da last 4 months I don't regret an won't take any of it back. Nigga yo' ass was my first an if all doesn't fell yo' ass will be my last feel me? Baby I don't expect no mo' dan ya give me, I realize chu don't do anything to please yo' self an I don't feel it's right, but I respect it, but da 4 months we kicked it I seen not one thing dat chu took time out to do fo' yo' self. It's been all 'bout me from pleasin' me sexually, my hospitalization, to watchin' me murk ma'fuckas an ya haven't left jet. Yo' ya played a big part in my move to East St. Boogie baby if dat means anything an I appreciate chu respectin' my gangsta so nigga remember I love ya." Curiously da 2 thought on da speech Queenie jus' gave 'em an of course dey knew she was sincere, but wut did she really jus' tell 'em. Tez looked at Cortez' an shrugged his shoulders, wit raised brows dey turned to Queenie an questioned in unison; "Yo' ma, baby girl wuts goin' on, wut chu conjurin' up? 'Cus right now it sounds like yo' ass talkin' in riddles?""Pooky" Queenie told 'em;"If I make it through tonight and tomorrow wit out Ola sniffin' me out, I'll make it to court an see wuts gonna happen to me an if I make it out to walk free, I'm gonna kill Pooky befo'I leave Chicago." Pooky, Pooky who da fuck is Pooky, Tez questioned 'em self."Ooooh shit Pooky dat use to run wit Skip? He use to bounce at da 50 fo' a minute, da nigga wit da limp? Tez asked. "Yeah dats da nigga,but da ma'fucka only limps 'cus he always got da bat in his pant leg. He jus' fronts like he hurt an shit." "So cuz dats da nigga Level was wit?" Cortez' stated; "Okay ma, but killin' dude will jus' put chu in mo' jeopardy an I'm not feelin' it. Sho' me where he be at day and night an I'll take care of it an dats on my strength. So don't think 'bout it no mo'." Queenie kept a low profile 'til it was time to appear in court, she stayed tucked away at da stash house. She pushed Cortez' and Tez away makin' 'em stay at his moms crib as planned so dey could be 'er ears an make sho' Ola wasn't lookin' fo' 'er. Queenie had Cortez' to drive 'er truck 'round since it was at da scene. Queenie wanted to make sho' it didn't get pulled ova an he wouldn't be harassed. Once she got word everything was cool da mornin' of court she had to be dere at 10:30am, so she had Cortez' and Tez pick 'er up at 8am,so she could go get rid of da truck. Queenie had already called da dealership an spoke wit da same young associate dat sold it to 'er. Dey pulled up at da dealership an da guy had made it where Queenie didn't pay anything she jus' did an even trade. She had to give up 'er red Lexus truck, but dude said dey had jus' got a brand new money green one wit gold flakes through it fully loaded wit Nitrogen boosters wit 200 hunnid on da dash. Queenie admit thought of da bike (motorcycle) she had done fo' Tez an told da sales man she was on da way. Queenie grabbed $3,000 out of 'er duffel bag an tossed it to da young nigga. Put dat in yo' pocket.” Den she jumped in da back an told Tez to drive to 'er moms crib. Since things took a different approach an it was only 8:30 now Queenie put a call in ova seas to change da date fo' da bike to be delivered, but some how dere was a mix up an it seemed to be already on it's way. Ma'am we are sorry fo' da mix up, but yo' order will be arrivin' 'bout 9 o'clock dis mornin'.” “Aiight dats fine matter of fact it's right on time. Thank ya.” Ring! “Hello, Queenie said.” “Baby dis auntie, it's 'ere.” “Where it at?” “I had 'em to put it up by da door, so when y'all pull up he can't see it.” “Aiight we'll be dere gotta stop to make first.” Liz got on da hitter. “Yo' wutsup ma, we'll be pullin' up in a minute, I'll talk to ya den love ya.” Tez pulled up at da house an dey all got out an Tez step to da side to take a better look. “Yo' cuz dis ma'fucka 'ere is sweet. Ya know dat paint go hard an ya know dose my colors lil' nigga.” “Yo' ya like dat huh?” Queenie locked 'er arm 'round he's an said jokin' “Nigga ya jonenin' but chu know dat ma'fucka got 200 on da dash right an it's fully loaded wit Nitro boost.” Jus' as dey hit da corner of da house she said; “Jus' like yo' Ninja, Happy Birthday nigga.” Tez picked Queenie up off da ground an spun 'er 'round tellin' 'er I love ya lil' nigga it neva amazes me wit da shit chu do. He finally put Queenie back on 'er feet. “Thank ya Ueenie, I don't know wut to say.” “Chu ain't gotta say nothin' fam' jus' know ya da only nigga in da city of Chicago wit it first.” Cortez' stated; “Niggas finna hate an da brauds will be flockin' and jockin' when ya get back to East St. Boogie homeboy.” “Oh I didn't stop to think 'bout dat, I'm finna ride dis baby back home. Oh shit I gotta get a matchin' ridin' jacket.” “Yeah yo' ass gonna need a fly ass helmet to protect yo' shit from da bugs on all dat open e-way.” Jus' den his moms and auntie walks out da house wit a box in each of their hands. “Ere baby I know it's early ya b-day is not fo' 4 mo' days, but niecy Poo told us y'all was leavin' afta' court, so I figured I couldn't let chu go incomplete baby." Tez ripped da box open an pulled a leather bomber jacket out. Money green wit gold 5 point stars 'round da portrait of Tez and Red. Off to da side it read "She was a ride and die bitch,chu was loved an will be missed" RIP August 22nd 1990. Tez hugged his mother an said; "Thank ya I love it." Liz chimed in "Ere baby happy birthday." Givin' 'em da box she step to da side. "Auntie dis kind of heavy wut is it?" Tez pulled out a matchin' helmet an tears filled his eyes at da sight of wut was written on it. Liz had a portrait of Red on one side wit their signature sayin' "We ride and die leadin' to da portrait of Blue on da utter side. Queenie also got teary eyed afta' seein' da helmet. "Dats hot ma I like dat." "Auntie it represents thank chu I appreciate it." Tez hugged his mom and aunt an kissed both of 'em on da forehead. Queenie said; "Aye y'all ready 'cus I'm startin' to feel nauseous, I need to get dis thing ova wit. Dese people been holdin' a ballot ova my head fo' to long now as it is, I gotta find out my destiny. Y'all feel me." "My baby goin' home free jus' as free as ya walkin' in dere." Liz told 'er. "I hope ya right ma, I hope ya right." "Tez chu ridin' yo' joint to da court house to test it befo' ya put it on da e-way homeboy?" "Yeah I think I jus' might do dat homeboy,so lets ride out. I'll see y'all dere if I don't beat ya dere." Chuckles filled da air, but Queenie had to reply. "Nigga don't fo' get I got Nitro to fam'. Ma y'all ride wit us unless y'all scared." Of course Liz gave 'er daughter da third degree 'bout 'er new truck, but Queenie jus' ignored it, but on a nutter note 'er aunt loved it. "Niecy Poo dis 'ere is a nice truck ya got an if I'm not mistaken it's da same color as Tez motorcycle. By da way dat was a very nice gift ya got 'em dats one he'll neva fo' get."

"So, ma how is work goin?"

"Baby work is work dey still got me on 12 hour shifts right now, but it's aiight." Queenie questioned "How are ya pockets wit out waitin' fo' an response she reached down in 'er duffel bag an pulled out 10 stacks den gave 'er moms and aunt 5 thousand each. Heather said thank ya baby, but yo' cousin jus' gave me, Queenie cut 'er off auntie it's cool I don't need to know wut Tez gave ya, but I am glad he on top of it. Jus' keep it dats fo' ya,so don't insult me." Queenie had a problem wit sayin' please to anyone, it wasn't 'cus she was bein' rude, but it made 'er feel as doe she was beggin' from someone or fo' somethin'. To 'er dat was a big ass pill hard to swallow, an 'er pride wouldn't let 'er so she didn't use da word. Dey arrived at da court house an Tez was dere already standin' wit Mr. D waitin' on Queenie to get dere. Tez smiled at 'er. "Look at dis nigga he think he did somethin' 'cus I let his ass beat me 'ere." Cortez' hit da alarm button chirp chirp an walked 'round to da front of da truck an placed his hand 'round Queenie askin' in earshot shawty ya good? "Yeah, good as Imma get I'm jus' ready fo' it to be ova. Yo' baby did chu take care of dat?" Queenie wanted to know if Cortez' had took care of da nigga Pooky like he told 'er he would do, so she looked into his eyes fo' any signs of da slightest lie. "So wut lil' mama ya got doubts 'bout wut I tell ya Imma do?" He kissed 'er an said; "Shawty I told chu I got chu, I took care of it last night. If ya don't believe me jus' ask Tez ya should know I ain't gonna lie to ya." "Dats cool, I believe ya it ain't nothin' personal I needed to make sho' ya feel me." "Wutup Mr. D?" "Nothin', but chu Ms. Miles. Are chu ready to do dis?" "Yeah I am sir." Mr. D. said lets go ova wuts gonna happen. Now dis is a trial, but da things dey ask will be to scare ya. Questions like how did da fight start, wut was it ova, why did ya hospitalize da utter girl by da way dey are callin' 'er da victim. We know dats not true, but since ya beat 'er so badly dey are callin' ya harmful to society. Everyone went on listenin' to Mr. D talk. "So Mr. D wut does dat mean fo' Queenie?" Tez asked. Well dey want to give 'er 5 years probation, but I talk to da DEA an dey can't seem to find their witness, so it jus' might be thrown out all together. All rise fo' da honorable judge Sykes. Ya may all be seated court is in session. Queenie, Tez, and Cortez' knew it was a good chance dat dey would be back on their way to East St. Boogie wit in da next few hours 'cus Red Bone was dead. Da DEA questioned Queenie on everything Mr. D said dey would. Mr. D even threw a few of his own questions in dere to make it look good. Judge Sykes asked da DEA if dey had any utter witness "No sir we learned 'bout 4 months ago our witness was murdered yo' honor, so we have no mo' witness on 'er behalf. "Well wit out a victim or witnesses dere's no reason fo' Ms. Miles to be charged fo' anything at dis time. Ms. Miles how old are ya? 'Cus ya look pretty young to be in my court room young lady." "Yo' honor I jus' turned 16 sir." "Well Ms. Miles ya to young and beautiful to be runnin' in an out of court houses fo' any reason, so stay out of trouble an out of my court room." "Yeah I mean yes sir." "Dis case is dismissed Ms. Miles ya free to go." Mr. D told Queenie and Tez I'll see ya guys 'round call me if ya need me again an he left da court room. "Yo' lets be out." Queenie wanted to get far away from downtown as possible. Cortez' asked; "Y'all hungry, do y'all wanta eat befo' we hit da e-way?" "Dats cool we can feed moms and auntie befo' we leave." "How 'bout Submarine Port we can grab some subs and soup wut eva y'all want." Queenie said. Tez hopped on his bike "I'll beat I mean meet y'all dere." "Oh ya got jokes huh? Well nigga I'm free now, but chu better be glad I got da ol' g's in 'ere, I'll see ya on da e-way." "Aye y'all better be cool wit all dat racin' we don't need any funerals to attend." It felt good to spend time wit their parents. Cortez' even fit good into da equation nicely. Queenie asked; "Are y'all ready to bounce now?" Liz stated; "Baby girl I remember it use to be a time when we had to dare ya out of da city." "Well ma Chicago can't see me no mo'. Dis 'ere is my home fo' eva I love dis city an Chicago loves me. I can come back at any time an still get da same respect I'm leavin' wit 'cus I am "Boss Queen" an everyone knows dis is my city, but now I jus' feel it's time to move on 'cus I've done a nuff 'ere an instead of lettin' Ola take me out of Chi-Town an disrespectin' my character, I jus' decided it's time fo' me to leave fo' awhile. Besides dat ma da life we built in East St. Boogie I feel in my heart is finna be a great one. I got Tez, Cortez' an befo' ya know it we'll have da 2 of y'all back where ya both originally came from." Tez told 'em; "Yeah we can't leave y'all 'ere fo' to long, so jus' prepare yo' selves fo' a move soon." Heather and Liz didn't know wut to say behind dat, but dey did know their children an it wouldn't be long befo' somethin' drastic happened. "Aye we'll talk 'bout dat later we gotta get on dis highway, 'cus I want Tez to get some day light, so his bike can floss in da sun." Laughter filled da air as dey all hugged an said their I love ya's.

Chapter Fifteen
"Trouble In Da South An She Goes By "Boss Queen"

Cortez' asked Queenie if she wanted 'em to drive, but she replied "Nah baby I can handle it ya jus' relax aiight." On da highway Tez pulled up next to da truck an locked eyes wit Queenie to say wutsup chu ready? Tez nodded an motioned his head down da e-way indicatin' he was ready to race. Da highway was fairly clear an wide open. Queenie touched Cortez' hand an asked 'em while still lookin' at Tez "Baby ya ready fo' dis ride 'cus Imma need chu to hold on." Queenie shot off like a jet, but Tez came up behind 'er jettin' 'round da truck an all chu could hear was a ssssst in da wind from da Ninja. "Damn dat ma'fuckan bike fast he gotta be doin' at least 90 miles." Cortez' exclaimed. "Nah baby he doin ova a hunnid 'cus we're doin' 115." "Damn shawty wut chu say dis bitch do?" "Yo' baby I can sho' ya better dan I can tell ya." Queenie press down on da accelerator an caught up to Tez. "Ma y'all got 2 ½ miles to da exit baby." "Baby lower yo' window. Yo' cuz we got 2 ½ miles so wut chu wanta do fam'." Queenie asked. Tez took off first Queenie came up beside 'em basically playin' wit 'em. Every time Tez picked up speed she would do da same keepin' an even flow wit 'em. "Yo' baby watch out fo' Ola nigga Imma end dis now." She hit da Nitro switch doin' every bit of 200 mph, but Tez did da same an dey played peek-a-boo 'til dey reached da exit. Back in town

"THROWIN' BRICKS AT THE PENITENTIARY"

4 days early Cortez' told Queenie to hit Saint Claire strip. Saint Claire was da main spot everyone hung out on. Dis was da same spot Queenie had 'er quarrel wit da brauds who hospitalized 'er. Queenie led da way an Tez followed. Cortez' flagged 'em to come 'round an he shot out like a rocket. Everyone was in awe of who it was on da bike. Queenie stopped in da middle of da street an waited to turn into da parkin' lot. Tez flew back up da strip an broke da gears down to a slow roll an pulled into da lot an Queenie pulled in slower behind 'em, so everyone could get a real good look at who was flossin' da Lexus. Someone screamed Whoa! Ya see dat ain't nothin' 'round 'ere like dat. Nigga dat shit don't come out fo' a minute cuz. Queenie gloated inside like 'er shit was top quality. She knew 'er taste was one of a kind. Queenie den made a mental note dat 'er archenemies were in da lot kickin' it wit some niggas off in da cut drinkin'. "Baby ya see dat crowd ova dere." As she parked next to Tez, Cortez' said; "Yeah ma I see 'em yo' ma yo' ass ain't fin_ Queenie cut of em off. "Nah nigga I'm not finna do nothin' dese bitches gotta pass today baby. Ya got my word an it's bond, so nigga lets jay down on a T-Bone steak baby. Queenie smiled at Tez as he got off his bike. "Yo' family wut chu wanta do?" "My Queen wanta get some steaks." Cortez' locked eyes wit Tez an nodded his head towards da crowd of people when Tez turned 'round to look he asked Queenie; "Cuz really today lil' nigga wuts really good?" "Look I jus' gave my word no matter wut dey gotta pass today fam' Imma be cool I'm jaunty jus' let me order my steak an eat befo' ya 2 piss me da fuck off."

Tez opened Queenie's door fo' 'er to get out da girl was fly. Wearin' a pair of black and white tight Levi's a white t-shirt wit a picture airbrushed of Blue cross 'er chest wit a pair of air force ones dat had a portrait of Blue on top of da shoe an Red on da utter one. Cortez' met da 2 in front of da truck where he put his hand on da small of 'er back dat's where he felt nina. Queenie had took off 'er jacket, so it was exposed fo' everyone to witness, but it didn't bother Queenie at all. As dey walked closer to da doors of da Waffle House is when da whisperin' began, but loud a nuff fo' 'em to hear. "Yo' is dat dat same bitch I beat wit a bat?" Queenie tried to ignore it, but inside it was botherin' 'er to da point she said; "Dats one bitch." "Aiight ma come on baby pay dat shit no attention." "Yeah, I shoulda killed dat bitch dat night, but dat bitch ass nigga ran up on me." Queenie told 'er self out loud repeatedly: "Word is bond, lil' nigga yo' word is bond an it's all ya got in dis world." Once inside Queenie walked all da way back to da back of da restaurant an took a seat. She She convinced 'er self dat today was not da day to jap out so she tried to relax.

"May I take y'all order, wit a smile on face." "Yeah I'm ready Queenie propped 'er leg up on da seat leanin' back against da wall. Let me get a T-Bone well done ova easy eggs, hash browns, pancakes jus' 2 and some OJ. "Hey ain't chu dat chic dey call "Boss Queen"?" Queenie didn't respond, but Tez asked; "Why who wants to know shawty?" "No one in particular it's jus' I was da one who waited on y'all dat night da fight broke out an ya jus' been da talk 'round 'ere. Everyone actually thought chu was dead, I was da one who called da ambulance." "Dats cool, but as ya can see I'm well alive and kickin' it home girl. Queenie questioned wit all da commotion dat night ya didn't get a tip did chu?"

"Nah, but it's cool." "Well take their order an bring us our food an I'll make sho' ya get da biggest tip ya eva got shawty." Da waitress eyes got wide as a deer in headlights she took da utter orders an in 20 minutes later she came back wit 2 trays ova 'er shoulder. Placin' 'em on da table behind 'er she distributed each plate to da rifle owners. Cortez' and Tez sat on da same side facin' da door entrance to see wut came in and out. Dis was one of da reasons Queenie sat in 'er seat, so she could look out da window an at da door. Queenie started up small talk; "So wutsup nigga how dat bike ride?"

"Cuz dat bitch ride proper dats wutsup." Tez exclaimed damn family fo' a minute dere I thought she was gonna get away from me it's so fuckan fast dat Nitro fam' afta' I jetted out, it jus' felt like I was floatin' on clouds an I ain't neva felt no shit like dat." Queenie said; "Dats why ya got it 'cus it will be a nutter 5 years befo' ya see a nutter one like it 'cus dats when it comes out. Nigga ya know we gotta be different at least fo' awhile anyway 'til one of dese busta ass niggas can get on our level an maintain da paper trail we get." Cortez' asked so wut up family wut chu wanta do fo' ya birthday? It's in fo' days correct?" Tez stated; "Shit I hadn't thought 'bout it homeboy wit all dats been goin' on." "Well yo' we gotta few up scale clubs we can hit if dats wut chu wanta do fam'. We can go pop some bottles shut da bar down an do it up right my nigga." As dey ate a loud crowd walked in da restaurant, da same group from outside still talkin' shit. Somethin' Queenie was not tryin' to hear, but told 'er self all in due time bitches. Yo' my niggas y'all ready to bounce it seems to be a lil' to crowded fo' my taste." Standin' from da table dey heard someone say bitches get outta dodge when it gets to hot in da kitchen Queenie tried to stay decent an not get outta 'er body wit dese bitches 'cus she wasn't wit all da talkin' when it came to getting down and dirty. Queenie felt dat she was to suave, but fo' some reason she felt like laughter an stated; "Only when wet dogs run in an smell up da kitchen. Wet bitches an heat don't mix." Tez and Cortez' couldn't help but to laugh. "Lets go fam' dese bitches tryin' to miff me an my gangsta is not to be tested. Not today." Ya surprised me lil' nigga 'cus I know dat took a lot outta ya to hold yo' composure, but chu conjured dat shit ma. Fuck 'em 'cus ya don't need any mo' mishaps." "Oh shit decipherin' shit to dose dumb bitches I almost fo' got to give ol' girl 'er tip." Cortez' said; "I'll go pay 'er ma." He didn't want 'er to go back in da inside since dey got 'er out wit no problems "Nah baby I got 'er, I'll be right back." Queenie stepped back inside da restaurant an called out fo' shawty. "'Ere yo' tip home girl." Queenie pulled off 10 one hunnid dollar bills an handed it to da waitress. "Yo' dis bitch thinks she ballin' or wut? I'll take 'er shit an beat 'er ass." "Aye shawty let me see yo' pen and pad." Queenie whispered in a low voice; "Call dis number ask fo' Lu and Chuck an tell 'em get 'ere now it's finna be a riot “Boss Queen” is back.” “Bitch yo' ass heard wut da fuck I said?” “Yo' call now! Was da last thing Queenie said befo' a gang of ma'fuckas jumped 'er befo' she could make it to da door. Tez and Cortez' rushed da door a few niggas held while da rest got da best of Queenie. Queenie held 'er own fo' awhile swinggin' landin' blows on niggas and bitches. 'Er conscience told 'er hold off a lil' longer da crew would be dere any minute. Queenie got knocked to da floor by some nigga, but she was still conscious bald up in a corner bein' stomped damn near unconscious she finally reached nina. Jus' as she came up bustin' 'er crew had made it dere an dey started puttin' it down. Droppin' niggas on da outside as dey ran out da door. Tez and Cortez' ran in to help Queenie an make sho' she was okay. “I got me cuz, I'm good y'all see I didn't start dis shit, I'm finna finish it doe homeboy. Now grab dat bitch dat crushed my ribs.” Cortez' did wut his girl said. “Yo' Tez give da owner 10 stacks fo' any damages dat was done an make sho' he stays quit. It was only three workers dat night 2 waitress and 1 cook give all of 'em $2,000 each fo' hush hush ya know how to do it.” She tossed 'em da keys so he could get da money from 'er duffel bag. Queenie ran out behind Tez an gave ol' girl a right hook dat's when Cortez' let 'er drop which made 'er stumble, but she popped back. “Bitch 'ere I am ya wanted me dead 'ere yo' chance home girl.” Every word she landed a punch. “Yo' I can't see ya shawty where ya at bitch? Can't fight as well as ya thought huh? Know wonder ya had to blind side me wit a bat yo' ass ain't got no wind, where yo' fight at bitch?” Queenie asked. Queenie realized why she didn't talk while fightin' it takes to much of ya wind. Everyone else stopped fightin' an had zoned in on da 2. One last punch an Queenie dropped ol' girl an walked away, but only to look fo' 'er next victim da reason she got hit wit da bat in da first place. Chuck and Lu wanted to know if Queenie had slipped into a trans or was she still in 'er right mind. “Yo' fam' is she still wit us?” Tez said; “Nah, my niggas she wit us.” Queenie yelled out; “Yo' razor bitch it's yo' turn shawty, Imma make ya swallow dat bitch. Lets squabble since ya feel ma'fuckas can't stand da heat in da kitchen. Lets sho' ya squad how much woman yo' ass is." Queenie taunted 'er prey to snuff 'er out 'cus she couldn't see 'er at first, but once she spotted 'er, Queenie broke out runnin' afta' 'er. Da braud broke out tryin' to get away, but Queenie was not far behind 'er an everyone else struck out behind da 2. Tez thought better of runnin' an yelled out squad up family wavin' his hand as he jumped on his Ninja tossin' da truck keys to Cortez'. Chuck and Lu was in da same car Tez pulled up an told 'em; "Follow 'em so we can throw dis bitch in da trunk." Tez and Cortez' were da first ones to reach Queenie of course, so dey witness Queenie run an jump up off da ground an drop kick da girl in da back. Dey both dropped an rolled a coupla feet. Chuck and Lu fish tailed to a halt jumpin' out da car dey grabbed da braud an threw 'er into da back seat den Lu got in beside 'er an duck tape 'er eyes and hands. "Ma get in da truck baby. Lets go." Cortez' yelled. Cortez' called Chuck's hitter. "Yo' fam' did y'all get da house sound proof jet?" "Yeah we did dat afta' y'all left it's done." "Well bro take dat bitch dere." "Baby I tried I tried. I didn't want dis today I had no attentions on puttin' my murder game down today." Queenie rant and raved on and on; "Dis bitch was supposed to be tortured slowly on my terms." Cortez' looked at 'er wit a raised brow of confusion. "Baby" callin' 'er out of da rage she was in. "My QUEEN, ma ya ain't gotta do dis. I'll have dose niggas take 'er some where an get rid of 'er ass so no one will eva find 'er ass. Baby I need ya to use yo' head on dis one baby girl whether dey get rid of 'er or ya do it yo' self remember ma she has 'er whole crew as witnesses an it's our word ova theirs an who's to say da ma'fuckas at da restaurant won't turn against chu? Baby ya know jus' as well as I do dat dis will fall back on chu ma." Queenie had to think fast. "Aiight listen baby dis is how it's gonna play out. I'm not gonna kill 'er, but I'm finna put a hurtin' on dis bitch she gonna wish she was dead straight up. Take me 'round da back of da crib I don't need any body to see me goin' inside, so tell Chuck make sho' dat bitch duck taped an sit dat bitch in a chair." Cortez' was a block away from da house so Queenie jumped in da back an went through 'er duffel bag in search of a black hoodie an a bandanna black sweat pants an jumpers changin' in da back she stated; "Baby call Tez tell 'em to clear da house everyone out except dat bitch. Yo' nigga usually I wouldn't say a word 'bout wut I'm doin', but since I got love fo' ya an ya bein' my nigga I feel da trust. If anything happens to me yo' ass and Tez split everything of mines an remember it's ride and die baby. I said dat to say I'm finna torture dis bitch 'til I get tired. Wut eva ya thinkin' I'm probably finna do to 'er Den Imma take dis bitch to da hospital an put on a big ass sho' like she's a friend of mines an she been hurt, by a gang of females an I witness 'er bein' beatin' in a gang way as I was drivin' by. I yelled out an dey all took off runnin' an I ran to 'er aid to see if I could help 'er. An instead of tryin' to find someone wit a hitter to call an ambulance I rushed 'er dere in my car. Yeah dats my story an Imma stick to it. So leave my truck in da back an jump in da car wit one of da fellas." Cortez' replied; "Yo' shawty I sho' hope dis shit works out fo' da good ma, but how in da hell will I know ya aiight?" He asked pullin' in da back of da house da privacy fence was standin', but not completed. Queenie kissed Cortez' so passionately, he actually thought dat would be da last time he would see 'er. "Baby no matter wut I will call ya one way or a nutter, I'm confident dis will be on point. Now go an let me do me. Y'all keep ya lines open give me at least 2 hours to complete dis." Queenie placed da bandanna ova 'er nose and mouth, so 'er vic wouldn't see who it was once da tape came off 'er eyes. Walkin' in da back door it was dark except fo' 2 candles sittin' on da floor. She knew Tez had did dat she thought good lookin' baby boy. Da guys had laid plastic underneath da chair so da mess made would be easy to clean up. Instantly Queenie swung an hit ol' girl breakin' 'er jaw bone. "Auuuugh! Ya bitch she muffled. Queenie snatched da tape off 'er mouth. "Did chu say somethin' I couldn't quite hear ya.

"THROWIN' BRICKS AT THE PENITENTIARY"

"Ya fuckan bitch." "Dats wut got chu 'ere ma yo' fuckan mouth." She swung again dis time she broke 'er nose takin' a razor Queenie sliced straight across 'er face an 'er flesh fell open. "Uh-oh shit!" "Wuts wrong shawty? Oops let me get chu a rag." Queenie picked up a bottle of rubbin' alcohol an poured it onto 'er face. "Uh-oh shit." She screamed. "Shut da fuck up was chu screamin' when yo' bitch ass was tryin' to stomp me out afta' ya girl crushed my shit?" Queenie was insanely agitated commence to swing a bat like she was hittin' home runs,first she broke 'er legs at da knees den 'er ankles den 'er torso da right den da left side breakin' every bone on 'er body. Buy now ol' girl was limp and numb from da pain an all da torture, Queenie realized she was fallin' unconscious so it was time to get 'er to da hospital. Queenie knocked 'er off da chair an pulled da plastic towards da door. She grabbed a blanket off da back of a couch an ran out da door an draped blanket ova 'er seat den went back an dragged da plastic to da truck. Queenie was strong fo' 'er size, she picked 'er up an set 'er in da front seat. Queenie balled da plastic up an took it back in da house along wit all da utter contents she had clothes, money an dropped 'em in da floor. She locked da door an opened da gate. Once at da hospital Queenie dialed Cortez' number it only rang twice. "Hello, ma?" All Queenie said was; "Go clean da house send Lu and Chaos." Click da line went dead. Queenie turned 'er hitter off an placed it da glove box,so no one could reach 'er 'til she was ready to be reached. Queenie ran into da hospital screamin' I need help please bring a stretcher. Hurry! Runnin' back outside to open da passenger door so da trauma team could get to 'er. She knew exactly wut she would tell 'em when dey gave 'er da speech 'bout not movin' 'er 'cus she could have punctured or fractured 'er seriously. "She's not respondin' take 'er straight to surgery. Da doctor was yellin' out different demands Ms. Please go to da nurses desk so we can get some info on dis patient. Queenie did jus' dat, but politely told 'er; "Ma'am I don't know da young lady, so I really can't tell ya who she is where she came from nothin' all I can tell ya is dat she was bein' badly beaten by a gang of people. Dis is how I found 'er an I woulda felt bad if I had jus' left 'er dere an I seen 'er hurt. Ma'am I jus' hope I got 'er 'ere in time fo' some help." Da nurse ask wut is yo' name den young lady? "Ma'am my name is Brandi, Brandi Stapleton." Well Ms. Stapleton da 2 officers ova dere would like to ask ya a few questions also jus' wut chu seen. If ya seen any faces. Da nurse flagged ova da officers. "Ma'am we need to ask ya a few questions?" "It's Brandi Stapleton I'm to young to be a ma'am." "Okay Ms. Stapleton how do ya know da victim?" "I don't I jus' saw 'er getting beaten by a large group of people in a gang way ova on Jump off way, so I yelled out an da crowd of people scattered. Dats when I realized da person on da ground wasn't movin' so I rushed to 'er aid. I had no phone so I couldn't call da paramedics, so wit out thinkin' I put 'er in my truck an brought 'er 'ere." Queenie put on a very good act fo' Ola. "Please sir's tell me she's gonna be alright, I hope she doesn't die." She asked da officers if dey were finish wit 'er 'cus she needed to get out of da bloody clothes she still had on. "I really feel nasty do ya think I need to get tested since I got 'er blood on me?" Queenie screamed an started to freak out 'bout da blood bein' on 'er person. "Oh my God." "Ms. Stapleton please calm down dey can test ya 'ere or if ya gotta a physician of ya own ya wanta see Monday mornin' ya can. Da officer stated; "We are done 'ere ya free to go have a good night." Queenie said to 'er self dis shit worked like a charm now let me get my ass outta 'ere. She headed fo' 'er truck as she pulled off she made sho' she was out of sight of da hospital she took 'er hitter out turned it on an called Cortez'. Jus' as she got ready to dial his number to ease his mind it didn't go threw. 'Er hitter rang. "Wutsup?" "Yo' baby girl wut da fuck, where ya at fam' ya got ma'fuckas 'round 'ere on da way to insanity. Is yo' ass aiight?" Chaos asked. Queenie got sarcastic; "Nigga didn't yo' ass jus' call me an I'm on da hitter talkin' to ya right? Now did y'all get my message to clean up?" "Yeah cuz we 'ere now." "Who is we nigga?" "Da entire family."

"THROWIN' BRICKS AT THE PENITENTIARY"

"Aiight tell everyone I'm cool, now hang up." Ring. "My QUEEN, wuts good baby chu aiight?" "Yeah baby Imma tell ya all 'bout it, grab my bags an meet me at home." Click da line went dead. Tez hitter rung he picked up on da first ring da line was silent fo' 30 seconds an den he stated; "Ma I'm glad yo' ass aiight lil' nigga, ya learn from da best so it wasn't any doubts 'cus I know ya study cautiously an adequate an dat brings advantageous. Jus' remember always give yo' self suffice time to make ya moves 'cus even bein' one minute ova da time ya set fo' yo' self will have niggas trippin'." Queenie understood wut 'er cousin was tellin' 'er basically she scared da shit out of 'em, but dat wouldn't be somethin' he'd admit to. "Aiight cuz I'm on my way to da crib is ya comin' wit Cortez'?" She questioned. "Nah cuz now dat I know yo' ass aiight I'll come ova first thing in da mornin' 'cus trust ya need to spend a lil' time wit dat nigga Cortez' I ain't neva seen my homeboy on edge like he is ova ya. Anyway Imma holla at shawty from da hospital." "Hospital oh cuz ya talkin' 'bout da nurse. I know it I got dat vibe she was feelin' yo' ass, but cuz ya mean to tell me while I was laid up in agonizin' pain yo' ass was puttin' yo' mack game down? Fam' niggas ain't shit, it's all good doe baby do yo' thang I ain't mad at chu. I'll holla at chu tomorrow." Queenie jumped out of 'er clothes jus' as she entered da house runnin' to da shower she barely let da water get hot she jumped straight in lettin' da water relax 'er. Da shower door opened an Cortez' stepped in butt naked wrapped his arms 'round 'er from behind squeezin' 'er tight, she smiled an turned to face 'em. His touch gave 'er a since of security, she noticed da hurt of pain in his eyes. Cortez' mouth I love ya ma.

"I love ya back daddy." Cortez' washed 'er from head to toe as he told 'er neva do dat to 'em again. "Baby I know ya a private person, but I want to know everything ya do ma, 'cus baby I don't wanta be in da dark 'bout shit ya do." Afta' he washed his own body he stepped out da shower an wrapped a towel 'round his waist. Queenie was fascinated how da water glisten off his chest. He den dried and wrapped a towel 'round Queenie's breast and torso, but not befo' he exam 'er scar from da surgery. Cortez' kissed it an said; "I love ya my QUEEN no doubt." She said; "Make love to me." He had no problem layin down da pipe when she asked.

Afta' words Queenie fell fast to sleep in his arms an he pulled 'er closer and tighter an told 'er; "I neva wanta lose ya ma." He to relaxed an went to sleep only to be waken by Queenie's voice.

Chapter Sixteen
"Lies And Deceit And Da Consequences"

"Daddy get my hitter." Queenie couldn't move 'cus of da grip he had on 'er. Reachin' ova 'em to grab da phone. "Hello!" Hello! She repeated. Da person on da utter end said; "Yo' family Chuck and Lu has been shot!" Queenie screamed; "Wut?" Wakin' up Cortez'. "Where dey at fam'?" "Ma at St. Joseph's hospital." "Fuck, Fuck we on da way. Cortez' we gotta go Chuck and Lu been shot baby." She rushed to get dress tossin' 'em some jeans and sweat shirt, as she tossed on a red and white sweat suit she snatched nina from underneath 'er pillow an dey ran out da door. Queenie peeped da scene ova Tez way but he wasn't home. "Where da fuck dis nigga at?" "Who baby?" Cortez' hurried towards da hospital. "Tez I'm talkin' 'bout Tez he wasn't home jet." "Baby calm down try to call 'em first 'cus if he hasn't called chu jet he might not know 'bout Chuck and Lu." She tried callin' Tez,but dere was no answer so she tried again an Tez picked up. "Wutup lil' nigga?" "Cuz get to St. Joseph's hospital fam' Chuck and Lu has been shot." Click Tez hung up wit no further questions. Tez prayed all da way to da hospital. "Lord dis 'ere is my family, my nigga, my right hand man. We grew up together dis nigga is mo' of a brother dan anything. Father I beg ya don't take Lu from me nor Chuck dats my homeboys bro an we all family, Amen." Tez was pretty shook from Queenie's call so he didn't wanta ride his motorcycle, so his new found soon to be woman drove 'em dere in 'er Gran Am. It wasn't much but it got 'er back and forth to 'er job at da hospital. Da 2 reached da hospital jus' as Cortez' and Queenie ran in da hospital goin' to da nurses desk. Da doctor walked out from behind some glass doors dat led to da surgery room jus' as Tez and Kandi rushed in all to hear; “I'm sorry neither one of 'em survive their gun shot wombs.” No, no, no, no, no's! Filled da room wit screams everyone screamed out in pain fo' different reasons. Tez dropped to his knees an questioned God why he had to take 'em? Cortez' flipped completely out he kicked and knocked ova everything an anything dat wasn't nailed down. Queenie broke inside, but she refused to let any tears drop from da wells of 'er eyes. She dropped next to Tez she leaned in close_ “I'm sorry baby Lu was our family he followed us 'ere 'cus we asked 'em to, so I can't help to feel dis 'ere is my fault fam'.” Queenie raised Tez head so their eyes met an she stated; “Cuz I can't bring ya bro back, but I will vengeance his death myself.” Tez said nothin' but Queenie recognized da person next to 'em tryin' to console 'em. “Yo' ain't chu da nurse who took care of me, yo' name Kandi ain't it?” “Yeah it's me.” “Can ya take care of my cuz fo' a minute I need to see 'bout my nigga an da rest of my family.” “Yeah I got 'em I won't leave his side.” Queenie told Kandi I like dat an she got up an went to tend to Cortez' and Chaos. Chaos couldn't handle dat his partna was gone dey did everything together even shared a place together, now his homeboy was fo' eva gone. Queenie sat next to Chaos an wrapped 'er arms 'round 'em. “Cuz sooner or later it'll be aiight fam', I know it's hard an we all finna go through it, but Imma need chu to hold it together. Let me check on Cortez' baby an we all gonna get outta 'ere.” Chuck was all da family Cortez' knew and had, both of their mothers passed away from drugs at an early age of their lives, so it gave 'em a close bond. Chuck was a coupla months older dan Cortez' dey found one a nutter on da streets tryin' to survive by doin' wut eva it took to hustle up on da next meal. Havin' no utter relatives Cortez' stayed low key from neighbors an continued to live in da house 'em an his mother stayed in. Afta' Cortez' had a run in wit Chuck tryin' to rob a local neighborhood corner store was how dey build a friendship, refusin' to be victims of da system dey help take care of one a nutter. Their bond grew stronger as time went on an da 2 raised 'em selves as 2 fine young men who called 'em selves brothers. "No, please bring my brother back nigga." Cortez' hurt turned into rage towards da doctor as he charged 'em he screamed; "Nigga bring 'em back!" Queenie ran an jumped between 'em an da doctor. "No nigga! Baby ya can't do dis. He not da problem baby. Queenie wrapped 'er arms 'round Cortez' neck an told 'em; "Listen baby yo' ass can't do dis come on he's gone I'm sho' he did everything he could, so I need chu to let me talk to da doctor." She wiped da tears from Cortez' face. "Is chu good, can ya handle wut he has to say or do ya want me to handle it alone?" Queenie looked ova at Tez an took Cortez' by da hand tellin' da doctor to give 'er a second. "Come wit me baby." Dey walked up to Tez an she called out his name an reached fo' his hand. She pulled 'em to his feet an she embraced 'em both. "I apologize I can't tell y'all it's gonna be aiight 'cus da only way to take away da hurt and pain is to bring da 2 niggas back which neither one of us can do fam', but wut I can tell' ya both is dat I will set it right. Chuck and Lu will not go down inveigh dis 'ere is an eye fo' an eye situation. Now if y'all can I need ya both to pull it together long a nuff so we can holla at da doc an see if we can find out wut happen. Tez so get yo' girl an hold yo' head high." Afta' Queenie introduced everyone as Chuck and Lu's family she questioned; "Doc can ya tell us wut happened, how did dey actually die?" "Well Ms. Miles dey both were brought in by da paramedics dere was a shoot out ova on Rosemonte an da 2 victims came in wit wombs to da chest, torso and back. From da looks of it someone had a personal vendetta wit da 2 'cus it was up close and personal. Da officers said da car was riddled wit nine millimeter bullets as well as 12 gauge buck shots." Queenie thoroughly analyzed da contents of da doctors conversation he was havin' wit da three of 'em an thought to 'er self; "Da only ma'fuckas coulda done dis was da crew dey fought at da Waffle House. Chuck didn't have any beefs an Lu definitely didn't 'cus he jus' moved 'ere, I will find out an I will clear out everybody." Thank ya doc, I will arrange fo' da bodies to be picked up in da mornin'. "Lets go baby." Queenie and Kandi were da only 2 dry eyed people in da whole waitin' area. She yelled out lets go family fo' da rest to follow an all ya could hear was a bunch of sniffles in da air. Outside she told everyone to meet up at da stash house. She told Kandi to follow 'er since she had Tez as 'er passenger. At da house Queenie told Skip to grab somethin' hard wit glasses from da bar. He came back wit 2 bottles of Hennessy and glasses as his boss asked. Queenie poured drinks fo' all da fellas an Kandi helped out an gave each one a glass. Afta' everyone had one in hand, Queenie raised 'er glass. "'Ere's to Chuck and Lu da most loyal niggas I eva seen ride wit Cortez' and Tez from day one no matter wut went down dey were dere. Tez and Lu stayed side by side he was Tez right hand man an me bein' me I had doubts when I first met 'em, but as time went on I excepted Lu as family I could always depend on fam' fo' wut eva he was a stand up nigga. So dis 'ere is fo' chu homeboy." Everyone threw their shots back an grabbed a nutter one fo' da next toast. "Chuck he was honest and loyal anyone of ya could say I'm sho' y'all knew 'em better dan me, but fo' 'em not knowin' me, he didn't mind steppin' up or takin' orders from a youngan. Chuck was down ready and wellin' to ride and die dat day at da mall when 'em brauds came at me an from dat day I knew he would be a nigga I could call on. So Chuck 'ere's to ya homeboy we gonna miss ya and Lu somethin' terrible, but y'all will always have a place in our hearts an trust both of yo' deaths will be revenged word is bond, "Boss Queen" will see to it." A tear rolled down 'er face an she called out to Skip come 'ere homeboy. "Wutsup boss?" "Let me holla at chu fo' a sec fam'." Da 2 walked away from da rest of da family. "I need chu to work da streets to see wut chu can find out fo' me since yo' ass a newer face in town. I'm sho' niggas not up on ya down wit dis family. Ya feel me I need to know their names, faces where dey hang out besides da fuckan Waffle House. I need to know where 'em niggas lay dey head at night.” “Boss ya want me to go get started on dat now?” Skip asked. “Yeah an soon as ya find out somethin' report back to me asap. I need one mo' thing befo' ya leave out grab a phone book an find da number to da funeral home 'ere, so Chuck can be buried. I gotta send 'em off proper. We gotta take Lu back to Chi, but I'll make his arrangements in da mornin'.” She made a mental note to check wit Tez to see where he wanted to bury Lu back home or where dey all reside. Queenie had to call Liz. Ring Ring_ “Hello, Queenie baby girl is dat chu?” “Yeah ma it's me, how ya doin'?” She asked. “Baby is everything okay, where is Tez baby is he aiight? Da last time I gotta call dis late it was 'cus ya was in da hospital.” “Ma it's neither one of us we're good, but it's Lu ma he_he's no longer wit us he got murdered to night.” Da line went silent all Queenie could hear was cryin', prayin', an den Liz let out a scream of pain. “Ma ya still dere?” “Yeah baby it's jus' Lu has been part of dis family fo' so long he's jus' like one of y'all. Yo' aunt and I consider 'em as one of our own. It's a longer story dan I wish to explain right now.” “Aiight ma when ya get yo' self together I need ya to call da funeral home an set up da arrangements an I'll have his body transported tomorrow first thing in da mornin'. Ma make sho' ya call me back wit da info, I don't wanta prolong it no longer dan it has to be 'cus Tez not 'em self right now.” She told Liz once da body arrived to tell da people dat she is gonna bring his outfit 'cus he's not bein' buried in no suit. So soon as dey gave 'er a date and time den she will have his stuff shipped to 'er. “Ma I got da funeral, but all I need is fo' chu and auntie to make sho' everything goes accordingly. Now I gotta get back an attend to Tez and Cortez'.” “How is Cortez' doin'?” “Not good he lost his brother also, 'em and Lu was together.” “Oh I'm sorry baby tell 'em both I said to try an be strong an dat dey are in a better place now. Imma call ya aunt an let 'er know wutsup so we can get dis done quick as possible. I love ya Queeine, oh how is Chaos holdin' up?”

“THROWIN' BRICKS AT THE PENITENTIARY”

Queenie had turned 'round to actually see how he was an she noticed at he was in a corner rockin' back and forth as he was inside da hospital. “Ma he doesn't appear to be doin' good at all he's cryin' an still rockin'. Let me go an check on 'em, call ya later.” She hung up an did jus' as she said she would. She kneel down in front of Chaos cuz stop rockin' my nigga how ya holdin' up? Do ya want anything? I got chu wut eva it is cuz I'm 'ere.” He jus' shook his head no. “Aiight if ya need to stay 'ere instead of goin' back to da house, let me know. Imma go ova 'ere an check on fam' and Cortez'.”

Cortez' and Tez stood off in a corner holdin' a conversation, when she walked up. “Wutsup ma, wutup baby girl?” askin' at da same time_ “Nothin' I jus' wanted to check on my 2 favorite niggas, so how are y'all holdin' up? Do y'all need anything?” “Nah we good right now shawty.” “Aiight well since I'm 'ere listen I put da funeral arrangements in motion already, so tomorrow I'll take care of da rest. We gonna try to have both of 'em buried on da same day if not Chucks will be first 'cus I'm taken Lu back home. Is dat cool wit chu fam'?” Tez responded yeah baby girl. Queenie stated; “I don't want y'all in no mo' pain dan ya already are feel me.” Da wells of Tez eyes filled up once again an he hugged 'er. “Thank ya cuz I love ya lil' nigga an I don't know wut I would do wit out ya if ya wasn't 'round. Tez kissed 'er forehead an let 'er go. Queenie ached deep down inside from da lost also, but she didn't want to break down in front of everyone, so she kept it strong fo' da rest of da crew. “Yo' family I don't like to see my niggas like dis, I hate dat our family circle has lost 2 great lieutenants, an shit from da looks of it we might end up losin' a nutter one in a mental state.” Pointin' into Chaos direction who was still rockin'. “Aye maybe y'all need to try an comfort 'em 'cus he seems to be takin' it hard. He was like dat at da hospital.” Da day of da funeral Queenie was able to send Chuck and Lu off in style da same day Chuck's sendin' off gatherin' was scheduled at 9am an ended by noon wit his burial. Lu arrangements were scheduled fo' 7pm dat evenin' since dey had to travel 'bout six hours to Chicago.

She sent both of 'em out in red and white Ice Burg gear. She made sho' all da flowers were to da same red roses, white roses, red carnations. Cortez' and Tez both purchased platinum chains wit diamond stud cross charms so their homeboys would be sent off right. Queenie made arrangements fo' 8 white stretch limo's fo' three days. In each limousine she had Hennessy and Champagne so da fellas could relax their minds, an of course dey had to eat so she had 4 boxes of pizza placed in each limo at da grave site jus' as it was ova. She had Skip to call da 50' yard line fo' da last viewin' of Chuck and Lu's life. Afta' Chucks burial Queenie went to each limo personally an let da fellas know wut was up she didn't want anyone getting to drunk befo' dey buried Lu. She made sho' dat Tez and his girl had their own limo so dey could be alone 'cus he hasn't been 'em self an da bad part of it all he was buryin' his nigga on his 19th birthday, so Kandi stayed by his side she seem to be da only one he responded to. Queenie and Cortez' was in da head limo told their driver to stop at Heather's house first so dey could pick 'er up den dey would go get 'er moms, but Liz was dere waitin' wit Heather which gave 'em a lil' mo' time to spare. Queenie stepped out in 'er red and white Gucci also wit a pair of all suede air force ones an all white leather jacket dat had portraits of Lu and Chuck on da back dat read; "Family Doves Flock 2gether Ride And Die." Embracin' 'er moms and aunt she could tell dey had been cryin' fo' awhile now. "Ma ya ride 'ere wit me and Cortez' an auntie chu ride wit Tez and jus' as she got ready to say Kandi's name da door opened an Tez got out. "Wutsup ma?" He hugged 'er an kissed 'er forehead an did da same to his aunt. "Where is Chaos dey asked in unison?" "He's in da third limo Queenie and Tez also said in unison. Queenie made a mental note to watch 'er cousin a lil' closer 'cus he was givin' 'er a unsettled feelin' in 'er gut, she needed to make sho' he was cool.

At da church Tez and Queenie had time to view an make sho' dat everything was good fo' Lu's final viewin' befo' dey sent 'em off. Tez sat Kandi in da front pew wit his moms and aunt Liz, as he took to Queenie's side at da casket. Wrappin' his arm 'round 'er shoulder sent tears rollin' down 'er cheek. She turned to 'em an held out a box, so he could place da necklace on Lu's neck da same way she did fo' Cortez' at Chucks funeral. Their parents made sho' everyone knew da colors so da church décor was beautiful even Queenie made sho' 'er family circle stood out from da rest. She bought everyone da same jacket as she. As da preacher asked if anyone had any last final words to speak on da behalf of Lu Miles, surprisingly Chaos stood to his feet along wit Heather and Liz. Dey locked their arms 'round his an walked up to da podium where Chaos spoke first, clearin' his throat.

"I jus' want to say I've been in an out of jail my entire life an I thought I had lost everything and everyone I had in dis world 'til one day I received a letter from my cousin 'ere tellin' me 'bout my son_ Lu Miles." Everyone was shocked specially Tez and Queenie. "Please hold on let me finish? Da letter said my lil' cuz Tez had a new friend an dey were real close homeboys so when she said it was Lu I asked 'er not to tell ya three 'cus I wanted to be da one to tell Lu first." Queenie could no longer hold 'er composure; "Nigga ya been home a year now an ya didn't tell da homeboy ya was his dad or dat he was our family!" Tez jumped up an grabbed his cousin to embrace 'er, but she snatched away an ran outta da church havin' da driver take 'er to 'er aunts house so she could jump in Liz car. Queenie gave da driver a note to give to Tez and Cortez' tellin' 'em she need time to 'er self an she would meet 'em at da 50', Love, "Boss Queen". Queenie gave da driver instructions to return to da church, den she drove off headed towards da Marriott Hotel to reserve 4 suites. Queenie placed da room keys in 'er jacket pocket an left so she could clear 'er head, but she couldn't do dat wit out seein' 'er homeboy Lu put in da ground first, so she drove to da cemetery. Jus' as she arrived from a distance she could see Lu's casket been carried to da spot wut would be his final restin' place. She wanted to show 'er presents, but thought better of it 'cus of how she was feelin' towards Chaos an didn't want to disrespect Lu in anyway. Queenie parked da car 'bout 50 feet away an stepped out da car so she could say 'er last good byes to 'er cousin Lu. "We had some good times baby boy, it was many time I wanted to kill ya myself fam',but findin' out now dat we blood, I'm glad I didn't." Queenie looked up an smiled "Nigga I know ya see me down 'ere. I always wondered why yo' features resembled Tez, so much, but I jus' figured 'cus y'all came so close ova da years my nigga. Lu ya was good peeps fam' an I wish we coulda had mo' time wit one a nutter I feel cheated homeboy. Cuz ya was a thorough nigga an da niggas who took y'all life Imma kill 'em all cuz, so ya can rest in peace." Tears rolled down 'er face as she turned an seen Lu's casket lowered in da ground, jus' den it started to rain once again she looked up an smiled as da rain washed 'er tears away. "I see ya nigga go head an lay it down fam', R.I.P Lu." Queenie backed out da cemetery da same way she came in so she wouldn't be detected. She picked up 'er hitter off da seat an listen to a few voice mails an one of 'em was from 'er mother. "Queenie dis is mommy we decided we should all sit down an talk 'bout dis baby." Da next was from Chaos_ "Boss Queen" I'm sorry cuz I neva knew dis would hurt chu like dis." She Skipped Cortez' an aunt Heathers message an listen to Tez message. "Cuz I know ya hurt 'cus I feel like I've been hit wit a double whammy myself. Lil' nigga I know ya like da back of my hand dats one of da reasons I let ya go but I do know chu were some where in da cemetery 'cus ya wouldn't let Lu be put in da ground wit out bein' present baby girl, so jus' call me an we can figure dis out together. I love ya Ueenie."

She started to cry again, but not 'cus of wut Tez said nor dat da three was neva gave da chance to know dey were blood relatives, but 'cus she knew in 'er heart dat tonight would actually be da last time she will see all of 'er family in da same room. 'Er word was given to Lu dat she would kill everyone who was involved in his an Chucks death. Queenie was all 'bout family an to find out dat Lu came from da same bloodline made it a lil' mo' personal fo' 'er. When she arrived at da goin' home

party all eyes were on 'er as she walked in an since she neva perpetrated 'er self to carry a phony act she jus' showed no emotions an stood in da middle of da floor. Tez and Cortez' walked towards 'er, but Tez whispered somethin' in Cortez' ear dat made 'em fall back. Tez asked; "Yo' baby girl ya aiight?" She jus' nodded 'er head wit out a word. She had anger and hatred in 'er heart from da situation. "Fam' I can't believe dat dey did dis shit all dese years Lu has been 'round us an dey didn't tell us cuz. Wut was da big ass secret an wut da fuck else haven't dey told us, huh?"
Tez hugged 'er tight an she placed 'er arms 'round his waist an gave da embrace back, but den nudged 'em away. "Nah nigga I'm tired of cryin' I ain't got no mo' tears, da stunt ma, auntie and Chaos pulled was foul cuz. Shit coulda been way different dan wut it was feel me." Tez knew deep inside his lil' cousin felt bad Lu wasn't seein' da paper he shoulda been even doe dey made sho' he was eatin' an had everything he needed, but it jus' wasn't da same an Queenie knew it an now she felt bad 'bout it.
"Lil' nigga look at me cuz, don't trip fam' we are gonna get to da bottom of dis situation befo' we leave Chicago. He could see da blank look Queenie carried in 'er eyes when she was ready to kill, so he told 'er; "Ueenie lets do dis right an send our family out in style an leave all da drama fo' tomorrow."
"My word is bond cuz, but I don't want talk or have anything to do wit dose three tonight at all."
"Aiight ma dats cool." Tez kissed 'er on da forehead an motioned fo' Cortez' to come ova. Den he went ova to his aunt, moms and Chaos an told 'em; "Look she'll be aiight, but in order fo' 'er to be 'ere to say 'er final goodbyes she doesn't want to talk to either of ya at all. Y'all know how she is stubborn an right now she feels betrayed, so jus' let 'er be an we can all talk 'bout it tomorrow." Tez kept it polite and firm, but dey knew better to question 'em when it came to his Ueenie. "My QUEEN ya wanta drink baby?" Cortez' asked handin' 'er a fifth of Hennessy. Queenie turned da bottle up an took it to da head. Bringin' da bottle down 'er and Cortez' walked ova to where Tez and Kandi were sittin'.

"Fam' ya aiight I seen ya turn dat bottle up like ya was a grown ass woman, nigga." "Yo' fam' I'm good how chu an yo' lady doin' ova 'ere? Oh yeah dat reminds me befo' I get to far gone 'ere is y'all room keys we stayin' at da Marriott presidential suites an da homeboys got double bed suites ya know how it goes. By da way give dis key to Chaos when we leave da party fam'." Tez had found 'em self an older woman who seem to be on his level. Kandi was finna turn 21 soon an da fact Queenie didn't get down wit females she figured long as Kandi had an keeps Tez best interest as 'er first priority she was good wit 'er. But Queenie knew better to trust anyone, so she did a lil' research of 'er own befo' she let Kandi in completely." "Wutsup Kandi how ya feelin', chu enjoyin' yo' self under da circumstances?" Queenie had a buzz goin' on, but she tried to have a good time. "Yeah my baby is da perfect gentleman. Kandi stated. Queenie raised 'er brow an said; "Yeah he is shawty, so ya might wanta hold on to 'em." Queenie told Cortez' lets go to da dance floor an slammed 'er bottle down on da table. Queenie was a great dancer an Tez loved to see his lil' nigga dance. She use to break dance against da neighborhood niggas, but on da dance floor ya woulda thought she took dance lessons. Queenie was a very classy youngan, but when it came to da dance floor she was down right nasty wit it 'cus she love da attention even doe she didn't need it. Da DJ had put on Lu's favorite house music an Queenie and Cortez' started to dance, but he pulled back an watched his perfect QUEEN do 'er thing. Kandi got hyped up watchin' Queenie an evidently started feelin' 'er self 'cus she told Tez she wanted to dance against 'er. Of course he didn't stop 'er 'cus he wanted to see wut she had an besides dat he knew his cousin wouldn't let 'er self be defeated she would make ya have a seat first befo' she let it happen. Tez took Kandi's hand an led 'er to da dance floor, whispered in Queenie's ear an tap Cortez' an motioned 'em off da floor. Queenie took off 'er red jean t-shirt an tossed it to Cortez' leavin' 'er in a red wife beater, but she fo' got all 'bout da burner dat was tucked in da small of 'er back.

"Yo' ma let me get dis burner." Ya could hear wows and whistles through out da club at Queenie's body no one had any idea dat da girl was so ripped she had da physic of a body builder by da arms but very sophisticated wit a washboard stomach, someone yelled out do it ma from da utter side of da room an Queenie and Kandi got it in an befo' ya knew it Kandi was on 'er way back to 'er table. Cortez' walked ova to Queenie to give 'er_'er shirt. "'Ere ma put yo' shirt back on befo' I have to do somethin' to one of dese niggas in 'ere." "Aiight. Yo' Skip family let me get yo' flag nigga to wipe off dis sweat." "Yo' ya got it boss." He handed 'er his flag an stepped off an Queenie slipped 'er shirt back on as she walked back to da table to give Kandi 'er props. "Yo' Kandi I like yo' style." Tez handed 'er nina back an asked; "Wut time y'all wanta leave?" Queenie stated; "When eva y'all ready shit it's 2:30 so lets go to Denny's 'cus I'm hungry my stomach touchin' parts of my body it shouldn't."Tez told 'er dat da ol' girls had put 4 carry out plates together fo' 'em befo' she got dere. "Yeah Queenie da spread was nice ya had."Kandi stated. Queenie had all da food catered which included: soul food, sea food, cajun food Louisiana style wit a desert table full of any cake or pie one person could imagine. "Well we can grab da carry outs an warm 'em later at da hotel, but right now I wanta go to Denny's." Queenie talked wit authority, no matter who was 'round. Ya had to love and respect 'er gangsta doe Tez and Cortez' did, dey loved everything she was 'bout, but Kandi didn't know 'er jus' jet, so she played it by ear, she decided to stay on da back burner fo' now an let Queenie shine. "Yo' fam' tell my moms 'er car is outside. Tell 'er to let Chaos drive it home fo' 'er an da limo can take 'em back to da hotel." Tez went an gave instructions to their parents and Chaos. Hugged and kissed da lady's fo' heads he embraced Chaos an handed 'em da room key, pickin' up their to go trays an da 4 bounce off to Denny's dey went. Queenie stayed low key so no one didn't know she no longer reside in Chicago.

Chapter Seventeen
"Respect Da Gangsta"

Once dey stepped inside of Denny's Queenie got da respect she always did as "Boss Queen", Queenie thought of 'er self as royalty an dat's how she carried 'er self, wit da niggas lovin' 'er an wit envy an da bitches gawkin' and hattin' on 'er. "Wutsup Queenie, wutup ma?" "Boss Queen"! "Yo' Queenie when ya gonna get back on da court ma?" Den dere were da whispers from all da females, talkin' stupidly while she walked pass. "Boss wutsup wit dat gear? It's tight." Someone called out; "Yo' Tez wuts happenin' homeboy, I ain't seen ya 'round lately." Tez threw his head up in a nod as to say wutsup. "Shit I been 'round homeboy." "Yo' where dat nigga Lu? Oh y'all gave 'em da night off or somethin'?" "Nah homeboy we jus' buried 'em, so shut da fuck up." Tez and Queenie tenacious afta' dude jumped up like he wanted to get buck. Queenie stood up in front of Tez placin' 'er hand on his chest an turned towards da dude wit a voice full of venom an stated; "Yo' dude we didn't come 'ere fo' dis homeboy an on top of dat yo' ass jumpin' up like ya tryin' to flex yo' muscles ain't gonna do shit but get chu a ass whoopin' ya definitely ain't gonna want." Cuz come on he ain't tryin' to see ya fam'. "My bad boss no disrespect intended, I didn't know fo' give me ma." Queenie told Tez; "Lets eat so we can get outta 'ere fam' we got a nuff on our minds. An on da real dat nigga is beneath ya nigga." Cortez' stepped 'round Queenie an whispered somethin' only fo' Tez to hear den patted 'em on da back "Now come on baby lets eat." Da 4 decided to eat at a table in da corner close to da door.

"Yo' ma Tez waved fo' da waitress to come ova." "Are y'all ready to order sir?" "Yeah,but ya ain't gotta call me sir shawty Tez will be fine. Once da food arrived dey ate an talked. "Yo' fam' I need to talk to ya and Cortez' 'bout somethin' in private befo' we leave Chi-Town." "Aiight how 'bout I come to y'all room 'round dark thirty an we can holla den 'cus I plan on takin' Kandi shoppin' an sho' 'er our city.” “Dats cool, 'bout wut time ya wanta go by ya ol' girls 'cus to keep it raw nigga I need some answers an I feel dey gotta a lot of explainin' to do cuz.” Queenie exclaimed. Their waitress came back to see if dey had any utter needs befo' she gave 'em da check, but dey had to be up pretty early so dey jus' asked fo' da check. Afta' payin' da bill dey were up and out. Cortez' wrapped his arms 'round his QUEEN'S waist an said; “Baby Imma have to take ya shoppin' also 'cus I can't have my QUEEN lookin' like today on tomorrow.” She responded sho' ya right, 'cus dat ain't cool baby, but it ain't necessary I got dat taken care of remember I've got plenty of gear in da closet at my ol' gs crib or did chu fo' get I wasn't able to return to get my things afta' all dat shit in East St. Boogie I jus' started a new wardrobe.” Cortez' said; “Ma cut dat shit out every time I say Imma buy ya anything wit out jus' goin' head an do it, ya always turn it down.” “Aiight once I get dress we can go find me a leather jacket to match my outfit, is dat cool daddy?” Cortez' picked Queenie up an said dat would be fine it was better dan nothin' den he told 'er maybe she could pick 'em an outfit out so he could see how well she could dress 'er man. “So now ya clowin' me my nigga? So wut chu sayin' ya don't think I can dress yo' ass better dan ya can do it?” “Nah neva dat baby, I know yo' ass can dress to impress fo' yo'self to a tee ma, but I jus' wanta see wut chu can do fo' me dats all.” “Baby dis wasn't planned but I did book our suites fo' three days, but I do have to handle somethin' befo' we leave, so I guess it'll workout. Well ya know I gotta take care of da fellas 'cus non of 'em know wuts goin' on, but I can't have 'em out 'ere bogus.” “Nah we gotta take care of 'em. Listen baby chu don't have to do shit by yo' self shawty. I told ya I'm 'ere wit chu dat means wut eva ya got goin' on ma. Anyway ya act like 'em niggas ain't gettin' money, ya know don't non of us go any where broke.” “I know daddy but dey didn't ask fo' dis I'm mo' dan sho' dey had a feelin' dat we was headed back to East St. Boogie at least by mornin'.” Cortez' pulled 'er in close to kiss 'er soft lips an stated; “Aiight ma tell ya wut we'll hit each nigga off wit 2 fits an a pair of jumpers an dats it dey can pay fo' their own meals. I know ya boss to 'em an dey give ya mo' respect dan dey give myself and Tez which is all good, but I feel yo' ass spoil da homeboys to much." "Baby wuts da problem we all family an dey take care of all three of us doin' wut eva dey told wit no hesitation. I guess I jus' got dat effect on ma'fuckas, but my ego won't have it any utter way, it's all part of my swagg 'cus dey ain't gonna find no utter woman to take care 'em like I do." Queenie said jokingly; "Baby yo' ass know dat. Now we can talk 'bout wut I do fo' da homeboys 'til da end of time, but where does dat leave time fo' us?" She asked wit a smile on 'er face. "My QUEEN dats da first time I've seen ya smile since, well it's a very good look on yo' sexy ass." Cortez' started to undress his QUEEN, when a tap came from da utter side of da door, Queenie looked at his Cartier an said; "Damn baby it's dark thirty already we been talkin' fo' awhile daddy dats gotta be Tez." Cortez' opened da door an dey both in unison said wutsup as dey embraced wit a tap of da shoulder. Tez kissed Queenie on da fo' head followin' wit a hug. "Wutsup lil' nigga?" "Fam' ya wanta drink?" "Yeah let me get one of dose homeboy." "Baby wut 'bout chu ma?" "Nah I'm good." He fixed two drinks an went back to da sittin' area handed Tez his drink an set da bottle on da table somethin' told 'em by time Queenie got done dey were gonna need da whole bottle. Queenie started straight in; "Family I'm 16 an I am $250,000,000 dollars strong I'm da youngest millionaire far as I know from Chicago to East St. Boogie an I feel it's time to move our parent back home,where dey came from. I bought dat big ass house up da block from us second one from da corner. I figure since we got da crew wit us dey can load up da trucks an drive 'em back." "Ueenie wut 'bout auntie job?" "Cuz I don't give a fuck 'bout 'er job, she love it dat much she can always get a nutter one down dere anyway we had already told 'em da time would come soon. Well dat time is 'ere no questions, besides dat I need 'em to be near cuz, 'cus ya will need 'em, ya both will when da time comes, y'all will need to comfort one a nutter." "Baby girl stop talkin' in riddles wuts goin' on wit yo' ass." Tez asked. "Nigga ain't no riddles, neither one of chu is dumb, further mo' cuz ya know how I move on dis chess board. 2 of my pawns were taken from me an ya know I will not let dat fly.""I'll hate to have to put one of dese niggas under fo' fuckin' ova ya I already feel responsible from ya bein' under my wing in da first place, so fo' ya to be snatched from under me is like pluckin' my feathers." "So ya know wuts 'bout to happen. I don't make promises, but I gave my word an it's bond an on top of dat dese niggas took my kin, so mo' or less ya right 'em niggas snatched 'em from under me like I ain't shit." "Ueenie ya do be listenin' even doe ya camouflage yo' self like ya not payin' any attention to a nigga." "Cuz all dat ya catechize me to do or not to do I always cohere it even me bein' stubborn it all has stuck wit me fam'. Yo' I know I asked fo' dis life an I love wut I can do fo' utters dis why I love da circle dats been built, dastardly I am not. Neva have I been bogus to anyone and I'm not a glutton person. Since I could remember all I wanted to do was play ball, but through all da snafu it was taken away from me wit a blink of an eye fam'." Cortez' said; "Baby ya 16 so ya can still fulfill dat dream." "Baby no, no I can't dat bitch on da court dat day fucked up dat. I won't lie dat part of my ego I had fo' da game won't let me. Da court was my comfort zone an I don't see it comin' back any time soon an even if it do it wouldn't be da same." Queenie drifted off to a visual of all 'em havin' a good time 'er Tez, Lu, and Chaos clubbin' an getting paper den wit da new family she has gained buildin' 'er family circle wit Cortez', Chuck an da rest of da entourage. She smiled at da thought, but as quick as it came it left an turned into a grimace look. Wit out warnin' she turned into da devils child jus' dat fast 'er eyes turned a cold black. Queenie said; "It's ride and die nigga." "Yo' ma wut ya 'bout to do shawty?" Cortez' asked. "Well like y'all been tellin' me all along I'm throwin' bricks at da penitentiary, well only way I see it. I'm goin' out in a blaze of glory fam' 'cus trust and believe I am finna deaden every last one of 'em bitch ass niggas who killed Lu and Chuck. Come on yo' ass don't take shit from me, I don't start shit, but better believe baby I'm gonna finish it, an I have no intentions on hidin' out, ain't no runnin', so Ola will be at me 'cus ain't no way I'm goin' to prison. I know y'all not feelin' me, but it is wut it is, dis da only way da game will stop me by taken da QUEEN off da chess board." When she finish talkin' she unfortunately saw da stream of tears fall down Tez and Cortez' faces. "Lil' girl wut da fuck ya talkin' 'bout, chu got ya whole life ahead of yo' ass." Tez was very pissed at wut he had jus' heard come out of 'er mouth an went on to say; "Lil' nigga I'm not finna let chu go out like dat, fuck dat." Tez stated. "Nigga yo' ass ain't got no choice 'cus I will not go to prison cuz, dat ain't da life I pictured fo' myself not even wit da hunnid murders dats under my belt dats gone unsolved Well dese 'ere cuz won't go unknown 'cus I'm at dese niggas how eva I get at 'em, but life in prison is not an option, so if Ola wants me dey gonna take me out in a body bag nigga 'cus I got to much pride to let 'em take me wit out a fight." Queenie had Tez and Cortez' on pins and needles 'cus dey knew da woman dey loved, so much was a tickin' time bomb. "So shawty how_ Queenie stopped 'em in mid-sentence, "Baby y'all know when dat time comes." As she walked out of da room she told 'em; "I love ya both neva fo' get dat it's ride and die." "Ma, baby girl, cuz dey called afta' Queenie she didn't respond an jus' kept walkin'. Back in East St. Boogie everything wasn't quit normal, but fo' Queenie it was back to biz'ness as usual an dat was normal to 'er. 'Er family was in place doin' wut dey were paid fo'. Cortez' and Tez watched 'er closely, but Queenie paid no attention to dat 'cus she suspected it from 'em, she had 'em spooked, but figurin' it was jus' da beginnin' dey better hold on tight 'cus da ride is finna get real bumpy. Between da both of 'em dey had no clue dat she gathered all da info she needed an it was jus' a matter of time befo' it all went up in flames. Queenie had da fellas move 'er moms and aunt into their big brick duplex. Dey both loved their new home, not dat dey really had a choice in da matter when ya jus' bein' told pack up 'cus ya movin', wut else is dere to say? Specially when it's ya kids throwin' 'round da orders. Once Liz and Heather saw da house dey looked 'round in amazement like lil' kids dat jus' got everything dey wanted fo' Christmas. Dey found a letter from Queenie sayin: "I love ya both know dis. I want y'all to enjoy it it's paid fo' an it's both of urns to share. I also had it put in da both of yo' names inside dat manila envelope is da deed to da house an $10,000 dollars fo' y'all to go shop fo' ya new home. I know ya wonderin' why I'm not 'round, well to be honest, partly 'cus I thought we all were better dan secrets. Dats somethin' I can't swallow family mean everything to me, so Lu bein' part of dis family shoulda neva been kept from me or Tez. Dis move was in affect fo' Christmas, but dis situation our family has encountered ya guys need to be closer to Tez 'cus he will need y'all and y'all gonna need 'em to get through dis. Ma I need ya to remember my safe combo."

P.S. I love ya both keep dat in mind always, I am my mother child
and I will not answer any questions.

Love, Queenie

Afta' readin' da letter Liz and Heather went into a frenzy 'cus dey didn't know wut to make of da letter, but to 'em it didn't sound good or like anything good was gonna come behind it. So da first thing Liz does is call Queenie's phone, but she got no answer. Queenie had already knew wut 'er mother would do dat's why she prepared 'er self fo' 'er hitter to ring off da hook. Liz called Tez an he finally answered. "Hello." "Tez baby we need to see ya at da house please. Hurry up baby an bring Cortez' wit chu." Tez didn't actually know wut was goin', but knew if she wanted Cortez' to come along it had to be 'bout Queenie, but he didn't want to think da worst jus' jet, so he called up his homeboy.

"THROWIN' BRICKS AT THE PENITENTIARY"

Ring! "Wuts good family?" "Shit nigga I need yo' ass to go wit me to da ol' gs crib. Auntie jus' called an she needs us to come by right now." "Where ya at homeboy?" "Yo' at home." "Aiight I was finna leave out anyway, so lets go." "Yo' nigga where Queenie at?" Tez asked. "She's upstairs fam' she said she gotta few places to go, some shit to handle." Tez and Cortez' rushed in da house wonderin' wut was wrong. "Ma, auntie where y'all at?" "We in da den baby." Liz responded. Huggin' da ladies dey wanted to know wut was da emergency. Liz handed Tez da letter an as he read it he said; "Damn! She movin' fast cuz an handed Cortez' da letter, so he could read it 'em self. Da frowns Liz and Heather had on their faces gave indication dat dey 2 better start talkin' real fast. "Tez talk to us wut is goin' on wit Queenie? Cortez' wut do chu know?" Heather cut in said boy ya better say somethin' tell us wut does dis mean. "Look y'all need to have a seat. When is da last time either of ya talk to 'er?" Liz replied; "Da day of da funeral when y'all picked us up from da house." "Aunt Liz ya know dats along time fo' chu and Ueenie not to talk, but wit da stunt y'all pulled on us at da church is one of da reasons she's not speakin' to either of ya. Dat has only added fuel to da fire an da utter reason fo' dis letter, well is 'cus Queenie has set in 'er mind to kill_ "Kill, kill who." Liz screamed. "Hold on let me finish, so ya know wuts goin' on. She set in 'er mind to kill da niggas who took Lu and Chucks life y'all know family means everything to Ueenie an she has neva been one to go back on 'er word 'cus by all means she goes by law an 'er word is all she has. Now it may not be wut chu wanta hear, but she stands on it an she will make good of da word she gave da homeboys as dey got placed in da ground. "She wasn't even dere when dey put Lu in da ground." "Auntie dats where ya wrong she was dere jus' non of us seen 'er, now trust me Ueenie is well aware of da consequences of goin' afta' dese niggas, but she told us she don't have no intentions of hidin' out dis time." "Tez baby she's gonna end up in prison if she does dis." Heather realized wut Tez had said, hide dis time. "Tez wut do ya mean dis time?" Liz asked; "Baby has my baby girl done dis befo'?" Cortez' looked at Tez wit raised eye brows. "Look, Tez got a lil' irritated by their questions an da fact he had let slip his lil' nigga was indeed a killa his voice filled wit venom as he spoke; "Dere is so much neither one of ya know 'bout Ueenie it ain't funny 'cus all y'all can see is da lil' kid in 'er dat goes wit 'er age, but dose blackout spells baby girl be havin' are not normal. Yeah cuz perfect on da outside, but we all know dat somethin' ain't right on da inside an wut eva it is dat triggers it off is when Ueenie snaps an it's hard to bring 'er back 'round. So to answer dat fo' ya no it's not 'er first time an yeah auntie yo' baby is a killa dat has a big vendetta wit da crew dat murdered Lu. Matter of fact it's da same crew dat beat 'er down."

Liz asked so is dat why she says 'ere ya guys need to be closer to Tez 'cus he will need y'all an fo' me to remember 'er safe combo? 'Cus she knows she gonna go to prison behind dis?" "Auntie I wish dat was so,but it's not dat simple. Queenie ain't got no intentions on lettin' 'em take 'er to da penitentiary she goin' out in a blaze of glory." As Tez eyes filled up wit tears Cortez's did da same as da pain struck 'em in da heart he placed his hands on top of his head an fell to his knees. Heather kneel down next to an put 'er arms 'round 'em tryin' to comfort 'em. "Baby it's gonna be okay. Tez baby pleased tell us ya gotta plan to stop ya cousin from taken such extreme measures of puttin' 'er life in danger."

"Da only thing we came up wit was to put a coulpa homeboys on 'er every time she leaves da house, but we can't sleep on dis lil' nigga 'cus 'er knowledge an intelligence makes 'er smarter dan we give 'er credit fo'. So tryin' to stay a step ahead of 'er will make ya trip yo' self. Honestly dere is nothin' non of us can do, but wait an pray Ueenie comes 'round an realize how crazy it is an dat it will not bring Lu and Chuck back." Da whole conversation had finally broke Tez down. "Man ma I can't lose my lil' cuz,she's all I got left, I shoulda neva introduced 'er to da street life." "Baby it's not yo' fault my niece woulda been put on if not by chu someone else, 'cus dats wut she wanted. "Er bein' introduced to da streets wasn't da problem son, it's wut eva ignites da fuse inside 'er head which could be a number of things. Who knows, we don't 'cus dey could neva find out anything." "Wut da fuck, so y'all knew all alone dat Ueenie had a problem an neva said nothin'?" Tez was furious."Wut else are y'all holdin' to ya chest?" Heather said; "Hold on I need both of ya to sit down, so we can explain somethin' to y'all. Listen son it's not dat we wanted to hold anything from chu or Queenie, but we thought it would be better to let 'er try an live a normal life as a child wit out 'er worryin' why she was different from utter kids. Yo' aunt and I actually thought wut eva it was would possibly go away least by time she got older." Liz told 'em; "Jus' by lookin' at Queenie ya see no different from anyone else, my baby is actually ova 'er IQ, but me listenin' to da fuckan doctors I held 'er back on da same level wit kids of 'er age. Now fo' along time I regretted it 'cus Tez baby when chu was a senior in high school Queenie was suppose to be one wit chu, but yo' mom and I figured it would make ya resent yo' lil' cousin, 'cus of da embarrassment of 'er bein' in da same grade." "Wut dats a bunch of bull." Tez shouted. "Tez baby she woulda been comin' out of da six grade son. Queenie should be in college at dis moment as we speak. Da doctor ran a many of test, but could neva find anything, but she was smarter dan da average kid. He'll actually she's smarter dan da average grown ass ma'fucka. I believe we knew it started when she was in da fifth grade when a lil' boy told 'er she was cute an 'cus she wasn't likin' lil' boys an didn't respond to 'em da boy an his friends called 'er a stuck up lil' bitch an dats was da day of 'er first blackout. She beat up his friends, but da boy dat called 'er bitch he was 'er main target." Liz said; "Dat day she damn near killed da lil' boy from constantly bangin' his head on da cement floor in da school gym. Dey called Ola on my baby an I went threw a lot of red tape to get 'em to let me keep my baby, dats when ya moms really stepped in an help me out. Once we seen dat chu had no problem wit bein' 'round 'er or 'er followin' up behind ya we jus' rolled wit it, prayin' dat ya would some how be able to control 'er, an we thought jus' maybe she wouldn't go into any mo' trans.'Til dat day at 'er game I neva had seen or knew da type of situation I had on my hands, now dat she's gotten older I've seen da killa in 'er an da next time I seen it was when Blue died an she put Red down. Dere was only one utter person we've eva seen da exact same way Queenie gets an dat was our father." Dats a nutter long story, but mother neva did know wut was wrong wit 'em, but he was a nutter one who neva got caught fo' any of da murders he committed." "So how did poppa Miles die?" Tez asked. Ring, ring! "Hello." Cortez' damn near lost control his heart skipped a beat from da voice on da utter end. "Wutsup daddy? I'm back where ya at?" He basically ignored da last question an said; "I'm on my way back home I should be pullin' up in three minutes. I needed to check on somethin' ya know my birthday is in a few days." "Yeah I know daddy hurry up I love ya." "I love ya to ma." Click she hung up."Family, Imma jet dat was my baby she back an I gotta spend as much time wit 'er as possible 'cus I don't know when time is gonna stop fo' us." "Imma head out wit chu." Dey hugged da ladies an bounced. Queenie had ordered da exact same Ninja she had bought Tez only difference was da colors Cortez' bike was red wit white flakes through it. On da back she had airbrushed "Ride and Die" she also bought 'em a brand new off da showroom floor big body Chevy Capri Classic dat she had tricked out. She had done somethin' no one eva thought of seein' befo' Queenie had suicide doors put on da car an had da car bullet proofed wit sounds an voice activated. She blasted da sounds so it would be heard an seen when he hit da corner, she even went as far as puttin' a big red bow on top of it. Salt and Pepper blared threw da speakers as she stood on da front porch waitin' fo' em to arrive.

Chapter Eighteen
"How Many Secrets Can One Person Take"

When 'em and Tez pulled up dey both were shocked. "Wutsup ma?" Queenie jumped in his arms an kissed 'em wit a remote in 'er hand she turned da music down an said; "Happy Birthday baby." "Baby it's not fo' three days." He stated. "Few days ain't gonna hurt shit." Queenie knew dat she probably wouldn't make it 'til his b-day 'cus she was feelin' blood thirsty, but she wanted to wait 'til afta' his day 'cus she didn't want to mess it up. Cortez' put 'er down an Tez walked up an kissed 'er on da fo' head. "Wutsup cuz, I see ya went all out fo' da homeboy huh?" "My QUEEN ya gotta nigga a motorcycle an a car? Ooooh shit Tez come check dis out my nigga. Tez went, but made mental note to talk to 'em when Queenie isn't 'round. Tez peep da bike first. "We can ride together now homeboy." Tez read da back fender "Ride and Die" "Check dis shit out. Baby yo' ma wuts da trick to getting in da car? Where da handles at?" Dey both asked in unison an da response she gave was; "Talk to yo' car." "Talk to it an say wut to it?" She said; "It activates by three voices only, so talk to it an tell it wut chu want it to do fo' ya." Cortez' said; "Open doors" an it did jus' dat all da doors open. Da front went up in da air an da back open da opposite way of a normal set of car doors. "Now ya try Tez." She exclaimed. "Aiight close doors" an all da doors shut. "Oh! Hell yeah dats da shit." Tez gave Cortez' dap an went on very excitedly. "Yo' calm down niggas an watch." "Driver door open._ Da door went up,_ "My QUEEN start up, Music QUEEN." An da radio popped on. "Dats cold shawty I like dis jank, I ain't eva seen no shit like it befo'." "Yeah lil' nigga I like da way ya sweeten dat shit up. Yeah it's right baby girl, but why ya put all our voices on dere?" "Jus' 'cus we family dats yo' homeboy, an dats my nigga anything could happen an one of us may have to pick it up or one of us jus' may wanta drive on gp an wit out keys it can't be done." Queenie told Cortez' da only reason she used my QUEEN to start

da car was fo' his protection an only da three of 'em know an far as da radio is so when he has his niggas in da car dey can't jus' play wit da radio if he doesn't have it on. “Yo' dere is one last feature dis beauty has.” “Shawty wut mo' can it have?” Cortez' asked. Queenie looked ova at 'em den at Tez an said; “Da entire car is bullet proof baby.” “Nah lil' nigga ain't no shit 'round 'ere doin' it like dat, so I know yo' ass bull shittin' right?” Tez looked at Queenie curiously say word lil' nigga. “Word is bond nigga, ya know how I do I'm not yo' average, so it ain't hard fo' me to pull off shit. Jus' like I got y'all Ninja's from ova seas, well I had dis ma'fucka shipped ova seas to have it custom da way I wanted it. Now I can sho' ya both better dan I can tell ya, so go ahead climb in an close da doors, turn off da radio an kill da engine an don't worry 'cus I already tested it an trust da bullets won't pierce through. Dere won't even be any bullet holes nor dints y'all know I will not put either of ya in harms way.” Cortez' and Tez sat in the car as she asked 'em to an afta' da car was shut down Queenie walked to da back car an activated da trunk wit 'er voice to open. Out of da trunk she came up wit an AK47 an from da back to da front wit no warnin' she sprayed da car endin' up in front of da car waitin' fo' da fellas to come back up from off da floor. “Yo' y'all can get out now.” Cortez' told Tez_
“Yo' ma'fuckan cousin is crazy homeboy.” Tez replied; “Welcome to da family nigga she's yo' woman an dats wut chu wanted remember.” Dey both broke out into laughter, so shook dey almost fo' got dey had to talk to da car in order to get out, so instead Queenie spoke fo' da doors to open.
“Yo' are y'all dat spooked ya can't speak to da car?” She asked. “Cuz when,where lil' nigga ya get a damn AK47 from? An why da hell yo' ass out 'ere in da streets wit it like ya Rambo baby girl? Put dat shit away fam'.” Queenie said; “I needed to give it a test run, ya like it, sweet ain't it? I jus' needed to sho' y'all da car was bullet proof dats all cuz.” She walked into da crib an put da AK47 back in it's hidin' spot only she would think to look fo' it. As da fellas looked ova da car fo' damages da bullets

caused, but dey found not one mark non wut so eva. Runnin' into da Cortez' called fo' Queenie.
"Yo' wuts good she yelled out as she skipped down da stairs. Yo' y'all wanta go out an eat?"
Tez stared at his lil' cousin he was glad to see 'er in a joyful mood, but he knew 'er like he knew his own self an figured somethin' wasn't right wit da picture she had painted fo' 'em. "Yeah lets go eat ma, where y'all wanta go eat at?" Cortez' asked. Queenie was hip to Tez so she let it be known:
"Cuz stop it 'cus it's not gonna work fam'. I've been 'round ya to long nigga an ya don't do it better dan me I'm da analyst so don't try to treat my life, so cuz take into consideration who I am an how high my IQ is fam' 'cus I'm far from slow cuz." Cortez' was puzzled he didn't know wut da convo was 'bout. Queenie told 'em; "Nigga I know ya may be hurtin' at da moment 'cus ya don't know when Imma strike an I'm positive of dis 'cus our bond is jus' dat tight, but Queenie is 'er own person an yo' ass of all people should know I refuse to let ma'fuckas know my every move. If I did dat I would be goin' against my own grain of livin'. Fam' we better dan dat ya wanta know somethin' ask me I don't lie an it's only 2 ways I can answer ya. One tell ya or two don't answer ya at all, but chu tryin' to analyze me ya gonna fall short every time, I love yo' ass fam' but don't treat me." He hugged Queenie an kissed 'er fo' head.
"Ya right baby girl dats wut I was tryin' to do, but it's all out of hurt an da love I have fo' ya lil' nigga. Cuz I'm hurtin' so bad I broke an told ya moms and auntie everything when dey asked me wut I knew 'bout da letter ya left 'em. Lil' nigga ya know we have nothin' to hide, so I won't start lyin' to dose 2 no matter wut." Queenie stated in a calm voice; "I expected ya to cuz, I know I've laid a lot out fo' ya to carry, but I feel in time y'all both will get ova it an move on wit yo' lives feel me. I want y'all to an continue to hold it down, now lets go eat 'cus I'm starvin' fam'." Da convo was ova fo' Queenie she tucked 'er nine in da small of 'er back an grabbed 'er leather. Cortez' shrugged his shoulders at Tez an said; "I don't know wut dat was 'bout, but come on lets jump in my new Chevy homeboy an go eat."

"THROWIN' BRICKS AT THE PENITENTIARY"

Cortez', Tez and Queenie went to Joe's Crab Shack an pigged out since it was so silent she started up a conversation. "Baby when is da next shipment comin' in?" "It'll be 'ere at midnight, wutsup ma?" Tez questioned wipin' his mouth; "Is everything on point are we good or does some changes have to be made?" "Nah all should be good, but afta' it's inventoried bring me 80 bricks an I'll get da rest later. It's time fo' me to sho' Skip his routes 'cus I need 'em to make some runs. Since all of dis bullshit an Chaos my paper has jus' been sittin' an I need it in my possession plus I got some shit dat needs to be delivered. Imma need one of ya to follow me in a rental, 'cus I don't need Ola all in my shit bein' curious of why it's 2 niggas and a chic ridin' three deep." "Ueenie ya ain't neva had anyone know da where 'bouts of ya clientele except fo' ya workers an dats always been Chaos. Now ya switchin' up cuz man I don't like dis shit at all lil' mama, but chu already know I got chu." "Cuz it's not like I brought an outsider in it's Skip an he's y'all boy on top of dat he's in da family circle an he's Chaos replacement. Chaos is still family, but I don't need his ass no mo' I won't swallow da bullshit he pulled at da funeral he shoulda knew da consequences workin' underneath me. I don't tolerate lyin', phoniness, fakes or fraud niggas. Keep it raw and funky wit me, I don't care wut da situation is feel me cuz? Yo' he better be glad cuz dat I didn't kill his ass. Neva da less cuz I'm lettin' 'em collect his pension fo' da rest of his life of 10 stacks monthly an he can keep da house I bought fo' 'em and Lu utter dan dat fam' I'm done wit Chaos word is bond." "Damn shawty dats a sweet ass game pension, cuz will be set fo' da rest of his life. Man ma I'm glad I'm on yo' team, but I hate I'm not one of yo' workers." Cortez' exclaimed. He tried to make lite of da situation an cut da tension in da room. Tez told Queenie; "Baby girl dats why I love ya_ yo' ass keep it raw no matter wut, straight to da point cuz." Queenie changed da subject fo' a second_ "My niggas how y'all feel 'bout leavin' out fo' Vegas afta' da shipment arrives doin' inveno only takes 'bout an hour. We can catch a three o'clock flight out an come back tomorrow on a noon flight an pick up from dere." Queenie was a very spontaneous at da drop of a hat she would jus' pick up an go. Money was no object to 'er long as she could do wut she wanted an needed to do wit 'er paper she was happy. "Lil' nigga if dats wut chu wanta do lets do it, but da fellas could handle shit 'til we return." Tez stated. "Nah dey goin' to cuz, dis is a family affair, da circle only." Cortez' questioned; "So do dat mean ya leavin' Chaos behind ma?" "Yeah baby dats wut dat means. Did ya not hear me say I cut his ass loose, in less one of ya niggas got some shit chu need fo' self an y'all gonna pay 'em or his ass gonna go get a 9-5 he's done getting money wit dis family baby. Only thing he will live off of is wut I give 'em monthly an when I leave dis bitch honor my wishes. I don't give a fuck how bad off he gets." "Ueenie ya serious 'bout killin' dese niggas an goin' out in a blaze wit Ola huh?" Tez finally broke an asked wut he had to know. Queenie leaned back in 'er seat wiped 'er mouth an made eye contact wit Tez an said; "Yeah fam' I am an I see no utter way my standards have been set high. Yeah da status I have could be carried on behind dose gray dingy ass walls, but dat ain't how I wanta live cuz. A great nigga as yo' self always told me neva feel defeated, let no one walk ova me, don't stand fo' disrespect an always give respect where it's due an to always stand up fo' wut I believe in an stand on it. So 'ere it is baby I'm standin' up fo' my family cuz. Fam' I know I gotta fucked up way of thinkin' an doin' things, but everything I am an everything I stand fo' is all 'cus of wut chu instilled in me fam', but don't take dat da wrong way 'cus to me it's a good thing 'cus as I grew it grew wit me I jus' so happen to put a lil' different twist on it. I know it's not yo' fault cuz how was chu suppose to know dat I wasn't right in da head?" Tears fell from 'er eyes wettin' up 'er face. "How was ya gonna know if dey held it from ya to." Cortez' took a napkin an wiped 'er face_ "Come on ma it's gonna be aiight, we can get threw dis if ya jus' let us help ya." "No it won't!" She said wit venom in 'er voice. "No it won't!" Tellin' Tez dis time; "Family my entire life has been a lie who does dat to their own child, huh? "Ueenie how ya know wut_Queenie held up a finger to 'er lips singalin' Tez not to speak. "Tez nigga it's not how I know it's wut I know an it's bogus fo' my moms and auntie to keep me in da dark, even if da doctors couldn't find out why da fuck I spazz out. I'm young ass hell an I should be livin' my life how I wish to carefree wit no stress dis is bullshit,but instead I'm 'ere da fuckan world on my shoulders. Let me ask both of y'all a serious question. Has either of one of ya took da time to realize I haven't mourned ova Lu, Chucks death or even Blue and Reds death? Let me answer dat fo' ya_ No ya haven't 'cus ya to worried 'bout me taken my life, but neither of ya have really asked why." Tez ya gotta know it's mo' to it cuz. All I wanted was to be young and rich yeah I love my boss status, but bein' a murder I neva visioned in my life. I don't wanta go 'round killin' ma'fuckas 'cus dey speak da wrong way, niggas I'm 16 an won't live to see 17 'cus I'm so fucked up in da head 'cus I can't seem to let certain shit go. Cuz my mama has hurt me so deep an da fact she hasn't been woman a nuff to step forward an tell me it's somethin' wrong wit me is fucked up. I checked out a few things out on poppa Miles when I found out he was carryin' da same shit 'round in his head also an da lie dats been fed to us ova an ova of 'em bein' killed all lies fam'. Poppa Miles killed 'em self afta' he killed granny an moms and aunties lil' brother. Dats a long story also cuz an I don't wish to explain,but yeah we had a nutter uncle da Miles women had 2 brothers it wasn't jus' 'em like dey had us to believe. Shit only safe thing to say is we've grown up in a fucked up family an our poppa went out like a coward by killin' 'em self, me I goin' out like I'm on top of da world like da bitch I be come a murderous "Boss Queen". "Ueenie lil' nigga I'm sorry fam' I wish I knew chu was carryin' all dis weight 'round we coulda tried sooner to get chu some better help." "I thought 'bout wut chu Cortez' an my moms kept tellin' me dat I was throwin' bricks at da penitentiary so honestly I had told myself afta' da shipment came in I would be out of da game fo' good once I got my paper_She stopped in mid-sentence an dried 'er face an stood up from 'er seat an said; "Man I'm done talkin' 'bout it lets go." "Cortez' baby call da fellas tell 'em wut eva dey doin' at dis moment to stop an go pack their bags 'cus afta' dey finish up at da warehouse tonight we leavin fo' Vegas an dey'll be dere fo' a week. Tez, cuz would chu like to take yo' girl to Vegas wit chu?" She asked. "Nah baby girl Imma spend dis time wit chu ma I don't feel like havin' a tag along. I got to much on my mind right now baby girl, but I appreciate da offer. Imma fly solo on dis one." In Vegas Queenie was amazed she was fascinated by da bright lights up and down da strip she had neva been in a place dat beautiful an it gave 'er a good feelin'. "WOW! Look Tez she pointed, screamed Ooooh, awes! Tez and Cortez' seein' da lil' kid come out of 'er an dey were in total awe 'cus it was da way she should be I a child's place wit out bein' stress out. Da life she took on at 'er age Tez knew she wasn't completely prepared fo'. Yeah he knew of 'er IQ an 'er intelligence, but at heart she was still a kid dat could be saved. "Yo' ma ya like dis shit huh? Well wait 'til we get inside da casino it's so fuckin' big an da rooms are all dat yo' ass gonna fall in love wit it." Cortez' retorted. Cortez' and Tez wanted to try an keep Queenie occupied afta' dey noticed how excited she was 'bout da city. Dey figured jus' maybe she to would want to stay da week. Queenie approached da desk to check in, den turned to 'er entourage; "Is all of ya niggas gonna stay da week an enjoy yo' selves?" Someone asked wut 'bout work. "Nah ain't non of dat dis a week paid vacation if ya niggas want it all expenses on me. Now I need to know if everyone is gonna stay." Skip asked 'er was she stayin'? "Nah I got some biz'ness to handle back home, so Cortez', Tez and I will be leavin' back out by noon." Skip said; "BQ if it's aiight wit chu I rather work ma." Skip had a thing fo' Queenie he wouldn't mind spendin' every moment of his life wit 'er, but he knew she was wit Cortez' an didn't want to lose cool points fo' tryin' to push up on 'er. Neva da less da chances he got to be 'round 'er he took advantage of it. "Dats cool anybody else, baby ya sho' ya don't wanta stay an bring yo' birthday in_in Vegas?" "Only if ya stayin' to ma utter dan dat I'm on dat big bird in da sky wit chu." Tez stated; "I guess we outta 'ere by noon cuz." Queenie shrugged 'er shoulders aiight turnin' back towards da lady standin' behind da desk she questioned; "Do ya have 4 rooms available?" Ma'am I need to see id first. So she handed da clerk a phony id dat read Brandi Stapleton. Thank ya Ms. Stapleton fo' 4 rooms?" She asked. "Yeah I would like 4 rooms three fo' a week from tonight an 1 jus' 'til noon tomorrow." Okay deres ya id back an will dat be cash or credit? "It will be cash deres no utter way." Well ya total is $7,000 an dats wit room service everyone will get three meals a day. "Dats cool." 'Ere are ya room keys Ms. Stapleton an behind da cage bars right ova dere ya can purchase casino chips an lets us know if dere is anything else we can do fo' chu. Utter dan dat ma'am ya all enjoy yo' selves 'ere at Las Vegas Le'Vitta Loca. Once upstairs, Queenie told all da fellas to come to 'er suite in 'bout 10 minutes. Knock! Knock! Cortez' yelled out "Yo' fellas it's open, come in." Tez led da pack an Queenie came 'round da corner out of da bedroom wit a Nike backpack. "Wutsup fam' ya ready to get it in on da crap table?" Tez asked. "Yeah cuz, but not jus' jet lets fall back an chill fo' a minute I gotta lot on my mind. Cuz my intentions is fo' y'all to enjoy ya selves, but I told ya da trip was on me, 'ere." She tossed each family member a wrapped bundle of $5,000 each. She toss Tez da first bundle an told 'em; "I don't wanta hear shit cuz jus' take it an go gamble fam'." Afta' everyone else savin' da best fo' last Queenie handed Cortez' his bundle den gave 'em a kiss. "Aiight now leave me I'll catch up wit y'all later. Cortez' walked out wit da crew, walkin' behind Tez he pulled his coat tail. "Homeboy Imma stay up 'ere wit my QUEEN I gotta try to talk to 'er I fill dis is da perfect alone time we need. I gotta get 'er out of dis slump she's in family. If not we gonna lose 'er sooner dan we think. Man go an try to enjoy yo' self an Imma see wut I can do, when I come down I'll make sho' she's wit me." "Aiight fam' givin' each utter a embrace Cortez' re-entered da suite. "Yo' ma!" Cortez' called out, Queenie exited da bathroom wit a bath towel 'round 'er breast and torso wit 'er nine in 'er hand. "Damn shawty ya so beautiful, why do ya wanta leave me?" He grabbed 'er 'round da waist pullin' 'er close liftin' 'er up an she wrapped 'er legs 'round 'em as he carried 'er to da bed. Afta' an hour of hot passionate love makin' Cortez' told Queenie baby we need to talk. "My QUEEN do ya love me?" "Come on wut kind of question is dat?" She asked. "Ma jus' answer it's me and chu baby so stop wit da "Boss Queen" position an give me da Queenie I witness earlier at da restaurant ma." Queenie responded back; "Yeah I love ya Cortez'." "Well why are ya finna kill yo' self shawty, I thought it was gonna be chu and me, baby all da way so it's jus' fuck wut we got huh, Queenie? Baby is it dat simple to let everything ya love go? Look baby girl I know I haven't been in yo' life dat long, but do ya feel dats fair to Tez? Ma my understandin' dis nigga has basically raised chu 'em self, an I think he did a damn good job shawty. Queenie it's tearin' my homeboy apart in da inside dats da reason he didn't wanta bring Kandi along 'cus he needed time wit chu, but he didn't wanta feel like he was resentin' 'er. Baby ya gotta know dat chu have all of us dysfunctional right now an wuts fuckin' wit me,so hard is I ain't neva felt dis way 'bout no braud. Baby I could kick it wit any bitch at any given time an let 'er walk away wit no problem an wouldn't give 2 fucks 'bout wut she did next. But my QUEEN ya came along an changed all of dat. I see somethin' in yo' ass ma I need chu chu have dat special quality in ya dat I haven't seen or found in any utter woman walkin' dis earth. Yo' look at me ma." Queenie's head was in 'er hands as he removed 'em he notice she was cryin'.

"Baby I know ya hurtin' right now 'cus to ya da world has been a total lie. I can't change dat part, but I need chu to know I love yo' ass an if ya give me da chance I got chu da best physician dat money can buy to find out wuts goin' on inside yo' head. Listen to me." Cortez' bent down in front of Queenie, so dey were at eye level again. "I know ya a woman of yo' word, so no I'm not sayin' ya can't get at 'em niggas I won't take dat away from ya, but all I'm sayin' is afta' ya do it lets jus' leave chu and me jus' so shit can cool off in East St. Boogie. We can go to Jamaica, I'll have it setup so no one will be able to point an say it was yo' ass at all ma. Please shawty wut do I have to do to get chu not to go through wit dis bullshit? How can I change ya mind ma 'cus I'm tryin' to see ya as my wife dats gonna have my child. I want us to be a family somethin' I neva had." As he talked Queenie heard every word he spoke, but wut touched 'er da most was 'em neva havin' a family an dat was somethin' she was big on.

Chapter Nineteen
"Give Me My Vengeance Niggas I Am God"

She dried 'er face an told Cortez' "Look daddy ya got me." "Yo' ma wut chu mean I got chu, tell me wut chu sayin' QUEEN.""I'm sayin' ya got me fo' as long as ya want me baby. I'll stay 'round an make a life and family wit chu daddy." Cortez' screamed at da top of his lungs"Woo! Thank ya ma." Queenie had jus' made 'em da happiest man walkin' da face of da earth he picked 'er up an spun 'er 'round. "Okay baby put me down 'cus ya really makin' me nauseous nigga. Lets go take a shower, so we can go break da house an win some of their paper." "Yo' my QUEEN can I get in wit chu?" She gave 'em a sexy look an dropped 'er towel an said; "Ya can do wut eva ya like daddy, but we showerin' not fuckin' an walked off towards da bathroom. "Ooooh! Shawty yo' ass a tease, how ya gonna act ma? Ya not right nah mean, but I'm comin' in anyway." Dey showered an Queenie got dress in a fresh fit she put in 'er backpack wit 'er money jus' in case. Queenie slipped on a pair of powder blue stretch jeans wit 2 wife beaters red and blue to match blue air force ones wit red embroidered BQ all ova. She placed 'er jewelry on givin' 'er self a once ova in da lengthy mirror. "Aiight ya look good ma." She told 'er self. "Yeah ya do shawty, chu came prepared didn't ya?" Queenie replied; "I gotta stay fresh baby, I know ya didn't expect me to keep dat same outfit I had on when we arrived." "Nah ya right I shoulda known better dan dat ma." Queenie placed nina into da suites safe an pulled out 10 stacks. "Yo' ya ready baby?" "Yeah,but let me ask dis last question is chu gonna stay da whole week now or wutsup?" "Nah baby, but if ya like I'll make a few calls an give ya an extra day down 'ere, but dat means we'll be goin' back home on ya birthday." "Why not afta' my birthday baby?" He asked. "'Cus honestly dats da day I assassinate does bitch ass niggas who killed our family an since I gave my word to stick 'round Imma hold chu to yo' word dat chu gonna take me to Jamaica." "Aiight I won't ask any mo' questions Imma take my baby off to Jamaica, so lets go rack up on dese people paper to take wit us. Cortez' said jokingly. He put his hand on da small of Queenie's back an off dey went to find da rest of their family. "Yeah I owe someone an apology fo' my irrational thinkin'." Queenie spotted Tez sittin' at da bar by 'em self havin' a drink, so 'er and Cortez' walked ova to where he was an she stated; "Damn nigga ya look like ya need yo' lil' nigga back." Tez raised his head from his sorrows an looked at Queenie she had a smile on 'er face dat brighten 'em up an she told 'em; "Don't worry nigga ya got me fo' as long as ya need me." Tez gave Cortez' a look an he nodded his head as to say yeah she's back. Tez jumped up off da bar stool an lifted Queenie off da floor an hugged 'er,so tight she couldn't breath. "Yo' fam' chu gonna kill me by squeezin' all da air outta me cuz." "Oh, shit my bad baby girl." "Cuz I wanta apologize I neva meant to hurt chu out of all people. It was brought to my attention dat I would be given up on da one person who truly gives a damn an took up da time wit me da same person who encouraged me to do wut eva I felt was best fo' me. An dats wut made me feel special dese years growin' up wit chu fam', yo' ass my brother nigga an I will always be yo' Ueenie yo' lil' nigga." Tez started to question 'er, but Cortez' stopped 'em an said; "Homeboy I'll fill ya in when we get back upstairs,but right now lets go to da crap table family an pocket some of dis paper." Tez kissed his cousin on da fo' head an da three went to gamble. Woo! Woo! Dey screamed Queenie was hot on da dice table within da 20 minutes dey were standin' dere she won half of a million dollars. "Yo' let me collect." Damn ya look a lil' young to be in 'ere on da crap table shawty. An older guy said to Queenie. She started to get irate wit da guy, but thought better of it an jus' told 'em thank ya fo' da complement. "But check it age is no barrier, it's a limitation ya put on ya mind. Tez, Cortez' lets go." Da 2 started to check dude an put 'em in his place, but realize she handled 'er self very well wit out makin' a scene so dey jus' followed 'er to cash in $30,000 of 'er winnins' an dey went a placed da rest in da suites safe fo' safe keepin'. Queenie gave Tez and Cortez' 10 stacks a piece. "'Ere y'all go I win y'all win." Neither one wanted to argue so dey jus' said thank ya an dey all went back downstairs were dey met up wit da rest of their crew. Everyone seemed to be doin' great,so she asked where could dey get a limo from dey all could fit in 'cus she wanted to go out an see da city while it was lite up at night. "Jus' go back to da front desk an tell 'em chu need a limo an dey'll provide one fo' ya." "Ms. Stapleton how long will ya need it fo'?" "Let me get it fo' da whole week, thanks." "Would chu like to keep da same driver fo' da entire week?" "Yeah I see no reason to change up." "Alright ma'am ya driver will be Stacey when ya ready go ova to da red phones chu see on da poles through out da casino an dial dis number an state yo' drivers name an within 10 minutes da driver will be out front. Would chu like to leave da casino now Ms. Stapleton, I can call fo' ya." "Yeah do dat if ya would." "Yo' baby see if da crew wants to roll out an if not jus' tell 'em we'll see 'em in a lil' while." Da crew got in da limo afta' their boss an wanted to know where dey were headed. "No where in particular, I jus' wanta see wut it's like it's late so I know ain't shit open. I jus' like da bright lights, dis shit is beautiful. Chicago ain't no where dis bright fam'." "Baby everything along dis strip is open 24/7. "Yo' ya bull shittin'! Yo' lets go shoppin' den we can go eat." Tez tap on da dividin' window an stated;

"Ma'am stop at da first clothin' store ya get to Ms. Stapelton would like to go shoppin'." Stacey da driver was a youngan 'er self who was also loved fashion an she peeped Queenie when dey arrived at da casino. "Sir if ya don't mind me sayin' I think a woman of Ms. Stapleton's status an persona she would like to see da finest delicacy stores dere are to go to dat fit 'er swagg." Tez made a mental note to check out da driver later. "Aiight start wit da top stores ma, by da way my name is Tez so ya don't have to call me sir." "Alright Tez I'm Stacey not ma'am." Queenie stood up hangin' out da sun roof of da limo wit 'er arms above 'er head an quoted; "I'm on top of da world, baby I'm on top of da world." Ms. Stapelton 'eres yo' first stop Levi's world. "Yo' dis my shit family lets go." Tez got ready to tap da window,but instead it jus' rolled down. "Yo' thank ya shawty handin' 'er a $100 dollar bill. "No I can't take dat, but thanks anyway." "Yeah ya can yo' ass gotta eat don't chu? Is dis yo' hustle? So take it besides ya really have no idea wut chu jus' done fo' me ma, now take it an trust dere's much mo' where dat came from." Queenie stood waitin' on Tez to get out da limo. "Cuz chu comin' fam?" She stuck 'er head back inside da car to see wut was up. "My bad nigga I didn't know chu fell back to put yo' mack down, but bring 'er wit chu fam' 'cus I want chu in da store wit me family. Yo' Stacey ya mo' dan welcome to jay down wit da crew hell ya finna be wit dese niggas fo' a week, so ya should get to know 'em ma." Stacey said; "But I'm not suppose to mingle wit my clients_ Queenie cut 'er off tossin' 'er $800 an asked; "Even if yo' clients need help carryin' bags huh? Now pick up yo' tip an every time ya stop da limo we get out yo' shawty chu get out even when we go to eat chu will eat wit us. Now come on Tez." "Man who is she?" Stacey questioned. She's pretty demandin' fo' a youngan does she always come off dat strong wit people she don't know?" Tez said; "Whoa pump yo' breaks shawty let me answer yo' first question ma. Dat dere is "Boss Queen" an dis is our family circle. Second age is only a number an 'er demeanor usually give people da wrong impression of who she is, which is a very nice nonchalant person ma. It's jus' 'er caliber she doesn't like signs of weakness an she feels it's no utter way, but to be firm." Queenie said; "Levi's Levi's dey got every type of Levi's ya can imagine." She picked up every pair she had neva seen befo' dat wasn't out back home. Dey were in and out of all type of stores dey all shopped, but Queenie didn't want to take all of their fun from 'em so she told 'em lets go eat 'cus she had in mind goin' back to da suite an puttin' it on Cortez'. Tez asked shawty where was da best place to get a T-Bone steak from an she told 'em Porter House dat was a lil' pass da casino. Dey served wut eva type of steak ya wanted. "Dats where we're goin' den." Queenie retorted. While everyone ate and drank Queenie spoke; "Yo' family instead of me leavin' today at noon we gonna be 'ere an extra day, but when we do leave out Stacey 'ere will continue to be y'all driver so make sho' y'all niggas treat 'er right. She's hustlin' to make a livin' also." "We got 'er boss, she's in good hands." "Aiight don't fuck up 'cus ya already know wut goes along wit it. Don't disrespect my character when I'm out of sight." Stacey was very intrigued by da authority Queenie had ova dis group of men an dat made 'er become envious of Queenie. She thought how could one person a young person have so much power ova anyone. Queenie could see da face expression Stacey carried, so bein' who she is Queenie questioned it. "Wuts good lil' mama, wut is chu so curious 'bout? Yo' ya know it's good to be curious an try to figure a person out, but wit me it's best fo' chu to jus' ask so wuts on ya mind?" Stacey replied; "I'm tryin' to figure out why dey keep callin' chu boss an why ya da only female amongst all dese guys? Wut makes chu,so special Ms. Stapleton?" "Yo' my name is Queenie dats wut I go by. Ms. Brandi Stapleton is jus' my alias to do me an get in such places as da casino. Now why does dis group of men keep callin' me boss, 'cus dats how I carry myself as such an 'cus I'm actually their boss. I am how dey eat an da provider of how dey make their livin', now don't get it twisted dis 'ere is my family an I treat 'em as such dey are everything to me. Dis 'ere is my cuz Tez dats my man

Cortez' an da 2 of 'em grew up wit Skip 'ere." An she went on and on of lettin' 'er know who everyone else was. "Yo' ask 'em fo' yo' self no matter wut their titles are or wut dey might call me I am "Boss Queen" an it's da name dey gave me, an who I am, an dey will neva disrespect me even doe I'm youngest of 'em all." "How young are ya exactly?" Stacey asked. "Yo' I'm 16 home girl." "A person would think ya was much older dan dat da way ya talk an throw money 'round." Queenie questioned "So how old is chu Stacey?" "I'm only 17." "Yeah I can tell chu still got a lot of growin' up to do. Listen I maybe young, but dere is no utter bitch young or old an dere's no nigga dat chu can put on my level. See shawty everything I am I learned ova da years to make it to age 16 I learned from one nigga an he's only 3 years older dan me. So see shawty it's not how young or old chu are it's how chu make yo' age work fo' ya." Queenie gave da girl no credit at all. "Now see wut I jus' said probably went ova yo' head." "Boss ya cold wit it baby girl." Cortez' whispered in 'er ear; "Baby ya ready to hit da suite?" He asked wit a kiss to 'er neck. "Yeah daddy_She rubbed between his legs to find out how ready he was. "Yo' chu ready to huh nigga." Standin' from da table Queenie told 'er crew to squad up, once dey returned to da casino Queenie and Cortez' disappeared back to their suite. "WOW! Ma I feel like I been on a actual roller coaster. Man shawty I don't know wuts been goin' on, but yo' skills have improved tremendously. Ah nigga needs to catch his_ooooh shit baby." Queenie finally got 'er chance to pleas 'em da way she wanted to bu give 'em a tea bag job. She damn near made Cortez' run up da wall from hummin' on his nuts, he didn't know whether to cry laugh or scream it felt so good to 'em. "Ma come sit on a niggas face an let me taste dat wet sweet juicy love box of urns." Queenie did jus' dat she sat on his face an rode it like he was a stallion as she bent ova an placed 'er lips 'round da tip of his dicks head. Sssst_Ooooh_Awe_Ma, Queenie quickly took all of 'em in 'er mouth wit no gag reflex. Wit one smooth motion she parted his thighs licked his ass an teased his sack wit saliva and soft breathin' givin' 'em a cool sensation. "Yo' ass a freak ma. I love ya." Cortez' turned Queenie ova as he repositioned 'er he said; "Let me wax dat ass from behind ma an sho' ya wut a real nigga workin' wit." Assumin' da position she backed dat ass up right on Cortez' pipe an da 2 went at it again fo' 'round 2 'til dey collasped into a deep sleep. Ring, ring, ring, ring, ring! Da call was ended as Liz said; "It's no answer." "Don't panic I'll call Tez, don't worry we'll get a hold of 'em." Ring, ring. Tez answered his hitter groggy_ "Wutsup who dis?" It's yo' mother son." Heather replied. "Yo' wutsup ma? "Tez baby listen to me, Chaos is in da hospital." Tez sat straight up in da bed an said; "Wut da fuck fo' ma?" "Baby he has been shot up pretty bad! Dey have 'em in surgery now an dey say dat dey not sho' if he's gonna make it baby. Where are chu an is Queenie wit chu?" "Yeah we together outta town, but we on da first thing smokin' back. Ma tell me wut happen." Tez stayed on da phone as he put on his pants and jumpers den grabbed his room key as Heather went on tellin' 'em wut she knew of da incident wit Chaos. "Baby he came ova fo' dinner to eat wit us an durin' dinner a conversation came up 'bout 'em bein' followed since he hasn't been 'round chu and Queenie. Well tonight I guess who eva da people are followed 'em to da house or maybe dey was jus' sittin' an waitin' on 'em, 'cus when he walked out an he got 5 bullets an even doe he had on his bullet proof he still got hit in da left knee an his left hip bone an da vest caught 2 and 1 in da neck." Boom! Boom! Tez tried to knock down Queenie and Cortez' suite door. Skip came out of da suite 'em an da homeboys shared wit a burner in his hand. "Yo' Tez wutsup homeboy. Wipin' cold from his eyes. Wuts good fam'?" "Get da fellas up we outta 'ere Chaos has been shot up." "Yo' niggas get up get y'all shit we outta 'ere on da next thing smokin' back home. Chaos been done up." He banged on a nutter door. "Get 'em niggas up." Cortez' snatched da door open an befo' he could say anything Tez said; "We gotta go home where is Queenie?" "Wutsup family?" Cortez asked. "Yo' baby girl! Queenie came out of da bathroom. "Wutup cuz?"

“THROWIN' BRICKS AT THE PENITENTIARY”

“Yo' ma I jus' got a call from moms_ He held up da phone an Queenie could see dat his hitter was still runnin' he still had someone on da utter line. We need to go Chaos has been hit 5 times an dey not sho' if he's gonna make it.” Queenie asked; “Wut da fuck happen fam'?” She signaled fo' Tez to give 'er his hitter. “Who ya talkin' to.” “Oh! Shit dats moms.” He stated. “Hello, auntie wut happen to 'em?” “Baby he's been shot 5 times his neck, his hip, his knee an he took 2 in his torso area, but da bullet proof vest caught does.” “Auntie Chaos ain't neva wore a vest befo' so wut he wearin' a vest fo' now?” “Baby all I know he came ova to have dinner wit yo' mother and I an was tellin' us dat since he hasn't been 'round chu and Tez any mo' he noticed he had been followed. Well I guess he slipped up an didn't notice it or dey had jus' parked an waited on 'em, 'cus when he walked out of our house dats when we heard da gun shots.” “Wut! Dese ma'fuckas brought it to my homestead?” Queenie fo' got who she was talkin' to at da time 'cus she snapped as she rant and raved wit annoyance. “Dese bitch ass niggas has touched a nutter one of my bloodline? Dey tested my gangsta fo' da last time dese bitch ass niggas will die today. We on our way!” As she ended da call da entourage stood in da middle of da room. “Boss everything has been taken care of. Da keys have been returned an da chic at da desk pro-rated our stay an she called da limo out front to take us to da airport ma.” Skip informed 'er. Cortez' had grabbed all of Queenie's things she had purchased da night befo' while she opened da room safe an gathered 'er jewelry, backpack of money an 'er nine. “Squad up niggas.” Everyone ran out da door an Skip yelled out; “Ma stop at da desk an get yo' money boss.” Once in da car Tez called his mother. Ring! “Hello, Tez.” “Yeah it's me, we on da way to da airport.” Cortez' was on da phone changin' their flights as Tez talked to Heather. “Yo' ma give me an up date, talk to me. Is he outta surgery jet, how is he?” “No he's still back dere an we haven't heard anything jet. Baby how long befo' y'all be 'ere?” Heather asked. “In 'bout 2 hours we should be arrivin', but Imma keep callin' 'til we

land, so if ya hear anything or somethin' changes don't hesitate to call me. Where aunt Liz?" "Right now she's ova talkin' to da nurses tryin' to find out any info she can on Chaos condition baby." "Aiight ma we finna board da plane." Dey all arrived at ST. Clarks Hospital dey rushed through da doors findin' Heather and Liz in da waitin' area. Rushin' to their parents sides dey asked in unison; "How is he? Y'all got word jet?" Liz and Heather's eyes were so puffy from all da cryin' Queenie asked; "Is chu 2 aiight?" Queenie knew dey had to be shaken up from da shootin' happenin' right at their door step. "Queenie told 'em dat dey were gonna stay in a hotel dat night an maybe fo' a coupla days 'til da shit was handled. "I can't chance dese ma'fuckas comin' back to da house tryin' to get at y'all to. I don't know wut dey might know, but I know one thang fo' certain dese ma'fuckas playin' fo' keeps an dat shit dere is to close to home, fuck dat it is home my nigga." Queenie ya don't have to put us up in no hotel baby girl. We not finna be runnin' from dese lil' punks." Liz stated. "Lil' punks huh?" Queenie retorted. Usually she would have put 'er foot down an demanded, but dis time she didn't. Queenie loved 'er moms and aunt Heather, but she was very furious wit 'em an felt dat bad timin' is neva presented on a good note, so as stubborn as she is she let it take ova 'er thinkin'.
"Yo' if dats da way y'all want it den 4 of da homeboys will stay at da crib wit y'all 'til dis shit is ova."
"Fam' lil' nigga watch yo' mouth dats yo' moms chu talkin' to." Queenie shot a look Tez way an he knew she was still feelin' a lot of animosity towards 'er moms mainly 'cus of all da info she wit held from 'er concernin' 'er life. Tez had also told 'em self dat he had jus' got Ueenie back from 'er own self destruction an dat all of dis could be to soon fo' 'er to handle. So he came forward; "Yo' ain't no disrespect intended, but she's right if y'all don't wanta stay at a hotel 'til dis is ova den 4 of da homeboys will be campin' out wit y'all, so get da spare rooms together an be good hostess."
Da doctor came outta no where an asked may I speak wit the Miles women alone? "Yeah doctor, but

we are all Chaos family, so wut eva ya have to say chu can say it in front of us all.” Okay, Mr. Miles is outta surgery an in ICU he can't breath on his own at da moment an it's a 60/40 chance he will neva again. Da bullet dat pierced his neck instead of it makin' a clear exit it ricochet tearin' his esophagus an it lounged into his left lung. He was hit wit a 22 pistol, an who eva done dis to 'em tried to take 'em out fo' good. His hip has been shattered an da knee far as da knee is concerned da bullet went straight threw, but it did a lot of damage to da cartilage, so befo' I can put dat strenuous pressure on Mr. Miles I need 'em to breath on his own an it's hard to tell if dat will happen any time soon at dis point. Jus' a lil' heads up if he stays like dat fo' to long he will need to be reformed. It will be like teachin' a child how to walk, talk an eat all ova again. He will need a lot of love and tender care, it will be a lot of work on jus' one person. Liz said; “I'm a nurse, I jus' relocated from Chicago Rush Hospital, so I'm a ware of how much work it is. If necessary my sister and I will take 'em in an care fo' 'em doctor.”

Liz and Heather had already talked ova da wut if's, so dey pretty much had prepared em' selves fo' da worst. Queenie had heard a nuff getting mo' pissed by da minute. “Yo' lets ride.” She yelled.

“Cortez' baby put Skip an three utters at moms crib. When dey leave dis hospital dey need to be in da car wit 'em an dey are not to leave an be alone fo' any reason.” “Squad up!” Queenie walked out da doors wit Liz yellin' fo' 'er to come back, but Queenie didn't look back. Tez and Cortez' hugged da ladies tellin' 'em she'll be okay, we'll make sho' of it. An dey to ran out da doors. “Family take care of 'em.” dey said in unison. “Yo' we got chu, but who knows who dese cats at or who dey are.”

Chapter Twenty
"Eye Fo' An Eye, Take Mines I'm Comin' Fo' Urns"

Queenie retorted; "I know everything 'bout dese bitch ass niggas an tonight is Friday an if dey ain't on da strip da niggas in da projects. I appreciate y'all bein' down, but dis my fight homeboys." "Nah we respect chu an all, but we family an chu was hurt befo' an it damn near killed all of us not knowin' if ya would pull through da ordeal, so fire us later, but right now we rollin' wit chu on dis one." a nutter voice said; "Lil' ma it's ride and die." "Well since y'all feel so strongly 'bout it get yo' ammo up 'cus we killin' da whole damn crew." It hit home when dey turned da corner an to their block an saw yellow tape in front of da ol' gs crib. "Yo' cuz ya see dat shit?" Queenie questioned. "Fam' dat easily coulda been one of our moms, dis lets me know dat dese ma'fuckas been watchin' us close. Dis ain't no fuckin' coincidence Chaos got hit dese ma'fuckas been plottin' on me jus' as hard as I been watchin' and plottin' on dey asses. Lil' do dey know dis shit ends tonight." Queenie ran in da house an hit 'er hidin' spot where she hid 'er AK47 an a sawed off shot gun. She had nina tucked in da small of 'er back already droppin' to 'er knees she grabbed a duffel bag from underneath da bed full of ammunition fo' all three guns. "Cortez' she yelled pull out yo' bullet proof baby." "She changed into all black jeans, t-shirt, jumpers an put on a bullet proof vest an threw a black hoodie on top of it. Runnin' back downstairs she yelled out; "Yo' y'all ready, where's Tez?" "He should be outside ma he went to go pull his Ninja out we gonna jet out on does." Cortez' said; "We'll be followin' chu an when we need it da car will be our shield feel me." Queenie replied; "Cool ya 2 ride wit me, baby boy yo' ass drive. Lets be out hit da projects first den da strip." "Boss I'm lovin' dat AK, bitch is sweet fam'." "She finna do damage wit dat ma'fucka trust and believe dat." Cortez' grabbed Queenie pullin' 'er back fo' a kiss. "I love ya ma, It's ride and die." She responded back; "Ride and Die baby." Passin' through da projects no one was 'round except a few young hustlers tryin' to get their serve on, so Queenie motioned fo' everyone to keep goin' to da next location. Queenie gave 'er driver a run down of how she wanted 'em to drive, 'cus she needed a clear shot befo' jumpin' out on dese niggas. "Yo' family I need chu to cruise by normal like we jus' hittin' da strip like everybody else fo' da night. We go down come back up an all hell breaks loose on dese bitch ass niggas." music my QUEEN she commanded da radio to come on an House Nation pierced from da 15's she had placed in da trunk.

"Damn boss dat shit hittin' ya hooked my homeboy up dis ma'fuckin' car is like no utter."

"Yeah, ya like it huh, aiight chu ain't seen shit jet. Chu drive dis ma'fucka like ya know how an don't wreck his shit." Queenie clicked every hammer she had in 'er possession lookin' into da back seat_

"Yo' fam' chu ready?" Cortez' and Tez did a few wheelies to stunt so dey wouldn't look suspect dey also did donuts in da middle of da street leavin' clouds of smoke so no one could see. Da 2 pulled up an drove slow along side of da passenger side of da car. Queenie rolled down da window. "Listen ride down slow make a u-turn an sho' out on da way back up, but stop at da top of da hill, but face us goin' back down hill." "Yo' ma ya suited and booted?" Tez questioned. Queenie raised 'er hoodie an told 'em; "Chu know it baby now hit it." Cortez' and Tez put on a sho' fo' all da on lookers dey raced back up da stretch. Jus' as dey had everyone's attention Queenie switched da music an told 'er homeboy; "To drive dis car nigga." All ya could hear was Tat,Tat,Tat,Tat,Tat. Queenie let da AK47 ride 'til it was empty da driver did a 180 an stopped in front of da Ninja bikes shieldin' Tez and Cortez' as da 4 of 'em continued to shoot Queenie spotted da nigga Tef 'lon tryin' to reload. Dis was da nigga who setup Lu and Chuck's murder, so she jumps out da car wit da moss berg in hand an 'er nine fully loaded. "Tef 'lon chu bitch ass nigga_ Thuf was da sound heard an Tef 'lon took off runnin' an behind 'em was Queenie like a track star. Pumpin' da shot gun again dis time she stopped aimed Boom! She saw his body drop to da ground an she heard da sound of a motorcycle in da distance an as she started runnin' to finish 'em Tef 'lon off Tez pulled up long side of Queenie wit out stoppin' he reached out his arm an Queenie grabbed hold an jumped on da back of his bike. Queenie toss da shot gun to Cortez' an pulled out nina as Tez got close to da body. "Ma finish 'em off." Queenie unloaded all eleven 'rounds. "Get ghost cuz." She told Tez. "Yo' ma chu outta 'ere ya goin straight to da airport cuz. Chu and Cortez' got da next flight to Jamaica baby girl an yo' ass is not to return 'til I call ya." Arrivin' at da airport da crew was waitin' fo' da three to sho' up. Cortez' had also arranged fo' Liz and Heather to be dere, so Queenie could say 'er good byes. Queenie stated; "No propounds huh, not even a proposition chu jus' gonna make me flee huh? So it's like dat? Well cuz why da hell does it feel like I'm runnin' from someone." Liz spoke; "Chu are runnin' from da penitentiary baby no one wants to see ya end up dere." Cortez' said; "Ma word is bond ya comin' back an when ya do everything will be all good. We gonna go have fun, so chu can relax fo' a while. Tez can handle everything 'ere." Tez said; "I give ya my word anything happens 'ere ya will be da first to know." "Ma I gotta helicopter on stand by fo' any time of da day now even doe ya against it we gotta catch dis flight." She hugged everyone, I guess I'll see y'all when I see ya." She hugged Tez da longest an dat brought a tear to his eye. "My nigga take care of my moms and aunt an take care of one a nutter I swear I can't lose anyone else." Cortez' gave dap to all his niggas an when he got to Tez he told 'em; "Yo' fam' keep me posted on Chaos." "No doubt family, take care of my lil' nigga." Tez handed Cortez' a duffel bag wit $60,000 dollars in it. "'Ere fam' y'all do it up big, an make sho' Ueenie enjoys 'er self. Try an keep 'er mind off of all dis an I'll let chu know wut da word on da street is in a coupla days homeboy." "Yo' ma straight? All I want chu to do is kick back and relax 'cus baby girl dis whole trip is 'bout chu my QUEEN. Jus' let loose an Imma take care of ya like a King should charish his

QUEEN. Nah mean ma?” Cortez' kissed 'er soft lips an wit a smile she retorted; “Nigga chu full of yo' self.” Cortez' said; “I got chu, we gotta bag full of money, so it's wut eva ya want or wanta do. I'll be yo' jenny only exception is ya can have as many wishes as ya would like, my love.” “Is dat right well wut if I jus' rather lay up under chu da entire time we in Jamaica?” Really he questioned; “Shawty if dats wut chu want we can do dat to we ain't neva gotta leave da bongo fo' anything. So I guess we should go shop befo' we shut ourselves in can't have my QUEEN lookin' like yesterday.” Dere was a limo waitin' fo' da 2, da driver held up a sign dat read my QUEEN. Queenie looked at Cortez' an asked; “Chu did dis? Baby ya so sweet, I didn't figure ya to be da mushy mush type.”

“If ya let up some chu can find out a lot mo' 'bout yo' mans.” Coretz' kissed da nap of Queenie's neck. “Mmmmm ya wanta be freaky huh? In da back of da limo?” “Does it bother ya to smash in da back of da car ma, 'cus if so we can wait 'til we get to da bongo.” Queenie pushed Cortez' backwards off of 'er an straddled 'em on da floor of da limousine an whispered; “Nigga it doesn't matter where we are as long as I'm wit chu. If ya wanta smash den baby dats wut da fuck we gonna do.”

Cortez' tapped on da dividin' window_ “Yo' my mans how long we got befo' we get to da bongo?”

“It'll be forty-five minutes my maan.” “Aiight thanks, baby dat gives us a nuff time,so come 'ere an let me pleas ya.” “Nah daddy Imma pleas ya first.” She unbuckled Cortez' pants takin' off his jumpers jeans, boxers den she removed his shirt. “Yo' ma ssssh.” Not sayin' a nutter word he pulled Queenie's t-shirt ova 'er head an unbutton 'er pants. “Ma take dat shit off.” He demanded pullin' an tuggin' at 'er jeans she finally let Cortez' pull 'em off. Queenie pushed 'em back down an sat on his chest wit 'er ass in his face. Cortez' was a freaky, freakier dan da freakiest of freaks so he didn't mind a lil' ass in his face at all. But Queenie knew how to tease 'em when she wanted to do 'er. “Spread 'em nigga.” Queenie let saliva drip from 'er mouth on to Cortez' nut sack dat slowly ran down to da crack of his ass. Takin' all of Cortez' into 'er mouth 'er finger tips massaged his nuts at da same time she blew his ass. "Damn ma chu good." Grippin' 'er ass cheeks all Cortez' could see was 'er fat pink love box. "Come on ma back dat shit up a lil' bit, stop teasin' shawty chu know wut I want." Queenie put 'er flirtation game down_ "It's urns daddy do wut chu want wit it as rough as ya want." Queenie lips made a poppin' noise on his balls it was jus' right so he would cringe an only he would get pleasure out of it. Dis made Cortez' toes curl as 'er tongue stroked his ass. "Mmmmm fuck ma, come 'ere ya finna make a nigga come." "Come daddy." "Not 'til I get inside of ya." He responded. "Aiight daddy make it rough daddy tear dat pussy up. Da_Ooooh! Faster, faster,faster, oh faster daddy_ I'm finna come." "Shit me to shawty." "Shhhh, baby da driver gonna hear us." She tried to muffle Cortez' grunts an loud growls pullin' 'em by da neck to bring his face closer to 'er breast lettin' 'em suck on like a baby's bottle. Cortez' sucked so hard to pleas Queenie she couldn't control 'er own screams; "Oh shit I'm comin' again baby." Pullin' out of 'er love box he stuck his face into 'er wet pussy an tasted every drop of 'er 'til she finished havin' 'er orgasm. A tap tap hit da window an Cortez' controlled da window on his side jus' a nuff so he could hear da driver speak. "Wutsup?" "Yeah maan we're 'ere." Da driver had heard da 2 sex battle, so he asked would chu like fo' me to open chu door now? Cortez' laughed out loud nah my man I'll get it he told 'em an handed 'em a hunnid dollar bill. "Yo' I need chu to stay out 'ere we'll be back out I gotta take my woman shoppin'." "Me wait 'ere maan_ he said wit a smile. Take care of e woman maan, me be waitin' right 'ere maan." Cortez' grabbed da duffel bag of money got out an helped his QUEEN out da back seat. Inside da bongo was beautiful, Queenie ran from room to room admirin' a coloration of each room. "Baby it's so colorful it's to beautiful." "I take it I've done good an it's up to yo' standards. Huh ma?" He asked as he walked up behind 'er kissin' da nap of 'er neck. "Yeah daddy ya did great. I wanta cook in dis kitchenette baby do dey have pots and pans in 'ere?" "Lets see baby." Dey pulled out drawers opened da pantry. "Bingo ma hell it all looks new an dere's even food in da pantry baby." Cortez' stated. Queenie opened da refrigerator an noticed it was packed wit all new bought groceries: milk, orange juice, eggs, bread dere were steaks, shrimp, lobster in da freezer. "Baby dere's a note attached to da refrigerator." Queenie read it: "Yo' surprise ma, I ain't seen ya in da kitchen a day in ya life except to eat shawty, but since I know ya can eat, I know ya can cook ya jus' don't 'cus da streets consume all of ya ma. Well I figure it can't do dat now in Jamaica so I decided to keep ya occupied. Now feed dat nigga of urns baby girl an relax."

Ride and Die, Tez

"My nigga he neva seems to amaze me. I don't know how he did it, but I love his ass." Cortez' said; "We can call 'em later, but now lets get in da shower so we can go shoppin' ma." East St. Boogie was home now fo' Tez, but unfortunately it was also a war field dat he couldn't get comfortable in 'til he finds out wut da streets were sayin'. Tez had continued biz'ness as normal as if Queenie was dere. Wit everything dat went on in da last 48 hours da shipment was behind on bein' distributed. He knew Queenie had money out dere to be collected well as 'em an dope needed to be delivered. Tez still had connects in Chicago he had to deliver bricks to. Givin' everyone their assignments, Tez pulled Skip to da side; "Look homeboy I need chu to make a run fo' Queenie to Detriot I don't wanta bother 'er, but baby girl got money out in 'em streets an ya need to drop off some packages, bad thing is only she can tell ya were to go and who to meet up wit homeboy." Ring, Ring. "Wutsup family, everything good?" Cortez' questioned. "Yeah my nigga jus' handlin' biz'ness, makin' sho' everybody's paper straight, so we can all still eat baby. Imma send Skip out, but I need to holla at baby girl to make sho' shit is legit since it's 'er connect." "Hello wutup cuz? I was gonna call ya later on fam' to holla at chu 'bout wut chu did fo' us. I appreciate it all day long nigga. Yo' ass always on point huh?" "Yo' my lil' nigga ain't nothin' to much fo' my baby girl, but speakin' of bein' on point I had to call to get yo' connect info, so I can send Skip to Detroit an handle dat biz'ness cuz." Tez retorted; "Can't let dis organization fall apart while boss is away. Now can I?" She replied; "Nah ya shouldn't nah wut I mean? Da circle still has to eat, jus' 'cus I'm away shit don't stop fam'. Yo' how Chaos any changes on his condition?"

"He's still da same as of now baby girl, but I know he will pull threw he's a Miles. Queenie dude has to get better ma dis family doesn't need to bury anyone else." Queenie said; "I feel ya cuz we could use a break at dis point, but jus' watch yo' back out dere fam' 'em streets is a war field." She gave Tez da run down fo' da delivery and pick up. "Aye cuz since dis is Skip first trip an I'm not dere send a nutter nigga wit 'em an tell 'em I said no fuck ups do it as I said an dey'll be cool." "Aiight ma everything kosha on dis end give ya a call in a coupla days an lil' nigga have fun." "Jamaica Queens Beautiful" Aye lets go in 'ere baby. Cortez' spotted lingerie on a store manikin in da store window.

"Since ya wanta stay in, I want chu to stay in dis shit ma." "Yo' it's yo' birthday, so I'll let chu have yo' way nigga I'll even give ya da opportunity to put me in wut chu would like to see me floss."

"Bet 'em up ma take dis black, red, purple, white green,orange, yellow an the powder blue." He picked jus' 'bout every color dere was in every style. He even went out on a limb an asked; "Baby can I get chu in some heels jus' while we're 'ere?" Queenie had a curious look on 'er face as she said; "Jus' one time nigga an dats only 'cus yo' birthday is tomorrow." "Wut 'bout dese ma?" Cortez' held a pair of red/ black wit a touch of charco-grey Chanel slippers wit a 4' inch heel. Perfect! She held up a red piece she picked out fo' 'er self dat she intended to wear dat night fo' 'em. She had found a strapless boastiee wit a spaghetti string thong an in da back dat came 'round in front like a tu-tu coverin' 'er pussy dat also had a long lacy robe dat drug da floor. In a messed up Jamaican accent Queenie asked;

"How me like maan? Chu can't see me nigga. Baby why so many ya gotta fetish fo' lingerie I know nothin' 'bout?” Cortez' replied; “Ma ya know how yo' ass get ya gotta change mo' dan one time a day, so ya always gotta have somethin' else to put on baby.” “Aiight daddy as long as we can go to an actual clothin' store also 'cus when it's time to go home I don't think ya want me to wear any of does on da plane.” She broke out into laughter. “Lets pay fo' dis shawty an we can be on da way to da next store.” Cortez' spent $1,500 alone on lingerie. “Yo' lets go in da store across da road, lets see wut dey have in 'ers and his.” Queenie exclaimed. Cortez' handed da driver da 2 bags to place in da limo.

“Come on baby.” Queenie was excited. “Stop actin' like yo' ass to cool to run nigga.” “Okay damn ma I'm comin' baby.” “Not jet ya ain't.” Den she turned an smiled. “Shit lets hurry dis process up den.” He tickled 'er sides makin' 'er conceal 'er laughter to a giggle. “Shit dis 'ere is wut I'm talkin' 'bout nigga some real clothes. Dey got Levi's, Polo, Gucci, Coogi.” Queenie was in heaven when she saw da different type of clothin' styles an brands dey had she whispered; “Baby I didn't know Jamaica had dis type of stuff.” “Dey human to ma so why wouldn't dey dress like everyone else. “Aiight smart ass I didn't mean it like dat. I jus' figured dey had their own culture a entirely different style.”

“Dey do shawty da older generation, but chu still got da younger generation comin' up seein' da world as it is today an dey wanta bring in da newer trends ma.” “Neva looked at it like dat I was jus' stuck on da fact dey had their own shit. I give ya props fo' schoolin' me on dat, but lets get back to wut we came in 'ere fo' homeboy. It's time to make yo' ass fly as me.” Jokingly she said if dat's possible nigga.

“Oh shit ma ya clowin' me shawty? On some serious shit doe ma yo' ass look gorgeous in anything even yo' birthday suit, but dressin' I seen no utter nigga or bitch out dress ya yet baby girl, so go head sho' me wut chu can do fo' me.” Queenie picked up a blue denium wash Coogi outfit an a pair of Polo jeans wit a matchin' Polo button down long sleeve and a Gucci sweat suit red and white stitchin'.

“Yo' my mans do ya do embroidery 'ere in da store.” She questioned. “Yeah me love, me can do it in de' store fo' 'er me also do de' airbrush 'ere tell me wut 'er want an me can get it done love."

"Aiight den let me grab wut I want done." Queenie snatched up 2 pair of matchin' fits fo' 'er and Cortez' to dress a like she thought wut could it hurt. She didn't know anyone in Jamaica except 'em, so wut da hell she thought. "Yo' my man put in red letters on both outfits. I want on da front of his shirt left corner embroider in small letters: Ride and Die in cursive on da back airbrush "My QUEEN. Now his jeans jus' da back pockets embroider King an down da back of each leg airbrush East St. Boogie in red only. An on da utter fit I need chu to do da same thing, but da back of dis shit airbrush "Da King" an far as da back pockets go put "Boss Queen" down da pants legs airbrush Chi-Town. Now how long will it take, an can I get 'em back today?" "Give me 2 hours love an me have it ready fo' 'er." "Aiight we gonna go shop some mo' an grab somethin' to eat an we'll be back my man."

"Yo' wuts da ticket on dat fam'? My bad maan wut do I owe ya?" "$200 dollars maan." Cortez' gave 'em da money an left out wit Queenie dey asked da driver where da shoe store was so dey could pick up some new kicks. "A coupla stores down on dis side maan. Do ya want me to drive de' dere maan?" Da reply he got was nah maan we are gonna walk an shop, but hold it down my man. Cortez' gave 'em a nutter $100 dollar bill jus' to stay put. Cortez' was mo' of a boot man, Queenie loved his swagg 'cus mainly it kinda reminded 'er of 'er own persona. She found some all suede B boots wit a clear gum bottom sole dat had caught 'er eye. "Baby wut size is it 10 ½?" "Yeah ma." He replied. On da jumper side Queenie didn't see not one pair of air force ones, so she jus' picked out a few pair of red, black, gray, and suede powder blue Nike boots. "Jus' a nigga size 6 ½ " She stated to no in particular, but Cortez' heard 'er an smiled. Puttin' a nutter $250 on da counter an picked up all of their shoppin' bags Cortez' asked; "Ya ready ma, lets go get somethin' to eat ain't chu hungry?"

"Yeah! I'm hungry, but lets jus' go to da bongo an I'll fix ya somethin', unless ya don't think ya can hold out fo' me to whip ya up somethin'." Cortez' gave 'er a suspicious look as to say whip me up wut. "At ease baby, it will be a meal dat chu will enjoy an it will be made wit much love, but it does take at least 45 minutes, so do chu think ya can hold out dat long daddy?" Queenie questioned. "Yeah ma I can wait long a nuff fo' ya to sho' me ya skills in da kitchen, but I can't say how much cookin' ya will get done afta' yo' ass put on one of does lil' sexy numbers we jus' got." Dey stopped an picked up their fits Queenie had airbrushed. Afta' lookin' 'em ova makin' sho' dey were to 'er standards she thank da man an left as da 2 walked to da limo Cortez' put his hand on da small of Queenie's back, waitin' fo' 'er to enter da car he told da driver to take 'em back to da bongo. "Yeah maan me on it me get chu dere." Da limousine driver was extra jolly 'cus he figured if he could keep dis couple 'round he would make plenty of money 'cus dey seemed to have much money to spend.

Chapter Twenty-One
"Surprises Come In Disguises"

"Yo' ma I gotta question fo' ya. How do ya feel 'bout kids, can ya see yo' self havin' any shawty?" Cortez' questioned jus' to see where Queenie's head was at on da subject. "Kids are cool I'm one myself. She said in a jokin' manner. "But of course on a serious note if ya askin' me how I feel 'bout havin' kids. Den I can tell ya dat I would love to have a son as long as it's by da right man and we are married. I neva wanta bring a kid into dis fucked up world wit out, 'em or 'er havin' 2 parents in da same home only 'cus it was da environment I grew up in, feelin' alone like I wasn't wanted by da man who knocked my moms up. Long as I can remember befo' Tez took me under 'em an raised me yeah I envision seein' my father takin' me to school, comin' to my basketball games even bein' at my track meets, but unfortunately I got now of dat. All I knew was my moms,and aunt gave my young ass cuzo' da responsibility of takin' care of me. Hell he was a baby 'em self, so it took away from his childhood also, but I commend cuz fo' wut he did and how he did it. Da nigga turned out to be a handsome, respectful young man_ Bein' cut off by Cortez'; "An he raised da beautifulest youngest entrepreneur, street QUEEN one has eva seen." Queenie couldn't help but to blush at da comment he gave 'er. "Thank Cortez'." "Seriously ma I am gonna be da one to marry ya an when da time permits itself I wanta have a family wit chu, but no mo' dan 2 kids. So tell me can ya handle dat or am I askin' to much shawty." "Nah it's not too much fo' me to handle, but let me turn 18 befo' we decide on anything baby we both still out in 'em streets an I wanta be out of da streets befo' I decide to bring our shawty's into dis cruel ass situation. Cortez' my children will be urns, so don't worry 'bout dat nigga. I'm not askin' chu to change or stop wut it is ya do. I jus' need to change my life style, but right now I'm in to deep, so dats why I ask ya to give me at least 2 mo' years on dat subject." "Aiight ma I can give ya dat one, but how do ya feel 'bout marriage at an early age?" He questioned expectin' along drawn out reason why she didn't want to get married, but Queenie took 'em by surprise wit 'er statement. "I told chu befo' age is jus' a number to me I respect chu fo' respectin' me. Yo' ass love me an my ass love chu wut else is dere? Da questioned is are chu ready fo' it, will yo' ass be able to handle it 'cus it's all or nothin' homeboy dere fo' is chu ready?" She asked. Cortez' stated; "I was gonna wait 'til my birthday_ as he kneel down on one knee takin' 'er hand he asked; Queenie Latrice Miles will ya marry me?" Placin' 'er hand ova 'er mouth as Cortez' placed a 10kt platinum diamond ring on 'er ring finger. She screamed yeah an as he stood up right Queenie jumped into his arms an he spun 'er 'round da bongo. "Thank ya ma yo' ass jus' made me da happiest man alive! Listen it's no presser, but next time dis year on my birthday I want us to get married. Is dat aiight wit chu? Chu will be 17 and Imma be 20, so ya good wit dat?" "We can do dat it'll give me time to lay out da weddin' I want seein' how

I don't know a damn thing 'bout no weddin'. Aye did chu tell ya homeboy 'bout dis?" She asked wit a smile. "Nah ma unfortunately I didn't, I wanted it to be a surprise not sayin' he woulda mention anything 'bout it, but I wanted chu to be da first to hear it from my mouth 'cus I needed to truly see if ya felt da same way I feel 'bout chu. Don't get it twisted shawty I know chu love me, I jus' didn't want to take da chance of ya bein' entice by anyone." "Ya should know I can't be enticed by anyone baby. I am my own person, I do wut I want, how I want and when I want, so fo' me to let any utter ma'fucka entice me to do anything, I would be a damn fool Cortez'." "Aiight ya right baby, so yo' are ya gonna call Tez or should I call an tell 'em?" "Yo' chu can call 'em afta' I feed chu daddy." She placed their plates on da table puttin' Cortez' at da head of da table as da King he was an took a seat on da side next to 'em. "Baby it smells good wut did chu fix yo' daddy?" Queenie replied; "I fixed some grilled lobster tails, broiled T-Bone steaks, baked potatoes wit butter sour cream fresh cheives fried bacon on top and fresh salad on da side. Ya got a bottle of Champagne dat was chillin' along wit 5 utters dat I found in a drawer of da refrigerator." "Ma thank ya I wouldn't ask fo' any mo' dan dis fo' my birthday. Yo' ass da best my Queen." Cortez' birthday came an went he was happy jus' bein' wit Queenie, he had no regrets of not kickin' it wit his homeboys like he has done every year spendin' time at da strip clubs pushin' up on different shawty poppin' bottles. Dis year was perfect fo' 'em he had Queenie his QUEEN which now was his fiance'. He was havin' da perfect time of his life wit 'er in Jamaica jus' layin' up. Queenie decided to call Tez, it has been 'bout 2 weeks since she heard from 'em an dat gave 'er an eerie feelin' dat mornin'. When she awakened Cortez' wasn't in bed beside 'er, getting out of bed she walked out outta da bedroom she smelled da aroma of waffles maple syrup, turkey bacon, grits and cheese eggs. In da kitchenette dere stood Cortez' rappin' he felt Queenie's presence, so he looked up an made eye contact wit 'er. "Wutsup baby, I fixed chu breakfast my QUEEN." Walkin' 'round da island he approached 'er an kissed 'er passionately to say he was excited dat she was woke. "Come sit and eat ma." Takin' 'er by da hand he escorted 'er to da table pullin' a seat out fo' 'er to sit down he den went an retrieved their breakfast plates. "'Ere ya go ma, I hope ya like it." Cortez' noticed she didn't look 'er self meanin' somethin' was wrong an dat made 'em puzzled. Turnin' away from his plate he took 'er hand into his an asked; "Ma wutsup, wuts good wit chu 'cus I can tell somethins' botherin' ya talk to me baby." "Baby I'm ready to go home. I can't explain how I'm feelin, but I gotta jet, I woke up wit an eerie feelin', I know we havin' a good time an I don't wanta ruin dat, but I know somethin' is wrong." "Aiight baby we can go, but let me call home first jus' to make sho' everybody and thing is straight an dat might ease yo' mind, so go pack an I'll call." Queenie walked towards da bedroom an Cortez' called out to get 'er attention; "Baby ya haven't ruined anything I had a wonderful time ma jus' da 2 of us fo' three weeks was off da chain fo' me, so if ya ready to leave it's cool baby. I can an will enjoy ya anywhere we go." Queenie smiled an turn back 'round an went to pack their things, while he was in da kitchenette makin' a call home. Ring, Ring, Ring, Ring! Tez finally picked up. "Hello." "Wutsup fam'?" Cortez' asked. "Shit homeboy." "Well tell me ain't shit wrong." Goin' straight into da conversation Tez said; "Slow down homeboy wuts good? 'Cus everything good on dis end, how y'all doin' in Jamaica?" He asked. "All is good 'ere, but baby girl woke up wit dis eerie feelin' dat she can't shake, so we finna jump on a plane an come home." "My nigga is ya sho' she's aiight, wut happen I thought she was havin' fun?" "Shit nothin' I know of dese last three weeks have been perfect bro,so I can't see wut would be wrong. She said dat she woke up feelin' dis way an she can't really explain da feelin', so she wanta come home. I jus' needed to call yo' ass an make sho' shit right wit da homestead, feel me?" Tez told 'em; "Yeah fam' all good on dis end, oh check it Chaos dat nigga gets to come home today. Dey pulled his tubes three days ago so he breathin' on his own an his mind is right, so he knows wut da fuck is goin' on, but he does have to learn how to walk again an it's gonna take awhile befo' he is completely back to normal. He'll have a therapist come out fo' as long as he needs an moms and auntie standin' on their word an let 'em stay wit 'em,so dey can take care of 'em. We gonna go in 'bout a hour to pick 'em up from da hospital, so call me when y'all get on da plane an I'll drop off da Chevy at da airport an set it up,so ya will have away home, 'cus I don't won't y'all waitin' to be picked up 'cus I know Imma have to help get his ass situated. Fam' call me doe jus' as soon as y'all touch down, so I can tell ya where to meet me at. Cuz I gotta get out 'ere doe an check on shit, so holla at me an tell my lil' nigga I love 'er an see 'er when she gets home." Dey hung up an Cortez' walked into da room an saw Queenie sittin' on da edge of da bed. He kneel down in front of 'er an asked wut was wrong? She replied; "I don't know can't actually figure it out, but I feel somethin' is not right." "Well baby I talk to Tez an everything back home is good he even said dat Chaos is comin' home today, so lets jump in da shower an get outta 'ere." Queenie had thoughts wit 'er self; "Could dat be it, could Chaos getting out of da hospital be givin' me dat eerie feelin'?" Queenie tried to let da thought go an jus' focus on Coretz' body in da shower, but not even his rippled body did da trick. Cortez' on da utter hand gotta woody from seein' da water rain down on 'er breast makin' 'er nipples hard da size of quarters. Closin' 'er eyes to relax from da thoughts she were havin' Cortez' softly bit 'er bottom lip an dis of course turned 'er on some wut den she felt Cortez' dick pokin' 'er jus' above da split of 'er pussy an da only thing she could do was moan. "Ma one last time in Jamaica please baby?" She didn't object an da only thing he heard was uh, huh an he knew he had to make it good. She mustard up a few words askin; "Chu want it 'ere in da shower daddy? I want it rough, fuck me wit everything chu got." Queenie wanted to get rid of da fucked up feelins' she was havin' an figured he could do exactly dat. Pushin' his head down towards 'er pulsatin' love box she told Cortez' to drink from 'er fountain. An he

did jus' dat once he was done he came up an Queenie pulled a acrobats move on 'em. She turned 'round bent ova an put 'er arms between 'er legs an raised 'er feet off da shower floor holdin' dat poise she said; “Now fuck me daddy.” Da girl had a very flexible body an bein' athletic workin' out made 'er very limber, but it was a shock fo' Cortez' he was sort of speechless, he had to ask 'em self; “Damn where da fuck she learn dis shit at? 'Cus I gotta freak fo' a woman an I'm lovin' da shit.” He snapped back an asked; “Baby girl wut utter stunts or tricks yo' ass got stored away?” “So ya like dat huh,well it's plenty mo' where dat come from now come on an pump hard nigga. Put it on my ass baby.”
“Oh ya gone scream fo' me ma?” She ignored da question he asked_Auuuugh! Tryin' to muffle da pain, but pleasure from da thrust of jus' da head of his nine inches in 'er anus made 'er want mo' of 'em. Cortez' said; “Yo' ma I want chu to scream baby chu want me to fuck ya in da ass den I need chu to scream.” As he pumped harder and harder Queenie wanted to holla,so loud she wouldn't allow 'er self to 'cus she wanted Cortez' to squirm an work hard fo' 'er,she didn't want 'em to think it was easy all da time. She was jus' fuckin' wit 'em it was a game a game dat pleas 'er. Although he knew da screams he wanted from 'er would come soon a nuff an dat would pleas 'em. “So ma ya not gonna scream huh? I got chu den.” Cortez' pulled on 'er body makin' 'er walk up da wall on 'er hands as he said; “'Ere ya go ma.” Bouncin' 'er up and down on all nine inches dat went inside of 'er asshole Queenie screamed so loud ya would have thought she was bein' murdered. “Mmmmm daddy it feels so good give it to me. Daddy watch me play wit my pussy.” Cortez' like da site of dat so he joined 'er wit his own fingers, as she started to remove 'er hand he told 'er; “Nah ma continue I'm finna come an I want chu to wit me.” “I got chu daddy pump faster as ya open up dat pussy. Ssssh_come on daddy I need chu to hit dat spot.” “My QUEEN mmmmm, I finna come ma.” An da 2 threw their heads back at da same time an felt da explosion of comin' together Cortez' gave 'em self double da pleasure as

all of Queenie's juices from 'er love box ran in da palm of his hand. "Ma I love da way yo' ass sex me chu make me feel like a King dats on top of da world. Shawty yo' pussy like dat first ma'fuckin' hit a fiend takes to get high." "So wut chu sayin' my pussy is addictive or dat yo' ass jus' a addict?" She broke out into laughter. "Dats funny to ya ma, 'cus a nigga addicted to yo' pussy or is it 'cus chu know yo' shit fye huh?" "It's no debate chu already convinced me fam' dat it's da bomb bomb digadity, so wut else is dere to say besides yo' addict ass has an addiction fo' yo' QUEEN'S addictive pussy." Queenie laughed as she tried to run out da shower, but befo' she could get away Cortez' smacked 'er ass cheek dat gave off a solid sound den he took off afta' 'er. He felt good knowin' dat he got his baby's mind off wut eva it was dat was botherin' 'er earlier. "Yo' ma da limo outside, I'll take da bags to da car while ya finish dressin' an den I'll come back in fo' ya an help lock up." "Aiight I'm 'bout finish Queenie decided to wear 'er new powder blue Nike sweat suit wit 'er same color suede Nike boots stadin' in a six foot body mirror she put on all 'er jewelry givin' 'er self a once ova to make sho' she was altogether. Cortez' walked in from outside an told 'er; "Ya look great ma, turn 'round. Shawty I can tell a nigga been layin' down da pipe right ma, 'cus yo' ass startin' to spread mo' like wild flowers." Queenie smiled an turned to look at 'er ass, but she didn't see wut he was gawked at 'cus 'er frame was tight. "Don't worry ma yo' ya ain't out of place shawty it looks good on ya, but I notice 'cus I pay attention to ya dats all. Chu ready ma?" "Uh huh_ Queenie put 10 stacks in 'er pocket dat he left on top of da dresser fo' 'er, but she felt half complete. She still missed one part of 'er attire an dat was nina, but she told 'er self dey would soon be reunited. "Baby befo' we leave Jamaica I wanta go to a gun store dat we seen on da strip in town, I need to cuff dat Uzi wit da hunnid 'round banana clip an ship it to da crib." Leavin' da bongo Queenie whispered in a low tone_ "We'll be back." Cortez' felt a chill go up his spine an he knew right den dat he had to get his baby back to Jamaica soon. Afta' she finished up 'er biz'ness in Jamaica dey got on da plane headed home an as soon as Queenie saw da archway she said; "Home sweet Home! We back in East St. Boogie baby." Queenie couldn't wait to land da three weeks seemed like an eternity specially been away from 'er cousin Tez. She had neva been apart from 'em so long maybe a coupla days, but three weeks was entirely to long away from da only nigga she trusted. Back on solid ground again da 2 retrieved their duffel bags as Cortez' carried dose she carried a duffel bag wit da money dat dey had as a carry-on. Afta' goin' threw da proper paper work to get da car Queenie told 'em; "Baby somethin' is not right dat eerie feelin' is back an it has me fucked up. Yo' call Tez an find out where he is I need to call a meetin'. If all is good since we been gone an everything is on da up an up ain't no way in hell I should be feelin' like dis at all somethin' ain't right." Cortez' said; "Shawty maybe it's jet lag dis time." She looked at 'em an said; "Baby don't patronize me." Givin' 'em a grimace look as to say nigga I'd outta fuck yo' ass up fo' even thinkin' dat shit let alone sayin' it. Seein' da look she gave 'em he jus' made da call as she demanded 'em to. "It's ringin' ma." "Hello wutsup family?" Tez asked. "Yo' cuz hold on." Cortez' handed his QUEEN da hitter. "Wutsup cuz she said an went straight into 'er conversation_ fam' where ya at 'cus we need to talk. I got dis fucked up feelin' an it's a eerie one dats tellin' me shit ain't correct it's somethin' wrong or goin' on wit my circle." "Lil' nigga wuts wrong 'cus everything 'ere has been goin' smooth as normal. Chu already know if it was anything out of da ordinary baby I woulda called ya, but all has been in order." "Cuz I'll neva doubt chu nah mean, but I always study, watch an analyzed every nigga/bitch dat has been 'round chu in yo' presents fam' an honestly if I wasn't certain shit woulda jus' slip threw da cracks, but don't take it wrong 'cus ain't no disrespect cuz it's not like ya not on yo' shit it's jus' lil' stuff ya don't pay attention to at all fam'." "Yeah lil' nigga yo' ass right dats where my lil' nigga always came in handy to keep me on my P's and Q's 'cus dats da type of shit chu stayed on. Ya

notice everything ma.” “Aiight call a meetin', so I can see if it's any glitches in our family circle an my word is bond if dere is a problem Imma let chu and Cortez' handle it how ya see fit my nigga.” Cortez' pleaded dat nothin' was wrong wit dis family circle 'cus dey had lost a nuff members already.
Tez told Queenie befo' he hung up; “Come to their parents house.” “Aiight cool nigga.” Cortez' had no clue of wut to say so he reached fo' Queenie's hand an said; “Baby it's gonna be aiight.” But he was shocked at da response she gave 'em back. “No da hell it won't be aiight 'til I'm fo' sho' no one in dis circle has bitched up on me an has become Ola out dis ma'fucka.” Cortez' smile faded away as his eyes turn back to da road. “Fuck how da hell does she do dat, she read my mind perfect.” He to had an eerie feelin' wash ova 'em dat made 'em look suspect. “Yo' baby go to moms dats where Tez at.” Fo' da next 2 blocks 'til dey turned da corner into da driveway behind Tez car she said nothin' Queenie jus' took in da scenery thinkin' to 'er self. Dey arrived an got out da car Cortez' was still amazed at his car how it worked off of his commands. Da 2 peeped da scene an both walked up da front stairs befo' she could open da door it swung open an Tez scooped Queenie off 'er feet. “Wutsup my lil' nigga?” twirlin' 'er 'round he missed 'er jus' as much as she missed 'em. “Damn it seemed like ya was gone fo' eva fam'.” Placin' 'er back on 'er feet he kissed 'er fo' head. “Shit I missed chu to cuz.” Cortez' told 'em; “Dats 'cus ya 2 ain't neva been apart it's like twins ya separate 'em an dey don't know wut to do.” Tez gave his homeboy a pound an embraced 'em as he said; “I missed seein' yo' face to nigga.” “Love ya to homeboy wuts good nigga?” Cortez' said. “Yo' where moms and auntie at an who dey got 'ere wit 'em holdin' shit down?” She asked Tez. “I got da lil' niggas Chris, Joc, Jo and lil' Man 'ere holdin' 'em down. I took Skip off 'cus I needed 'em to do da runs to Detroit an shit, but everybody's back dere in da den helpin' wit Chaos.” “So dey let 'em go huh?” “Cuz come on, don't act so enthused 'bout it smile lighten up baby girl. I know yo' ass will neva fo' get wut was done, but I ask fo' me jus'

let it be, put it behind chu aiight." "Aiight cuz only 'cus of chu we still family an I guess nothin' will eva change dat." Da three walked into da den ya would have thought dat Queenie was a superstar of some sort from da way da fellas called out to 'er. Dey were so happy to see 'er. "Wutsup boss glad chu back, we missed ya ma. How ya feelin' "Boss Queen" good to see ya back home shawty." Queenie nodded wit a smile; "Wutsup fellas, I hear y'all been holdin' it down an doin' wuts bein' asked of ya. I appreciate it big time." Lettin' 'em know dat da love is strong an she respects 'em fo' da loyalty dey bring to da circle. She told 'em; "Even doe dis 'ere is not in da job description dat chu fellas are use to, I know ya did it 'cus I'm yo' boss an ya got love fo' not jus' me, but da family which surrounds y'all." "Sho' ya right,but it's anything fo' ya ma. Wut eva chu need we got chu." Chris was a young handsome lil' nigga he had jus' turned 17an he looked at Queenie as his superior not as someone younger dan he was it wasn't da fact she was a girl, it was da thugg she had in 'er. Which meant to 'em all rolled up in one "Boss Queen" was a hood star an he knew as long as he played da game of 'ers right he to could live dat fabulous life as well. Queenie asked; "Do ya speak fo' everyone my nigga?" "Boss he can speak fo' us 4 dats ere' now. Jo spoke up an said_ Ma when ya met us out of da 11 of us we are da youngest 4 even if it maybe jus' by a coupla months or a year, we have a bond an chu can always find us in da same place at da same time an dats da way we met da rest of da entourage. Cortez' cut in he's tellin' da truth my QUEEN dats how Chuck an I found 'em together an dats how it's been since. Dey like a chain dey stay linked up. "Aiight we'll see if y'all done 'ere get cleaned up we gotta meetin' at da stash house in 'bout a hour." Queenie finally acknowledge 'er aunt Heather and 'er moms Liz. "Wutsup auntie, wutsup ma?" as she hugged 'em she said; "I see y'all got 'em up out da hospital huh?" Referrin' to Chaos like he was nothin' or he was in da room. "So da 2 of ya all good wit puttin' yo' lives on hold to take care of dis nigga 'til he gets better an fully recovers?" She felt bad 'cus of how da situation took place an damn near left 'em cripple, but couldn't sho' any sympathy once she got face to face wit 'em.

Chapter Twenty-Two
"Cut Throat Snitches Don't Get Stitches"

Compassion fo' dis nigga was no longer a feelin' she had fo' Chaos any mo'.

"Ma! Cortez' said wit a stern voice an everyone looked at 'em except Queenie_ "Will ya sho' some compassion or sympathy da man__ Bein' cut off by Chaos befo' he finished his sentence. "Yo' fam it's cool." Everyone den turned an looked at Chaos as he spoke. "She has every right to be on da out skirts wit me I betrayed a trust we had even doe it wasn't intentional baby girl I need fo' chu to believe me when I tell ya dat Queenie." She jus' stood dere an listen to wut Chaos had to say, but it didn't move 'er at all she jus' stared a hole straight through 'em. "Baby girl when I asked yo' mom and aunt not to tell ya and Tez dat da three of chu was kin it was 'cus I didn't want Lu to be scared off in away I would neva get to see 'em. Dats why dey jus' kept me updated on how ya three got along together 'cus see it's a lot y'all don't know 'bout me or dis family an I hate dat Lu ain't 'ere to find out who he is, but I feel it's time fo' chu lil' niggas to know wut time it is." "Mean to tell me y'all got mo' secrets chu holdin' on to? So wut since chu damn near met yo' maker ya feel da need to tell all now huh,an disrupt our lives. Dis ma'fuckan family is so dysfunctional an y'all sit an wonder why I do da shit I do, well listen to me good, so non of chu three will have to wonder why I'm tellin' ya dis. I know non of ya da only person in dis family I got is Tez da only nigga dat doesn't lie to me, from day one he has been my keeper wit no complaints or hesitation." Lookin' at Liz as she talked; "When chu so call didn't know wut to do wit me afta' da authorities didn't take me from chu afta' da incident in school happened, Tez stepped up teachin' me da best way he knew how hell he was a child 'em self. I'm pretty sho' he didn't want me 'round 'em an his friends all da time. Even Lu took to a likin' to me an come to find out he was my blood wit da same bloodline runnin' threw 'em. I said it once, but I'll say it again y'all robbed us of our own flesh of who we are an wut coulda been. Only if we knew halve da shit I know now."

"Yo' aunty don't think dat Imma make it easy fo' ya 'cus I practically lived at yo' crib an neva once did chu feel like ya shoulda told me anything since I was yo' favorite niece, hell I'm yo' only niece. Queenie was irate by da situation, but she continued to throw da questions at Heather waitin' fo' 'er to answer. "Oh! Wait or am I yo' only niece, 'cus fo' anyone 'ere dat doesn't know jet Lu wasn't yo' cuz he was yo' fuckin' nephew dats 'cus Chaos not y'all fuckin' cuz either he's ya fuckin' brother an he's da baby boy. Don't look so fuckin' surprise 'bout nothin' I'm sayin' 'cus da cats out da bag." Turnin' to Tez;

"So see cuz dey been holdin' lies an secrets to da chest like it's gold. Chu, Lu and me were all first cuzo's fam', but 'cus of yo' moms Lu's so call father and my moms non of us got to know who we really were cuz. But it's all good doe even doe we didn't get dat chance, Lu was family anyway an it's sad to say Lu mo' family to me dead dan da three of chu are alive." She turned 'er back on Liz, Heather and Chaos an told 'er crew to squad up an she walked out da house. "Yo' ride wit Cortez' and Tez."

She told da 4 youngans. "I'll meet up wit all at da stash house." "Yo' lil' nigga where ya goin'?" Tez called out afta' Queenie, but all he could hear was "Gotta" as she sprinted to da house. Queenie had three Uzi's shipped back same day delivery not knowin' when dey would make da delivery she made it to da crib jus' in time. When she shut da alarm off a UPS truck pulled up wit three long medium size boxes in his hands. "Hi I got three packages fo' a Ms. Stapleton is she 'round or could I get chu to sign fo' 'em?" "Yeah dats me ya can jus' set 'em down at da bottom of da stairs." She signed his board once he walked away Queenie opened da garage she hit da alarm fo' 'er Lexus dat was parked inside she put da three boxes inside da truck befo' goin' back in da house to search where Tez had put nina.

"THROWIN' BRICKS AT THE PENITENTIARY"

Findin' 'er nine underneath 'er pillow an 'er pump and AK in da corner of da closet she safely stored 'em in da comfort of a hidin' place only she knew of. Checkin' ova their home Queenie found all was as dey left it, so she jetted lockin' up she got into 'er ride a headed fo' da stash house. First she needed to ride threw da projects pass da house she purchased fo' Lu and Chaos. She had utter plans fo' dat spot goin' through 'er mind. 'Er word was bond she would take care of Chaos, but she knew dat he wouldn't be able to live by 'em self fo' long or again, so basically his pay dat he got from 'er would go to Heather and Liz to help take care of 'em since dey are his caregivers. Queenie told 'er self it's no since it jus' sittin' dere when it could be occupied 'cus 'er thoughts was she was in da biz'ness to make money not to lose it. Out loud; "Dats my second stash house right dere an I know jus' da lil' niggas to run it fo' me." Queenie walked in da stash house an noticed Cortez' and Tez went an purchase Krystal's fo' all of da fellas fo' their meetin'. "Jus' in time cuz we jus' walked in, so da food is still hot I got chu yo' usual baby girl." "Preciate it, but I'm good at da moment fam' yo' everybody take a seat at da table lets start dis meetin'." Queenie stared at each individual wit a blank expression showin' no emotions at all. "Now when we met I informed dis family circle I thought we all had a understandin'? Did or did I not warn each and everyone in da lil' interview dat if I was eva crossed I would deaden yo' ass, but I would send yo' ass out in style." Nodes were through out da room along wit raised eye brows as to say no one knew wut da hell was goin' on. All except one nigga his face expression neva changed. "Neva have I eva had a problem wit my biz'ness befo'. Wut is it, do y'all feel I'm dumb or jus' slow dat I wouldn't check up on my shit? Wut da fuck is it!? 'Cus family trust me I didn't get to where I am from bein' stupid. Imma very smart bitch an fo' does of ya who don't think so I'm always 2 steps ahead of da game nigga." By now she zoomed in on Skip eyes statin'; "I ended my fuckin' trip early all 'cus I woke up wit an eerie feelin' somethin' was wrong an I couldn't shake da shit, but neva will I ignore a bad feelin', so a call was made home. Tez said y'all was on point an deres no reason fo' me to questioned dis nigga 'cus I trust 'em wit my life. Neva da less he also taught me neva to trust anyone not even 'em, so afta' getting off da plane da fucked up feelin' I had came back ten times stronger. Neva second guessin' myself I actually had to stop an ask me wut da fuck did I do wrong 'cus I covered my tracks? Surveyin' every move I made in my head I found nothin' I did wrong 'til I made a nutter call. Still starin' a hole straight through Skip's cranium 'er voice stayed leveled, but everyone could hear da venom in it lettin' 'em know she meant biz'ness. "Yo' Chris." "Yeah boss?" As he walked close to 'er she told 'em out loud; "Go to my truck an bring in dose three boxes." She hit da alarm on 'er key chain. "Hurry I don't want chu to miss shit." Chris ran out an was back in 2 seconds wit da boxes. Neva breakin' 'er eye contact wit Skip she could see 'em swallow hard a vein in his neck was beatin' extra fast. "Now from da call I made I found out I did do somethin' wrong dat fucks wit my status an my credibility an dat fucks wit my pride nigga." Tez asked; "Wutsup, wuts goin' on baby girl?" "Well cuz it seems to be we have a bitch ass snitch in da circle, unfortunately one of our peeps got caught up wit 60 bricks on his way to make a drop and pickup. An in order fo' 'em to get cut loose guess wut he did da ma'fucka turned on me." Neva takin' 'er eyes off of Skip she could see fear in 'em. From my phone call Skip I hear ya told Ola a whole script on me. Lets see Imma QUEEN pin, da increments dat are made, da cars I've bought, dat I was da person who killed an murder da people at da Waffle House should I go on Skip? Fam' see wut chu fell to realize I'm da smartest bitch ya coulda eva met in ya life time. 'Cus even doe I hate da ma'fuckas wit a passion doesn't mean da ma'fuckas ain't on my payroll nigga. All ya had to do was let me know chu got caught up an I woulda taken care of it fo' ya. Why niggas feel da first options dey have is to run off at da fuckin' mouth to get 'em selves outta trouble beats da hell outta me." "So ma wut chu sayin' is ya fucked up now or wut?" Cortez' needed to know.

"Nah baby I'm cool, but dis nigga done fo' it was all a test an dis nigga failed big time. See my connect give my new runners a setup spill jus' to see how loyal dey are to me and 'em 'cus it's to much ridin' on dis fo' any fuck ups an ol' Skip 'ere fucked up. Dis nigga ain't loyal under presser at all family. Now Imma hold on to my word doe__ She told Skip an let my people handle it da way dey wanta." Queenie step back off Skip walked ova to Chris an took one of da boxes out of his hands, she placed da box on da table opened it an told Tez and Cortez' da utter 2 was fo' 'em. Den she pulled out a Uzi da entire room was shocked. "WOW! Oh shit dats sweet boss." As da fellas looked on she placed a hunnid 'round banana clip in an took a seat at da head of 'er table. "Now befo' our lil' session ends an we lose a nutter family member Imma be fair an give Skip a chance to plead his case. Befo' she could finish da sentence Skip tried to break out runnin', but Joc caught 'em in da jaw wit a left hook knockin' 'em back into da wall. Skip tried to gather his composure an steal on Chris, but unfortunately his utter three brothers rushed 'em as well. "Nigga try it." Yo'! Queenie called out . "My youngans chill he can't go no where family, he will soon be dismissed." Wavin' fo' da 4 to come sit she motioned fo' Tez and Cortez' to do wit 'em as dey pleas. Dey both pointed their Uzi's at Skip. "Hold on let me finish up first da number one ultimate philosophy I live by is death befo' dishonor fam'. Since I been in East St. Boogie 2 niggas in our family circle has been dishonest an very disloyal, but bein' lean as I was makes me feel like I showed a weakness. Youngans Imma give y'all a spot of yo' own da 4 of chu will run it together wit no fuck ups. I'm turnin' da spot I bought fo' Lu and Chaos into a nutter stash house, but I need to know right 'ere and now if y'all can handle dis? If ya don't think ya can speak now or fo' eva hold yo' peace family." "Yo' boss we can handle anything ya ask of us or put in our line of fye." "Boss if chu want us to run da spot chu won't regret it I can promise dat." Queenie stood up in a swift motion an asked; "Chu promise? Nigga don't promise me shit 'cus promises are made to be to be broken deres a prime example ova in da corner." She nodded at Cortez' and Tez givin' 'em a signal to fill Skip's body wit bullets an da room went silent givin' da sound of bullet shells hittin' da floor and walls. Queenie watched da faces of all 'er fellas in da room. "So is chu still willin' to make dat promise Chris?" She asked. Chris stated; "Boss I stand on my word if I don't know much I know a man is nothin' wit out his word. So yeah I can speak fo' me an my three brothers 'ere." Walkin' ova to Chris she stared 'em square in his eyes an told 'em; "I like chu lil' nigga, but if yo' ass fuck up on dis project 'ere I will personally kill all 4 of ya myself, startin' wit chu first fam',so make it ya biz'ness not to cross me. An dat goes fo' any one of ya keep it raw at all times an we can continue to eat together in peace as one. Dis house 'ere will be ran by Giz'mo and Stacks." Queenie placed da 2 together jus' 'cus dey are twins da only 2 real blood brothers in da clique. Dey have caramel skin, green eyes, medium build, low cut fades wit deep waves dat dey kept tight. Dey were 17 years old an da only way ya could tell da young men apart was from a scar Giz'mo wore across his left cheek. Queenie stated; "Same consequences apply fo' ya 2 as well we have rules in dese livin' quarters family. Dis 'ere is where ya lay ya heads, work, eat and shit cuz nothin' mo'. Don't bring yo' females 'ere to palay if ya wanta do dat go to their crib or get chu a room. Only people allowed at anyone of da stash houses are da niggas chu see befo' ya. Family! Yo' asses only conduct biz'ness in and outta 'ere do ya feel me? Now have I made myself clear a nuff? One last thing family if ya value yo' lives in anyway ya get in trouble in 'em streets remember y'all can come to me Tez or Cortez', it's jus' fare warnin'. An she said no mo'. 5 months had past by it was now March an everything had been runnin' smoothly a nutter year had come in wit no glitches she was still walkin' and breathin' on da face of earth. Trust and believe it even amazed 'er to have done all da bullshit she pulled off in da past year. Cortez' she yelled from upstairs to downstairs. "Yeah baby wutsup?" "Yo' Joc says da spot low, who at da warehouse?" Waitin' on an answer from Coretz'. "Baby I believe it's Flex and Tre'." "Aiight call Flex make sho' someone dere wit 'em first an if so tell 'em to run 4 bricks to da youngans, but if Tre' ain't dere call his ass tell 'em to get ova dere now an relieve Flex, so he can handle dat." Queenie live jus' down da block from 'er moms an hadn't spoken to 'er or anyone in da house fo' 7 months , only update she received on 'er moms an 'em was through Tez or Cortez' an dat was by force not choice. She would send Chaos no longer workin' pension to da house an see wut 'er mother may need threw utters. Cortez' and Tez both hated da way Queenie was actin' towards 'er moms, but neither one said anything to 'er 'bout da situation 'cus she was stubborn. Dey figured it would blow ova in due time. "Yo' homeboy wuts poppin' playboy?" Cortez' asked. "Yo' ass at yo' station, who do ya got on ya team?" "Yo' Tre' family." "Aiight cool da youngans need 4 dollars an Queenie needs ya to take it to 'em tell Tre' hold 'em down 'til ya return homeboy." Cortez' hung up an called Tez. Ring, Ring. "Wutsup my nigga?" Tez asked. "Shit cuz callin' to see wutup fo' today fam' can ya come out an play today wit yo' family?" He asked in a jokin' way Kandi not gonna trip is she?" Tez and Kandi had been together now close to a year, 'round da time Chaos came home is 'bout when Tez let 'er move in wit 'em. It started out as 2 teenagers in love like high school kids jus' kickin' it everyday. Unfortunately 'til Queenie returned home. Kandi turned straight she devil on Tez mo' of a bitch when Queenie returned from Jamaica as doe Queenie would be outta da picture fo' eva. Tez had no oblivious clue why Kandi's attitude had changed afta' three weeks an continued to get worse when eva he left da house or mentioned Queenie's name. Game was peeped once Queenie returned, Tez had invited 'er and Cortez' ova to his crib, so dey could catch up an have a few drinks. Queenie noticed den how tense and fidgety Kandi was she also notice how she would short talk 'er like she could careless of any conversation Queenie gave. Acknowledgin' dis made Queenie suspicious of Kandi on top of wut suspicion she already had 'bout 'er. Queenie didn't wanta crush 'er cousins heart since he seemed to be in love at least from da way he talk to Cortez' 'bout how she made 'em feel. Wit dat Queenie took to heart his feelin's an jus' decided to watch Kandi's every move. Neva one to fake da funk Queenie could no longer hold Kandi's hatred to 'er self, she felt Tez needed to know, so he would be aware of 'er next move. Ring. "Wutsup lil' nigga?" He asked. "Cuz wutup wit chu?" She asked. Befo' Tez could reply she went straight into wut needed to be said. "Look family I called fo' one reason to tell ya 'bout yo' girl Kandi. Yo' ass know I keeps it real wit chu of all people no matter wut, so let me bring somethin' to yo' attention den afta' I'm done chu can say or do wut chu want, aiight." "Aiight dats fare lil' nigga." "Yo' do ya remember when ya invited us ova fo' drinks, well dats when I peeped yo' girl eye ballin' me all reckless an short talkin' me like my convo was meaningless to 'er cuz. I also noticed how tensed up she gets when I'm 'round 'er family I don't have shit against yo' girl, but I got dis gut feelin' she doesn't like me in yo' presents. I know ya don't look at dat type of shit, but I'm finna sho' ya wut I see. Know I don't care how da next person feels or thinks 'bout me, but dis is ya girl an 'cus it's chu Imma look out fo' ya outta respect my nigga I will let chu handle it doe. 'Cus chu already know it ain't gonna be no mercy I get a hold to 'er fam'. I want y'all to come ova fo' dinner tonight 'bout 7 o'clock an I jus' want ya to watch 'er, from da time y'all walk through da front door. Jus' pay close attention to yo' bitches actions when she gets 'round me an da way she talks. Cuz it's not by coincidence dat y'all be havin' quarrel or dat she gets piss off when ya leave to be 'round me." "Aiight cuz we be dere she didn't have to work today, so it won't be a problem." In da kitchen Queenie threw down on da southern foods dat where fit fo' a King which Tez and Cortez' were to 'er. Queenie enjoyed cookin' an she let it be known. She didn't cook small jus' fo' 'er self an Cortez' when she cooked it was fo' 'er entire family circle. Dey were young so dey ate out, but she figure why should dey have to if she cooked a meal, why not let every one enjoy it. Queenie made sho' da youngans ate 'cus outta da 4 non of 'em could boil water, so she made sho' dey was da first ones she called or had food taken to their spot. Cortez' walked in da house yellin'; "Yo' shawty." "Wutsup baby I'm in da kitchen." He walked up behind Queenie an kissed da nap of 'er neck, forcin' 'er to turn 'round from da stove. "Nigga chu better watch it fo' we both be on da counter somewhere in a uncompromised position. Wutup doe baby." "Baby girl wut ya got cookin' in 'ere dat smells so good? My stomach touchin' my back." She replied; "Jus' a few of chu and Tez favorites dats all baby we got some fried pork chops, fried okra,turkey wings, mustard greens wit beef neck bones, cornbread (homemade) green beans white potatoes, sweet potatoes, baked macaroni and cheese,spaghetti, garlic bread and devil eggs." "Damn ma wuts da occasion ya cookin' like its a holiday." "Nah baby ya know how I get down I jus' cooked fo' everybody chu know I gotta feed my youngans__ She said jokingly_ Ya know dey can't boil water." Cortez' threw his head back in laughter. "Nah seriously I invited Tez an his girl ova fo' dinner." Queenie broke down da reason she invited 'em to Cortez'. "Baby ya sho' ya wanta do dis 'cus I don't need chu and Tez fallin' out ova dis braud." Queenie assured 'em dat 'er and Tez would neva fall short 'bout any bitch or nigga. "Baby dats my family a lot of things may transpire between us in our dysfunctional family, but neva have we let anyone come between us." Yeah baby, but dis is different homeboy is in love wit 'er it's like he tip toes 'round 'er to a certain extent. It's like he caters to 'er every need and wants instead of it bein' 50/50, but he seems to be cool wit it. Dats my homeboy we family, but I don't wanta cross any invisible lines dat I can't see by me tellin' 'em somethin' 'bout da situation an we fall out ova his braud selfish ass ways." "Well baby we gonna be jus' fine, so all I need chu to do is fall back an jus' peep how dis bitch acts when she gets 'ere. Dey should be 'ere in 'bout 15 minutes." Queenie fixed 9 Styrofoam carry trays fo' da fellas. "Yo' baby call da youngans an tell 'em to lock up an come get their food now while its hot. Flex and Tre' should still be at da warehouse tell 'em I said shut it down. An I will call Giz'mo and Stacks." As she went to make da call da doorbell rang. "Yo' come in cuz its open." "Yo' wut it be like ya reached Stacks." It was his voice mail. "Dis nigga an his fucked up v-mail she said huggin' Tez. Queenie spoke to da both 'em_ "How ya doin' Kandi?" Tez turned towards Kandi wit a smile to see 'er face expression. "Hi how y'all doin'?" Cortez' entered da room. "Wutsup wuts good wit chu two?" He asked. "Fam' y'all wanta drink befo' we eat?" He asked walkin' behind da tropical fish tank bar Queenie had placed in da den fo' 'em. "Yo' cuz I'll take a Hen on ice, baby chu want somethin' to drink?" Tez asked as dey walked to da den to be seated fo' dinner." Tez cuz call Giz'mo and Stacks tell 'em come get their food." "Ma dis spread looks delicious." He told Queenie as he waited fo' someone to pickup da line. Ring. "Yo' wutsup family?" Giz'mo questioned.

"Ain't nothin' family listen Queenie said lock up an come through an get y'all trays." "Oh! Shit boss cooked, hell yeah we on da way fam' thanks."

Chapter Twenty-Three
"Real Recognize Real"

"Y'all ready to eat?" Queenie asked. As da quad ate Queenie politely started up a simple conversation askin' Kandi how did she like livin' in da neighborhood makin' a slight joke she asked was 'er an 'er mother-in-law getting acquainted jet? She was speakin' of Tez's mother. Kandi replied wit a bit of sarcasm in 'er voice. "Da neighborhood is fine an I don't have a mother-in-law jet, but far as me getting to know Tez mother no I haven't." Queenie wanted to snap 'er neck, but she stayed cool 'bout da way she answered. Da doorbell chime dan Queenie excused 'er self fo' a second. Thinkin' of 'er next question fo' Kandi as she opened da door fo' Chris, Lil' Man, Jo, Joc, Flex and Tre' she embraced 'em all as dey said_ "Wutup Boss?" in unison's "Y'all know wut it is, gotta keep my family fed. Y'all know where its at on da counter in carry-out trays in case ya wanta leave wit it, but y'all mo' dan welcome to stay 'ere an eat.” Chris said; “We right 'ere boss.” Walkin' to da den dey all spoke to Cortez' and Tez givin' 'em dap an embracin' one a nutter. “Wut up fam', how is shit everything cool?” “Boss!” Chris called out; “Ma, we got dat earlier, but it was only a dollar left when we jetted to come 'ere.” Queenie said I__ Bein' cut off by Kandi wit; “Why do y'all call 'er boss or ma? Dats so stupid hell she's younger dan any of us in dis room.” Tez was able to get out yo' befo' Queenie said; “Nah, cuz hold on. Yo' chu finish Kandi or do ya have somethin' else on yo' chest?” Queenie asked. “As a matter of fact I do have somethin' else to say. I know Tez and chu are cousins, he's my man an I'm tired of every time chu say do somethin' he's jumpin' right on it an he always has yo' ass up under 'em like y'all fuckin' instead of me fuckin' 'em.”Queenie looked at Tez wit a smirk on 'er face, but Tez was piss at wut Kandi had jus' said. Tez thought to 'em self dat she was half way out da door wit dat last statement 'cus he couldn't believe she felt dat way. Out of all da conversation da 2 had he neva seen any signs of dis. He told 'em self at dat point; “Dat no bitch was worth his happiness, befo' she came along he was good at wut he did an whom he did it wit.” Tez sat back an gave Queenie a look as to say get 'er ass cuz handle yo' biz'ness Tez nodded an threw his hands in da air, but Queenie fell back an gave Chris da chance to roast 'er. Queenie said; “Go head baby boy.” Chris told Kandi_ “Dis 'ere is my boss an when we call 'er ma it's givin' 'er respect from da heart. Jus' like when a nigga calls yo' ass ma it's outta respect givin' ya props 'cus chu could as well be called bitch from da way chu jus' spoke up in 'ere an tellin' me dat I was stupid, but since I got love fo' my nigga 'ere ya gotta pass.” Queenie told Kandi as she stared a hole through 'er. “First off I think ya sick fo' even havin' thoughts of me an my cuz 'ere getting down wit one a nutter. I knew it was somethin' wit yo' bogus ass da night at da club, but 'cus of my family 'ere I fell back jus' so I could watch yo' fake phony bogus ass. Trust and believe my age has not a damn thing to do wit anything dat goes on in my life bitch. I'm older in da mind dan yo' ass will eva be an let me tell ya why. 'Cus any smart ma'fucka which ya not would not be up in my fuckin' crib talkin' shit." Cortez' saw da look on his girls face an said; "Nah, baby." "Oh I'm cool baby." Chris stood in front of his boss wit out touchin' 'er he told Cortez'; "I got 'er family." She pointed 'er finger an said; "Bitch dis nigga 'ere is my family always my fuckin' blood runs through his veins an vise-a-verse. Bitch I'm 'ere to let chu know dis man 'ere chu can neva tear us apart. Bitch he'll slit yo' throat befo' even havin' thoughts 'bout slittin' mines." Kandi jumped to 'er feet_ "Who da fuck ya callin' bitch?" Move Chris Queenie pushed 'em to da side wit 'er arm. She grabbed Kandi by da neck wit jus' one hand an da utter hand she snatched up Kandi's arm an twisted it behind 'er back. "Listen bitch I tried to get along wit chu even doe I don't fuck wit bitches, but now I see it's jus' jealousy wit chu, a sick jealousy." Kandi grasp fo' air as 'er feet left da floor an Queenie's strong ass got angrier by da minute. No one said anything everyone in da room was in a awe state at da whole situation. "Bitch ya don't have to like me, but chu will respect me an da man chu wit is my family whether chu wit 'em or not. I feel he can do much better dan chu anyway, but I'm not in da biz'ness of pickin' his relationships fo' 'em. But I'll tell ya dis I fuck bitches up fo' fuckin' ova mines. Now long as he's happy I'm cool." "Queenie let 'er neck go."Kandi drop to da floor coughin' out of control an hodlin' 'er neck tryin' to catch 'er breath as she heard Queenie's last words: "Bitch let dat be yo' last warnin' utter wise I will treat yo' life next go 'round." Kandi said not a nutter word she looked at Tez an walked out da door wit tears in 'er eyes. "Boss ya ruthless ma." Queenie asked wit a smile "Yo' anyone fo' dessert? We got sweet potato pie and German chocolate cake." Cortez' followed his QUEEN into da kitchen_ "Ma ya good 'cus I really thought chu was gonna kill 'er," "Nah I jus' needed to let 'er know where da fuck she was an who da fuck she was talkin' to. I'm not 'er home girl, but I know she thinkin' 'bout dat shit." Tez walked into da kitchen he knew Queenie didn't apologize fo' shit she did, but he wasn't expectin' one either 'cus he knew she didn't care one way or da utter. “My bad cuz, I didn't wanta fuck up yo' household, so maybe its still a good chance y'all can work it out. Cuz trust and believe I want chu to be happy an if Kandi is who makes ya complete so be it, jus' know I'm behind chu all da way fam', but jus' don't expect us to be cordial wit one utter 'cus afta' tonight dat bitch hates my guts cuz.” “Shawty don't even trip dat shit dere is done. I was practically tired of 'er ass anyway baby girl, I was jus' tryin' not to hurt 'er feelins'. But chu right I didn't know or pay attention dat she felt dat way.” Queenie said; “Cuz chu know I don't give no fuck 'bout how no bitch feels 'bout me an no nigga fo' dat matter. I got no love fo' 'er fam' my love is fo' yo' ass. So I do wanta apologize fo' steppin' on yo' shit, now whether ya stay wit 'er is on chu cuz. I'll stand behind chu always on wut eva chu decide, but I had to let chu know how she wasn't keepin' it real, it jus' wasn't somethin' I could know an not tell ya fam'.” “Yo' boss!” Chris yelled out walkin' towards da kitchen. “Ma chu good?” He asked as he gave Tez and Cortez' love. Chris looked up to Queenie as his protector. “Ma ya good we thought ya was gonna kill 'er. When ya lifted 'er up an 'er feet started danglin' seriously I knew she was outta dere, but I know why ya didn't fuck 'er up like dat 'cus of family 'ere.” Speakin' of Tez, Chris said; “Family no disrespect, but yo' girl don't know 'er place.” Tryin' to make light of the situation, no one knew dat Kandi was plottin' fo' revenge. It wasn't 5 minutes afta' Giz'mo and Stacks walked in bein' updated on da previous shit dat jus' took place minutes befo' dey arrived is when a loud crashin' of glass came thrushin' to da floor. Everyone ducked an pulled out their burners, a brick slid half way across da hard wood floors wit a note attached landin' by lil' Man's leg. “Yo' boss 'eres a note.” Dey passed it to Queenie, but Cortez' read it first out loud bitch ya fucked wit da wrong one ya dead. Furious at dis point not sayin' a word Queenie slid backwards on da floor an pushed da refrigerator to da side wit force. On da side of it was a hidden compartment she tapped 5 times an a panel fell off an she retrieved a sawed off. Da fellas looked on in awe 'cus who would eva think of dat shit. Jumpin' up from da floor she dashed fo' da door wit Tez, Cortez', Chris an da rest in tow bullets ricochet da front of da house. Tez yelled; "Down." Queenie saw a bullet whisk pass Cortez' body an landed in da aquarium bar, fish and water flooded da den. Queenie thought to 'er self_ "Dis bitch is tryin' me 'ere she tryin' to get at me an I got my family in dis ma'fucka dis bitch has lost 'er fuckin' mind." "Yo! Dats a .380 dat bitch is shootin' fam' where da fuck she get dat fam'?" Tez questioned out loud. Queenie said; "Count 'em shots, fuck 'er." She stood up snatchin' da door open blastin' Boom! Boom! Queenie jumped off da porch runnin' to da middle of da street she pumped again as she seen da tail lights of Kandi's car. Da crew ran out to make sho' Queenie was aiight. "Baby girl, ma, Ueenie, boss ya aiight, ya good?" Dey all asked. "Cool dat bitch jus' signed 'er death certificate she shoot up my place wit my family in it. Dis bitch coulda hit either one of chu." Queenie looked at Tez wit a blank look in 'er eyes statin'; "Dis one is mines fam'." Ring, Ring, Ring! Cortez' answered his hitter, "Hello!" "Yo' I hear sirens, somebody called Ola." Dey all ran fo' da house_ "Wait fam' its a ambulance." Cortez'! Liz screamed from da utter end_ "Somebody shot threw da house_she cried hysterically_ Lookin' down da street Cortez' shouted; "Yo'! Dey at moms and aunties house." "Wheres Tez, Heathers been hit." "Yo' Tez" Cortez' called out as he dropped his hitter an took off runnin'_Heather's been hit fam'." Dey all took off behind 'em towards Liz and Heather's crib tears streamed down Tez face as he feared da worst his moms had been shot. Not givin' a damn 'bout nothin' at dat point, but to see his mother dey all ran pass Ola an a second set of paramedics dat arrived to only be stopped in his tracks to find his mother unconscious on da floor wit a bloody hole to da abdomen. Paramedics worked on 'er tryin' to help 'er regain consciousness placin' tubes in 'er mouth to help 'er breathe wit IV's. Tez cried uncontrollably wit

Queenie by his side she wrapped 'er arms 'round his waist squeezin' tight screamin' "No,no,no,no,no, not again God don't take 'er please let 'er live." Tez held 'er tight an kissed da top of 'er head. Da paramedics put Heather on a stretcher an rushed 'er out da door an put 'er in da ambulance. "Yo' wut hospital she goin' to?" Cortez' asked. A paramedic said ST. Joseph's Hospital. Liz grabbed 'er purse an road wit 'er in da ambulance. Queenie had pulled 'er self together an told Tez; "Cuz chu go wit auntie an give me dis." Snatchin' his burner out of his waistline. "Now go we on our way." At da hospital dey were on stand by fo' Heather to arrive so she could go straight to surgery. Da bullet had tore through her intestines an she was in surgery fo' 5 hours befo' anyone came out to give da family an update on how Heather was doin'. Once Queenie heard da news of 'er aunt pullin' threw da surgery okay, but dey had 'er heavily sedated an da next 24 hours will be critical. Afta' dat been heard Queenie eased out of da hospital doors getting in 'er truck she left da hospital in search of Kandi. Returnin' to da block first where it took place she went into 'er house an grabbed 'er nine, puttin' it in 'er waistline she also grabbed da Uzi and AK47 an walked out da house like she was starin' in "Rambo" or some shit. Thoughts filled 'er head of all da things dat have happen. She realize everything dat has happen from Lu and Chuck up 'til 'er family circle to 'er aunt Heather has been all 'er fault. An even doe she hasn't regretted anything up 'til dis point in 'er life Queenie felt da guilt and remorse fo' wut had happen to 'er aunt. Tears rolled down 'er face an she could no longer muffle 'er cries. Sittin' in da driveway she screamed beatin' and shakin' da steerin' wheel out of anger furious, frustration,hurt da pain in 'er heart ran so deep it blurred 'er vision. Queenie anguished all she could take now was time fo' 'er to give some of da pain back an neva da less Kandi was 'bout to feel da wrath of how she felt. Back at da hospital everyone was an emotional wreck. Liz was not tryin' to loose a nutter siblin' specially Heather. Da 2 had such a close bond to be sisters 'cus usually sisters couldn't stand one a nutter, but dese 2 were thicker dan thieves. Liz said a silent prayer beggin' God to watch ova 'er sister an to let 'er pull through dis ordeal. Tez needed his moms to pull through dis she was all he had an Heather was his heart, his world. He knew if she didn't make it it would be curtains fo' 'em. He would be loopy fo' da rest of his life. Cortez' and Liz tried to comfort Tez helpin' 'em get 'em self together an when he realized da picture 'round da room was outta sink he sucked his tears back an ran his hand cross his face. "Yo'! My nigga where is Queenie questionin' everyone particularly. Chris ran outside, runnin' back in from da parkin' lot. "Yo' fam' boss truck gone." "Dammitt!!" Cortez' and Tez sang in unison's. "Fuck! Cuz stay 'ere wit yo' aunt make sho' yo' moms good." Givin' Tez an embrace an Liz a kiss on da forehead lookin' at 'er weary face he told 'er; "Ma don't worry we'll find 'er." Cortez' took charge in a desperate need of findin' his fiancee'. "Yo' squad up." Tez yelled out to Flex_ "Yo' family leave me yo' hitter." "No doubt fam'." Flex left his hitter wit Tez, so he could stay in contact wit Cortez' on his search fo' Queenie. It was no secret why Queenie was not at da hospital any mo' an Tez knew exactly how his lil' nigga would get down. He knew his lil' cousin all to well, so he asked his aunt; "Auntie can chu handle bein' 'ere alone? I need to be 'ere, but I gotta find__Liz said "Shhhh baby go find yo' cousin an bring 'er back safe please, I'll take care of my sister." Tez gave Liz da number to Flex hitter. "Auntie call me if anything changes befo' I can get back 'ere." "I will, now go baby." Liz told 'em. Kandi had no idea dat she damn near killed Tez's mother when she shot through da picture window of Tez and Queenie parents home. She even figured dat she would not be found either since she had no plans on goin' back to da crib she shared wit Tez. Kandi was goofy 'cus she went out to a club called "Home" in East St. Boogie further out west. Who knew which way da wheels spent in Kandi's head or wut she thought 'bout, but it was definitely not 'bout wut she done to Queenie dats fo' sho'. Kandi walked into da club as if she hadn't done anything 2 hours prior.

"THROWIN' BRICKS AT THE PENITENTIARY"

Queenie pulled 'er self together da excruciatin' pain in 'er heart and soul turned into agonizin' hatred fo' Kandi dat made da heart in 'er chest turn into a iceberg. "I will find chu bitch." Queenie turned every block dere was ridin' down da strip lookin' fo a new purple Chevy wit gold trim an 17" Datins. She hit every club from da south to west side Queenie made a vow to 'er self she wouldn't rest 'til she found da braud an she was dead. While Queenie looked fo' Kandi da rest of da crew looked fo' 'er. Tez called Cortez'. "Wut up fam'?" "Yo' chu ain't found 'er jet fam'?" "Nah, cuz we searched da south side we gonna ride out west an look out dere." "Yo' where ya at dis moment?" Tez asked. "Finna drop Lil' Man and Joc off at da house to help out Chaos 'til we know wut da fuck goin' on." "Cool! Imma block away Imma jump in wit chu." "Wut!" Was wut Tez heard befo' he hung up da phone. Da loud screechin' of tires were all could be heard as Tez turned da corner he seem to be on 2 wheels pullin' into da driveway. Door open Tez command jumpin' he gave a command fo' da door to close. Cortez' pulled out like a bat outta hell. "Homeboy wutsup I thought chu was gonna chill at da hospital wit moms." Cortez' questioned. "Nigga I got faith moms gonna be good my aunt is wit 'er, my baby is out 'ere homeboy an we both know wut she's capable of doin' fam',so I'll be truly be fucked up if anything happens to 'er." Tez pounded his fist in his palm_ "I shoulda neva let dis bitch in my world." "Cuz jus' pray we find shawty befo' she finds Kandi." Queenie spotted Kandi's car in da parkin' lot of club "Home". Queenie pulled in an parked in a far corner of da lot by da back door of da clubs exit. She placed da AK and Uzi on da back seat since da spot was dark no one would be able to see inside. Queenie put nina in da small of 'er back an put on a black hoodie an sleeveless red vest ova it. She walked to da front of da buildin' where dere was sort of a line dat she by pass. Approached by da bouncer; "Wutsup lil' mama?" He asked. Queenie said nothin', but pulled out $400 dollars an placed it in his hand an in ear shot she told 'em; "Let me threw." He looked at his hand an stepped to da side to let 'er pass. "Ya got it lil' mama." He placed da money in his inside jacket pocket. "Yo' Tez, da truck ova dere family." "Where?" "At da club Home cuz." Cortez' bust a U-turn, but inside da club Queenie spotted Kandi on da dance floor an da chaos dat was 'bout to explode da club was not ready fo'. Queenie pulled 'er hood on 'er head wit da strobe lights it was hard to see, which made it convent fo' Queenie as she pulled nina from 'er back. She walked up to Kandi on da dance floor dancin' wit some nigga an as she turned 'round to drop it low she caught a smack from da handle of Queenie's burner. "Come on bitch!" Queenie grabbed Kandi by 'er hair an drug 'er towards da door. "Wut da fu__ Queenie raised up nina in dudes face an screamed; "Wut nigga try me." Kandi struggled tryin' 'er best to get free from Queenie's grip. Queenie had no remorse fo' human life at dat moment specially Kandi's. She slung 'er into da street, but out of 'er peripheral vision she saw a nigga runnin' up on 'er. She turned aimed an fired a warnin' shot. Kandi tried to gain 'er composure an make a break fo' it, but Queenie thought better of an did a 'round house on Kandi. "Bitch where chu goin' yo' ass jus' tried to kill me an my family oh ya gonna take dis ass beaten." Queenie fell into a trans state as swung left,right,left,right. "Ma'fucka chu put my aunt in da hospital fightin' fo' 'er life. 'Ere I am Kandi kill me bitch." Queenie demanded as she smash in da side of 'er face wit da gun. Cortez' slammed on breaks once dey spotted Queenie in da middle of da street stompin' Kandi a new asshole. He almost fo' got to put da car in park da 4 jumped out so fast. Cortez', Chris, Tez and Jo took off runnin' up da block as dey called out fo' Queenie to stop. "Boss!" Chris yelled hearin' sirens in da back ground nearin' quickly. "Ola ma lets go Ola's comin' boss." Queenie feelin' dat dis beatin' was not adequate a nuff she wasn't coherent to anything or anyone 'round 'er 'er conscience told 'er to shoot an dat's exactly wut she did. Queenie unloaded every bullet left in 'er nine into Kandi in da mist of Ola turnin' da corner. Chris made it to Queenie first snatched da burner from his boss hand an kept on runnin' non stop. Tez and Cortez' noticed it was a dead body riddle full of holes an a gang of witness an baby girl standin' ova da body. Tez snatched Queenie up befo' Ola got up on da scene he prayed dat dey could blend in wit da rest of da crowd , but he knew in da back of his mind dat dere would be a snitch somewhere in da crowd. Ola questioned everyone dat dey thought coulda seen anything to help 'em do their job fo' 'em. Fortunately no one gave any info up. Tez still hadn't brought Queenie out of 'er trans jet. Dey didn't want to move 'er jus' jet 'cus dey didn't wanta look suspect wit da 4 of 'em standin' along da wire fence dey disguise Queenie jus' to be upset from seein' da young lady laid out on da ground dead. Ola started clearin' out everyone at da club. Chu 4 lets go move it, we need to clear dis area fo' da paramedics can get in 'ere. Tez walked Queenie to 'er truck tryin' to pull 'er out of it. "Yo' fam' well met chu three block up." Cortez' and Jo got back in his ride an Cortez' called Chris hitter. Ring,Ring,Ring. No answer. Chris ducked off into a 7-eleven an called Cortez' back. "Wut up family?" "Yo' Imma 'bout 5 blocks up my nigga at da 7-eleven on Walhbash Ave. homeboy." "Hang tight lil' nigga I'm on my way." Hangin' up he called Tez. "Fam' has she come out of it jet bro?" "Nah, fam'." "Aiight listen Chris 5 blocks from 'ere at 7-eleven, so go dere an we gonna see wuts wit 'er." Tez talked to Queenie as he drove; "Baby girl I know ya somewhere in dere I need chu to come out of hiddin' baby girl. I'm not mad at chu fo' wut ya did it's all good I know ya did wut chu felt was right fo' ya family an I'll neva take dat away from ya lil' nigga. I'm jus' glad chu aiight." He squeezed 'er hand an called out; "Ueenie please lil' nigga snap out of it, I need chu to help me get through dis wit da ol' girl. Jus' then a tear rolled down Queenie's cheek some wut snappin' 'er out of 'er trans. Pullin' up at da spot dey were meetin' Cortez' at he parked an looked at his lil' cousin. "Baby girl is chu wit me?" He asked. "Yeah fam' I'm wit chu." "Baby girl I'm glad chu 'ere." "Wut happen cuz?" She asked as Cortez' snatched da door open. "Ma is yo' ass aiight?" Wipin' tears from 'er face. Queenie told 'em;

"THROWIN' BRICKS AT THE PENITENTIARY"

"I need to see my auntie an if y'all 'ere wit me who's wit 'er?" "Yo' moms wit 'er at da hospital."Cortez' told 'er. "Look into his eyes she said; "Take me to da hospital to see my aunt." She was so adamant 'bout seein' 'er aunt Heather, Cortez' told Chris to drive his car as he hopped in da back. "Fam' pull ova to my car so I can command da bitch." Chris and Jo ran to da car an Tez pulled up an spoke fo' da doors to open and close. "QUEEN start, music QUEEN an da Chevy started an da radio came on. "Follow us youngans." On da ride to da hospital Queenie need answers she told 'em only thing she remember was bein' at da hospital 'cus 'er aunt was shot. Dey ran everything down from dinner to 'er sneakin' out da hospital an wut dey saw once dey got to da club. Queenie looked at wit a curious look on 'er face. "Cuz tell me it ain't so tell me dat bitch wasn't at da club yo'." "Oh shit baby. Fam' we gotta go to yo' house first cuz." "Wutsup?" "Baby gotta Uzi and AK on da seat fam'." Afta' droppin' da guns off dey headed to da hospital where Liz was sittin' in da room wit Heather watchin' 'er breathe. Heather had went unconscious twice, but each time she came back out of it. Now she was restin' comfortable wit da morphine dey were givin' 'er. Makin' it to da hospital Queenie had an eerie feelin' dat made 'er stomach feel like somethin' was crawlin' inside of it. "Its somethin' wrong cuz." Queenie told Tez as she looked back at Cortez'. "Wut, wut is it baby?" "Yo' my gut tellin' me shit ain't right." Jumpin' out da truck Queenie ran towards da hospital doors wit Tez, Cortez', Chris and Jo behind 'er. Queenie told 'er self right 'cus Ola seen da tapes from da club surveillance cameras dat caught Queenie in action an dey were on their way to apprehend 'er. At da nurses station Queenie demanded to see 'er aunt. "Wut room is Heather Miles in ma'am?" Da patient is in ICU at da moment. Smakin' da desk wit 'er hand_ "Wut fuckin' room is she in!" 21-C da nurse said nervously an Queenie took off down da hallway. ICU was at da end of da hall off to da right. "We'll be right 'ere family." Chris yelled out to Tez. Finally makin' it to 21-C Queenie eased da door open an dey walked in. Liz was,so happy and relieved dat 'er child was unharmed she ran to Queenie. "Baby girl momma's so glad ya aiight." "Ma I can't breath." "How is she auntie?" Tez asked as Queenie walked away from Liz to be by 'er aunts side. "We lost 'er twice 'bout 2 ½ hours ago, but dey bought 'er back an she's bein' sleepin' since. She's heavily medicated right now,so she can be comfortable. She was woke fo' awhile 'bout 30 minutes ago. Da doctor said constantly talk to 'er like ya would wit a patient dats in a coma."

Chapter Twenty-Four
"I Am Da Devils Child Who Open Da Gates To Hell"

Queenie started to cry_ "Auntie I don't know if chu can hear me or not, but know I love ya an I neva meant fo' any of dis to happen chu or moms not even Chaos or Lu. Holdin' Heather's hand she told 'er; "Its 'cus of me all dis has happened." Heather eyes opened as she told Queenie; "Baby girl nothin' chu do is yo' fault. Yo' mind not bein' right ain't yo' fault.""But auntie I jus' killed da girl dat shot chu." Liz clutched 'er chest like she could not breath air any mo'. "Sit down auntie." Tez told 'er helpin' 'er to a chair an Queenie finished; "Da sad part 'bout it auntie I feel no remorse fo' doin' wut I did, but dis time somethin' is different 'cus as I'm standin' tellin' chu dis my body has an eerie feelin' lettin' me know somethin' is wrong an I damn near snapped on dese 2 to get 'ere. An dis feelin' is growin' stronger by da minute." Tez heard sirens of squad cars she knew right den she would see da inside of a prison. "Auntie I love ya I need fo' chu to get better fo' me." She started talkin' super fast tryin' to get everything out she needed to say, she hugged each an everyone of 'em. "Ma my combo da same ya gonna have to use it 'cus I know dese people comin' fo' me." Queenie knew it was long ova due. "Tez cuz I love ya fam' get Mr. D. down 'ere asap. She pulled back to look in Tez eyes_ "Nigga I kept my word I'm not goin' out in a blaze of glory, word is bond, but tell Mr. D. to get me outta dis cuz."

"THROWIN' BRICKS AT THE PENITENTIARY"

Kissin' 'er on da fo' head he said; "Don't worry lil' nigga I'm on top of it." Cortez' grabbed Queenie an hugged 'er an whispered; "Baby I love yo' ass an we will get through dis chu comin' home shawty den we gonna walk down dat isle baby." "I love chu Cortez'." Chris and Jo ran full speed to ICU yellin "Yo' boss Ola on da way, we dipped when we heard 'em pigs at da nurse desk askin' if Queenie Miles been up 'ere to visit Heather Miles." Queenie hugged 'er moms "I love ya take care of yo' sister and brother." Lettin' go of Liz she embraced Jo den Chris in ear shot she said I appreciate chu youngan chu a real nigga." Queenie pulled away an tossed 'er nine to Liz. "Ma put dat in yo' purse I don't need 'em rushin' in 'ere an up settin' auntie she's my heart." Openin' da door Queenie made it three steps down da hallway wit 'er family in tow. It seemed like all of da Ola's in East St. Boogie had their guns drawn on 'er. "Turn 'round put yo' hands on back da back of yo' head. Get down on da ground on yo' knees." Dey shouted. Queenie complied, slowly she turned wit a grimace look on 'er face dat seemed to say y'all luck I gave my word utter wise I would take dese punk ma'fuckas wit me. As she got on 'er knee's Queenie's eyes neva left 'er families presences 'til Ola grabbed 'er wrist cuffin' 'er as da officer kicked 'er in da back forcin' 'er to lye down. "Yo' all dat ain't necessary is it?" Cortez' asked. "She's not resistin' arrest!" Tez yelled. As 'er rights were bein' read a nutter officer pull a picture from his pocket an pointed his finger at Chris. "Chris Toy chu under arrest turn 'round an put yo' hands behind yo' back." Chris assumed da position an Liz questioned; "Wut are dey bein' arrested fo'?" Ma'am who is chu da Chief of police asked? "I'm Liz Miles their mother. Now wut are ya arrestin' 'em fo'?" "Ms. Miles 'ere fo' murder an Mr. Toy interference of a crime scene takin' a muder weapon from da scene." Da officer snatched Queenie off da floor by 'er cuffs beside a um-mm dey heard she said not a word. Holdin' eye contact wit Tez she grinned showin' Tez dat famous dimple of 'ers to let 'em know she's good dat dey couldn't hold 'er down. Queenie looked at Lil' Chris an nodded. Dis was da first time fo' 'em locked up an Queenie didn't want Chris to feel defeated or intimidated 'cus of da situation. Queenie finally spoke; “Youngan hold yo' head up nigga neva let me see chu hang yo' head low fam' yo' ass good.” As she winked at 'em 'er aunt words played ova and ova in 'er head; “Its not yo' fault, nothin' chu do is yo' fault.” Queenie knew exatly wut she had to do to get outta da situation she was in an hopefully Tez caught on to 'er vibe. Down at da precinct Queenie and Chris were separated into different integration rooms where Queenie went into deep thoughts as she waited to be questioned. Sittin' still and quiet inside 'er head she talk to 'er conscience; “Yo' don't fo' get who chu is when on da outside ya “Boss Queen”, but bitch prepare yo' self fo' wuts 'bout to take place on da inside behind dose walls. Remember ya done a lot of shit to utters an chu neva know who ya might run into on da inside.” “Man I ain't worried 'bout no utter bitch steppin' to me it is wut it is.” 'Er conscience spoke back. “Yeah but ma'fucka yo' ass better be worried 'bout a nutter charge bein' held ova our head.” She thought 'bout it bein' put in a situation dat would send 'er in a trans dere wouldn't be anyone to bring 'er back 'round like Tez or Cortez'. Further on in 'er thinkin' she thought 'bout Chris an how he was holdin' up. Were dey tryin' to break 'em, was he scared or had he already given 'em everything dey wanted to know 'bout 'er. Queenie told 'er self; “I pray chu hold to yo' guns Chris 'cus ya fuck me family I'm gonna kill ya.” Outta no where da door swung open, but it didn't bother 'er,Queenie kept 'er eyes straight ahead lookin' at da double mirror. As Ola questioned 'er she held to 'er thoughts dat went back and worth in 'er head. “Yo' Mr. D. I'm sorry to bother chu so late, but look Queenie has been charged wit murder can chu come to East St. Boogie tonight an find out wuts goin' on wit 'er?” “Is dis Tez?” Mr. Demontea questioned. “Yeah my bad Mr. D. dis is Tez, I apologize I'm talkin' so fast I didn't even say hello first, so wutsup Mr. D. can ya make it 'ere? Dey got 'er down at da 5th precinct. Reassurin' 'em money is no object I jus' need chu to take dis case Mr. D.

Queenie has neva been locked up ova night, so I don't know how its gonna affect 'er." Tez played his sympathy card to get Mr. D. dere to help 'er quick as possible. "Yo' I'll pay fo' yo' gas jus' put it on my bill plus I'll put chu up in a hotel,so ya can go ova da case." "Okay son I'm on da way, I'll be dere jus' as fast as I can get dere." Tez gave a node to Cortez' and Liz to say Mr. D. gave his approval of comin'. Mr. D. told Tez once he was 'bout 2 hours into his drive he would call,so he could fill 'em in on wut took place wit Queenie, but Tez needed to know if he could take on a nutter case 'cus he needed Chris out of da jam also. "Mr. Demontea a nutter one of our family members has also been charged wit interferin' wit a crime scene. His name is Chris Toy he is also at da same precinct.""Mr. Miles how old is dis young man?" "Mr. D. he is only 17 an dis is his first time in trouble wit da law sir." "Okay I will take his case also, now I'll talk to ya soon I'm on my way." Three hours had passed an Queenie said nothin' she hadn't even budged from da chair she sat in. Ola was pissed at da fact dey were talkin' to 'em selves. "So dats how ya gonna play it huh? Ya ain't got nothin' to say in yo' defense,well dats cool ya ain't gotta talk to us home girl. I know some people dat will make ya talk take 'er ass to lock up." He told Queenie getting up in 'er face tryin' to scare 'er into talkin'. "Dey'll have a good ol' time turnin' yo' pretty ass out." Mr. Demontea stood on da utter side of da glass mirror watchin' da 2 officers torment his client. He noticed dat it was not affectin' 'er at all it was actually amusin' to 'em to see his client make 'em break a sweat. "Excuse me gentlemen." His voice came through as da door opened, may I have a word wit my client?" Thank ya. Somethin' lite up inside of Queenie to see Mr D. it gave 'er comfort dat it all was goin' to be okay. "Ms. Miles,so wutup?" He asked settin' his briefcase on top of da table. "I hear ya a busy young lady." "No, sir I haven't been busy at all,an call me Queenie." Givin' 'em a smile. Within da last several hours dis was 'er first time changin' 'er face expression. "Queenie do ya know why ya 'ere?" "Sir I actually don't, dey say murder, but murdered who and when did I do dis?" She asked."We need to talk in private,so lets get yo' bail posted an get ya away from 'ere,so we can talk 'bout dis case." Queenie asked 2 questions; "How much is my bail an where is Tez?" "Well fo' ya to walk out of 'ere it's $60,000 an Tez yo' mother and Cortez' should be outside wit Mr. Toy." Queenie gave Mr. D. a smile wit a node to say thanks dats wutsup. When an officer opened da door an said Ms. Miles ya free to go he had a dumb look on his face. Mr. D. put his hand in front of 'em an told 'er afta' chu Ms. Miles. Queenie rise from da table nonchalantly an she walked pass Ola wit a swagger,so arrogant as to say fuck ya bitch ass nigga. As Queenie strutted pass each officer she could hear whispers of how did she make bail, wut baller pockets she in? I don't know but we'll get 'er she won't be free fo' too long. One officer went as far as to say damn she's a fine ass specimen of a woman, how old is she again? Only 16 my friend only 16. Damn kids are not kids any mo' when it comes to body. Blushin' as she reached da door Mr. D. open it fo' 'er,so she could walk out first. Instead of Tez standin' dere it was Cortez' she saw first. "Baby wutsup shawty?" He asked as he picked 'er up off 'er feet. Queenie kissed 'em passionately like she neva wanted to let go. "I missed chu to baby." Da three walked up da stairs to da street where she saw Tez, Liz, and Chris. Throwin' 'er hands in da air like she jus' did a long ass bid, Tez walked up to 'er an hugged 'er an grabbed da top of 'er head an asked; "Chu good baby girl?" "Yeah I'm good fam'." Tez asked 'er jokingly; "Ya didn't break did chu, ya didn't go tell on yo' self?" Everyone broke out into laughter. "Nah fam' I didn't but I need to know if anybody did dat fo' me?" Lookin' in Chris direction, she walked ova to 'em standin' toe to toe wit Chris she looked into his eyes not breakin' 'er stare she asked "Mr. D. how long befo' ya see my 4-12?" "I'll see it tomorrow when I meet wit da states attorney. "Now Chris chu know I got love fo' ya youngan we family, but is dere anything chu need to tell us befo' we depart from dis area?" Queenie asked wit a serious demeanor an in ear shot,so only Chris could hear fo' respect of 'em. "'Cus family if da lawyer tells me any different I'm gonna kill ya where chu stand youngan like I neva knew yo' ass." Tez and Cortez' already knew wut dat ear shot was 'bout an all dey could do was ask God to have mercy on Chris soul if he did open his mouth. "Boss I would neva cross ya ma, ya my homeboys QUEEN. Ma I neva had a woman in my life dat I eva respected, shit to be honest far as I can remember I had no one. My ol' g was a addict an she ran off wit 'er pimp leavin' me behind to fend fo' self an if it wasn't fo' Chuck and Cortez' who knows where I would be. Maybe dead or stuck in one of doe's ma'fuckas fo' life,but den chu came 'round kickin' it wit my mans. It gave me somethin' in my life I didn't have a family an wit chu bein' 'round all us fellas completes da picture an I said it befo',but I'll say it again. Even doe I maybe older dan chu ma I still look up to ya ma. Yo' I'm not tryin' to lose dis family. An he shot back in 'er ear; Trust me I seen ya in action first hand,so I know wut yo' ass capable of ma." She stepped away from Chris an hugged 'er moms askin'; "How is auntie doin'?" As she embraced 'er daughter back she replied; "She's restin' now I jus' got off da phone wit da hospital,but I'm worried 'bout chu is chu okay an how is yo' back?" Liz questioned. "I'm good, but seriously I know I probably gotta big boot print in da middle of shoulders its a lil' sore." "Well I already talk to Mr. D. 'bout suin' da precinct and da officer dat kicked chu 'cus it was no reason fo' dat when dey had da cuffs on already. He said dat could be done." Cool, cool. Mr. D. wutsup ya wanta talk 'bout dis ova breakfast? We could go to da Waffle House an sit if ya like." "I will make it easy as possible we can jus' go to my hotel room an order dere while I try to figure dis out an get a better understandin'. Liz said baby girl do chu want me dere or need me 'round?" Queenie replied; "Go be wit my aunt an if I need chu I'll call ya aiight, but fo' now jus' keep me updated on auntie." "Aiight!" Liz hugged everyone an gave Mr. D. a hand shake an left as Queenie said. Tez and Cortez' took care of all of Mr. Demontea's expenses dey put 'em up in da Marriott fo' 2 days,so he would be comfortable workin' on Queenie's case. "Lets get down to business, I need to know exactly everything dat happened up 'til chu ended up at da precinct." Queenie said maybe it's best fo' 'em to tell ya 'cus I don't remember anything afta' leavin' da hospital,so beyond dat I don't know.""Okay dis is gonna help a great deal." "How is dat?" Cortez' asked. "Fortunately Queenie's condition is a great thing in 'er case, don't get me wrong it's a very bad state fo' a young lady of 'er age to be goin' through,but da present time it will help 'er out of dis situation. Queenie have ya eva been diagnosis or treated fo' dis problem ya have wit yo' brain?" "Far as I know my mother and aunt tried to find out wut was wrong, but da doctors couldn't find anything wrong." "Well have ya been tested recently." "No I was suppose to,but I neva found da time.""Well baby girl I think dis is da time 'cus yo' life of goin' to prison or stayin' out of it depend on dose test. An I need dose papers from yo' mother statin' wut da doctor said den."

"Yo' I'll call auntie right now an get 'er on dat, I gotta check on moms status anyway." Ring, Ring_

"Hello." "Wutsup auntie hows my moms?" "She good dey say she's out of da woods,so dats a good thing. Would chu like to speak to 'er she's woke." "Yeah, but hold on befo' ya put 'er on I need chu_ well Mr. D. needs chu to get all da test results dat chu and mom had done on Queenie's brain."

Liz said; "Okay when does he need 'em?" "Asap!" Tez told 'er. "I can get 'em to 'em first thing in da mornin'. Does he think dis will help 'er?" Tez heard his mother in da back ground say it will help 'er, dat baby don't know wut she be doin' when da shit attacks 'er, it's not 'er fault. She waved fo' Liz to give 'er da phone. "Son listen chu tell dat lawyer of 'ers dat I want to see 'em an maybe y'all can get 'em up 'ere tomorrow. Shit dey not 'bout to send my niecy poo to no damn penitentiary fo' some shit she has no recollection of doin'. Baby I'm good don't chu worry 'bout dis ol' woman, chu take care of lil' cousin she's all ya got, now handle yo' biz'ness son." "Aiight ma, I'll get 'em up dere, but chu can tell 'em how ya feel den. Yeah I love ya an I'm dere jus' as soon as I'm done 'ere." "Okay baby mama loves chu to."

Tez walked back to da area where everyone was sittin'. "Yo' she says she can have 'em first thing in da mornin' fo' ya." "Good, good!" "Also my mother Heather wants chu to come to see 'ere tomorrow so she can talk wit chu 'bout Queenie's situation." "Okay I can do dat, how 'bout chu jus' pick me up 'round noon 'cus I have to meet wit da states attorney at 9 am, but I should be back by noon. Now since I got a since of relief wit a heads up on da paper work fo' Ms. Miles lets discuss Mr. Toy_ yo' charge could give ya jus' as much time as Queenie 'ere if not mo',but ya in luck I'm sho' I can get yo' charges dropped wit out dis even goin' on ya record. Do to da surveillance tape from da club yo' face was not shown clear a nuff to say it was chu." Mr. D. tried to lighten da room up a lil'_ "Son do ya or have ya eva ran track 'cus if dat was chu on da tape it was like a bolt of lighten dat went across da screen, so dere is no way in hell dey can say it was actually chu." "Well why would dey call me by name at da hospital an arrest me fo' somethin' dey couldn't identify?" Chris asked. "I am goin' to keep it real wit chu it's only three ways I see it. One someone seen yo' face knew who ya were an snitched. Two ya been in trouble befo' an turned snitch to get yo' self outta hot water__ "Man scratch dat one cus' I neva been in trouble out my life of bein' in da streets an I damn sho' ain't no snitch."Chris stated. "Or three Ola is watchin' ya fo' some utter reason an knows yo' name, but I bettin' it's door number three my friend." Tez stepped in an said; "Dat means if,so an it's truth to any of dat_ fuck dat means Ola knows utter shit on Queenie already." "Yes dis could mean dat dey already know wut she does, wut chu all do,but I'm figurin' if dey didn't add a nutter charge on top of da murder one I'm gonna take a wild guess dis is one of da reasons dey set 'er bond,so high jus' to release 'er tonight. An since y'all paid it dey will be watchin' things tough, so wit dat bein' said Queenie be cool. Lets get cross dis bridge befo' ya get caught up in anything else." Mr. D. smiled an said; "Okay?" An change up any routines dat y'all may have dat chu do daily. I'm not sayin' stop 'cus I know everyone has to eat,but wut

I am sayin' is be on ya P's and Q's stay cautious of da surroundins' chu keep even doe's from a far. Okay not to rush y'all off,but I gotta lot of work to do befo' 9 am,so if y'all excuse me I will be puttin' ya guys out now." "Aiight Mr. D. we feel ya, see ya tomorrow." Silence filled da car ride on da way to da hospital it was a quarter to eleven an Queenie broke da silence. "Yo' family." "Wutup cuz?" "Nah fam' I'm talkin' to da youngan." "My bad boss wutup?" Chris questioned. "I don't apologize to many fam',but Imma be da bigger person an put my pride to da side 'cus I got love fo' ya fam', I apologize to yo' ass youngan fo' puttin' ya out dere like dat 'cus honestly I don't feel ya opened yo' mouth,but neva am I stupid,so I will check dat 4-12 out baby boy. My gut tells me chu are a stand up kid,so I don't see chu goin' against da grain,but shit I didn't see Skip ass goin' against his own either, but look where dat got 'em. Chris don't take dis apology fo' a weakness fam' 'cus my word still stands." "Don't worry 'bout me boss like I said chu my "Boss Queen" fo' life ma. I'd tell on myself befo' I eva tell Ola 'bout chu ma,an dats my word on me family." A tap at da door startled Liz from a node. Peckin' 'er head through da door Queenie asked; "Auntie chu woke?" "Yeah baby I'm woke niecy poo come 'ere baby girl." Heather reached 'er hand out fo' Queenie an she hurried to 'er bedside takin' 'er hand. "Wutsup aunty?" "So dey sprung ya from jail huh?" Heather asked tryin' to laugh_ Ooooh shit. "Ma chu aiight, chu know dat chu can't be doin' no jokin' mess 'round an bust a gut ol' lady." Tez said. "Son I'm good I jus' need to brighten up da room, y'all need to stop all dis tip toein' 'round me like Imma die any minute 'cus I ain't goin' no where,but to da court house when it's time fo' my niece to appear." "Heather how are chu gonna manage dat?" Liz asked. "Wit da help of y'all. Ya take care of da jus' an I will gather my strength to hold up my appearance an dats my word niece." Heather had 'er own plan she had already thought out to help niecey stay away from da penitentiary. "Ueenie give yo' auntie a hug baby girl." Queenie hugged Heather da best she could wit out hurtin' 'er an kissed 'er fo' head. "Auntie I love ya mo' dan chu know,but I jus' need chu to get better lady,so ya can get outa dis place." She looked 'round da room an stated; "I hate hospitals wut has da doctor said anything at all?" "Of course dey are still keepin' a close eye on 'er instead of every hour dey come in every three now,so dats kinda good." Liz said. "Sometime tomorrow she will start therapy sessions to get thinks back functionin' properly." "Not lookin' forward to dat, but da solja in me says it needs to be done I don't jus' wanta lay in da bed fo' eva." Tez kissed his moms on da fo' head an said; "Ol' g chu a go getter,so ya be up outta dis bed befo' we know it,but look we gonna get outta 'ere so chu can get some rest an we'll see ya in da mornin'. Aiight?" He demanded mo' dan askin'. Cortez' placed his arm 'round Queenie's neck, shawty_ "I love ya jus' wait 'til I get chu home__ooooh shit fam' I fo' got all 'bout home dat shit fucked up homeboy. I can't have my fiancee' stayin' dere wit windows busted out an walls full of bullet holes family. My QUEEN looks like we'll be at a hotel 'til dat shit gets fixed."

Chapter Twenty-Five
"Always Consequences Fo' Wut Chu Do"

"Nah cuz y'all jus' stay at da crib wit me y'all know I got da space an da rooms in dat big ass empty house. Remember its only me so chill no need to spend dat money on a room when ya got a free one across da street from yo' own crib. Dis way chu can pay attention to da ma'fuckas who gonna fix yo' shit." "Cool dats straight chu wit it ma?" "Fo' sho' baby, no doubt." Tez stated wit laughter; "Homeboy dat money chu tryin' to get a room wit chu better hold on to 'cus Mr. D. finna hit our pockets fo' da situation dese 2 in." "My nigga I got a lil' change put away dat I can put up also. I don't wanta feel like no charity case fam'." "Yo' youngan hold on to yo' chips fam' we got dis." Queenie stated. "I take care of my own, besides once dis is all ova chu gonna need dat fo' dat next family trip

we finna take feel me." Tez spoke up pullin' to da curb to let Chris out turnin' in da seat to look 'em in da eye. "Yo' lil' nigga I'm gonna give chu da benefit of a true young blood dat yo' word is bond. 'Cus keepin' it raw on da real my first mind told me to keep yo' ass hostage fo' da night 'til we see wut baby girls 4-12 has on it,but unfortunately Imma follow my heart on dis one family an let chu breathe easy." Tez said nothin' to anyone,but he made a call earlier lettin' Chris brothers know wut was up so jus' soon as Chris walks in da house he was not to leave fo' any reason. Tez had placed a number on his head if shit was not on da up and up. Chris nodded his head an asked; "Fam' wut time chu gonna pick me up or should I jus' meet chu at da hospital." "Yo' be ready by 9 an I'll swing by and scoop ya youngan." Queenie retorted. "Aiight boss Imma be on point." Enterin' da front door of Cortez' and Queenie's home standin' in da foyer she stood in an awe state, not believin' 'er eyes. She questioned "Wut da fuck happened, baby look at dese big ass holes in da walls. My floors are ruined why?" She questioned walkin' towards da den. She saw dead fish an gallons on top of gallons of water all ova da bar dat once stood in a corner of da den was no longer dere an it was a very loud stench of alcohol through out da room. "Shawty don't worry Imma get somebody on dis shit first thing in da mornin'." Cortez' exclaimed. "Yo' jus' go get some things together to take to Tez's crib." Queenie took da stairs 2 by 2 reachin' da top she went to 'er bedroom closet an pulled 2 Nike duffel bags an packed their things fo ' at least 2 weeks. Even doe she knew dey would be jus' across da street Queenie didn't want to go back to 'er home 'til it was back to normal fo' 'er to live in once again.
Queenie conscience tapped 'er in da back of da head; "Yo' ain't chu glad dat bitch dead 'cus she caused mo' trouble dan she was worth. Yo' my nigga, Kandi dat was trash a undercover hood rat from da gutta. Its a good thing chu gotta 'er away from cuz 'cus it woulda really been his down fall." Cortez' asked Queenie; "Baby is ya gonna make it through dis I know its a great deal ridin' on dis meanin' yo'

life. So ma please don't put on a front wit me 'cus I understand da pain of yo' situation is inevitable. Baby girl try not to sweat it 'cus Gods gonna work it out fo' ya fo' da simple fact he knows its a birth defect somethin' ya have no control ova ma. I could look at it from a different aspect if chu were jus' out 'ere killin' ma'fuckas in yo' right frame of mind, den I would have questioned it." Queenie turned to face Cortez' wit a tear streamin' down 'er cheek an she whispered; "I love ya." "No doubt I love ya to ma." "Cortez' if da worse comes outta dis baby let me go. Go on wit yo' life an do chu like ya want to." "Ma wut da fuck ya talkin' 'bout? If worse does come to worse I will be right 'ere fo' chu, Queenie stop talkin' to me like dat shawty. Queenie could hear da venom in his voice dat told 'er he was sincere 'bout his statement. "Listen ma ya my QUEEN an I be damn if I let chu think da penitentiary will change dat, chu hear me? Ya mines, ya belong to me an dats straight from my heart." Cortez' hugged 'er as tight as she could bare__ "Chu got me fucked up wit one of dese busted ass niggas out 'ere dat doesn't care, but dat ain't me. I'm right 'ere always." Tez tapped on da bedroom door wakin' Cortez' 'bout 7 am he eased out of bed,so he wouldn't wake Queenie jus' jet. "Wuts good homeboy?" Cortez' questioned in a whisper. "Jus' givin' y'all heads befo' I roll out to make my daily appearance ya know da early bird gets da fresh worms first my nigga. So fam' how did Ueenie hold up last night?" "Not really good cuz, she cried in my arms fo' 'bout an hour." Cortez' covered his head wit his hand rubbin' 'em down his face_ "Fam' we need to talk later on afta' everything is handled. Tez noticed his homeboy expression an didn't like wut he saw it kinda made 'em uneasy. Suggestin' drinks later Cortez' told 'em dats wutsup. "Queenie said she needed to spend time wit yo' moms today anyway." "Cool!"Tez gave Cortez' a hand shake an pulled 'em close to embrace 'em. Cortez' said; "I'll catch chu in a minute." As he walk back into da bedroom where he found Queenie sittin' on da bed in 'er bra and panties. "Good mornin' my beautiful wife." She smiled retortin' I'm not yo' wife jet nigga.

"THROWIN' BRICKS AT THE PENITENTIARY"

Come 'ere daddy." Layin' back on da bed Queenie spread 'er legs eagle style. "Come talk to us daddy." Rushin' between 'er thighs Cortez' wasted no time to pull 'er panties off wit his teeth roughly caressin' and massagin' 'er quarter size nipples he kissed from 'er neck all da way to 'er love box. He stated; "Ummmm ma da fresh smell of pussy da first thing in da mornin' turns dis nigga on." Only thing heard from Queenie was grunts and moans as he breath of cool and warm whispers hit da inside of 'er pussy walls. Cortez' knew da hummin' he did while he ate out Queenie's love box would make 'er go wild like a buckin' stallion. A arch of da back an screamin' at da top of 'er lungs_ "oooooh shiiiit dad_awe." Spreadin' wider she pushed Cortez' head deeper into 'er love box. "Daddy get it all." Queenie pumped,rolled and swayed 'er hips side to side. Risin' from his breakfast buffet he flipped 'er ova like he was da chef an on all fours Cortez' went in from da back teasin' Queenie wit da head of his dick an she yelled out in pleasure givin' 'er a on da spot orgasm. "Damn ma chu doin' it like dat fo' me?" Watchin' Queenie's cum slide down his penis excited 'em. "Ya ready ma, how ya want it slow,fast,soft and gentle or rough and thugg?" "Give it to me rough and thugg daddy." She moaned while she rubbed 'er pussy fo' em. Dere was no mercy on Cortez' end at all thrustin' as hard wit much force one would have swore he was tryin' to knock 'er insides out, but not Queenie she loved every bit of it, it brought mo' of da freak out of 'er. "Yeaaaah daddy beat dat shiiiit up give it_an Queenie screamed in a sexual pleasure. "Imma give it long as chu can take it." Cortez' came abrupt halt an slid out of 'er love box nice an slow. "Come on baby now ya teasin' me, wut? She looked back at Cortez' sexy sweaty ass body seein' his ripped physique made 'er pussy pulsate mo'. Cortez' parted da ass cheeks of Queenie's voluptuous curvey ass sittin' up in his face, he licked 'er ass hole 'til it was moist a nuff fo' 'em to enter. "Ma chu ready?" Wit out waitin' fo' a response Cortez' push half 'em self in Queenie's ass. Twistin' 'er torso like a pretzel he kissed 'er passionately to muffle da cries and

screams she let out. In and out Cortez' plowed da rest his dick in an she gave a node to say it's in don't stop. He felt 'er body relax an he heard a sigh of pleasure comin' from 'er,so gently he let 'er lips go. Dey together played wit 'er pussy roughly__ “Ummmmm daddy I'm finna cum all ova da place.” Pumpin' in and out she threw da ass back to 'em which he was dere to catch 'er water fall.
“Oh I feel dat shit!” Damn Cortez' exclaimed. “Chu wanta taste it I'll feed it to ya.” She moaned as Cortez' grip got stronger an mo' firmer. “Ummmm! Fuck shawty I__ooooh cummin'!” Dey sound in sink wit one a nutter as he exploded inside 'er pullin' out Cortez' smacked 'er ass an said; “Ma I know ya gonna be sore afta' dat ain't chu?” “I'll be good don't worry 'bout dis ass.” She joked. “On da real baby wut time is it?” Cortez' looked his watch an responded it 8:25 ma. “Damn we gotta be outta 'ere by 9 am I'm suppose to pick up Chris,so we can meet wit Mr. D. on top of dat I got utter shit dat needs to be handled.” “Aiight slow up baby I'll call Chris hitter an tell 'em ya be dere by 10 afta' 9. Imma be at da house handlin' dat shit ova dere, but I'll be at da hospital by noon on point.” “Cool.” Queenie told 'em walkin' in da shower_ “Whoa fuck dats cold!” She shouted. “Yo' baby girl, Tez already picked up da youngan he said he'll meet us at da hospital afta' he pickup Mr. D..” Queenie stepped out da shower an Cortez' walks in an tells 'er; “So see slow down lil' mama, when dis is all ova I want a son. Look at me ma seriously I need chu to have my shorty.” He pulled 'er close as he spoke an it was somethin' 'bout da way Cortez' told 'er wut he wanted and needed dat gave 'er a warm sensation between 'er thighs. “Aiight daddy was all she could conjure up to say.” Queenie dressed in a Gucci outfit green and gold nothin' special jus' some skin tight jeans wit a long sleeve button down wit a fall vest jacket wit removal sleeves. Afta' puttin' on jewelry she dab on some Ici perfume on. “Now I'm ready. Damn shawty chu look good in wut eva ya put on.” She told 'er self.
“Sho' do sexy Cortez' said as he walked into da room wit a smile on his face. “Yeah dats wutsup,but

I'm not complete jet." "Why not wuts wrong shawty ya look fine." "I ain't got nina nor do I have my daily pocket change. It's cool doe 'cus Imma 'bout go get right wit both of 'em." He jus' looked at 'er wit a raise brow, but said nothin'. "Yo' baby meet chu at da hospital nigga lock up on yo' way out." "Queenie!__ he called afta' 'er_ "Yeah!" "I love ya shawty." He yelled. "True dat I love chu too." Givin' 'em a wink as she walked out da door, Queenie den jumped in 'er Lexus an 'er mind went into ova drive. 'Er thoughts were on da charge dat hung ova 'er head an 'bout Tez an how he was really feelin' since Kandi wasn't 'round an 'bout da youngan Chris if he sold 'er out. Den dere was Cortez' bring to 'er attention he wants 'er to have his seed. Queenie picked up 'er hitter an called Tez. Ring! "Wutsup cuz how chu feelin' baby girl?" "Man cuz I was cool 'til I left da crib. It feels like anxiety is tryin' to take ova my body, somethin' ain't right cuz." Starin' at da review mirror she said; "Cuz where chu at dis exact moment an do chu got Chris wit chu?" "Yeah he wit me baby girl wutsup an we on third and Taylor. Why wutsup cuz?" "Yo' family I'm headed towards third I'm bein' followed an I'm naked out 'ere fam'." "Lil nigga be cool I swear chu don't need any mo' trouble. Wut color is da car ?" "Its black or navy blue Benz." "Ma its probably jus' Ola in plain clothes." Tez told 'er. "Cuz when Ola start ridin' on rims? 18's to be exact." "Ueenie turn off an let me know wut da car do,but don't do anything foul do da speed limit." "I'm comin' up on ya we 2 blocks away cuz." "Yeah dis ma'fucka followin' me an I'm getting irritated now I'm 'bout ready to pull ova an ask wuts da fuckin' problem feel me cuz." "Nah I'm right 'ere comin' up on da side of da car now, ma chu keep drivin'__ Chris ask 'em fools wutsup." Hangin' out da window Lil' Chris threw his hands in da air suggestin' wut was up wit 'em. Da driver window went down an da passenger was pointin' a Tek 9 at Chris and Tez. "Yo' its a hit family." "Yo' ma U-turn!" Tez yelled in da hitter an it dropped to his lap, makin' a quick turn off he damn near caused a wreck. Queenie knew she couldn't end da call she had wit Tez 'cus he wouldn't be able to answer again, but she needed to call Cortez' an let 'em know wut was up,but jus' so happen Cortez' was tryin' to get through on da utter end. “Yo' baby!” She screamed somebody tryin' to kill me an dey afta' Tez and Chris! We on Hampton by da cemetery I'm naked!” Queenie hurried an clicked back ova to Tez line, so she could hear wut was goin' on inside a car. Queenie heard da sound of bullets, but didn't know from wut type of guns. She could hear voices,but not loud a nuff to hear wut was bein' said. Chris told Tez his clip was empty. “Family yo' take mines.” Chris grabbed Tez glock an continued to shoot back. “Fuck fam' I'm hit ugh shit!” Tez also squealed in pain, Chris bullet from his shoulder hit Tez in his right thigh. “Family! Queenie screamed at da phone an afta' getting no answer seein' Tez car swirl out of control she got 'er thoughts together hung up an called Cortez' back. “Baby dey been hit!” Queenie pushed da nitro button an was on da scene wit in seconds as if she was Ola 'er self. Cortez' could hear da screechin' of tires as he called out; “Yo' ma I'm 'ere I see ya.”

Dey all jumped out of three cars tryin' to get to Tez and Chris at da same time. Tez car was cocked up on da curb, Chris had went unconscious an Tez was losin' a lot of blood da entire crew was dere to help. “Yo' we gotta get 'em to da hospital we can't wait on no ambulance.” Queenie demanded hurry don't let dese niggas die on me baby.” She locked eyes wit Cortez' an he seen tears well up in his girls eyes. Queenie said; “Scoot 'em ova or put 'em in da truck an I'll get 'em dere myself. Yo' y'all get Chris put 'em in da truck, cuz help me pick up Tez.” Queenie ran to da truck an let da back seats down. “Lay 'em on da floor of da truck an call mama an give 'er heads up 'cus I'm bring 'em to ST. Joseph's.” “Cortez' yelled out da window as Queenie pulled off; “Squad up.” Pointin' to his car an Tez ride grab doe's. Cortez' called Joc's hitter; “ST. Joseph family.” Slammin' his foot against da dashboard to hold 'em self still in his seat as Queenie dipped in and out of traffic an runnin' every red light dere was. He called Liz phone. Ring, Ring_ “Hello, Cortez' wutsup baby?” “I'm good ma, oh shit!” “Wuts wrong son?" "Look ma we on our way to da hospital Tez and Chris has been shot have da doctors and nurses outside wit 2 stretchers we a light away ma do it now." Da line went dead an Cortez' hope dey made it in one piece da way Queenie drove da truck. Screechin' an squealin' of tires could be heard 'bout 2 blocks away pullin' up to da hospital she slammed da truck in park an 'er and Cortez' both jumped out openin' da doors. "Come on, come on don't let dese niggas die." Da paramedics placed Tez and Chris on gurneys an ran 'em to surgery. "Yo' Jo park my shit fo' me family." Queenie demanded. "Got chu boss." He responded. Inside da hospital was pure chaos Queenie showed up an showed out as dey would say. No one knew wut da fuck went on, but only da ones involved an Queenie didn't know da niggas 'cus she couldn't see da driver only Tez and Chris could reveal dat. But if Queenie didn't calm down no one would know how dis came 'bout. Liz said; "Somebody has to go get Mr. D. or call 'em an let 'em know wut happen,so he can be present 'cus we know Ola is comin' to question 'em all." "Aiight ma,but we can't let 'er slip into no trans. She's so irate right now it sounds like she's talkin' in tongue." "Nah baby da way she's talkin' to God, she sounds like da devil right now." Queenie screamed lookin' up at da ceilin'; "Wut da fuck do chu want from me dude,why da fuck do chu feel da need to keep takin' my family away from me? So wut is it fo' everyone I take chu hurt or take, chu hurt or take three or four of mines? Is dat how dis work my nigga?" Droppin' to 'er knees in da middle of da waitin' room. Why not jus' cut straight to da problem? Me I'm da problem take me ma'fucka, I'm da devils child." 'Er body heaved up and down like she was exhausted an da room got quiet. " Yo' boss." "Shush!" Cortez' motioned his hand like dis was gonna make everything go away an Queenie would snap back jus' like dat. Queenie had already fell into a trans by da time she hit da floor, 'er head snapped 'round in da direction of Lil' Man who was now standin' by Liz and Cortez'. "Oh fuck! Sorry ma." Lil' Man told Liz as he jumped behind 'er; "But did y'all see 'er eyes?" Dis was da first time dey had eva seen 'er eyes up close while in a trans. Even Liz had neva really seen da way 'er daughter eyes looked up close. Cortez' yelled; "Squad up I don't give a fuck wut she does to any of ya don't let shawty out dis hospital or outta yo' sight. Mom I gotta bring 'er back an I believe she's gonna have to see and hear Tez and Chris voice, so see wut chu can find out 'bout 'em an call Mr. D. an y'all get 'em 'ere now. 'Cus if Ola arrives befo' I can bring 'er back ma ain't no tellin' wut dey will do to 'er." Queenie's cryin' session turned into anger to da point she started to throw da hospital furniture at 'er crew. Cortez' needed to grab 'er from behind, but in order to do dat he needed to stay out of 'er vision which seemed impossible at dis point 'cus he seemed to be 'er main target. "Yo' fam' chu gonna have to tackle 'er like a quarter back." In da back dey had Tez bandaged up, his bullet went straight threw it was a clean shot. Chris on da utter hand da bullet shattered his collar bone, so he was still in surgery. "Doctor please tell me how long befo' Tez Miles will be able to come out?" Tez walked out on crotches behind da doctor. "Wutsup auntie I'm right 'ere." "Tez baby Queenie's in one of 'er trans again baby please." "Fuck! He yelled_ grab dat wheelchair." He demanded. Da doctor rushed 'em to da da front of da hospital jus' as dey entered da waitin' area he heard sirens of Ola. Standin' from da wheelchair he handed his crutches to his auntie an yelled; Ueenie an befo' she could turn 'round he bear hugged 'er. "Ueenie its me Tez baby come on back to me baby girl. Please lil' nigga snap out of it ma." While Tez tried to bring his lil' cousin back reality, Cortez' pleaded wit da doctor explainin' Queenie's condition dat he really know nothin' 'bout. "Look doc Ola 'ere an my girl is in a nuff trouble please sir I beg of chu don't press charges against 'er. Dis 'ere is 'er mother she can vouch fo' me I'll have dis whole area remodel fo' ya jus' please help 'er we need to find out why she goes into dese spells." Da doctor said say no mo' once he brings 'er back 'round I will admit 'er,so I can run test on 'er admittedly. He gave his nurses orders to setup an get a room ready an to get da information on Queenie from 'er mother. “Yo' baby girl snap out of it ma its me cuz, its Tez please lil' nigga I'm good,but I won't be if Ola comes in an try to take ya from me.” In earshot Tez whispered; “I'm cool ma, I'm good baby girl please, please.” Ola ran through da doors guns drawn pointed at Queenie and Tez. Da 2 had jus' dropped to da floor in a fetal position, where Tez covered da top of Queenie's body to shield 'er. Mr. D. had jus' ran through da door also an Liz screamed; “Wait wait she's my child an she's finna be admitted.” Liz pushed da medical records he requested into his hands. “Hold on I'm 'er lawyer withdraw yo' weapons.” Da doctor stated; “Dis is my patient all of dis is not necessary officers. He tried to reason dats 'er family member an he's jus' tryin' to bring 'er 'round.” “Can ya hear me Ueenie?” “Umph?” “Listen to me I don't trust Ola, so Imma pick ya up off dis floor when I say,so rise up wit me an I will not leave yo' side feel me?” Queenie nodded 'er head in his chest. Tez waved fo' da wheelchair, now lil' nigga an da 2 stood up which gave Tez a weak feelin' in his stomach not knowin' if Ola was gonna gun 'em both down where dey stood. “Nurse get me a nutter wheelchair fo' Mr. Miles he needs to be restitched.” Tez was saturated wit blood dere was a puddle on da waitin' room floor. “Yo' doc can ya put us in da same room?” “Mr. Miles its not possible fo' me to stitch up yo' womb in da same room.” “Well I'm good jus' put a clean dressin' on it doc 'cus I'm not leavin' 'er side fo' nothin'. Dats my lil' cousin an I jus' gave 'er my word an my word is bond.” “Tez baby chu need to be treated befo' chu get infected boy.” “No! dats my baby, my lil' nigga an dis bond 'ere is ride and die. I won't leave 'er side.” Cortez' stated; “Mom its no use arguin' wit 'em on dis dats his baby an ya know already dey thicker as thieves. Ma he'll be aiight.” “Imma go check on Chris.” Liz said feelin' hurt due to she knew she was losin' 'er daughter 'er only born. Liz went into prayer as she walked da halls to get to da recovery room. “Which room is Chris Toy in?” Liz asked da nurse. “How is he doin' did his surgery go okay?” Da nurse told 'er yes his bullet hit his collar bone an broke it in 2 places,so da doctor had to put 4 pins in his shoulder to connect it back. He's in a partial body brace to help hold 'em in place, so dey can set right. He's in bed 5 straight ahead." "Auntie!" Chris said a lil' groggy wit a dry mouth. "Hey baby how chu feelin'?" "High auntie I feel high, can I have somethin' to drink?" He asked. Liz picked up a water pitcher an pored 'em a small amount of water in a cup wit a straw. "'Ere chu go baby drink it slow." "Auntie, Tez how he doin?" Chris prayed she didn't say he was dead. Hysterically in a frenzy he asked; "Where is lil' mama, auntie where is "Boss Queen"?" "Chris baby calm down their both upstairs." "Upstairs? Wuts upstairs ain't dat where dey admit patients?" "Yeah baby it is. Queenie had a nutter one of 'er episodes in da waitin' area when dey brought chu and Tez in an no one could bring 'er out of 'er trans, but Tez. An da police came Cortez' had to plead wit da doctor not to press charges on 'er fo' tearin' up da place den da doctor took 'er as his patient to run test,so Ola couldn't take 'er." Tears rolled down Liz face__ "Auntie don't cry she's gonna be aiight yo' daughter is a solja like no utter. Come on auntie take me to see 'er. I need to make sho' my family is aiight fo' myself." "Sir ya can't leave jus' jet." "Ma'am I'm a nurse also an I'll take full responsibility, his love ones are upstairs bein' admitted an he needs to see 'em to make sho' their okay." Chu know how dese kids are chu can't tell 'em shit,but I will make sho' he's not away to long." Upstairs as Queenie laid in a cat scan tube da doctor did make a exception an stitched Tez up in da same area so he could still be in view of his lil' nigga. "Chris baby wut happened, why is dis happin' to y'all?" "Auntie I don't know all I know is some niggas were followin' boss an if we wouldn't showed up when we did boss would be dead, 'cus she wasn't strapped." Chris knew who da passenger was 'cus he saw 'em in da middle of da street at da club dat night, but dis wasn't somethin' he was 'bout to tell Liz. Getting off da elevator Chris spotted Cortez'. "Yo' fam' wutsup?" Chris threw his hands in da air. "My nigga wuts good how ya feelin'? Wuts all dis my nigga? Man youngan I apologize I wasn't in recovery when ya came outta surgery, but we had a episode downstairs wit Queenie.” “Yeah, auntie told me dats why I had 'er to bring me up 'ere, but its cool fam' I wouldn't want it no utter way. We gotta make sho' boss cool,but fam' where Tez?” “He's inside wit Queenie he refused to come out 'til she's done he gave 'er his word he wouldn't leave 'er side.”

Chapter Twenty-Six
“An Operation Will Kill 'Er If Da Streets Don't”

“Dats wutsup, but let me holla at chu homeboy. Excuse us auntie.” Chris said.

Cortez' push da wheelchair outta earshot of Liz an Chris started talkin'. “Yo' bro right 'ere is good Cortez' walked 'round to face Chris. “Wutup lil' fam'?” “Fam' I didn't want to say in front of auntie,but remember dat night at da club da dude Queenie shot at?” “Yeah dat tall black ass nigga I know if I saw 'em, but wut 'bout 'em?” “Well bro dats da nigga who was trailin' yo' girl an da ma'fucka who tried to take us out tonight fam'.” Cortez' punched a hole in da wall__ “Fuck man dis is some bullshit I love shawty in dere, she's da only thoroughbred woman I dan met she's da only ma'fucka who has touched my heart family. I'm diggin' 'er an Imma make 'er my wife dats da woman who's gonna give birth to my seed. Now chu tellin' me niggas out 'ere tryin' to off 'er an 'cus she wasn't in 'er right mind to know who she shot at jus' means dis ma'fucka has one up on my QUEEN which puts me on charge.” Cortez' was an optimism he handled things in a nonchalant laid back cautious manner. Dat's 'til he started kickin' it wit Queenie, but within da year da 2 been together he went from jus' laid back to straight intrepid to I don't give a fuck thugg. Cortez' told Chris; “Its time fo' da streets to see me again an feel my wrath again fam'.” “Bro chu ain't gotta tell me how yo' ass was, remember dats how me an da bro's met chu and Chuck. Trust and believe I damn near felt it myself to say da least, but yo' fam' I know chu may not approve of da shit boss do, but its somethin' chu gotta deal wit 'cus reality is dat its 'er an it may neva go away." "My QUEEN, I won't give 'er up fo' shit in da world fam', shawty is intoxicatin' to me when she's 'round I'm high as fuck, but when she's not I'm down like I've lost 'er fo' eva fam'." Chris stated; "Yo' family ya really in love dats deep I ain't neva seen chu jones ova no braud, so I know "Boss Queen" got chu open wide cuz. But don't feel shameless, boss is a good woman she young an neva da less she takes on a lot of responsibilities shawty has a big heart an chu know family is everything to 'er. Bro how I see it chu got a special lady an she's like no utter, now lets go see wutsup wit 'er." Down at da 5th precinct Ola was buildin' a strong case against Queenie an 'er family circle. Captain Nuts gestured wit a pointer_ "Right 'ere we have Queenie Miles aka "Boss Queen" to da streets an dis 'ere is 'er family circle she built dat consist of Tez Miles 'er first cousin, Cortez' who's 'er fiancee' now. Den we have Chris,Lil' Man,Jo and Joc dese 4 stick together an dey do nothin' wit out da utter dey also live together. Dese 2 'ere are twins Giz'mo and Stacks dey also live together, an dere is one utter person Chaos dis is 'er uncle, but he is no longer part of their circle he is da guy dats recoverin' from gun shot wounds da incident dat happened 'bout a month ago. Dat also reminds me dat dese 2 'ere Chris and Tez was jus' gun down tonight an we gotten word dey survived. Now Flex and Tre' runs a warehouse Queenie has an dats da only place dey been spotted. It was unfortunate fo' dese 2 Chuck and Lu,but are no longer wit da circle dey got murdered. Dose were da guys murdered on da strip 'bout six or seven months ago it was personal. My fello colloquies it doesn't seem we are goin' to get dis lil' kid on da murder charges 'cus of a medical technicality." Excuse me. "Yes officer Fields?" "Wut do ya mean lil' kid how old is dis woman?" "Dats jus' my point she ain't no woman jet, Queenie Miles is only 16 an she turns 17 on June 22nd ." "An she's a Queen pin?" "We're not fo' sho', how much money she has, but da word on da streets is she's a millionaire already from da things dat have been bought. It seems dat money is no object to 'er or to dese 2 Mr. Miles or Mr. Fabs.” Back at da hospital Queenie's physician walked out of da exam room leavin' Tez to be wit 'er. “Wutsup doc, wut did chu find out?” Coretz' asked. “Well Ms. Miles brain is not normal. Its like dis where we all have a brain dat has an upper part called Cerebrum an a lower rear part called Cerebellum. Now Ms. Miles brain works fine 'til she's provoked she can feel fear whether its 'er own or a love one. Den da lower part of 'er brain cut off from da main part of da brain an becomes paralysis, which is called Cerebral Palsy. Its from a lesion on da brain.” “Yo' doc can it be removed? Can chu fix my girls head?” “Yes an no.” “Wut do ya mean by dat?” Cortez' questioned. “Mr. Fabs to answer dat fo' ya, yes it can be removed,but if I did dat Queenie would not live 2 hours an from da scan shows it's still in someway attached,but it functions on its own,so its like dis say it has a mind of its own. Dis has become a part of Ms. Miles life,so let me be honest wit chu wut y'all have been seein' is wut chu will continue to get out of 'er. Dis is not goin' away an deres no medicine dat will keep 'er from fallin' into dose trans.” Da doctor looked 'round to make sho' no one was listenin' befo' he said; “I'll tell ya dis to help yo' girl out of trouble da charges dey are tryin' to hit 'er wit in 'er condition dey will neva stick son,so talk to 'er lawyer 'cus if she's convicted of anything y'all can have a lawsuit 'cus Ms. Miles isn't 'er self when she goes in a trans an I seen it fo' myself tonight.” “Thank ya,so much doctor.” Liz spoke up an shook his hand. “When will she be able to leave?” “She's free to go now. I know dis will be pretty impossible to do 'cus ya not 'round 'er 24/7,but da calmer and happier she stays da few of dese episodes she will have.” “Doc can I?” Cortez' pointed at da door wantin' to go in da room wit his girl an da doc gave 'em a node to confirm he could enter. “Ma wuts good chu okay?” He hugged and kiss Queenie on da fo' head. “Yo' fam' chu good homeboy?” “Yeah I'm cool.” Tez neva was da one to bite his tongue so he jus' went in hard on who eva an dis time he had to let his homeboy know wut da deal was 'cus he had a bone to pick wit 'em. "Look family I gotta bone to pick wit yo' ass us bein' boys from knee high to a duck I love yo' ass like a brother,so we family in many ways now even mo' so,but nigga dis 'ere is my bloodline dat my blood flows threw an dat situation downstairs shoulda neva happened. Yo' ass suppose da be able to handle it. Bro I'm not gonna be 'round all da time_wut if jus' wut if I would not have made it bro? Was chu gonna jus' leave 'er like dat fam'? I'm sho' da doctor told y'all da same shit he told us, she's like dis fo' da rest of 'er life family. So Imma need chu to step up to da plate my nigga an take control of da situation when da shit presence itself. Feel me. Fam' yo' ass know I don't mean any harm,but when it comes to dis lil' nigga all love goes out da window." "Yeah I peeped how chu treated yo' auntie 'bout baby girl,so I know damn well I won't get no respect on da situation."

"Yeah well nigga she's finna be yo' wife,so do wut chu need to do 'cus yo' ass can't be scared fam'. When da time comes an she falls in a trans yo' ass gotta be on point chu gonna have to be rough and gentle deres no way ya can hurt 'er shit she'll hurt chu if anything,but wut I mean by rough chu gotta grab 'er from behind in a bear hug an gentle well shit yo' ass dan seen me wit 'er its jus' dat simple chu gotta to get 'er to realize who ya are an wuts goin' on. Its like a soothin' transaction,but make sho' ya always drop to da ground wit 'er specially if its a crowd or Ola pops up. Wut eva happens try yo' best not to let anyone see 'er eyes an at all times keep 'er body shield. Got it fam'?" "My nigga I got chu,but speakin' of Ola did da doc put y'all up on dat shit 'bout 'em not bein' able to charge chu ma wit 'em murder cases? Yo' ass can't be charged fo' non of doe's murders at all shawty." Cortez' went on to tell 'em wut else da doctor said an tellin' da lawyer so he could get on top of it. Leavin' da hospital Tez refused a wheelchair jus',so he could walk beside Queenie while she pushed Chris in his wheelchair. Queenie finally got to see da waitin' area an said; "Whoa! Hold da fuck up fam' did I do dis?" She had neva seen any of da damage she caused 'cus either she was still in one of 'er trans or dey had already left da scene befo' she came 'round. "Man nah I can't leave 'ere wit out talkin' to da doc I gotta pay fo' dis my reputation means way mo' to me to jus' bounce like ain't shit happen." Cortez' said; "Baby I spoke wit 'em 'bout it, Imma take care of it aiight." "No its not aiight, excuse me nurse can chu call da doctor back out 'ere fo' me?" "Is dere a problem Ms. Miles?" "Yeah it is I didn't know 'til now da damages I done an I would like to pay fo' 'em." "Well yo' fiancee' and I already discuss dat,so its taken care of." "I don't mean to sound rude 'cus I do appreciate my guys gesture,but I pay my own debts." Queenie let 'er pride get in da way, but dey all decided to let 'er have it 'er way. She told da doctor; "Imma be back less dan a hour to bring chu $30,000 dollars dat should be mo' dan a nuff to remodel dis an some extra fo' da kids ward maybe." "Oh yes Mr. Miles yo' mother should be released in a coupla days she pulled through dat ordeal like a trooper an 'er therapy is goin' great. She said somethin' 'bout she was a mission fo' 'er niecy poo." "Thanks doc I know exactly wut she's talkin' 'bout. I'll be up 'ere in da mornin' to visit 'er." Queenie thoughts ova ran 'er brain which ova whelmed 'er. Back at da house da three ordered pizza an drank Hen fo' their choice of beverage. Sittin' up on da edge of da couch placin' 'er head inside 'er hands. "Wutsup ma?" Cortez' asked. "Yo' fam' my life is crazy,but its sweet dey can't charge me fo' any of da murders I done, but dat ain't got shit on da drug charge dey finna hit me wit." Tez retorted; "I see ya been thinkin' baby girl." "Always nigga dats all I do day and night even when I'm a sleep my brain is workin' ova time. Look I know its a matter of time befo' dey come fo' me fam' an when dey come da ma'fuckas comin' hard. Every place dey think I got somethin' to do wit will be bum rushed cuz." She stood up an said; "I know wut Mr. D. said dat night at da precinct was true an it confirmed it when he said Chris didn't say shit to Ola. Right dere let me know dese ma'fuckas been watchin' me an our circle an y'all know dat means in order to get to me dey will take every last one of chu down. I got dis gut feelin' afta' I appear in court dats when Ola will make a move." "Baby dats next Friday ya gotta go to court." Cortez' looked wit raised eyebrows. "Yeah baby it is,so its not a lot of time to do wut needs to be done." "Baby girl wuts yo' next move?" Tez asked curiously. "Yo' fam' we finna shut it down fo' a minute 'til dis shit blows ova at least jus' 'til I can get some of dis heat off me ya feel me." "Yeah lil' nigga I feel ya,but jus' how do chu plan on doin' dat?" "Fam' trust me chu gonna find out in due time, give me an hour an I will answer yo' question. I need both to call up da fellas fo' a meetin' at da hospital." "Baby da hospital why da hospital?" "Yeah da hospital aunties room is where we will meet an da only place we will 'til I figure out a a different place." "Aiight ma, we're on da same page." Tez responded wit a suspicious look on his face. She told 'em; "I would hope,so cuz 'cus all our lives and welfare depends on wut we 'bout to do." When da sun peeked through da blinds an beamed on Cortez' face he turned to wrap his arms 'round Queenie to only find 'er not dere_ "Aye shawty!" He called out thinkin' she may have been in da shower already, but dere was no Queenie. He got out bed adjustin' his erect penis__ "Yo' shawty!" Callin out again openin' da bedroom door. "Wutsup homeboy?" Meetin' Tez head on in da hallway. "Shit wutsup bro, chu seen Queenie?" "Nah, fam' I jus' got da shower_ lookin' at his watch_ hell its only 7:30 am I thought she was in dere wit chu." Tez told Cortez' "I'll call an check up on 'er while chu get in da shower homeboy." "Aiight cool fam' give me 20 minutes an I'll be ready bro." Cortez' thought to 'em self "Damn I know dis girl ain't no punk an can hold 'er own under any pressure, but da shit does scare da fuck outta me when she's out 'ere doin' 'er while she has in da streets tryin' to get at 'er head. Wut da hell does she have a death wish?" Queenie placed a call at dark 30 in da mornin' askin' to meet wit 'em by six o'clock am an once he agreed she showed up at Mr. Demontea's suite wit a lot of demands questions an 2 Nike duffel bags full of money. Knock! Knock openin' da door Mr. D. stood on da opposite side_ "Yes Ms. Miles come in." He questioned. "It must be very important wut eva ya need fo' chu to bring yo' mother out dis early?” “Good mornin' Mr. D.” Liz spoke. “Queenie wut do I owe dis visit?” He asked. “Mr. D. I thought a great deal 'bout wut chu said da utter night we were 'ere an I understand I won't go down fo' murder 'cus dey can't hold dat on me. Some wut chu both know wut my life style consist of: drugs I am a Queen pin an I am known to most as “Boss Queen” in da streets from 'ere back to Chicago. Anything I set my mind to I do, can and will accomplish 'cus I'm a thoroughbred,so I make no mistakes an I have no remorse fo' human life. Imma be honest as I will eva be breathin' in air,only people I care 'bout is my family from moms to da niggas in my circle utter dan dat I give not a fuck 'bout anyone else not even my damn self.” Mr. D. and Liz looked at Queenie like she was crazy,but said nothin'. “Dat brings me to say and ask chu to take dis money 'ere an get it cleaned up befo' Friday? Dat gives chu six days.” “Queenie chu talkin' 'bout money laundrin' I___She cut 'em off. Mr. D. don't bullshit me on dis I appear in court Friday mornin' an my gut tells me dat Ola will be all ova me den an I refuse to make their job easy fo' 'em. I already have three strikes against me

1. I'm 16
2. I'm a murderer
3. I'm ova a million dollar drug Queen pin

so Ola is requital fo' theirs an will not stop 'til dey have me,so Mr. D. I need chu to clean dis money up an take care of all da paper work on all 5 houses where Ola can't have 'em seize an I need chu to take dis hitter.” “No Queenie I can't do dat I have a phone already. I can't except dat phone Ms. Miles.” “Yeah chu can Mr. D. its so I can get in touch wit chu, I will no longer be usin' da ol' number chu have fo' me,so 'ere ya go. Only I have da number to dat hitter an if anything does happen to me destroy dat hitter. Mr. D. I'm holdin' my last meetin' today at da hospital in my aunts room in 'bout 2 hours dat be 9:30,so be dere.” She looked at 'er diamond Fossil watch an stood from da chair an told 'er moms lets roll. “Queenie! _ he called out behind 'er,but how much is in da bags?” Queenie's response was

"Dat will be $120,000 its $60,000 in each." She pulled 'er hood ova 'er head an walked out da door. Queenie an 'er moms went to da bank dat Liz had been bankin' wit since Queenie was 5 years old she needed 'er moms to open up a illegitimate account fo' Queenie's college basketball tuition fund she had Liz to put $80,000 in dis account. She knew Liz was da only one who had a legit job an had held on to it fo' ova 10 years. Liz phone rung an she let it ring 5 times,an when Liz answered it. "Hello baby let me call chu back." Tez held his phone up in front of his face,an retorted; "Wut da fuck,no she didn't jus' short talk me an hang up like dat." He said to Cortez' who sat in da passenger seat. "An when da fuck did Queenie phone get cut off?" Cortez' questioned. Tez knew dat was not like his lil' cousin so he let Cortez' know dey needed to get to da hospital fast. Heather had gave no notion at all to as why everyone was dere in 'er room fo' Queenie's meetin', she jus' acted surprise to see all da fellas as dey started walkin' in da door. Lil' Man and Chris even bought 'er balloons and flowers. "Wutsup fellas dats sweet of y'all to come an visit an ol' woman, pull up a seat." "Yo' wutsup auntie how chu feelin'?" Chris asked. "Damn I seemed to be a lil' better dan chu youngan, wut da fuck happen nephew?" Befo' Chris could reply back Tez voice come from behind da fellas standin' 'round. "We were in a lil' altercation." Seein' 'em walk in on crutches freaked Heather out. "Wut da hell happen to y'all son?" "I'll tell chu in jus' a second auntie." Queenie said as 'er and Liz walked in. She walked ova to 'er aunts bedside an kissed 'er on da fo' head. "Wutsup aunty how chu feelin' today are ya up fo' dis?" "Yeah anything fo' my niecy poo. An yo' meetin' will not be interrupted 'cus I already had my mornin' session of therapy an I informed da nurses to leave me alone 'til 2 o'clock,so I could have my visitors dis mornin'. So we good an baby da floor is urns. "Ma let me find out chu in 'ere demandin' shit." Tez said jokingly finally kissin' 'er on da fo' head. "Aiight since we all 'ere everybody knows except aunty dat someone's tryin' to kill me." "Wut!" Heather said jus' above a whisper. "Yeah auntie dats wut happened to yo' baby and Chris dey saved me by puttin' 'em selves in danger. But unfortunately family we got a bigger problem dan dat." "Wuts dat boss?" Chris questioned. "Ola youngan Ola. My intuition tells me dat Ola is comin' fo' all of us,but we all know dey want me especially since dey can't touch me on da murder charges,so dey will get me any utter way possible. So da reason we all 'ere today is,so we all on da same page family." She looked 'round da room at all of 'er family an stated; "We finna close up shop, shut it down fo' a minute family. I love each an everyone of y'all an I feel bogus to let my family take a fall fo' my shit. Look I had shit legitimized dis mornin' all 5 spots da paper work is bein' handled as we speak. Moms opened a college trust fund,so dats legal at least to da naked eye, Ya feel me? Mr. D. is handlin' some utter things fo' me dat he'll let me know 'bout in a coupla days." She looked at Mr. D. as to say right? "Yes by Friday everything will be in order fo' ya Queenie." "Now I want da warehouse cleaned out of any drugs Flex and Tre' wuts left?" "Boss its 60 bricks total." Tre' nodded his head towards Mr. D. as to say did chu fo' get he was in da room. Queenie chuckled an said; "Baby boy trust and believe I'm not illiterate at all not to put chu on da spot,but don't worry its a reason I had Mr. D. Come 'ere fam' an dats,so he will know wuts goin' on, he knows he can leave at anytime he wishes to an it'll be cool 'cus I know dere is a such thing called a lawyer and clients confidentiality. Ain't dat right Mr. D.?" She questioned. "An besides dat Mr. D. knows where his bread and butter is comin' from wit dis family." Nonchalantly she stated; "Da mo' he knows da deeper he's affiliated wit us." Tez made eye contact wit Queenie an winked. "Now everybody take one of dese phones dat moms has. Dis hitter is only fo' chu to contact me I have each one of da numbers an every 2 months chu will get an updated one, neva da less if somethin' should happen to me destroy doe's hitters admittedly. Dis number is setup to where it can't be traced at all, but jus' fo' yo' safety be cautious." Cortez' said; "Baby is dat why yo' phone was off 'cus we tried to check on ya earlier shawty.

"Yeah I destroy it soon as I walked out da house dis mornin' an Friday my whole life will be basically wiped clean, but dis won't stop 'em from comin' fo' me family,but it will make 'em work extra harder to prove anything. Yo' Flex I need 30 of doe's bricks an da rest y'all split it up an get rid of it fast. Far as da stash houses I want 'em boarded up leave da furniture, but remove anything dat can and will be traced back to me or yo' selves. An 'til all dis mess is ova wit moms and auntie will put up Giz'mo and Stacks. Flex and Tre' will live wit cuz an da youngans will live wit Cortez' and me. I hope y'all have stacked yo' paper fo' a purpose as of such 'cus y'all gonna have to live off of it fo' a hot second. On Friday everyone should be settled in yo' perspective livin' quarters an everyone will receive their bonus pay. Add it to wut chu got already an fellas spend it wisely." "WOW! Boss I neva heard chu use doe's words befo' ma." Da entire room started to laugh even Queenie threw 'er head back in laughter. "Yeah well I guess I knew it all alone, but neva followed my own advise 'cus I jus' spent recklessly 'cus I got it like dat an didn't give a fu_ I didn't care,but its different 'cus I'm thinkin' 'bout y'all my family. An if I go down I need fo' all of chu to be straight. I believe dats all,so go do wut needs to be done." Queenie said; "Aunty when dey lettin' ya up outta dis joint?" "Should be in two or three days, fo' sho' I'll be out befo' next Friday." "Aiight auntie dats cool." "Boss when chu want da bricks?" Tre asked.

Chapter Twenty-Seven
"All A Setup Fo' 'Er Take Down"

"I need 'em tonight Cortez', Tez and myself are takin' a trip to Detroit an we'll be leavin' out 'bout six,so get 'em to me in da next hour. Now is dere any mo' questions befo' we get outta 'ere? If not lets squad up family an make dis shit happen." Da fellas said their good byes an left to handle biz'ness. "Baby 'bout dis trip ain't chu,we a lil' to hot to chance dis move?" "Yeah baby we probably would have to worry 'bout Ola if we drove ourselves, but its not gonna happen 'cus we not. I'm havin' a limo pick us up from Tez house,so dress up my niggas 'cus we goin' to a weddin'.” Queenie was a master mind at wut she did so she left no wheels unturned. 'Er thoughts ova loaded 'er mouth so she blurted; “Imma make dese ma'fuckas work hard fo' my ass an by time dey finish I'll have their heads spinnin' dey won't be able to recall wut dey did last.” “Yo' baby girl chu aiight?” Tez asked snappin' Queenie back to reality. “Yeah cuz I'm good jus' thinkin' y'all ready to bounce I gotta drop moms off an run by da stash house.” She needed to count up 'er paper she needed to know exactly wut was wut 'cus da rest would remain locked underground. “Baby!” Cortez' called out. “Yeah wutsup?” “Aye I need to go to da house an see wuts wit da workers an put a rush on dis,so it'll be done by Friday ma,so why don't I take yo' ride drop moms off an meet y'all back at Tez crib an Tez can take ya to da stash house.” He replied; “Dats cool is dat cool wit chu fam'?” “Yeah I'm cool wit it dat makes a lil' mo' since anyway.” At da car she asked Tez if he wanted 'er to drive an told 'er hell yeah help a handicap brother out shit a nigga don't mind bein' chauffeured.” “Yo' cuz I think we need to talk on some real shit.” Tez turned da music down. “Wutsup Ueenie its jus' me and chu baby girl. Wut chu got on yo' mind?” He asked. Tez wanted to know exactly how she felt 'bout Ola comin' fo' 'er an Queenie tried to keep dat stern tough demeanor she carried 'round to protect 'er ego and pride,but it didn't fly wit Tez. “Look ma I know its fuckin' wit chu 'cus I can see da shit in yo' eyes it has finally hit home.” Queenie pulled up in da back of 'er stash house got out an open da gates while Tez put his leg across da seat an drove inside an Queenie shut 'em back an got back inside da car befo' she entered da house to finish their conversation. “Aiight cuz preciate dat now as chu was sayin'.” “Baby girl I know yo' ass an maybe no one else can see it,but I know da shit has hit home. When chu start doin' shit of da normal its 'cus yo' ass nervous lil' nigga, so tell me wuts goin' on in yo' head baby.” “Look fam' its mo' like paranoid 'cus ma'fuckas finna kick in doors at any minute an to be honest it makes me nauseous. Its like dey have a hold on me already an I been tryin' to picture how behind 'em walls gonna be,but I come up wit is wut chu see on television where ya got ma'fuckas shankin' or a bunch of butches runnin' 'round bein' carpet munchers.” “Ueenie is dat wuts botherin' chu baby? Chu can't believe dat mess ya see on T.V..” “My nigga its not so much dat_my thing.” Queenie got choked up an tried to swallow da lump in 'er throat an looked at Tez. “Yo' Imma be gone from chu fam' dat hurts me da most cuz, an ain't shit sayin' Imma make back home alive. Jus' wut if somethin' happens I neva been away from yo' ass mo' dan wut three weeks at da most when I went to Jamaica wit Cortez',so yeah cuz I gotta lot of shit goin' on in my head. Family I ain't stupid,so I know Ola mad 'cus dey can't get me on da murder game I put down,so of course it will be no mercy dey gonna try an treat my ass on da time. I tried to keep dat faith in Mr. D. dat he will work his magic, chu ask me its not lookin' to good fo' da home team nigga.” Tears dropped out of 'er eyes as she went on to say; “Its not even 'bout da money cuz its all 'bout family. Keepin' it raw doe da reason I wanted to sale drugs like yo' ass fam' was 'cus I seen da way moms and I lived. Even doe she worked 'er ass off it still didn't seem like she was makin' ends meet,so I vowed dat I would take damn good care of 'er an get us up out da hood. Only thing was doe I figured I would go to da pro's an make dat happen,but once I got down wit chu cuz an da money started to flow heavily I guess chu can say I got greedy in a since 'cus it felt good to have in my possession at all times on point. When I needed and wanted I could go get it. Yeah I got a lil' ova whelmed by da fact I could give moms thousands to jus' put in 'er pocket fo' 'er to pamper 'er self. An yeah it gave me great pleasure to hook my people up wit money wit out 'em askin' fo' shit,so no doubt da paper was a plus,but dats not wut made me doe. Nigga all 'em prop's go to chu yo' ass built da young ass teen ya see befo' chu bro. Wit out chu “Boss Queen” wouldn't be.” “Yeah well if I wouldn't have help build dat person I wouldn't be feelin' all fucked up right now. If I had put my foot down an told chu to pick somethin' else fo' ya birthday gift chu wouldn't be preparin' yo' self to go to prison lil' nigga,so in all rawness don't give me prop's 'cus I coulda done better an dats real talk." "Cuz dis ain't yo' fault I'm not blamin' chu fo' anything I got careless wit da spendin' an I let one-two many people know who "Boss Queen" is knowin' ma'fuckas run off at da mouth like sittin' down to take a piss. But its cool fam' ya already know I can hold my own cuz." "My point exactly baby girl dats one of my main concerns right dere. I know chu can hold ya own, but chu not seein' da big picture 'ere Ueenie. Da penitentiary is not where yo' ass need to be wit yo' condition yo' brain is not stable fo' dat. 'Cus da first time a bitch says anything outta pocket an chu blow a fuse who gonna bring yo' ass outta dat shit? 'Em ma'fuckin' CO's won't give a damn if yo' ass is hurt or not dey'll let chu die up in dere an we'll be da last to know. Tez questioned an do chu wanta know why? Queenie jus' stared at 'em_ "'Cus baby girl chu belong to 'em chu have no say so." Queenie looked puzzled as 'er tears ducks filled wit salty water 'cus wut Tez said hit home an reality slapped Queenie in da face. "Don't cry ma I'm not tryin' to scare chu, 'cus ya gonna be fine. I jus' need chu to try an hold yo' composure a lil' better dan chu do out 'ere in dese streets baby girl, an long as Mr. D. do wut I know he's capable of doin' shit should be good." "Cuz chu my protector an have been now fo' 16 years an I love and appreciate dat from da heart nigga. Chu been through so much wit me it'll be impossible fo' me to fo' get dat, fam' chu actually made me solid to say da least. I did wut chu told me, I followed yo' lead now I need chu to trust and believe dat yo' lil' nigga still has da situation in control. Remember I am always still be 2 steps ahead of da game an dat even includes Ola baby. Tez Imma always remember one of da many things chu drilled in me. Neva let 'em see ya sweat 'cus it will sho' weakness. Well nigga I sho' no signs of weakness an if I figured it out correct afta' Mr. D. do his thing in court I will only have to do a year hopefully. Queenie said confidently six months at da most, so ya see cuz dey are da ones who will be sweatin' somethin' fierce fam'. Look afta' dis run I need fo' us to have a family gatherin' all of us,but we need to do dis Friday afta' court is ova." Speakin' 'er thoughts out loud; "Imma confuse da fuck outta da ma'fuckas, let da chess game begin." "Yo' baby girl yo' ass aiight?" "Yeah cuz jus' let me grab dis loot den we out." Queenie threw 4 big duffel bags in da back seat an hopped back in da drivers seat. Da limo was right on time an Tez yelled out fo' Queenie "Yo' lil' nigga da limo outside. Chu ready jet?" "Aiight cuz I hear chu." She told 'em as she started to walk down da stair case in a Louis Vuitton designer dress which was fit tight strapless dat stop at da knee wit a long lacy train flowed behind. "Damn shawty chu look beautiful." Cortez' was mesmerized by how gorgeous she was his mouth dropped open as his heart skipped a beat. Tez walked ova an stood at da bottom of da stairs an put his hand out,so he could help 'er down da last few steps. "Ueenie ya beautiful ma, I neva seen ya dis dressed up. Chu look good doe cuz, but chu say we goin' where again?" Queenie said; "Baby its all a disguise da whole get up, we finna go make dis last delivery,but in order fo' us to do dat wit out bein' suspicious an lookin' suspect I had us to dress as doe we goin' to a weddin'. Ya feel me? So is y'all ready?" She asked. "Lets do it shawty." Cortez' replied as 'em and Tez step back an watched Queenie walk to da door. "Umm_Uh_Umm homeboy I gotta hurry up an marry all of dat fo' some utter nigg tries to push up on wuts mines fam'." "Yeah my baby girl is skillful she can get wut she wants,when she wants it. Long as chu treatin' 'er right yo' ass ain't gotta stress ova 'er goin' no where else fam' chu feel me? She's in love wit chu homie, dats fo' damn sho'." Enterin' da limo dere was a bottle of Hennessy and Champagne on chill fo' da three along wit 2 big duffel bags packed wit clothes and drugs. Befo' da bag of gear was open Queenie grabbed three glasses an pop da top off da Champagne. Holdin' their glasses in da air she said; "'Ere's to life, its ride and die fam'." Tez and Cortez' in unison's repeated; "Its ride and die we love chu shawty_lil' nigga." An wit dat said dey threw da Champagne back an Queenie pulled out their gear handin' Cortez' COOGI jeans casual COOGI sweater wit a pair of TIMBERLAND boots an she dressed Tez in GUCCI jeans wit a long sleeve GUCCI button down shirt wit air force ones to match. Da 2 changed while she turned 'er head even doe it was 'er nigga an 'er cousin she didn't feel da need to watch 'em get dress. “Aiight ma we done.” “Cool turn y'all heads,so I can get dressed now.” Tez and Cotez' said we midst well pop da Hennessy open an while dose 2 rambled through da mini bar Queenie dressed in all black Louis Vuitton skin tight jean suit wit Louis Vuitton wife beater and black and white air force ones. She swooped down in da seat to pull up 'er jeans statin; “Gettin' dress in a car is a ma'fucka. “Yeah shawty it is,but yo' ass has become a pro at it.” An dey all broke out into laughter an Tez passed 'er a glass. “'Ere Ueenie, baby girl let me ask chu outta curiosity how ya come up wit dis shit.” Tez asked. “Skills and intelligence.” “Aiight I'll give ya dat, but answer dis how did chu get_ nah let me rephrase dat where did da driver get da bags from 'cus Flex neva brought 'em to da house ma. An how do chu know he didn't check fo' wuts inside 'em?”Cortez' and Tez were pegged an looked at Queenie curiously “Yo' chu niggas trippin' fo' questionin' me,but 'cus I love da shit outta both of y'all Imma give chu a pass an tell it today. Look our meetin' we had at da hospital when I told Flex to bring dat shit to da house,well all dat shit was setup like dat it was a decoy fo' who eva might have been listenin'. I ain't stupid an I don't sleep on shit all of dat was fo' Mr. D's ears an any utters listeners.” “Well hell ma why have 'em dere if chu think he's gonna snitch?” “I'm jus followin' his advice he made to be cautious dats all I'm doin' bein' cautious wit everything I do. Hell I gotta have a lil' faith in his ass since I keep havin' 'em represent my ass. Anyway I wanted to make sho' dat he wasn't bugged 'em self comin' up in da meetin' dats all,so if chu actually wanta know how da bags got in da car wit out Flex doin' it it was Mr. D..... Dis mornin' me and moms left out early dis mornin' an I met wit Mr. D. at his suite to get everything squared away far as da legal paper work done. Well when I through da 2 duffel bags at his feet an told 'em wut was up he basically had no utter choice, but to do wut I said 'cus in any form I thought he was bugged I wouldn't be sittin' 'ere wit chu 2. When we were leavin' da limo was jus' pullin' up which was perfect timin', so I sat in da cut of da parkin' lot at da hotel jus' so I could see Mr. D. get in da back seat wit da 2 bags da driver closed da door an got back in an pulled off givin' Mr. D. further instructions on da utter 2 duffel bags in da back seat dat sat where da 2 of chu are sittin'. Doe's 2 carried da money I needed 'em to make good on. I knew if he got in dat limo we were all gravy but at da meetin' an since it was a hospital I still needed to be a 100% sho' dis ma'fucka was on da up and up fam'." Cortez' questioned; "So chu felt like chu couldn't share dat wit us? Wut we snitches now to?" "Nah, I don't feel like dat at all." Lookin' Cortez' in his eyes she had a stern voice. "Listen I jus' got my own set of rules I live by an dats neva let my right hand know wut my left hand is doin'. Baby I know its only been a year,so Imma advise chu to ask ya homeboy 'bout me 'cus I'm not gonna explain myself." "So chu changin' on me now, right?" Cortez' asked as he took da seat next to Queenie.

"Nah I'll neva change on yo' ass,but I can't do da phony an I don't know how else to be,but real so trust and believe I will keep it raw and funky wit chu at all times." He whispered in Queenie's ear;

"I love ya ma no matter wut,but don't do me like dat." "Wait 'til y'all asses get back home fo' all dat shit. Baby girl chu gonna finish da script or not?" "Oh shit yeah cuz huh poe me a nutter one. Now far as da driver he's straight now turn 'round an say wutsup to Caine." Queenie let da divider glass down an Caine spoke; "Wutsup fellas its good to see y'all again." "Wut up homeboy?" Dey asked in unison's an den turned an looked at Queenie as to say wutsup ma,wuts really good? Queenie stated; "From 'ere on out Caine is our driver an dis 'ere is our own personal limo." Tez smiled an said; "Chu didn't cuz yo' ass bought da limo company out." She nodded 'er head to say yes. "Da only person I kept was

“THROWIN' BRICKS AT THE PENITENTIARY”

Caine I had employed 'em da day afta' Chuck and Lu's funeral. “So chu tell us chu been owner of da limo service since last year sometime?” Tez inquired. “No I been Caine's boss since den an da limo, but far as da biz'ness itself goes I_we jus' became owners of da limousine biz'ness. Dis biz'ness 'ere is one of many dat will laundry my money.” “Cuz chu been workin' wit Mr. D. all along?” “See I figure dats how I could find out if he decided he wanted to play by Ola rules or if he would stay true to da bitch dat feeds 'em,but either way he'll fuck 'em self. Dats why I made dat statement at da meetin' he was dere 'cus I felt he was already into deep,but he still had da opportunity to leave wut he do? He stayed I am his source of bread and butter now.” “Boss!” Caine's voice came through da intercom; “We will be pullin' up at da spot in 'bout 5 minutes we're 2 blocks away.” “Aiight no chance of us bein' followed?” Queenie questioned. “Non boss I followed all da instructions ya gave me an I stayed under da radar. Okay boss we're 'ere.” He put da car in park an got out an walk to da back an open da door fo' his passengers to exit. Queenie stepped out wit a duffel bag in hand followed by Cortez' den Tez. Inside da big brown stone Mr. Cho who was a ol' head gracefully greeted Queenie wit open arms as usual. He kissed 'er hand an said; “Boss Queen” How are chu?” “Fine Mr. Cho' I'm doin' good honestly.” Mr. Cho' shook his head no, no, no, no, “I know dere is somethin' wrong 'cus ya neva come to do yo' own biz'ness transactions an dese are 2 new faces I am seein' wut happen to da Skip guy?” “Chu mean da same one chu talked to me 'bout dat got down wit Ola? Well unfortunately I had to cut 'em loose Mr. Cho' if he felled a dummy setup chu know I couldn't keep 'em in my circle.” Mr. Cho' said; “Dats why I love 'er she's very smart.” Queenie said; “Far as me bringin' dese 2 wit me I felt it was time to introduce da three of chu. Mr. Cho' dis 'ere is my soon to be husband Cortez'.” Cortez' stuck his hand out to shake Mr. Cho's,but Queenie intervened by placin' 'er hand on top of his hand shakin' 'er head to say no. “Baby Mr. Cho' doesn't shake hands 'cus dats a sign of disrespect

towards 'em." "Cortez' apologized quickly to Mr. Cho' 'cus he didn't want to make any problems fo' or wit his girls connect. Mr. Cho' dis 'ere is Tez my cousin who I will ride and die fo'." "So dis is da non utter dan Tez Miles huh?" Mr. Cho' bowed his head an Tez returned da gesture. "Mr. Miles may I call chu dat?" He asked. "Yeah." "Well Mr. Miles I've heard so many wonderful stories 'bout chu. "Boss Queen really looks up to ya she is yo' young protege'. She tells me ya taught 'er everything dat she knows an dat she consider chu as 'er brother instead of 'er cousin. Now dats a close bond dat no one can eva rip apart an dat dere is wut chu call family bond neva let anything happen to 'er. Always protector 'er. Mr. Fabs chu finna be 'er husband?" Cortez' said; "Yeah sir Mr. Cho' I am. Cortez' nodded wit a proud stance. "Well do chu have any idea of wut yo' roll is or yo' position chu play?" Queenie seen da offensive look on Cortez' face, but said nothin' she jus' let Mr. Cho' speak. "Mr. Fabs no disrespect to chu son,but chu have to realize dis young lady 'ere is worth millions an has plenty haters out dere in 'em streets. Queenie's very intelligent an very well rounded. Dat means do everything in yo' power to make sho' 'er well bein' is protected even if dat means chu takin' a fall fo' 'er den do it or it may be takin' a bullet and dyin' fo' 'er den do it. As 'er King wit a woman of 'er status and statue as "Boss Queen" she will need chu even doe she is very stubborn chu gotta take control at some point." Queenie said; "Mr. Cho' dis da reason I needed chu to meet da 2 men who means da world to me 'cus Ola is on my ass an I know dat dey will be comin' fo' me soon. Tez and Cortez' will be da ones handlin' all of my biz'ness an holdin' my circle together,so dat speech chu jus' gave I appreciate it,but a nuff bullets have run threw my family. Besides I need both of 'em on da streets holdin' things down."
Mr. Cho' got a lil' chocked up an as he cleared his throat he asked; "Boss Queen" "How long will chu be down? I mean how do chu know dis an wut can I do to help? "Boss Queen" wut are dey tryin' to charge chu wit?" "Somethin' 'bout bein' da biggest Queen pin from Chicago to East St. Louis." She

said nonchalant like it was no big deal. Mr. Cho' looked in 'er direction as doe he was scared fo' 'er, she reassured 'em she would be aiight. “Mr. Cho' don't worry it won't be long fo' chu see me again I'll be back at chu.” “Of course chu will an I will be dere wit open arms as usual.” Queenie had thought 'bout da phony ass smile on his face an she decided against callin' Mr. Cho' out on not speakin' his mind or wut was on his chest jus' 'cus she has much respect fo' 'em so she neva said anything out of pocket afta' all she knew he had neva steered 'er wrong. Mr. Cho' was da biggest drug lord in Detroit, but when he went into retirement he had plans on doin' somethin' fo' da lil' ghetto kids. So he became a scout. Scoutin' da basketball courts to sponsor talented unprivileged kids an yes Queenie was one of dose kids who grew up in da ghetto,but wit Tez in 'er corner far from unprivileged. Neva da less Mr. Cho' sponsored 'er trip fo' a basketball tournament ova in Japan at da age of 14. Queenie and Mr. Cho' had been in contact every since,so when he found out dat she was in da streets an makin' major moves he got word to 'er dat he needed to see 'er. Back in East St. Boogie Queenie had instructed da driver to go to da hospital an he could leave from dere. Queenie said; “Lets go up 'ere an see wutsup wit auntie. Baby call Giz'mo an tell 'em pick us up 'ere at da hospital.” “Wutsup auntie?” Queenie said wit a cheerful tone she den bent ova da bed an kissed Heathers fo' head. “Aye ma how chu feelin' up in dis peace?” Tez questioned. Den he gave 'er a kiss on da fo' head an Cortez' follow suit. “Yo' auntie chu leavin soon?” Queenie asked. “I'm fine and I should be leavin' tomorrow hopefully if not it will be da day afta'.” “How long chu gotta be in da crib befo' chu can move 'round?” “Hell niecy poo dese sons of bitches don't want me to rest. I gotta come up 'ere fo' therapy 3 times a week.

Chapter Twenty-Eight
"Family It's Time To Make Moves"

"Aiight listen auntie I came to tell chu I got dat limo biz'ness straighten out an its in yo' name. All da major paper work is taken care of, so to be honest I need chu to start befo' Friday if ya think ya can do it. I jus' need to setup everything befo' dey come get me. I need to make sho' everybody has a job an knows their part." "Ma wuts da deal is chu gonna be able to pull dis off?" Tez asked. Befo' she could respond Queenie cut in. "Why wouldn't she specially when she got chu 2. Auntie is jus' da front man fo' us an chu and Cortez' are da behind da scenes keepin' da fellas in line an on que. Keepin' da books straight 'cus wit me bein' away I don't need or want any money fuck ups. If auntie is eva questioned 'bout 'er employees all she needs to tell 'em is dat she's a one woman sho' its 'er an 'er drivers. Besides 'em she has to manage 'er books." "Okay baby girl wut did chu name it or did chu leave it da same?" Tez asked. "Nah fam' I changed it to Blue and Red Limo Service. It was 2 utter names I wanted, but considerin' da situation da family is in I went against it. I figured no one knew our babies beside us,so I felt it would be da perfect name." Tez felt da connection an Queenie could see da wells of his eyes tear up. Huggin' 'er he told 'er; "I love yo' ass baby girl." "Fam' I know chu do, but don't be goin' all soft on me nigga." She said jokingly. Heather asked curiously wut was da utter 2 names did she pick out. "Auntie I had thoughts of Chuck and Lu's Take It Home Limo Service or da utter one woulda been TCQ, but decided Ola woulda put 2 and 2 together." "Smart thinkin' cuz I like da one chu got." Knock, Knock, someone shouted; "Wutsup family y'all back huh? How chu feelin' auntie?" Giz'mo asked as he walked ova to Heathers bed an planted a kiss on 'er fo' head. "Oh baby I'm good. How chu doin'?" "Auntie I'm suave its all good, jus' waitin' on chu to blow dis place."

"It should be tomorrow,but I'll definitely be dere by time chu and Stacks move in baby." "Auntie we beat chu to it. Boss we cleared out an cleaned da stash house and boarded it up jus' as chu wanted." Queenie stated; "I'm impressed chu niggas still had a few days left, but y'all decided to end early huh?" "Yeah auntie welcomed us wit open arm, so we closed shop. An we'll be done wit da few bricks by Friday fo' sho'." Tez cut in; "Where y'all put dat shit?" "Yo' family it's buried in da back yard of da stash house." Friday came to fast fo' Queenie an she refused to sho' 'er family any signs of fear dat she was endurin'. Queenie had thoughts of fleein' da country, but she couldn't see 'er self runnin' from anyone or thing. Den 'er thoughts of goin' out in a blaze of glory came back an said fuck it she would end 'er life all together. She quickly decided against dat one 'cus she wasn't a coward, so instead she put a blank look on 'er face. Tez knew no matter how hard she tried to hide it she was in fear of wut was 'bout to happen an goin' to da penitentiary. All he could do at dat point was stand by 'er side an be dere fo' 'er. His thoughts were if he could do da time fo' 'er he would do dat wit no questions asked. Cortez' stepped in front of Queenie an wrapped his arms 'round 'er waist as he squatted to look into 'er eyes he said; "Ma quit yo' worryin', aiight. Lets jus' get through dis 'ere first baby. Mr. D. said dat he would get chu da less time as possible he could get chu." Queenie shook 'er head up and down wit out sayin' a word she jus' dropped 'er head in Cortez' chest. "Its cool ma chu gonna be aiight." While rubbin' 'er back he told 'er dey we're gonna make it through it together. Queenie walked inside da court room wit 'er entire entourage behind 'er. Queenie leadin' wit Mr. Demontea' by 'er side den followed Tez, Cortez',Flex, Tre', Giz'mo, Stacks, Chris, Jo, Joc and Lil' Man. She spotted 'er mother and aunt Heather sittin' in da front row of seats behind da lawyers bench where 'er an Mr. D. sat. "All rise fo' da honorable judge Websters chu maybe seated." Da bailiff told da courtroom. Blaah, Blaah was all Queenie heard comin' from da states attorney's mouth, 'er ears felt like dey had noise blockers in 'em an everything dat was said sounded muffled to 'er. Even when da judge told 'er lawyer to state his case it even sounded irksome, to da point she jus' wanted to lay down wit no fight. Da very last thing Queenie heard clearly was judge Webster say was; "Mr. Demontea I don't want to believe dat dis young lady committed any of da murders dey have charged against 'er an I am anxious to get 'er some help, but from da reports I see dere's nothin' dat can be done to save 'er life at dis point wit out killin' 'er. Da judge paused an turned his attention towards to Queenie. "Ms. Miles are chu coherent?" Mr. Demontea' nudge Queenie's arm. "Queenie da judge is speakin' to ya now. She turned an looked at Mr. D. wit a set of da coldest black eyes he had eva seen befo'. "Queenie its almost ova I need chu to answer da judges question. Dis means chu have to look up at 'em Ms. Miles." "I got chu Mr. D.." Queenie coached 'er self I can do dis, 'er head was flooded wit wut Ola was planin' on doin', clogged 'er brain,so much she couldn't focus an dat only frustrated 'er mo'. "Come on baby talkin' to 'er conscience I gotta hold my composure, dis is our life. Queenie took a deep sigh an held 'er head high. "Yes yo' honor." "Ms. Miles I should send chu to juvenile 'cus ya still a baby fo' wut dey say ya done, 'til chu turn of age an send chu straight to da penitentiary, but fortunately I have a heart an today is a good day. I don't think dats da solution fo' dis condition of urns, but I do want to mandate chu to go see a psychic twice a week an Ms. Miles take care of yo' self da best chu can."Judge Webster said; "All charges of murder against Queenie Miles have been dropped dis court is a journ." Da judge hit his gavel against da small mallet. Queenie mouth Thank chu to da judge nonchalantly turned to 'er lawyer an hugged thankin' 'em. Queenie said in earshot; "We need to talk, Imma call da red phone in a hour." Tez could see his cousin was not right an wanted to run straight to 'er, but decide to fall back peep da vics 'er eyes fell upon. When he noticed 'er starin' Ola down he gotta eerie feelin' dat shit was finna get real ugly, so he needed to retrieve his baby girl an get da hell outta da courtroom. Cortez' was a lil' slow on da draw,but soon caught on. "Dis may jus' be da day dat dey take chu down lil' nigga ." Tez put on a big front in front of Ola tryin' to throw 'em off as he put a smile on his face an threw his arm 'round Queenie's neck. "Yo' baby girl chu ready to go through wit dis game of chess chu got goin' on Ueenie?" Shakin' 'er head as to say yes an once outside she told 'em; "Take y'all places chu know wut to do." "Squad up family." Tez shouted. Queenie had it setup,so when Ola came tryin' to take each individual dey would get a slap in da face when dey smash in da door would be a known Mr. D. fo' 'em. Queenie had da fellas to leave each an every door wide open on every house she owned even da warehouse includin' 'er moms and aunts house. "If Ola wants me 'ere I am baby." Queenie shouted at da gatherin' table sittin' in Tez's dinnin' room. Liz and Queenie had fixed a feast fit fo' a King,but in dis case it was fo' a QUEEN. All gathered as one big happy family dey laughed, talk an enjoyed one a nutter company as if nothin' was 'bout to happen. "Boss 'eres to chu ma." Chris said wit a smile on his face. "We love ya baby an remember dey can't hold a good woman down." Holdin' up his glass. "Baby afta' dey get chu processed me Tez, Chris and moms will be up dere, so I can marry chu. Den afta' chu get home we can have da weddin' chu dreamed of wit all da family." "No baby I don't want dat leave everything as is 'til I get back home." Mr. D. chimed in; "She's right even doe it sounds like a good idea its best if she stays Queenie Miles 'til she gets home 'cus Ola at dis point has been a vendetta wit 'er 'cus she's been treatin' their lives fo' sometime now. 'Em bein' annoyed by our actions in court today, dey will try da best of their ability to make it hell fo' 'er an da rest of ya. I advise all of chu to jus' follow wut eva Ms. Miles instructed chu to do 'til she gets back to y'all." Cortez' picked Queenie up an spun 'er 'round_ "Okay shawty I'll do it yo' way." Kissin' 'er on da lips passionately in earshot; "Ma jus' hurry back home to me, Imma be waitin'." Queenie's red phone went off. "Dis is it ma." Cortez' said knowin' it was only one person who could be callin'. "Hello." Queenie said to Caine who was on da utter end. "Boss dey jus' hit both stash houses an da warehouse."

“THROWIN' BRICKS AT THE PENITENTIARY”

“Wut damage did dey do? She questioned. “Non boss wut could dey do wit da doors wide open, but I can see dat dey are pissed an dey are headed yo' way full force an fully loaded.” “Dat many huh?” Queenie gave out a big sigh an stated; “I guess dis is it family dey on da way, so see chu when I touch back down.” “Boss Queen” Keep yo' head up ma.” Caine told 'er as dey ended da call. Queenie shook Mr. D's hand tellin' 'em; “Thank ya Mr. D. I'm expectin' chu to handle yo' biz'ness an turn dis shit 'round an get me a shorter stay.” Cortez' hugged is baby 'round da waist from behind an told 'er; “I love chu ma an I ain't goin' no where, Imma be right 'ere.” Queenie looked at Tez an reached out 'er arms wrappin' 'em 'round his neck. “I love yo' ass family chu know its ride and die wit us right? Cuz make sho' chu take care of dese 2 beautiful women 'ere.” Queenie motioned 'er hand fo' 'er moms and aunt as 'er and Tez walked towards their parents. Da 4 had a group hug an told Queenie dey loved 'er in unison's. Liz said; “Take care baby an no matter wut try to hold dat temper of urns please.” “Aiight ma I will.” “But don't let 'em bitches see no weakness either an don't take no shit from nobody chu a Miles an we don't raise any punk-asses chu feel me.” “Feelin' chu auntie.” Queenie individually kissed their fo' heads an said; “I love chu an I love chu.” She gave Chris an da rest of da fellas hugs and dap, pounds as Liz told everyone to sit fo' dessert. “We got German Chocolate Cake and sweet potato pies.” Throughout da room ya heard da awes, oooohs, hand claps and lips smackin'. “Let me give my QUEEN da first piece.” Jus' as Liz placed Queenie's slice of sweet potato pie in front of 'er dis was where 'er game of chess began an it was 'er against 'em. She had all of 'er people ready an in position on da floor face down wit their hands on top of their heads except 'er aunt Heather who had to stay in 'er wheelchair, but she to assumed da position wit 'er hands on 'er head also. Queenie could hear 'em comin' runnin' into da house yellin' get down, get down an nobody move assume da fuckin' positioooon. “Wut da fuck?” A officer said seein' everyone laid out across da floor. Queenie put 'er fork down done eatin' 'er pie she took a napkin off da table an wiped 'er mouth, an officer walked ova an said; "Queenie Miles chu are under arrest fo' traffickin' drugs. An blaah, blaah was wut she heard afta' dat 'er rights had been read to 'er, but neva once did dey come in wit papers fo' da raid of 'er properties. Queenie scooted 'er chair back listenin' to Ola try an down grade 'er, callin' 'er every name in he book dat wasn't a child of God. Once she stood from da table all guns were pointed at 'er cocked and loaded ready to take 'er down. "Chu lil' bitch wut did chu think dis lil' fiasco chu planned would make yo' ass look any cutter?" Da officer got all up in Queenie's face. "Bitch dat lil' stunt y'all pulled off in court today was funny, but I bet dis 'ere ain't funny. Now is it?" Dey were reckless pushin' 'er down ova da table an den he slammed Queenie's head into a Champagne bottle which broke an cut 'er ova da eye, dat gave 'er a big ass gash which needed admitted attention. She tried to hold 'er tongue, but da pain in 'er eye would no longer let 'er. Tez, Cortez' and da family were furious, but dey remained silent out of respect fo' Queenie an how she mapped it out fo' 'em.

"Yo' fuck chu nigga all chu Ola bitch ass niggas, where I'm from y'all pigs ain't no better. Gotta beat on a kid to boost yo' ego huh? Well go ahead nigga do chu." Queenie said; "Get my lawyer." Lookin' directly into da officers eyes wit 'er blank stare an 'er cold black eyes wit venom in 'er voice she told 'em; "Get me a ma'fuckin' ambulance chu see all dis blood gushin' outta my head." "Officer Ted call dis lil' bitch a ambulance an lets get 'er fixed up,so we can run 'er ass in." An dey all started to laugh at Queenie's expense. "I maybe young an a bitch to chu,but I can assure chu an all yo' colleagues I will take chu on yo' best day pig." Ola had pissed Queenie off, but challengin' 'em was not wut she was suppose to do, neva da less he had got under 'er skin wit all da abuse an da bitch word. "So ya challengin' me huh?" He asked laughin' tryin' to be funny as possible to cover up his embarrassment.

"Ms. Miles chu know dats a nutter charge I could add to yo' shit right, but I won't do dat 'cus I know chu ain't got no win, I'll jus' take it as illusional talk from da pain in yo' head." "Ma'fucka chu'll take it as dat 'cus dats wut punk ass bitch niggas such as yo' self do when their scared. An knowin' dat all yo' fellow brothers 'ere seen ya get yo' ass whipped by a young ass bitch will truly be somethin' da precinct would neva let yo' punk ass live down pig." "Everybody get up off da floor an stand against da wall." "Boss chu gonna let dis lil' kid talk to chu like dat? Give dat lil' ma'fucka wut she's not lookin' fo' somethin' 'er daddy should have given 'er ass along time ago." Da whole force was in accomplice wit their fellow officer getting at Queenie. Da paramedics arrived an stitched 'er up on da scene like Ola had 'em on call already an dey left da scene jus' as fast as dey appeared. Cortez' couldn't hold his tongue any longer; "Yo' wut chu need to do homeboy is fight a nigga 'cus seems like a real bitch move to be fuckin' wit a female." "Dats 'cus Ola ain't shit." Chris spat. "Awe chu don't want to witness yo' lil' bitch get 'er ass stomped, by a man. Well don't worry Imma go easy on 'er, but of course afta' I'm done beatin' 'er ass chu can be next." Queenie spat; "Yo' ain't non of dat necessary." She looked at 'er family to say I got dis. Queenie looked at Mr. D. an he patted his chest an gave 'er a slight nod lettin' 'er know dat he had it all. She den made eye contact wit Tez an she could see da fire in his eyes. He didn't approve of how Ola treated his baby girl an he was unsure of 'em provokin' Queenie to fight. Tez mouth I love chu, do chu ma, but don't kill 'em." "Bitch wut chu lookin' at 'em fo' dey can't help yo' ass. Awe she needs help." Smack Ola stole off on Queenie. "Dat shit ain't cool, take da bracelets off 'er an give 'er a chance to at least fight back an defend 'er self." Everyone yelled. She stumbled backwards, but held 'er weight. Stumblin' she fell back against Tez and Chris. "Ma I'm not down wit dis dis ma'fucka is not gonna fight fare, but handle yo' biz'ness ma." Ola snatched 'er up off of Tez by da cuffs. "Yo' take da cuffs off 'er an let me sho' 'er young ass dat we run dis shit 'ere in East St. Boogie." As da cuffs came off Queenie's mind and body dropped into a trans. "Yo' boss its somethin' wrong wit dis lil' bitch." Officer Nut Sack said. I__ ouuuuch was da sound dey heard as Queenie swiftly caught da officer in his throat an pushed 'em across Tez dinner table. Click, Click. "No hold yo' fire da officer said. "I got dis." Holdin' his hands up to stop his colleagues from shootin' 'er down. One utter punch was all da officer could get off. Queenie felt she had took a nuff abuse and beatin' dat she was 'bout to stand fo'. She had no remorse or respect fo' Ola anyway, so she went hem, afta' da first punch landed Queenie let loose an went all in on da officer. Da smacks from da punches was all ya could see and hear,she decided not to say a word befo' she fell into 'er trans. Everyone could see da officer barely standin' Queenie had caught 'em in a weak spot right between his abdomen and rib cage. Constantly jabbin', jab afta' jab she neva realized she had broke his ribs. He fell to da floor an Queenie dropped on top of 'em wit a jaw breaker punches. Left, right, left, right, Ola could no longer see wit his eyes damn near closed shut. "Yo' stop da fight!" Tez shouted. Knowingly Queenie was in a killa's mode at dis point, Tez tried to reason wit da officers he tried to persuade 'em to let 'em get 'er. "Yo' let me get 'er under control,so y'all can take 'er to da station an tend to yo' officer." One of da officers waved his gun signalin' 'em to go ahead an get 'er calmed down. Tez den grabbed his lil' cousin up from behind an whispered softly in 'er ear; "Its me ma, close yo' eyes baby girl." Tez quickly turned 'er to face only da family to shield 'er eyes from Ola. He shaked 'er softly__ "Come on ma I need chu to come back to me. Listen to my voice baby girl its da same routine I need fo' chu to drop to da floor wit me, keep yo' eyes close please nod yo' head if chu understand me. Dere was no response an while Tez tried his hardest to get Queenie to snap back while da paramedics tried to bring da officer back 'round out of his unconsciousness. "Ueenie do chu hear me baby girl its Tez, please nod yo' head if chu hear me."

"I hear chu fam'." She told 'em in a low whisper. "Good, good lil' nigga listen I'll explain all dis later, right now try to focus. Ola is finna take yo' ass to jail don't say anything jus' go an Mr. D. will be dere an y'all will go from dere." "Cuz why my head hurt so bad?" Puttin' 'er hand up to 'er head. "Sssss_ouch wut da fuck! Yo' why all y'all bloody?" Stand up lets go an officer shouted at Tez. Its time to go pushin' Tez to da side an snatchin' Queenie up off da floor, dey put hand cuffs back on 'er an walked 'er out to da squad car. Outside stood da whole neighborhood full wit on lookers. Cain was also positioned,so he could take photo's since he was da only member not in da house 'cus Ola had no clue he was on Queenie's payroll. Cain entered Cortez' and Queenie's house through da back door an posted up jus' in case any foul play went on afta' Ola entered Tez house. Ola put Queenie in a integration room an left 'er dere fo' ova an hour an within dis time she tried to put things in prospective an figure out why she had a cut ova 'er eye. "Wut da fuck happen." She questioned 'er self, not makin' any emotional face expressions 'cus she knew Ola was watchin' 'er through da mirrored picture window an she knew any sudden moves she made dey would be like white on rice pressurin' 'er to tell 'em somethin'. "Think Queenie think." She told 'er self ova and ova. "Chu gotta find out wut happen." 'Er conscience told 'er to ask fo' 'er phone call, so she could hit Tez up 'cus he could explain." Jus' as she got ready to demand 'er phone call, Mr. D. walked in an Queenie's face lit up like a Christmas tree on a beautiful Christmas day. "Queenie how are chu, how is yo' head? Are dey treatin' chu okay?" "Nah, I been sittin' in dis room since dey brought me 'ere. I was actually jus' finna go hem 'cus I ain't got my phone call jet,but I'm glad to see chu 'ere Mr. D.." "Queenie have a seat, so I can talk to ya." Dey both sat down an dose were da only words spoke. Mr. Demontea' took out a pad and pen dat already had a few questions dat he wanted 'er to answer. Ms. Miles take dis read it carefully was wrote on top of da paper in big letters. "Queenie I don't want chu to say anything verbally 'cus I know dey are watchin' an I am pretty sho' dey have da room tapped. Now don't worry I got all da evidence we need from da moment Ola walked into da house. I also got da pictures from Cain. I called in a favor from judge Webster to get chu in court tomorrow mornin'. Queenie dis will play out nicely da judge will be leaned on chu, but he still has to do his job to protect da people. Da district attorney didn't like wut da judge had to say an dat was 'em givin' chu a deal 'em self instead of givin' chu 30 years he will expect chu to do 4 months in da penitentiary dey have a drug treatment group dat will mandate chu to attend. From dere chu will be shipped to a treatment center fo' women to get dat psychic help he wants chu to get.” Afta' readin' and answerin' questions Queenie flipped to da next sheet of paper an wrote Mr. D. 'er own lil' note. “Thank ya Mr. D. fo' everything, I know meetin' me has been probably a obstreperous. I appreciate all da shit chu have had to pull off ova da last year fo' me. I know wit my loopy ass condition and track record I carry wit da court system it hasn't been a walk in da park fo' chu. So of course chu will be compensated a great deal.” Queenie slept in da holdin' cell dat night alone.

Chapter Twenty-Nine
“Hands Can Be Da Best Defense Fo' Da Offense”

Every utter persons dat dey had in da cell when she came in were no longer dere, each one had been assigned to a cell. Queenie was glad to finally be alone, but either way she thought 'bout it she knew Ola was fuckin' wit 'er 'cus she beat da shit outta one of their pig brothers. Lookin' 'round da holdin' cell it was flithy somethin' Queenie couldn't register in 'er mind. Unfortunately she did grow up in da heart of da ghetto in Chicago, smellin' da pissy hallways and stairwells dat ya had to take 'cus da pissy elevators were out of order. So it was no doubt she had seen filth,but it was a big difference from den and now 'cus back den she had a choice an now she felt she didn't 'cus da law said we got yo' black ass now an chu have no say so in wut chu do. Queenie setup all night long smellin' piss dat offended 'er nose as she watched a coupla mice play in a corner of da cell. Queenie placed 'er back against da wall bendin' 'er knees to 'er chest puttin' 'er chin on da bends of 'er knees an closed 'er eyes. Shift changed a CO yelled out; "Yo' Miles get ready 10 minutes chu go on a rid." He tossed 'er a bag wit a toothbrush and toothpaste in it. Afta' brushin' 'er teeth she looked at 'er face in da smudged reflectin' plate da cell had as a mirror. "Yo' CO wuts a rid?" She questioned. "Ya goin' to court, turn 'round an put yo' hands through da bars. A van waited outside fo' da inmates to aboard so dey could be transported to da East St. Boogies court house downtown. Climbin' in da van Queenie saw a few utter faces she had seen 'round town, mainly niggas dat tried to get down between 'er legs or utters dat knew 'er line of work an wanted to be on 'er team. A few greeted 'er wit some wutsup "Boss Queen" an utters whispered and hated. Queenie nodded 'er head to say wutup back to dose who acknowledged 'er, an fo' dose who stared and whispered she put on a smile 'er face an ignored 'em. So aye yo' chu "Boss Queen" Huh?" A voice of a CO said; "So yo' lil' ass da one who fuckin' beat Steve's ass an put 'em in da hospital?" He asked wit his fist up to his mouth. "Oooooh shit lil' mama chu did his ass crucial." His colleague nudged his arm an asked; "Who side chu on?" "Dude I know wut side I'm on,but chu gotta admit she whoop dat nigga ass an he's_ Lookin' at Queenie's file fo' a second_ She's only 16 come on an she's a girl.....Ah stop bein' a hater chu gotta give it to 'er, she banged dat ass good. One nigga in da back said wit excitement; "Yo' ma chu da one who dey call "Boss Queen" huh? Damn chu was da one who beat Ola ass?" Queenie knew she couldn't say anything to incriminate 'er self,so she jus' turned 'er head 'round an winked at da fellas in back. "Oh shit dats wuts up we got mad props fo' chu ma." Queenie turned back 'round facin' front so she could keep 'er eyes on da CO's. Walkin' into da courthouse shackled to 9 utter men Queenie lead da pack, wit a CO in front of 'er an one in da back of da line dey entered da courtroom an had a seat where only criminals sat right next to da judge. Half da courtroom was filled wit 'er family she saw Tez and Cortez' seated next to 'er moms and auntie. "Yo' I love yo' ass ma." Cortez' mouth first an as she look Tez, Liz and Heather it was like a domino affect dey all mouth da same thing. Queenie said nothin' she jus' nodded 'er head. Mr. D. walked ova to da CO an afta' their conversation da CO uncuffed Queenie ankles, so she could walk out da courtroom to speak wit 'er lawyer. All rise fo' da honorable judge Webster once he entered da courtroom an took his seat everyone else had a seat. Da courts call Queenie Miles. Queenie stood next to 'er lawyer wit a sort of cockiness 'bout 'er. "Ms. Miles its really not a pleasure seein' chu back so soon, but since ya 'ere lets get dis ova wit. Ms. Queenie Miles da charges dat have been charged up against chu are as followed: bein' da biggest Queen pin from 'ere to Chicago, conspiracy of attempted murder against an officer, an ya bein' charged wit assultin' a nutter police officer. How do chu plead?" "Not guilty yo' honor." Queenie said. Mr. Demontea' where is da evidence of dese false allegations chu say has been misappropriate charged against yo' client?" "Yes yo' honor,I do have 'ere exhibit one a small tape recorder,where officer Steve an his colleagues tortured, intimidated and agonized my client an she fell into 'er mental state of mind. Exhibit two we have 'ere photo's of how she was bein' mistreated in da midst of bein' apprehended. While 'er fate was bein' decided by dis big black man sittin' behind da huge Mahogany Oak desk. Queenie drifted off into 'er own thoughts once again. "I guess I'm 'ere an dis shit is real some where I neva considered bein' at all even wit my mom Tez and Cortez' tellin' me to always slow down 'cus I was "THROWIN' BRICKS AT DA PENITENTIARY." No yo' stubborn ass didn't listen to well at da words chu were given. Fuck now I gotta..... "Ms. Miles." Queenie shook 'er head to shake off 'er thoughts wit 'er conscience. "Yes sir yo' honor." Judge Webster said; "Ms. Miles chu will spend six months in DCC fo' women an chu are eligible fo' days on good behavior. Once chu earn dat it cuts yo' time in half. Ms. Miles afta' three months chu will be sent to a treatment center fo' women only, so chu can be treated by a psych doctor." Queenie felt degraded bein' stripped into da prison wit a bunch of utter females in da same room. A girl next to 'er saw da disgust on 'er face an she said; "Get use to it 'cus 'ere ya stripped and search when eva dey tell chu ma." Queenie stated; "Preciate da heads up, but not ya ma home girl." Da girl got a lil' offended at da way Queenie praised 'er an at da same time stomped on 'er like she was nothin'. "My bad." She put 'er hand out to shake Queenie's hand. "My name is Rochell." Queenie look down at 'er hand dat she let gravity hold up. "Boss Queen" I go by "Boss Queen". "Oh shit chu "Boss Queen"? Chu a legend in Chi- Town if ya da same person." "Yeah its only one "Boss Queen". "Word is "Boss Queen" single handed kill da biggest Kingpin dat ran halve of Chicago. Triple was da man he had a master plan an a million dollar operation goin' on." Movin' to da next processin' procedure da girl started to get on Queenie last nerve. "Yo' Rochell is it?" Queenie questioned. "Why da fuck chu ridin' a dead mans dick,so hard? Are chu related to 'em, was he yo' nigga or pusher? Wut tell me 'cus Triple is dead no longer 'round fo' ya to jock home girl,so wut is it to chu who killed his ass? 'Cus it won't bring 'em back." "Nah it ain't nothin' like dat at all. I jus' was askin' 'cus it seems a lil' strange to me chu look like a baby by da face. If chu don't mine me askin' how old are chu?" At first Queenie started to jap out 'cus she felt ol' girl was bein' a lil' to nosy, but den 'er conscience kicked in to gear an told 'er to use everything to 'er advantage. "I'm 16." She know da word would get 'round da prison dat "Boss Queen" was a 16 year old kid an she was up in da joint an wasn't to be fucked wit. Queenie thought she would jus' lay back,so she wouldn't get into any trouble an try to ride 'er timeout wit out any problems or altercations,but dat of course didn't last long. An altercation she found 'er self in only afta' a month dere, she walked through da chow line to get a tray of slop da institution called food an some huge big foot woman who had a look of a rough ass man asked some one repeatedly; "Is dat dat "Boss Queen" bitch?" She was egged on by da entire cafeteria. Queenie slapped da braud wit 'er entire tray home girl lose 'er balance an fell back on a nutter table den she was pushed to da floor. Queenie pounced down on top of 'er an started bangin' 'er head on da cement floor. Queenie was drugged to da hole where she stayed da remainin' of 'er time. 4 long months wit no visitors or contact wit love ones makin' Queenie feel alone 'cus she knew nothin' not even why she was out population. But now it was time to go to da second part of 'er program. "Wutup cuz?" She ask da person on da utter end of da phone. "Oh fuck baby girl I'm glad to hear yo' voice lil' nigga. Wuts good baby? I thought I was gone loose my damn mind 'round 'ere, every time I would come to see chu dey would turn me 'round 'cus chu had went to seg fo' assault on a nutter inmate. Cuz dey didn't tell me if chu had an episode or if chu was aiight nothin'. Dey wouldn't tell us shit,so all I could do was keep moms and auntie in prayer dat yo' ass pull through dat shit okay. Cuz when dey let chu out of da hole lil' nigga?" Tez asked. "Aye yo' I hit yo' books up,so dey tight have dey let chu go shop jet?" Tez was jus' full of questions he was,so excited dat he was able to talk to his lil' cousin finally.

"Yo' fam' slow down nigga. I'm cool I made it through dat shit,but I don't know how 'cus I can't remember a damn thing really except I was in a fuckin' hole fo' 4 months nigga an dey snatched my ass from dat cold ass hole put me in a van an dey shipped me out 'bout 4 days ago." "Hold, hold on ma where chu at lil' nigga? Where did dey ship yo' lil' ass to?" "Yo' fam' I'm in Chi- Town, yeah find out from Mr. D. how long I gotta be 'ere 'cus I'm not feelin' dis place or da bitches livin' 'ere cuz." Queenie told Tez its a tragedy waitin' to happen in dis ma'fucka. Yo' I figured y'all didn't know I was 'ere 'cus I hadn't seen or heard from any of chu, so where is moms and Cortez' at?" "Baby girl Cortez' had to go up to Blue and Red's to handle somethin' an auntie should jus' be getting home from work she's back to pullin' doubles. Yo' lil' nigga we gotta lot of catchin' up to do, when can chu get passes to move a 'round?” “Hell my psych already gave me my passes fo' my movement, but chu know cuz I ain't finna walk no where. Fam' call Mr. D. tell his ass to get ova 'ere asap 'cus I need to talk to 'em I gotta get da fuck home cuz. Matter a fact chu and Cortez' need to camp out up 'ere 'cus shit I need to be able to move 'round everyday an if I gotta move 'round in Chi-Town chu already know wut it is. Yo' pull three niggas away from Blue and Red's an bring 'em wit, an make sho' one of 'em is Chris.” Wut eva way anyone looked at it Queenie still had authority an shit still went 'er way even out of sight. Tez knew requistion was his job to give Queenie wut she wanted afta' all dat was his baby. “Yo' lil' nigga Mr. D. will be dere in da next hour,so be patient an we will be. We leavin' out tonight 'cus I need dese niggas to finish up their shifts befo' we head out. Baby girl I can't wait to see yo' ass ma, an everybody gonna be trippin' to hear chu in Chicago. We can come get chu in da mornin',so we'll have mo' time 'cus I know by time we get dere it'll be to late.” “Yeah fam' do dat 'cus I need to go to somebody's store to get some fresh gear, so I can't get up out dis bullshit ass clothes dey got me in.” Knock, Knock “Yo' bro its me.” A voice yelled from da foyer. Cortez' shouted; “Nigga where da hell chu at?” Tez couldn't hear 'em 'cus he was in his bedroom on da phone laughin' wit Queenie. “Yo' family!” “I'm upstairs nigga.” “Damn bro I haven't see yo' ass laugh or crack a smile in 'bout 5 months nigga. Wuts good?” Cortez' asked. Tez tossed 'em da phone ova da banister. “Yo' catch bro.” “Hello.” Silence filled da lines, den outta no where he heard da sweeties, sexiest, flirtatious voice he hadn't heard ova 5 months. Queenie's voice was music to his ears an a mend in his heart. “Baby is dat chu?” Tears dropped out of Cortez' eyes as he tried to grasp reality dat he really had his fiancee' on da phone. “Listen baby I'm cool, I love chu an I will explain wut I can tomorrow.” “Tomorrow?” Da only word he could get out his mouth befo' time ran out on da phone call. Queenie started to call back,but she decided against it. She loved Cortez' wit every inch of 'er bein', but knew if she left 'em in suspense it would be dat mo'

excitin' when he saw 'er. Neva da less she would let Tez fill 'em in on da rest. Hangin' up da phone she heard, Queenie to 'er session wit da psych. As she walked da hallways to 'er session she went into deep thought knock knock its yo' conscience. "Who da_wut da fuck chu takin' me to dis loopy ass bitches offices fo'? It ain't shit wrong wit us, at least nothin' she can fix." "Yo' I gotta stop havin' dese conversation wit myself, but it is true no one can fix me." Da softer part of 'er conscience kicked in an said; "Hold up think Queenie chu gotta at least make dese people think chu doin' better in order fo' chu to leave 'ere permanently ma." "Aiight dat is true." She thought as she knocked on da office door.
A voice said; "Come in Ms. Miles I didn't know if chu knew we were havin' a session today dats why I had chu paged." The doc told 'er. "So how are chu feelin'?" "I'm feelin' good, actually I feel rejuvenated bein' able to talk to my cousin fo' da first time in 'bout 5 months,so it exactly felt good. Talkin' to 'em made me feel gaiety." "Ms. Miles dis is good a very great start. Chu have already been issued yo' passes fo' da month,so when eva dey are ready to come get chu chu are free to use 'em at anytime. Ms. Miles__ "Stop callin' me dat doc jus' call me Queenie. I know its professionalism to call me by my last name, but it makes me feel older dan I am. Ms. Miles is my mother an every time chu call me dat I feel dats who ya talkin' to." Queenie told 'er in a nice polite way dat she's not 'er mother.
"Yes Queenie is wut chu prefer den dats how I'll approach chu, 'cus I try to make all my patients comfortable. Now da question I was 'bout to ask chu are chu engaged?" Queenie shook 'er head as she looked into da doc's eyes. "Well we only suppose to give ova night passes to dose who are married already, but I will make an exception an give chu a all day an ova night pass. Dis way it'll give chu time to spend quality time wit yo' soon to be husband." Ova da loud speaker came Queenie Miles chu need to report to da visitin' room fo' a attorney's visit. "Aiight doc I gotta go,but when can I get dat pass,so I go spend time wit my fiancee'?" "Come see me afta' yo' visit is ova an I'll have it ready fo' ya

Queenie." "Aiight doc, I'll be back later." She had a big cheesy smile on 'er face once she walked out da office. Queenie knew da doc had jus' started 'er chess game fo' 'er all ova again. It was only one person dat coulda been dere visitin' 'er an dat would be Mr. D. 'cus Tez an da fellas wouldn't be dere 'til tomorrow. Queenie gallivanted ova to where she spotted Mr. D. sittin' wit a certain gleam 'bout 'er self, he to was also happy to see Queenie. One could tell by da way he hugged 'er instead of da normal hand shake. "Wuts good Mr. D.? I see life has been treatin' chu well." "Wut can I say_ poppin' his collar he replied; "Wut can a man say chu have treated a man pimpish." Queenie broke out into laughter; "Oh shit Mr. D. yo' ass slingin' words like yo' ass hip, chu been hangin' 'round da family to much." Dey joked 'round fo' a minute den Queenie took a serious tone and facial expression. "Now lets get down to why I asked fo' chu to get ova 'ere asap. She told 'em leanin' in closer,so only he could hear 'er. "Look Mr. D. I need chu to get me outta 'ere, talk to da judge again tell 'em my sessions have been goin' great at least dats wut da psych says. Mr. D. chu already know can't nobody fix da devils child chu feel me? Da doc already gave his diagnosis,so ain't no way in hell dis is finna help me. Mr. D money talks an chu can't get me to believe dat yo' honorable judge Webster is one of doe's docile niggas dat can't be bought, 'cus I know he can be trained wit dat paper. Wut eva it takes make dat ma'fucka bow to chu, da money ain't no object wit me I jus' want my freedom back. I wanta go back home to my people." Queenie looked in Mr. Demontea's eyes an said; Mr. D. chu got a week to get me outta dis 'ere an I wanta be back in East St. Boogie wit my family." Mr. D. understood perfectly well how his client felt an how adamant she could be. Dere fo' he needed to be adequate in pursuin' is friend judge Webster to discontinue his clients treatment wit money. "How much should I offer 'em?" He asked Queenie. "Start wit 10 stacks an go down, tell 'em dats my offer an my only offer,so every time he refuse go down a thousand. Regardless wut postion he's in he's still a hustler an money talks fo' an to da best of us, but I think he will recognize my generosity as a beneficial towards his kids trust fund.” Mr. D. realize by 'er speech how eva it played out if his friend wanted longevity dat he would need to be feasible. Utter wise his client Ms. Miles would have 'em dealt wit. In earshot Queenie told 'em; “Once I'm free from dis place chu will receive a nice healthy commission.” She could see da glisten look in his eyes when she mention commission at dat point she knew she had Mr. D's glutton ass eatin' out da palm of 'er hand. Queenie sat back in 'er chair put a grimace half cocked grin on 'er face an told 'em; “See money is da rule of all evil. Even a ruthless savage as myself can pull yo' puppet strings an make someone of yo' credentials perform fo' money.” She chuckled slightly an said; “Now get to work an make shit happen.” Mr. D. was warned mo' dan asked. “Alright Ms. Miles yes I will get started on dat right now an I will be back to visit chu on Friday.” “Nah yo' Mr. D. I'll call chu an tell ya where to meet me.” He had irony written all ova his face like somethin' she said he was confused 'bout, but didn't say anything. Queenie couldn't sleep 'cus she felt ova excited to see 'er people specially Tez. Don't get it twisted she damn sho' couldn't wait to see Cortez' not jus' 'cus she needed a good fuck,but 'cus their bond had grown,so tight an when dey were alone jus' da 2 'em she was da perfect woman fo' and to 'em. 'Er hard shell on da outside was reversed to soft. Soft as a candy gummy worm in da inside and soft as a teddy bear on da outside. Queenie thought she would neva change anything 'bout 'er self, but she found it amazin' how when dey were alone he brought da femininity out of 'er. Cortez' could look at 'er an she'd cum all inside 'er panties dat was one of da effects he had ova 'er. Queenie would neva let 'em know dis 'cus she would neva let 'em know he had dat much power ova 'er. Queenie knew 'er family should already be dere in Chi-Town,so she called Cortez' hitter at 7am. Ring. “Hello! He said wit excitement. “Damn wut took chu so long to call me ma?” “Yo' how did chu know I would be callin'?” She asked teasingly. “So I take it chu missed me huh?” “Shawty stop playin' 'round man chu know damn well I been missin' da fuck out chu ma an den chu go an pull dat lil' stunt yesterday. Why didn't chu call me back baby, yo' ass gotta nigga all worked up I couldn't sleep fo' shit. Den my homeboy 'ere wanted to take his ma'fuckin' time on fillin' me in on wut da hell was goin' on."

Chapter Thirty
"Lets Get Dis Paper"

"Awe dat baby miss me, don't worry baby da feelin' is mutual if it makes chu feel any better I got somethin' fo' yo' ass an its been waitin' fo' 5 long months,but chu might have to knock da cobwebs off of it but trust and believe nigga it will be well worth da wait chu had." "Damn chu nasty ma,so hold fast 'cus we should be dere in 'bout 20 minutes. An Imma tell chu how I feel 'bout dat situation. Queenie said; "Aiight, but don't tell me shit nigga sho' me." Tez, Cortez', Chris, Flex and Tre' rolled to Chicago together. Tez knew his lil' cousin had somethin' goin' on inside dat lil' pretty head of 'ers when she requested fo' 'em to bring three of da fellas an makin' sho' one of 'em was Chris. He knew no matter how much time Queenie got it wouldn't stop 'er from bein' in da game 'cus it was 'er lifeline now. "Yo' Tez I gotta serious question homeboy." Cortez' stated. "Shoot fam' wuts on yo' mind?" Tez replied. "Yo' I know certain parts of Queenie, 'cus she's my rib da love of my life an I always told 'er from day one dat she would be my QUEEN fo' life. An I will make dat happen by marryin' 'er so she could sit on da throne next to 'er King as corny as it might have sounded, but den I actually fell in love wit 'er crazy ass." "When did chu actually figure out chu fell in love wit my cousin?" "When dat shit happen wit Tef 'lon at da Waffle House an we had to jet to Jamaica, bro dats when it really hit me. Dat yo' cousin was da thugg hearted woman I wanted to spend da rest of my every wakin' and sleepy nights wit 'er,but of course yo' ass 'er cousin an chu know every inch of 'er seein' how chu raised 'er,so my question is do chu think she's really ready to be married an have kids? An besides dat do chu think Queenie is ready to stop da street life?" "Listen fam' Imma answer yo' last question first. No I don't think. I know Queenie will not give up dis street life wit out a lil' persuasion an even den its gonna be a hard task to accomplish. Yo' we all know Queenie is very stubborn, but marriage bro is not gonna stop 'er, 'cus long as we are in da streets dats where she'll be in da streets. Now only thing I know dat will slow 'er down would be havin' yo' seed cuz." "Why chu say dat will be da only reason." Cortez' asked. "Nigga look at it like dis, wut makes Queenie happy?" Tez responded befo' he could answer. "Its family cuz, family is wut she's so protective ova. Chu act like dat was hard, aiight nigga answer dis wut does Queenie do wit 'er money? Tez retorted she spends it on us 'er family makin' sho' all of us are takin' care of. Ueenie doesn't give a fuck 'bout da money only reason she got in da game was to take care of 'er moms, so my aunt wouldn't have to struggle to live or keep a roof ova their heads. Nigga wut chu need to do is pay mo' attention to yo' woman if chu say chu in love wit 'er, 'cus dis game 'ere has be come a power trip fo' da lil' nigga. I won't say she gets off on it,but its mo' 'bout da props she gets from da streets. Everyone recognizes 'er street credibility da young girl is a street legend at da age of 17 an nigga chu gotta millionaire on yo' arm. I don't know anyone who can say dat, but my thing is dis don't try an trap 'er into havin' no kid. Sit down wit 'er an talk 'bout it jus' to make sho' she's on da same page chu on,an if she do agree I know dat will be da best an only way fo' 'er to stay out da penitentiary an da streets. Hell who knows it might even slow 'er murder game down." Tez told 'em she's gotta nutter year left,so time will tell if she leaves da game on 'er own fam'." A chuckle came from da back seat. "Wutsup fam' why yo' ass laughin'?" Tez asked Chris."Yo' family ma ain't goin' fo' now of dat shit y'all airin' 'bout,dis my mentor y'all talkin' 'bout. No disrespect fam'_ he told Cortez',but I know mo' 'bout 'er dan chu do my nigga. Family listen ma ain't goin', yeah she gone marry chu 'cus she loves chu

no doubt fam' she even gonna give chu dat seed on 'er terms,but not fo' a coupla years. Why?" Chris asked a question to answer his own question. "'Cus she not ready to let da streets go only 'cus da game is to sweet an its a priority fo' 'er to have a nuff money to make sho' all 'er love ones are set fo' life even afta' she' long gone. Dat even means yo' seed fam'. If ma had yo' child now it wouldn't be right 'cus da way she thinks da paper is not where she wants it. Further mo' not bein' visible in da streets,but in da streets is a rush to 'er. She's jus' like a nigga once he steps out in da streets an bitches and niggas start to praise 'em, it gives 'em extra swagg 'bout 'em self. Well ma da same way in a sense. 'Er swagger is already tight niggas love 'er ass an bitches hater an dis is wut makes 'er confident doe. Da demeanor she has 'bout 'er self family she's da type of person who doesn't demonstrate shit. Yo' nigga is very nonchalant an myself I love dat in 'er, 'cus she gonna keep ya guessin' an cuz chu neva gonna know wuts next wit lil' ma. But all chu gotta do is like cuz said pay mo' attention to yo' woman."
Ring Ring Ri_ "Hello wutsup baby girl we outside." Queenie hung up da phone an went outside she jumped off da porch an ran an hopped in Cortez' arms an excitedly out came; "Wutsup baby I missed yo' ass. She planted a nice sexy kiss on Cortez' dat gave 'em urges to fuck 'er right dere on da spot. "Yo' shawty I'm so glad to see yo' ass ma." "Damn fam' can da rest of us get in a hug?" Cortez' put Queenie back down an she jumped straight into Tez's arms. "Wut da fuck up lil' nigga_awe shit its good to breath yo' fresh scent baby girl. I missed chu cuz." Tez continued to squeeze his Ueenie. "Yeah family I missed yo' ass to cuz." "Ummm can we sho' some love to?" Chris asked in a jokin' matter holdin' out his arms fo' Queenie. "Yo' ma wuts good how dey been treatin' chu boss?" He stepped back to check out 'er physique. "Damn! Ma no disrespect,but chu gotten thicker dan dat thang. "Chris!" Cortez' warned 'em watch yo' self homeboy." "Nah mean no harm done family,but chu took it wrong. I'm sayin' "Boss Queen" physique is bigger dan urns an mines. Fam' look at doe's guns."Jokingly Chris

told 'em shit chu better watch wut chu say fam' 'cus she jus' may knock yo' ass out." Everybody started laughin'. "Wutup Flex and Tre' how y'all feelin'? I missed y'all fellas." "Aye lets get my baby up outta dis bullshit she got on." Cortez' stated. "Yo' hit up Ju-Town first afta' wards we can go back to da hotel so she can change." Queenie smiled at Cortez' an said; "Chu think chu know me huh?" "I really would like to think I do ma." Cortez' had a look of confusion on his face an Queenie made a mental note to talk wit 'em later when dey got alone. On da ride to Ju-Town da fellas wanted to know how Queenie was,so Flex started da convo off. "Yo' boss so wut went down inside dere did chu have any confrontation?" She said; "All I can tell y'all is wut da CO's told me on da day dey transported my ass 'ere." "Wuts dat shawty?" Cortez' asked wit curiosity in his voice. "I was told dat I damn near killed a nutter inmate somethin' 'bout me slappin' 'er wit my tray in da chow hall. Dey say I jumped down on 'er an banged 'er head on da concrete floor den dey hall my ass to da hole fo' 4 months actually 5 'cus dey added a month to my shit." "Well ma how chu get dat big if dey jus' had chu in da hole all dat time?" Chris wanted to know. "Family I jus' did bed dips and push ups along wit only eatin' breakfast, so y'all know a ma'fucka hungry fo' some Southern home cookin'. I need some soul food." Steppin' out da car in Ju-Town made 'er feel like a kid in da candy store,so she took in a deep breath__ "Ahhhhh da good ol' smell of Ju-Town. Mr. Cho wuts good sir?" Throwin' 'er hands in the air, Mr. Cho didn't speak very much English,but Queenie was his favorite very well known customer. "Awe_Queen_me's favorite_cust_e_mer. How_ye_been?" "I'm good Mr. Cho, but I need some gear." "O_ye_need_made cust_um?" "Nah I ain't got time fo' dat today,but Imma be back next week,so I can tell chu wut I need. Fo' now let me get dat Guess fit dat red and black one. Yo' Mr. Cho wuts new Levi jeans chu got in?" Mr. Cho said; "Wait!" On his way to da back of da store. "I got somethin' fo' chu I jus' got in dat_has not_put_ouch_yet." Mr. Cho came back to da front wit a soft pink and powder blue Levi jean outfit matchin' jacket wit a pair of Tim's dat were also soft pink and powder blue. "Oh so chu remember my size huh?" He smiled an shook his head as to say yes. Queenie took da items out of his hands. "Give me dat, y'all gonna stop actin' like ya know me." She told 'em as she walked in to da dressin' room where she changed everything. Dis even included bra, panties den she put on 'er fresh gear an 'er fresh pair of kicks. "Yeah a bitch is back!" She jus' blurted out loud as she studied 'er own body in a lengthy mirror Queenie liked 'er physique. Queenie den told 'er self; "Ma chu a sexy ma'fucka." Cortez' made his own comment underneath his breath,so no one could hear 'em. "Damn ma I thought chu said chu had stop eatin'." "Boss Queen" is back niggas." Chris looked at his boss an retorted; "Ma chu rockin' dat fit." "Preciate it my nigga." "My QUEEN" Cortez' called out to Queenie. As she turned to acknowledge 'em he told 'er holdin' up a new flat thick choke chain wit a name plate made out of nothin', but diamonds dat read: "Boss Queen". "Turn 'round shawty, so I can put it on chu." Afta' he clamp da clasp he said; "Now "Boss Queen" is back do chu ma." Queenie mouth I love chu an turned back Mr. Cho an told 'em; "Yo' give me doe's red Tim's along wit dat black and gray Levi outfit dere an I want doe's gray suede air force one's wit da black swoosh sign an dat will be all today." "Ye_sho'?" Mr. Cho asked. "Yeah I'm sho' Mr. Cho Imma be back next week,so chu jus' be ready fo' me den aiight." "Okay ye_tot_is_$500." Cortez' dug in his pocket an pulled out a roll a hunnids,but Tez stopped 'em. "Hold on fam' I got it." He den to pulled out a big ass roll an peeled off $500 fo' Mr. Cho register a nutter $200 fo' his tip fo' jus' takin' his time away from his utter customers an givin' all his attention to Queenie. Chris and Flex grabbed Queenie's bags an put 'em in da trunk. "Where chu wanta eat at baby girl?" Tez questioned. "Family lets hit up DUSTIES,so we can chat I got somethin' we need to discuss dat will benefit us all. Da whole family." Everyone in da car was silent wit a curios written all ova their faces. Queenie changed da subject. "So how my moms doin'?" "Yo' cuz auntie good. I damn near gave 'er a heart attack when I told 'er dat dey transported chu to Chicago. 'Er and moms cried wit joy, dey been so worried 'bout chu since 'em dumb fucks at da prison wouldn't tell us shit 'bout da state of yo' condition. Dey wanted to come,but I jus' told 'em straight dat dis trip 'ere was a biz'ness trip an chu would be home soon. Auntie was da one who called Mr. D. fo' me,so ain't no tellin' wut she said to 'em." Wuts goin' on wit my auntie is she back to 'er ol' self?" She asked. "Hell yeah auntie doin' 'er, she got dat ma'fuckin' limo service off da chain. Biz'ness is boomin' ma." Chris told Queenie from da back seat. "Ma she got all of us drivin'." He sounded,so excited as he was tellin' 'er, but den quickly apologized. "My bad ma." Queenie turned in 'er seat to look at Chris. "Chu cool fam' wut da fuck chu apologizin' fo' my nigga?" "Nah mean chu was talkin' to Tez an I jus' chimed in." "So wut yo' ass dan turned soft on me now? Chris chu know me don't do dat shit fam',we all family_ nigga in my eyes chu a grown ass man,so act like it." Instead of Chris lookin' Queenie in da eye he dropped his head. Chris was 18 now an he had love fo' his boss,but it wasn't sexual 'cus he neva wanted to hurt his bro Cortez',so he held his feelins' back. Chris knew dat da woman he grew attached to ova da years an took a hold to as his mentor would soon be leavin' 'em,but he didn't know how. "Yo' fam' chu tryin' to piss me off? Yo' pull dis ma'fucka ova." Tez pulled in DUSTIES parkin' lot towards da back,so no one would be able to hear or see Queenie. "Chris get da fuck out da car." Queenie stepped out da car from da front passengers seat an walked 'round da front of da car where she met Chris. "Nigga wut da fuck wrong wit chu fam' 'cus yo' ass actin' real bitchy right now? Why da fuck chu keep droppin' yo' head homeboy? Do I intimidate chu or somethin'?" She asked. But befo' he could answer Queenie told 'em; "Look fam' I got love fo' yo' ass 'cus we family an chu my niggas lil' nigga an I look at chu as my lil' protege', but nigga dis ain't da Chris I left behind. So I need chu to man da fuck up or yo' ass ain't gonna make it." Wit dat said Queenie left Chris standin' dere to marinate on wut she jus' said. "Squad up!" Inside dey all sat a da family booth to pig out on some collard and mustard greens, fried chicken, smoother pork chops, cornbread, corn on da cob an da list went on. "Yo' I want all y'all to know I missed da fuck outta all of chu an I wish we was all back in East St. Boogie right now havin' dis meal at our own table,but unfortunately we not. So 'eres da deal da six of us dat are 'ere will discuss biz'ness an y'all will take it back wit chu an jus' let da utters know wutsup. Now da reason I had chu three brought along 'cus I'm back in da Chi an whether or not Mr. D. gets me cut loose from dis home da judge has me in I'm not leavin' Chicago fo' a while. Dis 'ere is my stompin' grounds an I'm finna work it even if I gotta be in dis treatment center feel me." "Huh?" She heard da table say. "Yo' no matter where I am my money don't stop flowin'." Lookin' 'round da table she stated; "Dat even means when I'm dead and gone." Dey all looked at Chris an da thought of his statement to Cortez' crossed their minds. "Yo' shawty_ Cortez' tried to say, but Queenie threw 'er hand up an said; "Wait let me finish baby." As she looked at Tez_ "We openin' da stash house back up tonight. I holla'd at Detroit,so he'll be 'ere tonight at da spot 'round 9pm." "Hold up lil' nigga!" Tez spoke Detroit he questioned in a whisper; "Ma when Detroit comes he don't come small." "Cuz I know he's bringin' in 2 semis an I want chu to have 'em parked inside da privacy fence. Chris, Flex and Tre' unload one of da trailers an stash da contents in da basement. Da utter trailer is already sold,so leave it alone, I gotta guy comin' threw by midnight to calm it. I'll be dere by 11pm,now each truck has packed 400 bricks in it dats pure uncut, raw cocaine straight from Mexico family,so no fuck ups. Reason dis shipment is so big is 'cus I need to make sho' my family is set 'cus as chu know I'm finna marry y'all homeboy 'ere an its only right to give 'em his first born. He or she will be da next protege' of dis family if he or she wishes to be." Queenie said; "Imma be behind close doors takin' care of my family afta' dis shipment I'm pullin' out goin' legit dats why I open da biz'ness an will be openin' a coupla mo' befo'

I go behind da scenes." Chris said; "So ma chu finna go into retirement, huh? Well let me ask chu dis A long pause filled da air wit silence befo' he spoke. "Ma everybody don't know chu like I do." Wit out sayin' any names Chris looked at Queenie in da eyes an stated; "Boss chu don't eva plan on quitin' da game 'cus chu still on da chess board ma. Chu jus' removin' yo' self from da eye of da streets an da people dat lurks in 'em an lettin' da money work fo' chu instead of chu workin' fo' it." Queenie said; "My lil' nigga, my lil' protege' I see yo' ass found da Chris I know an brought 'em back. Chu right homeboy dats why everything we own y'all will work from now on. Instead of y'all handlin' dope, from now on only thing y'all will handle is money dats made off of drugs,by of hands dat belong to da biggest dope boys,big time drug dealers and Kingpins. We will no longer be of service to da community except fo' 2 biz'ness dat we will supply an doe's are a neighborhood grocery store an a laundromat. "All da rest only accommodates da hustlers, ballers and Kingpins,of course I know y'all peeped da clientele dat has come through Blue and Reds." Queenie stated; "Biz'ness is boomin' 'cus an ol' wise man made dat happen fo' me an in return all he wants is fo' me to be is safe and happy wit dis man right 'ere." Tez and Cortez' knew exactly who she was talkin' 'bout. "I'm curious baby girl why only one laundromat an one grocery store, why not a chain of 'em?" Tez asked. "'Cus fam' we only got one moms a piece. I'm taken auntie out da limo biz' an givin' 'er 'er own store front dat she can call 'ers. I don't care which one she takes, which eva den moms gets da utter one, so she can finally quit dat punk-ass hospital job she at." "So chu makin' da Miles women biz'ness owners of their own huh? Tez questioned, but wut 'bout yo' uncle their brother?" Queenie looked at Tez wit a grimace look on 'er face. "How is Chaos cuz? She asked wit some sincerity in 'er voice. "He good baby girl,but I gotta admit fam' he been buggin' 'bout a job. He's ready to work' again." "Yo' fam' I told chu if one of chu wanta let 'em get down wit y'all dats aiight wit me." "Nah, mean he wants to work fo' chu again cuz." Queenie thought 'bout it since she's been away on jus' stoppin' Chaos cash flow altogether. "Yo' I thought 'bout puttin' a halt on his life long commission checks anyway. My word is still bond cuz,but I will give chu and Cortez' heads up if y'all wanta make 'em feel like he's apart of somethin' dat means he can only work where eva y'all put 'em 'cus I will not give 'em his own biz'ness. He will jus' earn his pay check, feel me." Back in da car Tre' stated; "Boss I like how cold yo' heart is ma, chu keep it real wit us all. Uh a nigga can't help,but to love chu ma,'cus speakin' fo' myself I love yo' swagg an ain't no utter ma' fucka like yo' ass,but da next bitch I get has to be in yo' league if she ain't got a swagg where she can be sexy,sophisticated an carry 'er self as a woman an still have dat thugg in 'er den da bitch ain't fo' me." Dey all broke out into laughter as Chris said; "Yo' family chu stupid yo' ass gonna be lookin' fo' along time bro 'cus it ain't no bitch out dere remotely like boss. Dere is an will always be only one "Boss Queen"". Queenie said lets fall up in da hotel fo' a minute_where y'all at anyway?" "We at da Double Tree downtown shawty 2 rooms since we didn't know wut to expect, I knew chu and I had to have our own." Cortez' replied. "Yo' Ueenie wut time chu gotta be back at da spot?" "Oh shit da psych gave me a 2 day and night pass since she knew my fiancee' was comin' up. She said its 'cus Imma showin' progress,but only if da bitch knew,so we good." At da hotel Queenie had da fellas grab 'er bags from da trunk of da car an on da elevator she told Tez; "Give me 'bout three hours an we'll be ready to roll out." Tez smiled an shook his head at his lil' cousin knowin' she was 'bout to get 'er freak on. Tez kissed Queenie on da fo' head an said; "See ya in a minute ma." "Aiight yo' I appreciate it family y'all jus' put 'em bags on da floor right by da door an I can get 'em." Cortez' put da latch on da door behind 'em. "Shawty I missed chu?" He exclaimed as he pulled Queeenie clothes off one piece at a time like he was sight seein' 'er body fo' da first time in life. 'Er shirt as he massaged, kiss and caress 'er breast next he unbutton 'er jeans. Cortez' pulled 'em down off 'er ass along wit 'er panties down to 'er knees. As he kissed 'er love box he laid 'er down on da bed an pulled 'er Tim's off den jeans, panties,so he could really taste wut he had been missin' since she's been away. Cortez' dropped to his knees an put his whole face in between his QUEENS legs lettin' his tongue bring down da first orgasm of many. “Yo' daddy yo' ass miss dis shit huh?” She asked as she pushed Cortez' head deeper into 'er pussy an his response was “Ummmm, huh!” Comin' up fo' air he told Queenie; “An I'm finna beat dis shit up like I missed it to.” “Do as chu please daddy, sho' mama wut chu workin' wit. Nigga sho' me how much chu missed me,daddy chu want me to have yo' youngan?” “Um, huh.” “Well make it tonight daddy,let dis be da night our child is conceived on.” Cortez' felt a since of serenity come ova 'em dat gave 'em dat feelin' 'em and Queenie were on da same page. In a soft but stern voice Cortez' told Queenie I got chu shawty an from dere da 2 fucked sucked an made love fo' 2 ½ hours. As dey got dressed da 2 talked 'bout their future an dere of it to come. “So ma wut utter biz'ness chu wanta open up?” Queenie replied; “A car wash, strip club of course a barber shop_Gotta keep y'all niggas lookin' fresh and fly. A playaz lounge an well da rest I'll figure out as we go along.” Queenie said; “Yo' y'all niggas strapped up?” “Yeah ma wutsup?” “I jus' feel naked out dis ma'fucka.” “Yo' lil' nigga chu know I ain't finna have yo' ass out 'ere like dat.” Tez said bend down an put yo' hand in da vent an pull out yo' burner. Queenie did jus' dat an came back up wit a all black baby glock. “Now dats wut I'm talkin' 'bout cuz. Aye we got some major weight an I need all 400 bricks gone by da end of da month. Which is very feasible 'cus we got some major playaz comin' through fo' da shit,be on point doe 'cus most of dese niggas gone be sendin' bitches or their flunkies feel me. Tez and Cortez' will let y'all know wit a heads up, but family if it don't look right, feel right even if chu smell some foul shit always trust yo' first instinct 'cus it'll neva steer yo' ass wrong so go wit it if chu feel somethin' ain't right. We all been 'round long a nuff to know dat if da area yo' ass in smells fishy move da fuck 'round." Da truck had been unloaded an it was 10 'til midnight so Queenie an da fellas sat inside da stash house talked and played da game system while dey waited on Tez phone to ring. Ring_ring_ring_ring. "Yo' fam' pick it up on da fifth ring." She had told Tez den da phone rang once mo'. "Hello!" "Yo' homeboy let me speak to "Boss Queen"?" "Hold on homeboy." Tez said wit a lil' frustration in his voice an passed da phone to Queenie. "Baby girl who eva dat nigga is chu better tell his ass to watch 'em self." "My killa nigga wutsup? Chu 'ere,well come on an make it happen, jus' pull in da back." Chris and Flex opened da gate an killa backed up da cab of his semi to connect to his trailer den he hopped out da cab an opened da back door an pulled out 10 duffel bags an placed 'em on da ground. "Dere chu go "Boss Queen" doe's contain $5200000 dollars."

"Chris take it in house an put it through da money machine lil' nigga." Killa asked; "Queenie chu need me to fall back while its counted up?" "Dat won't be necessary, but Killa jus' know if its not all dere I know how to find chu fo' sho'." Da truck pulled out of da yard an da gates were locked back an 'er crew went back into da house. "Yo' family Killa ain't shit chu see how I jus' punk his ass." "Yeah, ma I peep dat." "Dat nigga sneaky doe,so watch out fo' dat nigga when chu dealin' wit 'em." "Fo' sho' cuz." Tez replied makin' a mental note of wut Queenie told 'em. "Yo' ma its all 'ere all $5200000.

I put it all 10 thousand stacks 'cus dis crazy ass nigga jus' had it thrown in da bags."

"Dats Killa sloppy ass fo' ya." "Wut chu want us to do wit it ma?" Chris asked. "Nah mean nothin' fam' Imma put it away, but wut I do want chu to do since chu put 'em in stacks of $10 toss a stack to Flex and Chris an take one fo' yo' self fam'." "One love ma, good lookin', but we gotta ask wuts it fo'? "Its fo' y'all to do wut chu feel yo' asses need to do wit it. But I gotta question do I spoil y'all to much?" Queenie looked 'round da room do y'all niggas need to be weaned off da titty fo' real. Yo' I need shit to be tight an on point 'cus if anything was to happen to me on da outside my world is finna be in yo' hands an I need to know dat I can jus' fall back an relax wit out shit on my conscience tellin' me I fucked up down da road." Tez told Queenie; "Baby girl chu already know we were built on in and 'round dis shit,so we will conduct biz'ness da same as usual 'til chu say different ma."Da next mornin' Queenie spent majority of 'er time wit Cortez' laid up. "Ummmmm baby its been along time since I've woke up next to da nigga I fell in love wit 2 years ago." "I've missed yo' presents to shawty it has been along time even doe 5 months don't sound long,but it felt like an eternity when a piece of chu is gone an yo' ass can't touch or talk to 'em." Cortez told Queenie as he kiss da nape of 'er neck. "Well daddy I gotta chess move fo' dat, I should know somethin' on Friday." She went on to tell Cortez' wut she was havin' Mr. D. work on. "So baby if da judge doesn't want to comply den point blank his ass will die word is bond." "Shawty chu puttin' da judge under if he don't release chu from da treatment center? Ma knockin' off a judge will get us life under da penitentiary." "Oh,so chu down?" Queenie asked. "Damn right I'm down chu my baby an its ride and die wit us right?" Cortez' asked. Queenie kissed Cortez' all ova startin' wit his chest. "Dats_right_daddy_its_ride_and_die_wit_us_ baby." Makin' 'er way to his erect dick, "Ummmm_some_body_is_happy_to_see_me." Takin' all of 'em into 'er mouth she made his toes curl. "Ahhhh,aye,awe shiit ma. Ummmm its been a while baby." Cortez' placed his hand on da back of 'er head an grind his hips slowly,so she started to hum on his pole which made Cortez' go loopy wit in seconds. "Ooooh suck dis dick ma, please don't stop." Queenie started to tease 'em when she felt da vein pulsate in Cortez's dick. "Come 'ere ma ride me, bounce dat ass up and down on dis dick." Queenie did as he requested, she put it on 'em,so good he wanted to ball up an go to sleep,but Queenie wouldn't let 'em. "Get up baby!" She told 'em as she smacked 'em on da ass; "Lets order room service 'cus I'm starvin' yo'. Anyway chu can't go to sleep we need to call Tez 'cus its time to hit da streets tomorrow is Friday." "Friday wut is,so special 'bout it?"

"THROWIN' BRICKS AT THE PENITENTIARY"

"Yo' I find out wut judge Webster decided." Friday came Mr. D. showed up fo' his and Queenie's visit wit good news.

Chapter Thirty-One
"Home Is Where My Heart Is But I Gotta Go"

"Ms. Miles da judge considered da proposal we offered an he has released chu from dis treatment center jus' as soon as da doc signs yo' papers." "Good, good now everyone can remain in one piece." "I got chu Mr. D. I'll meet chu at DUSTIES in Dalton 'bout 2 hours." She told 'em as she ran off to get 'er things an call Tez. Ring, "Hello." "Yo' nigga come pick me up fam' I'm out dis joint." "We'll be dere in 20 minutes baby girl we comin' off da Ryan." Once Queenie got 'er papers from da doctor she waited on da porch fo' 'er ride. Queenie hopped off da porch an jumped in da car. "Wutsup my niggas?" She asked. "Yo' take me to da stash house first,so I can make sho' dese three know wuts goin' on den I need to grab a hitter den we can jump on da e-way headed back towards East St. Boogie. I need to sho' my face an ease moms and aunties minds, let 'em know baby girl is back an I'm all together. I also need to see da rest of my circle,so I can feel 'em in on a few things." Back in East St. Boogie Tez drove straight to da store front Blue and Red's Limousine Service an Queenie stepped out da car to stretch as she made da statement; "Awe shit back in East St. Boogie." Queenie walked inside. "Excuse me ma'am can chu help me I need a limo to take me far as I can go." She had said to 'er aunt Heather. Heather turned 'round awe shit my nicey poo is home_give me some love. "Why didn't y'all 2 tell me she was out." "Ma we didn't know she was getting out,so soon." "Where my moms at." "She'll be right back, she didn't have to work today,so she's been up 'ere wit me helpin' out. She's gonna be ova joyed to see 'er baby girl dats fo' sho'." Liz came through da door lookin' down at da packages in 'er hands an wit out lookin' up she asked 'er sister when did Tez an 'em get back?" "Today afta' dey picked me up." Queenie said an Liz looked up an screamed. "Awe my baby's home." Queenie replied; "Yeah and no." As she hugged 'er mother. "Wut do chu mean?" Liz asked. "Well I'm home fo' a few hours I had to come check on y'all an make sho' things were straight. An no 'cus I'm goin' back to Chicago fo' 'bout a month to handle some biz'ness I gotta handle an neva da less I need to talk to chu both. Look Imma open up a laundromat an a grocery store an since y'all 'ere now chu can decide who wants wut. Dis will be yo' own biz'nesses, chu hire yo' own people an run it how chu feel it needs to be ran. Queenie told 'er moms chu need to retire from da hospital asap. Liz said; "No mo' has to be said." While Queenie had da meetin' wit da rest of da family lettin' 'em know 'er next chess move Liz and Heather had prepared a feast fit fo' a QUEEN. Convincin' Queenie to stay wasn't very hard to do to da fact she was starvin' fo' a good home cooked meal. "Man ma chu and auntie hooked it up it looks like a Thanksgivin' feast goin' on up in 'ere an y'all did all fo' me huh?" "Yeah we did, but we really didn't think we were gonna be able to pull it off, but wit da meetin' chu had den Tez and Cortez' help, 'ere we all are well except three. Now come on baby sit down let mama fix 'er baby plate." Queenie said cool an everyone had a seat,so dey could all eat as a family. Back in Chicago Chris, Flex, and Tre' had da stash house bangin' like dey were back in East St.Boogie workin' their own area. "Yo' bro's we keep workin' shit like dis we'll be done befo' da month out." Flex stated. "We've already let a 150 bricks go fam' an boss only been gone 'bout six hours." Chris said; "Yeah give or take a few, boss and 'em was jus' getting into East St. Boogie when we got 'em off. I think boss will be pleased 'bout dat, but we may need to go head an call 'er jus' to keep 'er on point wit da count." "Yo' my nigga." Tre' yelled out. "Off doe's 150 B's we jus' made $2250000 dollars I jus' dropped in da floor." Ring,ring,ring,ring. Tez answered; "Wut up family who dis?" "Yo' fam' its Chris."

"THROWIN' BRICKS AT THE PENITENTIARY"

"Shit cool, wutsup?" Tez asked which drew Queenie's attention from 'er plate of food sittin' back in 'er chair she drank a tall glass of Kool-Aid waitin' fo' Tez to get off da phone. "Nah fam' ain't shit wrong its actually good. I jus' call to talk to boss an give 'er a count dats all my nigga." "Aiight hold up. Tez walked back ova to da table an handed Queenie his hitter. "Its all good ma, dats Chris." Queenie sat at da head of 'er mothers dinnin' room table like da QUEEN dey treated 'er as. "Hello." On da utter end Chris said; "Wut it do ma?" Queenie stayed silent an let 'em talk. "Boss I was callin' to let chu know we let a 150 white doves go outta da cage 15." No questions needed to be asked 'cus she already totaled da figures in 'er head quick as 1,2,3. Den a smile crossed 'er lips. "2250000 huh dats wutsup." She told 'em. "So my lil' protege' how chu like 'em numbers fam'? Y'all pulled dat off in wut jus' 'bout six hours huh nigga." "Boss yo' chu sho' dis gonna be it? I'm jus' sayin' dis shit right 'ere is sweet." "I feel chu nigga we gonna holla 'bout dat at a later time I'll see wutsup when we get back,but befo' ya hang up I need to know is chu niggas cool wit da position y'all in?" "Wut chu mean boss?" Chris questioned. "Yo' I'm askin' ya do ya wanta stay in Chi-Town or would chu like fo' ya brothers to come an relieve y'all,so yo' asses can get back to East St. Boogie?" "Boss I'm tryin' to be where chu at ma,but I can ask da fellas real quick. Yo' boss said y'all good 'ere in da Chi or do y'all want some of da bro's to come take yo' places?" "Nah mean we good 'ere fam' tell boss we gonna stay if its aiight wit 'er." Flex and Tre' sang in unison's. "Boss we all gonna stay ma." "Aiight cool, check dis out we gonna be headed back out in 'bout 45 minutes an moms gonna send y'all some plates back. I know y'all hungry 'cus it ain't to much dere to snack on,but don't trip doe I'll go shop at da grocery store when we get back to fill up da frig an da pantry since y'all gonna be dere fo' a minute. Yo' tomorrow we'll go see 'bout getting a rental,so y'all can get 'round when y'all want to. Better jet fam' fuck dat Imma go buy a car, I'm not finna rent shit. We can holla 'bout it when I touch down peace family." She hung up da hitter an handed it back to Tez. “Ueenie everything good?” Tez asked. “Yeah cuz its $225000 dollars good. Yo' lets finish up 'ere,so we can get back, man fam' I like da way dat lil' nigga reminds me of us.” Tez raised his brow as Queenie went to say; “Jus' how I look up to chu cuz an me bein' yo' lil' protege' keepin' me under yo' wing. Well dats how I see Chris I think he's gonna go far.” “Queenie.” Queenie had drifted deep in thought. “Baby girl!” Liz called out snappin' 'er out of 'er train of thoughts. “Yeah ma wutsup?” “Baby y'all wanta take some of dis food back wit y'all?” “Nah ma chu can jus' fix Chris,Flex,Tre',Tez and Cortez' some carry out boxes, I'm good.” Liz questioned Queenie; “Chu sho' ya don't want me to fix chu non baby?” “I'm sho' I'm straight ma I really haven't had much of an appetite in da last few days,so chu can jus' fix da fellas somethin'.” Cortez' said ma talkin' to Liz; “If she gets hungry she can eat my plate.” Wut he jus' said gave Liz da go head to add extra to his tray in case,so dere would be a nuff da both of 'em. “Yo' cuz I need to push da Lexus back its time fo' me to dump it change da color or somethin'.” Cortez' chimed in; “Why don't we all jus' drive our whips back dat way when we need to move 'round no one will be on stuck if shit jumps off.” “Yo' dats cool.” Queenie told 'em. “Yo' I'm wit dat, lets do dat.” Tez said. Pullin' up at da house Tez replied; “Yeah it is time to roll in somethin' different I can have one of da fellas drive my shit back when its time 'til den I'll park my baby in da fence behind da stash house.” Chicago a place Queenie and Tez grew up in a place she neva thought once she moved 'er moms away from dat dere would be any reason fo' 'er to go back,but I guess its like da sayin' goes chu can take da girl out of da city,but chu can neva take da city out of da girl. 'Cus she will always return to it an dat's exactly wut Queenie has done, returned Da three pulled back up at da stash house carryin' bags and bags of groceries. “Yo' family y'all go get da rest of doe's bags out da cars.” Chris rush to his mentors aid an took all da bags she carried in from 'er hands. “I got 'em boss why chu carryin' dese? We can get dis shit, ma chu don't need to be doin' nothin', jus' relax." Queenie smiled,but befo' she could say anything Cortez' replied; "Nigga she stronger dan yo' lil' ass,chu actin' like shawty sick or pregnant or sump." Chris said nothin',but looked at Cortez' as to say she could be as much as y'all be at da hotel fuckin' chu dumb ass nigga. Chris held it to 'em self 'cus dat was his bro an he would neva disrespect 'em in anyway. Da next mornin' Queenie was up bright an early 'cus she needed to handle a lot of stuff it would be rush hour 'cus it was da weekend a nutter reason she felt sick at da stomach,but didn't want to alarm Cortez' 'cus he was,so ova protective an she knew he wouldn't let 'er leave da hotel jus' so he could make sho' she was aiight. Queenie neva had thoughts 'bout bein' pregnant 'cus 'er mind was focused on back makin' money,so she could get 'er moms and aunts biz'ness up an runnin' befo' 'er own birthday came 'round in 2 months. So da fact she could be pregnant neva crossed 'er mind. Ring,ring,ring_ "Yo' who dis?" Chris answered da phone groggly. "Dis yo' boss nigga get yo' ass up an brush yo' mouth fam' sounds like dat shit stank." She said jokingly. "Yo' ma my bad I'm up boss its jus' afta' y'all left shit picked up again. Guessin' 'cus its da weekend." Chris yarn. She cut Chris yarn short. "Man go wash yo' ass an get 'em niggas up an we'll be dere in a hour. Queenie didn't want to talk ova da phone,so she cut da convo short. Cortez' she whispered; "Get up baby we got shit to do very important an its gotta be handled today." She kissed Cortez' on da lips an grind 'er pussy against his erect dick. "Baby if chu get up now an go to da car lot wit me we can be back 'ere by three o'clock an I can be fuckin' yo' brains out daddy." She told 'em very teasingly. Cortez' eyes shot open an he grabbed 'er 'round da waist pullin' 'er down on top of 'em. "Yo' ass sho' know how to get me all worked up don't chu? Why chu always know da right shit to say to get yo' way huh ma huh?" She replied; "I guess I'm jus' good like dat don't hate da playa hate da game nigga." She said wit a smile as she hopped off of 'em. "Now lets go." "Yo' shawty chu gonna let me shower wit chu?" He asked. "Yeah of course no freaky shit doe 'cus we ain't got time right now." Befo' she could get into da shower 'er hitter rung,so she answered it on da first ring. "Yo' hello." "Wutsup baby girl, good mornin' to chu." Queenie let da caller control da call. "Y'all love birds up lil' nigga chu know its da weekend an its time to make some donuts." "Yeah cuz we up I was finna jump in da shower as yo' call came through. I called Chris an told 'em get up an wash dey ass, so dey'll be ready by time we get dere. So give us 'bout 20 minutes fam'." Cortez' walked pass Queenie an smacked 'er ass as she pushed end on da phone. "Da shower all urns ma, I needed a cold shower anyway." "Did chu huh?" She said as she snatched his towel from 'round his waist an ran to da bathroom lockin' da door behind 'er. Dey all drove to da stash house in separate cars givin' Queenie a few minutes to 'er self wit 'er thoughts alone. "Boss Queen", wut chu gonna do ma chu gotta big decision to make is chu stayin' in da streets or is chu gonna work da game from behind close doors?" Queenie thoughts ran wild non stop talkin' to 'er self out loud_ "Listen we are goin' behind da scenes, an we'll no longer be in da streets, but befo' we do Imma make one last call an double da shit we received befo' dats if my mentor can respect dat since dis was suppose to be da very last shipment. Maybe as long as I still play it from da utter side of da fence it'll be cool wit 'em." Queenie pulled up first in front of da stash house den Cortez' an comin' 'round da corner wangin' was Tez wit his double 15" kickers blastin' some new joint by 2 Pac. Cortez' and Queenie stood on da sidewalk an watch Tez bob his head to da music waitin' fo' 'em to turn off da engine. Queenie called out to Cortez'; "Baby I been feelin' nauseous at da stomach fo' da last few days." "Shawty why didn't chu tell me earlier, chu wanta go back to da hotel an lay down?" "Nah baby I'll be aiight I jus' wanted to forewarn chu in case ya see me bent ova somewhere callin' earl. Of course I wanted to tell chu, but I knew how chu would act wit yo' ova protective ass." Queenie chuckled an broke out into laughter at his expense. Tez walked up an asked; "Wut chu laughin' at cuz?" Cortez' told his homeboy; "She thinks its funny or some type of joke when she tells me 'er ass sick.” “Wut chu mean sick, wuts wrong ma?” Tez asked bein' concern. Queenie shook 'er head; “Its nothin' cuz I jus' told 'em I felt a lil' nauseous fo' da last few days so if he seen me bent ova callin' on earl don't be alarmed, dats all.” Tez raised a eyebrow at Queenie as he looked at 'er. “Ueenie do chu think chu could be pregnant?” “Nigga chu crazy cuz, nah I ain't pregnant.” Queenie turned an walked into da house feelin' a lil' frustrated wit all da questions Tez was throwin' at 'er. “Its not time jet fo' dis to be happenin'_I'm not married jet an I still got much to do befo' I bring a shorty into my world,dis world.” “Wutsup boss?” Chris snapped Queenie back from 'er thoughts she had been,so deep into. “Yo' wutsup fellas?” She spoke to all three of 'er solja's. “How y'all feelin' today y'all ready fo' dis we gotta big day ahead of us.” “Yeah we game.” Tre' replied. “Yeah lets get dis paper boss.” Flex retorted. As Queenie walk toward da bedroom to retrieve da stash da fellas made da night befo' she got dizzy,but held 'er balance. Chris was followin' 'er an givin' 'er da run down of wut happened last night. “Neva da less boss we only gotta 110 bricks left an today ain't even started jet,so I doubt if it last da night.” “Fam' I got chu don't worry let me count dis den I'll make a call an by dis evenin' shit should be back thick 'round 'ere ya heard.” Queenie stood up an said; “Now get me da money machine.” “Ma chu good 'cus yo' ass don't look well at all. Do chu need to sit down?” An befo' Chris could get his next sentence out Queenie's eyes rolled in back of 'er head da 2 duffel bags she held drop to da floor an she fell back goin' through da bedroom window. It happen wit in seconds an 'er young protege' wasn't able to catch 'er in time. “Yo' fam' call 911 he yelled as his boss body fell through da window. Cortez' and Tez damn near knocked one a nutter down tryin' to get in da room where Queenie and Chris were. “Wut da fuck goin' on?” Dey asked in unison's “Ah fuck no Ueenie please don't be.” Cortez' in a panic asked; “Wut da fuck happen to 'er fam'?” Chris quickly sums it up as tears streamed down his face; “I don't know!” He was in shock as he tried to hold Queenie's head up from a very compromised position. She had a thick piece of glass piercin' through 'er back dat was pokin' threw 'er chest on da left side of 'er body. Chris had caught da back of 'er head jus' in time befo' it snapped backwards onto da glass dat was pointed at da center of 'er neck. “Yo' Flex go outside fam' an break da glass dats jabbin' 'er neck please bro.” Chris cried; “Boss come on ma chu gotta make it through dis dis ain't yo' fate ma chu been threw way mo' dan dis fo' it to be da end now. Tez she losin' way to much blood fam'.” “Yo' fam' I hear sirens close.” Tre' told 'em. Chris, Tez and Cortez' tried their best to hold 'er dead weight up off da glass wit out movin' 'er 'til da paramedics arrived. “Right 'ere!” Tre' flagged down da ambulance. “She's in dere hurry!” Da paramedics rushed into da bedroom wit a stretcher. “Wut happen?” Dey had questioned,but non where bein' answered. “We're gonna need chu to let us get in 'ere to get 'er secured.” “Man we can't jus' let body go like dat.” Tez responded. “She has glass through 'er shoulder an ain't no tellin' where else.” “Okay, okay fellas lets all switch positions one by one. I move in an chu move out, Imma need some one to go outside an on my count I need chu to break da glass from da window pane dats threw 'er back Tez ran outside at da window he said; “I'm ready.” “On three be very careful, 1,2,3!” Tez broke da glass as instructed. He stayed on da outside to help support Queenie's head up. “Give me dat sheet dere so I can place ova 'er face, so no glass will cut 'er face as we pull 'er back threw da window.” Chris handed da sheet to Cortez' an he placed it ova 'er face. “Alright lets lift 'er easy an place 'er on da stretcher, she's lose,so much blood we will have to work on 'er on da way. We're takin' 'er to U of I its closer to 'ere.” “I'm ridin' wit 'er.” Cortez' said. “We right behind y'all fam'.” Tez stated an 'em Chris, Tre' and Flex ran out da house. Tez tossed his keys to Tre'_ “Drive my whip fam'.” An 'em Chris and Flex jumped in Queenie's truck da three rode in silence fo' a coupla blocks den Tez asked Chris; “Fam' wut happen while y'all was in da room.” Chris gave Tez play by play of wut 'em and Queenie did.

"Fam' afta' she stood up rom da safe I told 'er she didn't look well an did she wanta chair, next thing I seen was 'er eyes roll back in 'er head da bags drop to da floor an she went back into da window fam' an I_ I barely made it_a pause silence da car as he started to cry again. Fam' if I hadn't caught 'er head an neck dat shit woulda went straight 'er neck family." Tez grabbed his lil' homeboy by da head tryin' to comfort 'em by makin' light of da situation dat he knew at any moment could take a turn fo' da worst.

"Family listen to me Ueenie she's gonna make it, my lil' nigga has been through hell an back she will not let dis defeat 'er y'all feel me. Dats my solja in back of dat truck." He mainly tried to convince 'em self wit dat speech. Pullin' up behind da ambulance Tez and Tre' parked da cars an dey all jumped out an ran to da trauma center where da medics ran Queenie into. Dey met Cortez' at da nurses desk dey wanted to know from Cortez' wut dey did fo' 'er in da back of da ambulance. Cortez' said; "Dey gave 'er IV's oxygen an dey got da bleedin' to slow down, but dey said da doctor has to pull out da glass,so dey jus' shot 'er to emergency surgery an da nurse said dey'll come out an let us know somethin' soon." "Excuse me sirs,but who can I get some info from on da patient dat jus' came in." Dis felt like de'ja'vu all ova again fo' Tez. He looked at da nurse den looked at his homeboy Cortez'. Den Cortez' looked back at Tez an said; "Chu gotta call Liz. Tez told da nurse; "Dis is 'er fiancee' and I'm 'er first cousin,but we don't know all da answers to yo' questions,so Imma call my aunt fo' chu."

"Dats fine go ahead." Da nurse told 'em. Ring,ring,ring,ring,ring__ "Hello, Liz speakin'."

"Yo' auntie." "Aye nephew, I ain't received a early phone call from chu__wuts wrong wit my baby? Where is Queenie?" She said frantically an Tez jus' passed da phone to da nurse. "Mrs. Miles hello my name is Aeries Kelz I am a nurse 'ere at da University of Illinois an we jus' received yo' daughter 'ere in da trauma center an unfortunately she has to have emergency surgery,so if chu could be of some help fo' me an give me a lil' information,so I can put into 'er files." Liz said; "Yes I can do dat." Afta' da nurse finished wit all of da questions she had fo' 'er she said; "Thank ya Mrs. Miles now I'll return da phone back to ya nephew." "Hello, Tez wuts goin' on? Wut happen to Queenie?" "Auntie she fell out an when she did she fell straight throw a window." "Excuse me do either one of chu know if Ms. Miles has eva been pregnant or if she maybe pregnant at dis time?" Da nurse asked. Liz ova heard da convo Tez had wit nurse as he got back on da phone. Liz asked; "Why do chu think yo' cousin is pregnant?" Wit 'er bein' a nurse 'er self fo' many years Liz wanted to know everyone of 'er daughters actions since she's been away from da treatment center. "Auntie Imma let chu talk to Cortez' or Chris 'cus I jus' found out a coupla hours ago dat Ueenie has been feelin' sick." Liz questioned sick? "Tez has Queenie been eatin' like she usually does?" "Come to think of it no ma'am she's jus' been pickin' ova 'er food. Da last time I really seen Ueenie get down on a plate of food was da day dey let 'er out an we all went to DUSTIES.""Yeah it was strange of 'er not to eat much when me and yo' moms cooked all dat food when y'all was 'ere. I'm on my way wit yo' mother." She told 'em. "Instead of driven yo' selves jus' call up Caine,so he can bring y'all 'ere in da limo,he'll get chu 'ere quicker. Matter of fact jus' get ready I'll call 'em myself to pick y'all up." Liz hung up da phone befo' she could hear anything else Tez said. "Hello." Caine spoke. "Yo' family dis is Tez homeboy, I need chu to stop wut eva it is chu doin' an go pick up moms an 'em at da house an get 'em 'ere to Chicago asap." Cortez' paste da floor as well as Chris, Flex, and Tre'. Tez afta' he got off his hitter he stood at da window an stared out on to da world as he searched fo' answers. Jus' da 15 minutes dey had been at da hospital seem like a life time it was movin' so slow to the 5 of 'em while dey tried to wait patiently to hear somethin on Queenie's condition. Back in East St. Boogie, Caine picked up everyone except Chaos an dat was only 'cus his physical therapist was at da house, utter dan dat he would have had someone put 'em in da car also. Liz couldn't stop or make Queenie's entourage stay behind 'cus once dey heard

"THROWIN' BRICKS AT THE PENITENTIARY"

Liz tell Heather and Chaos wut happened da fellas were admit 'bout seein' their boss. Caine made it his biz'ness to get to Chicago as fast as possible as Lil' Man called his bro Chris to see wut was up. "Who dis?" Chris answered da phone in a distraught tone. "Wutup bro dis Lil' Man, wuts good wit boss fam'?" "We ain't heard shit jet she still in surgery bro." Lil' Man told Chris; "Hang in dere bro boss is tough hell she's "Boss Queen" she's gonna make it." An hour and half pass by an still no word, but dat she was still in surgery. Cortez' told Tez; "Family I feel,so hurt da woman I love is on a operatin' table once again. She's been threw,so much shit an she don't deserve any of it, I feel like all dis is my fault fo' wut eva reason cuz." "Don't beat yo' self up fam' even if she is knocked up Ueenie played 'er part in it also man. Chu already know dere is not much yo' ass can tell 'er dats gonna slow 'er ass down." "Yeah I know,but I shoulda paid mo' attention to da signs she gave off. Hell my lil' bro seen mo' dan I seen." Dey both looked in Chris direction as Tez stated; "Man chu can't let dat beat chu up 'cus chu feel family knows mo' 'bout 'er dan chu, remember he is 'er protege' an all he does is study Queenie. She has become his mentor,so don't fault 'em actually cuz yo' ass need to be thankin' 'em fo' catchin' da shit chu not." Wut Tez told Cortez' made 'em think long and hard. Da hospital doors opened an Liz and Heather rushed in followed by da rest of da crew. "Any word jet, how is she, wuts goin' on?" Liz and Heather had all type of questions,but no one could answer. A phone rang at da nurses desk an once she hung up 'er receiver, she walked ova to Tez an said; "Excuse me Mr. Miles dey jus' called from da back Ms. Miles has pulled threw da surgery jus' fine an da doctor is on his way out to give chu mo' details on 'er condition." Tez nodded his head an thanked da nurse. "Da Miles family?

Chapter Thirty-Two
"De'ja' vu Wit A Twist"

I'm doctor Kennedy I performed Ms. Miles surgery." "Jus' call 'er Queenie she hates when people call 'er Ms. Miles." Cortez' explained to da doctor. "Okay den Queenie pulled through jus' fine it took a lil' longer dan I thought it would do to da fact da glass had slice threw one of 'er arteries an it had to be mended back together. Right now she is in da recovery room,once she awakens we will move 'er to room 502. I want 'er to remain in da hospital fo' a week,so I can keep an eye on dat arm,da glass damaged 'er artery pretty bad an I need to make sho' she gets feelin' back in it an 'er nerves are functionin' properly. Last,but not least I did have a pregnancy test ran an Queenie is pregnant an befo' she leaves da hospital I will do a full examination on 'er,so we can see how far along she is." Three weeks went by an Queenie refused to go back to East St. Boogie,so she remained in Chicago laid up in da hotel suite 'er and Cortez' had,it was official Queenie was indeed pregnant, 2 weeks to be exact. She wanted no special treatment,Queenie didn't want to be treated differently 'cus of da state she was in. Da doctor told da family it wasn't uncommon dat she passed out from bein' pregnant it was jus' away 'er body reacted,so she could find out dat dere was a nutter life inside 'er. His main concern was 'er havin' function in 'er arm again. Queenie did listen to da doctor an stayed in bed,so she could recuppe, but fo' 'er he said nothin' 'bout 'er workin' from da bed. She called shots from da bed in 'er hotel suite an she made dat call to 'er mentor like she told Chris she would three weeks ago. Ring_

"Hello! "Boss Queen" how are chu feelin'? I hear chu banged yo' self up pretty bad." "Wutsup ol' man,how did chu find out so fast?" She replied. "Awe I know everything Queenie,jus' like I know chu want one last run befo' chu settle down an take care of yo' baby." Queenie started to question 'er mentor, but thought better of it an jus' ended up smilin' an told 'em; "Yeah ya,so right ol' man now can we get down to biz'ness,so I can go back to restin' sir?" Queenie went on to tell 'er mentor wut she needed,so Detroit could get it to 'er asap. "I need double of wut was sent befo' instead of da 800 send 1600 dat last batch didn't last a week." "Boss Queen" I will give chu wut chu ask fo',but movin' merch like dat only brings heat an draws suspicion to da game not only wit Ola,but my people will start to look at it suspect. Queenie chu don't need to draw any mo' attention to yo' self movin' dat many bricks in a weeks time will land chu in one of two places: dead six feet under or da penitentiary. I prefer neither one fo' chu,but of course chu a very stubborn young lady an chu will do Queenie. Jus' be be careful chu will receive 2 rent-'em u-haul trucks midnight tonight an we'll convo later 'bout da tab. "Boss Queen" do chu, but watch yo' back dat baby needs chu." Once off da phone she dialed Cortez' hitter. "Yo' wutsup shawty is chu still restin' ma?" "Yeah baby I am in da bed as we speak. Look Cortez' I need fo' y'all to come to da room." "Who dat ma,me and Tez or chu need to see all of us?" "Aye I need all 5 of y'all asap an we'll talk when y'all get 'ere." She den asked Cortez' was he ready,but Cortez' thought befo' he answered 'er. "Ready to wut marry yo' ass ma?" "Yeah chu ready to marry me." She repeated. "Hell yeah I'm ready I been ready shawty, but da question is wut chu waitin' on ma?" He asked in a sexy thuggish tone. Queenie replied; "Yo' fo' da time to be right, but it jus' neva seems like it eva will be. 'Cus on my end its always some shit thrown in da game. So tell chu wut nigga lets jus' do it we can have a big weddin' later down da line aiight, 'cus truth be told we keep puttin' it off my ass jus' might end up dead an we still won't be married baby.""Yo' shawty stop talkin' like dat nah mean yo' ass been through a hellva lot, but yo' ass ain't goin' nowhere, we finna have a family soon,so chill out wit all dat negative bull shit." Cortez' spoke befo' he thought 'bout wut he was sayin'. No one knew dat Queenie was a wanted youngan in da city of Chicago not even she knew. Da fellas walked through da door an she asked 'em how were things at da stash house. She questioned; "Is everything

everything 'round 'em parts?” “Yeah boss all good everything is straight we jus' waitin' on chu to say wut it is.” Chris stated. “Well wait no longer lil' nigga 'cus tonight y'all got 2 rent-'em u-hauls comin' in 1600 bricks. Now dis shipment is double from da last one an y'all already know wut to do same as befo' store of 'em in da basement, but dis time y'all will be unloadin' both trucks. An da last thing dis 'ere will be last an final shipment an afta' we will be headed back to East St. Boogie to start yo' new lives wit one of yo' own biz'nesses feel me. Dis is my last run fellas an I'll be givin' my protege' his own light to shine,so he can bring his “A” game. Chris will call shots wit Tez and Cortez'.” A coupla months passed an Cortez' and Queenie tied da knot at da downtown court house in front of a judge wit Tez Chris, Flex, Tre' an of course 'er moms an auntie on 'er 18th birthday. Queenie's belly started to show she was 4 months along an Cortez' couldn't have been any happier. He married his QUEEN which was a dream come true an in 5 months she would give birth to his son. Dey found out Queenie was havin' a boy da next heir of da family an dey had already had decided his name and nickname which would be Cortez' LC Fabs an his nickname (Tez). “I love chu Queenie yo' ass has made me da happiest man alive today an fo' eva ma.” “I love chu also an I will always love yo' ass fo' an eternity.” Givin' 'em a long passionate kiss tellin' 'em don't eva fo' get dat daddy. Queenie said; “Now lets go to DUSTIES an eat I feel like I can eat a race horse. Queenie put 'er arm 'round 'er moms waist an rested 'er head on Liz shoulder an asked 'er; “Ma chu ready fo' yo' gran baby to get 'ere?” “Yeah I am an chu better be takin' care of yo' self an my gran son. Chu comin' home to have 'em right?” Liz asked. “Yeah ma lil' Cortez' will be born in East St. Boogi jus' like his daddy was.” Chris asked Queenie; “Ma I know I can be his God Father right?” She stated; “Yo' chu gotta take dat up wit his #1 God Father.” As she looked at Tez. “Cuz dere is da perfect man who raised me dats if he wants da position an da title. “Lil' nigga chu know I'll be honored to be cuz's God Father I won't have it any utter way.” Cortez' chimed in;

"Congratulations homeboy I wouldn't of picked anyone nigga better fam' fo' my son to look up to either. Yo' did she tell y'all da name we chose fo' 'em? My lil' solja name will be Cortez' LC Fabs an his nickname Tez." Tez sat at da table an smiled wit a tear streamin' down his face. "Dats wutsup baby girl." An nodded his head in approval lettin' 'em know dat was wut was up. "Wut do da initials LC stand fo' boss?" Chris asked curiously. "We wanted Lu and Chuck's name in dere, but it woulda made his name to long,so we decided to jus' give 'em their initials LC." Da lights up ova da families table da lights blinked off and on 5 times an everyone 'round 'em looked in an ahhhh state. Liz said; "Lu and Chuck likes dat idea jus' fine." She looked up towards da ceilin' an whispered; "Y'all watch ova my babies." An once again da lights blinked off twice. "Yo' auntie chu serious 'bout dat stuff wit Lu and Chuck?" "Nephew dey say we all have guardian angels,so I truly believe if chu loose someone dat was as close to chu as Lu and Chuck was to all of chu den yeah I believe dat was a sign from 'em. We pray every night dat he gives y'all special angels to watch ova all of yo' asses 'cus God even knows he can't do it by 'em self wit everything y'all go threw." Liz had da full attention of each an every last one of Queenie's crew. "Queenie chu my child my baby an I am not tryin' to lose chu baby girl fo' any reason. Ya married now an chu jus' turned 18 an on top of it all an chu gonna be someones mother I can,but I won't tell chu wut to do,but I will suggest an give my opinion an say chu will do da right thing. We all know yo' ass stubborn,so we know Queenie is gonna do Queenie. All I ask of chu is think 'bout yo' child 'cus he deserves all of chu not jus' part of chu." Queenie knew wut 'er mother was getting at, it was all 'bout 'er bein' in da streets which really started to piss 'er off,but she decided not to feed into da convo, 'cus today was 'er day. So instead she asked was everyone done eatin' 'cus she was ready to go out to da lake front an chill out. Queenie didn't want to think 'bout wut 'er moms had said she didn't want to think 'bout da streets or wut needed to be done in 'em. All she wanted to do was relax an enjoy 'er b-day peacefully. "Yo' tomorrow we all will go back to East St. Boogie I got somethin' to sho' everybody." Cortez' and Tez had a raised eyebrow lookin' in 'er direction tryin' to figure out wut she had done now. "Yo' Tez baby call Mr. D. an tell 'em to meet us in Boogie by 1o'clock tomorrow fam'." Tez got on top of Queenie's request no sooner dan she finished 'er sentence. "Yo' lil' nigga its done he said he had been waitin' on yo' call fo' a few days. He said he'll be dere by noon." Queenie replied; "Dats wutsup lets walk ova to da Navy Pier. She waved da family on in dat direction an dey all had a ball. Dey walked da pier rode rides at least ones Queenie could get on. Chris and Tre' went to da navel shops an bought a few disposal camera's, so dey could all take pictures of da memorable day. "Yo' boss dese pictures 'ere chu can start da baby's photo album wit,to sho' 'em his mom,dad and family liven it up." Dey all laughed joked took pictures an drank, except Queenie she jus' sipped on apple juice all night 'til it was time to leave. An eerie feelin' came ova Queenie afta' 'bout 5 hours into their outtin' she felt as doe someone was watchin' 'er,but she refused to alarm da fellas so she watched 'er surroundins' 'er self. To 'er surprise it was a group of females dat followed 'em every where dey went,but from a distance,so she figured dat da girls were some young groupies dat wanted to holla at da crew. Only later a few hours as it started to get dark did she realize somethin' strange of one of da chic's in da group. Queenie finally gotta good look at da leader of da pack. It was one of Tez ex-girls. Da last girl he had in da Chi befo' Queenie cock blocked. Queenie saw a problem wit 'er money hungry ass an she brought it to Tez attention. Afta' Queenie requested fo' Tez to come to East St. Boogie all of da girls cash flow stopped fo' sho' 'cus he had jus' up and left. "Yo' Tez." Queenie called out to 'em. Tez along wit everyone else stopped in their tracks. "Wutup ma?" "Yo' cuz ain't dat yo' long time ex ova dere eye ballin' me fam'?" Tez looked on an da girl spoke; "Tez don't act like chu don't know who I am, dat bitch of a cousin of urns know to." "Oh shit Queenie no!” Tez tried to jump in front of his lil' cousin, but Queenie threw up 'er hands. “Don't touch me Tez I'm cool I jus' wanta ask 'er wuts 'er problem.” “Tez man don't let 'er go ova dere. Fuck 'ere we go.” Cortez' stated. Chris walked behind his boss as well as Tez as Liz shouted; “Queenie chu pregnant yo' ass don't need to be fightin'.” Da chic told 'er girls; “Oh shit dis bitch is pregnant.” By dis time Queenie screamed; “Moooova lookin' from side to side at da utter girls as she grabbed their home girl by 'er neck wit 'er left hand. “I need to know why da fuck chu keep callin' me bitch when chu damn well know my name?” Not knowin' whether Queenie would toss 'er ova da rail of da Pier da girl struggled to keep 'er feet on da ground as she held on to da rail fo' dear life. She tried to pry Queenie hand from 'round 'er neck. “Yo' ma let dat bitch go she ain't worth it at all baby girl think of yo' shorty lil' nigga.” Tez tried to convince Queenie to let 'er go. Tears rolled down da girls face an she started to turn purple. Queenie leaned in,so only she could hear 'er; “Yo' shawty listen an hear me clear home girl today is yo' lucky day 'cus chu musta fo' got who I am, but dis da deal afta' I drop my load I will see yo' ass again,so be prepared to give or either take a beat down, but either way chu will regret eva usin' da bitch word.” Queenie opened 'er fingers like she was throwin' away some trash an walked away leavin' da girl gaspin' fo' air wit 'er crew tryin' to help 'er to 'er feet. “Squad up! I'm ready to bounce.” She shouted. No one said anything to Queenie 'bout 'er actions dey jus' were relieved dat da situation didn't escalate into anything mo' knowin' dat woulda been stressful on da baby. “Cortez'!” “Wutsup baby?” “Get everybody rooms fo' tonight an we will all leave out in da mornin'. Get moms an auntie a double bed suite dey can share an da rest chu already know wut to do. Aye cuz lets go to Kenny's ribs ova in Harvey real quick an grab some ribs fam'.” “Damn cuz chu hungry again? Shorty gonna have yo' ass wide as a house or chu gonna have 'em comin' out lookin' like a lineback baby girl.” Queenie hit Tez in his arm. “Can we jus' get da ribs nigga? Mr. ha ha funny man.” She said jokingly.

“Aiight, aiight we goin' cuz calm down. Yo' I'm glad we rich doe 'cus if we were broke wit yo' appetite we would be messed up on da real cuz.” “Homeboy leave my babies alone dey both gonna be jus' perfect.” “Ah nigga shut up I'm jus' sayin' wut chu won't say 'cus chu scared cuz can't take critism. Cortez' chu should know by now dat dis lil' nigga can take anything chu throw at 'er ass an can dish it out jus' as well fam'.” While dey talked and joked Queenie place da order of a pan of rib tips half wit sauce an half wit out sauce. A large pan of fresh fries a small pan of coleslaw, bake beans an to top it off she ordered a whole chocolate German cake. “Yo' total is $220.06 ma'am.” Da lady behind da cash register told Queenie which made everyone's head snap 'round. “Damn ma wut chu order?” Voices chimed out an she snapped back; “Food niggas now grab da bags an stop questionin' me.” An she walked out da door. Afta' arrivin' at da hotel Liz and Heather turned in fo' da night tellin' 'em dey would see 'em in da mornin' an to enjoy their food. “Yo' ma_auntie y'all don't want to take some food wit y'all to da room?” Cortez' asked. “Nah baby we're still stuffed from da food at da lake. Chu kids enjoy an have fun son.” Liz whispered. Queenie an 'er crew gathered in one room ate talked shit, laughed and cracked jokes on one a nutter. Queenie laughed,so hard she caught sharp pains in 'er stomach. “Yo' ma, no one said anything earlier,but I gotta ask wut was goin' threw yo' mind when chu grabbed ol' girls neck like dat? 'Cus honestly a few mo' seconds an da bitch woulda flat line fo' sho' boss.” All da fellas laughed and joked 'bout da situation except Tez and Cortez'. “Actually nothin' Chris, I wasn't actually thinkin' 'bout shit lil' fam' an if I wouldn't have heard Tez tell me da bitch wasn't worth it I probably woulda killed dat bitch. I felt my hand crushin' 'er esophagus I felt my adrenaline rushin',but cuz stopped dat.” Chris said; “Ma let me ask one mo' question if I can?” “Shoot lil' nigga.” She told 'em. “Wut did chu tell ol' girl in ear shot befo' chu let 'er go?” “I said yo' shawty listen an hear me clear 'cus chu musta fo' got who I am an today was 'er lucky day an afta' I drop my load she will see me again,so to be prepared to give or either take a beat down,but she will regret eva usin' da bitch word. Word is bond." Chris said; "Ma I'm kinda glad Tez spoke up 'cus I wouldn't wanta see lil' family get fucked up." "Yeah I know." She rubbed 'er stomach an said; "I gotta hold shit together 'til Mr. Fabs gets 'ere or his daddy jus' might flip out on me 'em self or faint. Jus' jokin' nigga. Baby I'm ready to go lay it down. Family I'll see y'all in a few." She hugged Tez an he kissed 'er on da fo' head. "Aiight see chu in a minute baby girl get some rest." Cortez' gave a pound to each one his family members an placed his hand on da small of Queenie's back leadin' 'er 2 doors down da hall to their suite. Once inside he laid Queenie on da bed an undressed 'er 'em self. She lied motionless while he pulled off 'er shoes,socks den unbuttonin' 'er pants an pullin' 'em off as he den pushed 'er shirt up ova 'er stomach. Dat's where he stop to gently kiss it all ova in a circular motion. "Ma dats my son inside dere." Tellin' 'er instead of askin' 'er,but she stayed silent an jus' enjoyed his soft lips and warm breath on 'er skin. Queenie was horny as hell,but da 2 decided not to have sex 'til afta' da baby was born since Queenie had gotten so big dey didn't want anything to go wrong since it was their first pregnancy. Cortez' pulled Queenie's shirt off ova 'er head an played wit 'er breast an sucked on 'er nipples which made both of 'em hot. Den came da partin'_ "Baby chu sho' we can't fuck?" She asked. "Nah ma we not finn chance it, I'll neva fo' give myself if I damaged my son shawty but tell chu wut I will do, I'll go downtown an clean yo' love box fo' as long as chu want me to aiight." Queenie shook 'er head yeah as she grabbed da top of his head pushin' 'em towards 'er pussy. It wasn't wut Queenie wanted,but she loved da feel of it since she couldn't have Cortez' dick inside of 'er. Respectin' Cortez' wishes fo' his reason of not wantin' to have sex made 'er love 'em jus' dat much mo'. Well it was time to head back to East St. Boogie,but befo' doin' so she had to return to da stash house to retrieve 'er paper an Tez needed to get his drop top. Queenie had also purchased 2 Mustangs

5.0 GT fully loaded wit horse power. One was 'ers an da utter she had bought fo' da fellas to get 'round in,but now da time had come, Queenie's biz'ness an 'er flawless was done in da city of Chicago. Queenie paper was long she was $2805000 dollars to da richest. Tez bought 'em self a new bubble Chevy windows tinted, Chrome tail pipes sittin' up on 18" rims fully loaded. Queenie had da fellas board up da stash house once again leavin' Chicago in da wind. Queenie yelled out; “Squad up fam' lets ride out.” Chris drive my truck, Imma drive my 5.0.” “Yo' Flex fam' drive my drop fo' me.” Tez retorted. Giz'mo rode wit Tez, Lil' Man rode wit Chris. Stacks drive my shit fam' Imma ride wit my wife. Tre' jumped in wit Flex, Joc and Jo jumped in wit Stacks into Cortez' box Chevy. Of course Liz and Heather rode back in da limo wit Caine drivin'. Ridin' down da highway it looked like a beautiful parade of cars alone da e-way. It was a sight to see each car shined like dey all jus' came off da showroom floor. “Baby wuts next on da chess board?” Cortez' asked; “We got 4 months befo' da baby gets 'ere. Are chu ready shawty?” “Yeah baby wut utter choice do I have he's in dere growin' big an strong now. Da question is chu ready to be a father sir?” “Baby all I gotta do is setup his nursery. Don't worry 'bout dat ma I jus' need chu to relax aiight. So tell me ma wut chu gotta sho' everybody once we get back home.” “Nah mean chu can't wait 'til we get dere an see like everyone else?” “Nah ma now wutsup why chu holdin' out on ya own husband?” “Oh shit so yo' ass gonna try an play da husband card on me huh? Nigga dat shit ain't gonna work like ya think it is, but I got chu doe. Listen Mr. D. got doe's properties I wanted dats all. He got da grocery store front da laundromat an da barbershop,so dats my surprise baby I'm jus' tryin' to put my people to work so da cash flow will continue on a regular basis.” Caine's hitter rang.

Chapter Thirty-Three
"I'm Takin' My Family Off Da Streets"

"Hello" "Wutsup homeboy I jus' need chu to listen to me. Remember da store fronts I showed chu fam', well go to da grocery store first." Dey all pulled up at da store once Cortez' helped Queenie out of da car an da fellas gathered on da side walk Queenie signaled Caine to let 'er moms and aunt out of da limo. Queenie walked toward 'er moms an put 'er arm 'round Liz shoulders an said; "Dis 'ere all chu ma." Mr. Demontea' walked out of da store lockin' da double doors in a open position. "Ms. Miles its all urns." Pointin' to da sign dat read Liz Community Grocery Store. Mr. D. handed Liz keys to 'er new biz'ness an open his arms pointin' towards da doors fo' 'er to walk threw. Tears of joy fell from da wells of Liz eyes. "Thank chu baby dis 'ere is,so beautiful my own biz'ness named afta' me how sweet." She hugged Queenie,so tight she almost fo' got dat 'er child was pregnant. "Everything has been newly remodeled an updated,every shelve has been stocked an every cooler and freezer has somethin' in it. Dis 'ere is jus' to get da ball rollin' when time comes to re-up its all chu lady,to buy an do wut chu want. Chu also got a butcher spot in da back,so if anyone of chu niggas wanta go to school an learn da proper way to butcher up shit 'ere would be yo' first job. Ma when every chu ready to open it up its all good." "Yo' lets move on I got somethin' else to sho' y'all." Everyone headed fo' da cars,but Queenie said; "Yo' lets walk family." Dey were all shocked an a lil' surprise dat their boss an love one wanted to walk considerin' she walked no where. "Damn yo' don't look so surprise its not dat far its in da same neighborhood fam'." Dey walked 2 blocks to get to Heather's Community Wash Services. "Yo' dis 'ere is sweet cuz." Heather jumped up and down as she den bent ova in tears. "Thank ya niecy poo I feel so blessed to have chu fo' a niece, neva would I imagined bein' a owner of anything let alone,my own boss of my own biz'ness. Thank chu thank chu." Queenie hugged 'er aunt; "Its cool auntie jus' stop cryin',so chu can see da inside.” Tez took his moms and Queenie by da hand an walked 'em inside da laundromat it was freshly remodeled wit big boy washer fo' blankets. Top load washers and dryers it even had a behind da counter snack venue where chu could order nachos,hotdogs,chips,pop and mo'. A game room off in da back fo' dose who come to wash an got bored. “Auntie chu also got a service to da public where dey can drop off their laundry to be cleaned, deres yo' weight station chu can weigh da laundry baskets or bags by da pound an it'll give chu a total price. It prints da tickets an dats how chu get paid fo' yo' services. Auntie who eva chu decide to hire is on chu an when eva chu ready to open 'ere go yo' keys its all urns.” Walkin' back outside da family was met head on by some of da people from da neighborhood wantin' to know when da only laundromat in their neighborhood would be open fo' biz'ness? Some even wanted to know if dey were hirin' an could dey get applications. Queenie said; “Yo' y'all need to talk wit dat pretty lady right dere 'cus she's in charge.” Dat put a bigger smile on Heathers face as she raised 'er hands an said; “Okay to answer yo' questions da laundromat will be open tomorrow at 7am I'm not hirin' jus' jet,but chu can pick up applications between 7am and noon.” I'm so glad chu openin' up a laundromat 'round 'ere in da hood 'cus we ain't got nothin' 'round 'ere no mo'. I'm tired of takin' a cab or walkin' wit all doe's bags 12 blocks jus' to wash my kids rags when I stay 4 houses down ova dere.” “Well we glad we can be of service to y'all an yo' families.” Queenie told 'em. Da lady shouted out God bless y'all all as Queenie an 'er people left. Da next stop was “PAY 4 YO' LADYS 2 PLAY SPA”. “Yo' “Boss Queen” wuts dis ma?” Chris asked. “Dis 'ere is a all women spa ran by jus' men,so dat means chu even got men receptionist who answer phones da whole nine yards fam'. Dis 'ere is fo' does women who plays wifey,who considers 'em selves as da shiiiit. Feel me an dis 'ere spa only a real boss can afford now lets step inside.”

“Whoa,wow,damn ummmm dis is plush! Shawty dis 'ere is King status half da women dese niggas have as wifey not even worthy of dis kind of treatment." Queenie said; "I wouldn't give a damn how, dese hoes look or wut dey worthy of, all money talks an long as da niggas can pay den dey bitches can play. Excuse my french ma and auntie." "We feel chu biz'ness is biz'ness." Heather stated; "Some of da women dey house do be hood ratz, but I guess everyone deserves a chance an dey say pussy ain't got no face." Tez said; "Ma!" An dey all broke out into laughter. "Aiight Tre' and Stacks y'all up." Queenie held out da keys fo' 'em both to take, but either of 'em budge. "Do y'all wish to be proud owners of "PAY 4 YO' LADYS 2 PLAY"?" Tre' and Stacks at da same time in unison's responded; "Nah mean no disrespect ma, but we wanta go to school." Which kinda shocked most. "If I didn't know any better I would think chu 2 were twins instead of Giz'mo and Stacks. So y'all prefer to go to school instead of runnin' yo' own biz'ness?" "Yo' boss if its okay wit chu."Queenie told 'em; "Yeah dats cool dats wutsup family,so if y'all don't mind me askin' wut would be yo' profession? Wut chu lookin' to get out of school?" Stacks told 'er; "I wanta take up da butcher sanitation course,so I can work in da store wit auntie Liz if she don't mind." "Baby I don't mind at all dat job will stay open jus' fo' chu baby." "Aiight Tre' an wuts yo' plan fam'?" She asked. "Boss I wanta take 2 if dats okay wit chu. I want accountin',so I can be quick wit countin' money like yo' self." "Huh." Queenie said. "Yeah boss I see da way chu can jus' add shit on top of yo' dome its like yo' ass a genius when it comes to numbers 'cus I neva see chu write shit down or use da money machine an I want dat. I wanta be able to count my shit quickly wit no mistakes orhave reason to leave any paper trails boss. An da utter course I wanta take is is barbershop cosmo,so one day I can own my own spot." "Aiight chu 2 we'll talk later on tonight if school is wut chu wanta do first den Imma make it happen,but in da mean time dat means I still need two fellas fo' dis biz'ness 'ere." Queenie said; "Yo' how 'bout pretty boy Giz'mo and playboy Jo?" "Ahhhh yeah!" Da 2 rubbed their hands together an stated; "Yes, yes, yeah boy we in da house wit da honeys.” Thank ya boss da 2 sang in harmony Queenie pulled Giz'mo and Jo by da hands closer to 'er in earshot. “Don't make me look bad, fuck up an dats yo' asses.” “We got chu boss we'll neva make “Boss Queen” look bad.” Across town da club Home was shut down,so Mr. D. purchased it at his clients request. “Yo' ma ain't dis da same__” Queenie cut Cortez' off. “Yeah baby dis is da exact same place I murdered ol' girl an shot at dude dat tried to sneak me an hit Tez and Chris instead. But now of course it belongs to chu, Tez and Chris dats if y'all wanta be da new proud owners of da biggest strip club in all East Boogie baby.” Da sign above read CTC STRIP CLUB. Tez asked curiously wut did CTC stand fo' since all of da sign wasn't unveil yet. “Yo' fam' first off its all three of yo' initials an it stands fo' “CUTTIES TOO CUDDLE”. Once again family its only women throughout da whole club. Strippin', bartenders even yo' money collectors at da door only male bouncers chu will have will be dat of da circle. I know I don't have to tell chu or remind chu of my reputation dis establishment is legit and legal its fo' yo' ballers, playas, and kingpins. A place niggas go to get away from their partners, wives, chu will even have bitches dat get down like dat come threw,but I ain't seen or ran cross a nutter braud dat has dat boss status or type of paper to be able to play in da big leagues jet.” Queenie said; “If dey can't afford da door admission chu already know da deal. Yo' its up to y'all make sho' dat everybody dat works 'ere is screened and auditioned thoroughly. I don't want any low class hood ratz in 'ere dat don't know how to act fam' bringin' da place down befo' it takes off, at anytime should biz'ness be discussed inside yo' establishment y'all feel me.” “Cuz I gotta hand it to ya chu really did yo' thang up in 'ere baby girl 'bout how many girls,dancers can be employed up in 'ere?” Tez asked. “Well da capacity of da place is 3,000 people which includes yo' staff,so jus' a suggestion if chu wanta get paid I would pack 2,000 customers in 993 brauds to strip an yo' staff three bartenders, one person at a time collectin' money off da door. Hire 4 of yo' brothers as da bouncers,but do it da way chu see fit. Jus' so y'all know dat way will give y'all da most money. Only thing I request of y'all is da brothers chu pick it can be da same 4 or it can be a different 4 each night I really don't care how chu do it, but doe's 4 chu will pay a $1000 a night. Trust an believe $4000 a night is not gonna hurt yo' biz'ness 'cus y'all finna quadruple dat every night." Tez kissed Queenie's fo' head an Cortez' grabbed his wife from behind kissin' da nap of 'er neck as he whispered; "Thank chu ma." Chris stood in front of 'er an took 'er by da hand an kissed it like da Queen he respected 'er as. "Thank ya boss chu da best ma."

"Yo' dis is a birthday gift to chu 2 also 'cus I won't be able to party wit y'all dis year. Chris I made chu part owner also 'cus yo' ass has showed me a lot ova da years an dis is my gift to chu. Jus' to sho' my appreciation lil' fam' chu will always be my protege',so do da right thing family." Queenie told 'em;

"Everything is setup legal except da liquor licenses. Its on da wall statin' y'all all got 'em already, but on da real I need fo' y'all to go get 'em asap. Chris wit chu only bein' 19 I had it setup,so chu can take da test,but chu will not receive yo' legit license 'til chu turn 21 lil' nigga. Tez chu an Cortez' will be right on time 'cus ya birthday's are in a coupla months. So at all times family keep yo' fake ID on chu jus' in case Ola pops up fo' any reason." Throwin' 'er arms in da air an twirlin' 'round tellin' da three;

"When eva its all urns homeboys." Queenie told 'em; "We got 2 utter spots, but considerin' one of our family members want to go to school to get his barber licenses I will hold da shop fo' Tre' an once he gets his paper sayin' he official den he can hire who he wanta." "Preciate it boss fo' my barber licenses I only gotta do 4 months an 2 months hands on,so maybe when dat time comes 'round chu can open up so I can do my hours?" Tre' suggested. "No problem fam' chu got it." "Boss wuts da utter biz'ness chu got?" Lil' Man asked curiously. Queenie said; "Its called "GET YO' SHOE SHINE DETAIL SHOP"."

"Huh?" Lil' Man questioned. "Come on y'all ah see." On da same side of town Queenie bought an old outside do it yo' self model car wash an turned it into a newly remodeled let us do it fo' chu wash detail an shine yo' rims while chu lay back relax an enjoy yo' piece of mind. "As y'all can see dis 'ere is not yo' ordinary car wash. Hangin' from da ceilin' in each corner of dis buildin' chu got 50" flat screen tv's ova dere chu got a wet bar which will have one woman an one man workin'. Only reason fo' a man 'cus y'all know jus' as well as me its a few under da radar ballers out in 'em streets__ Queenie broke out into laughter__ I'm jus' sayin' fam' y'all know wut it is. Aiight ova in dis its setup fo' 'em niggas who wanta come out an watch da games on Sunday and Monday night football an need dat famous excuse to get away from home,so dey say dey goin' to wash da car." "Damn ma chu pulled out all stops huh shawty?" Cortez' asked; "So Mrs. Fabs who will run dis fine establishment?" She replied; "Dis right 'ere belongs to Lil' Man and Joc, so wutsup y'all down fo' da crown homeboys or wut?" She asked. "Hell yeah ma,boss chu will not be disappointed in dis one 'ere." Lookin' at da two Lil' Man and Joc got excited. "Same rules apply to da both of chu jus' like da utters, its urns y'all partners an family is family, so do right by each utter. Fo' each and everyone of chu I would take up one or two of dese trade of yo' fello' brothers 'cus neva know when yo' ass may need to take his place fo' wut eva reason. 'Cus non of us will be 'round fo' eva feel me." Queenie held out da keys a set fo' Joc an a set fo' Lil' Man. "Y'all now are da proud owners of "GET YO' SHOE SHINE DETAIL SHOP" enjoy fellas an I know it will be a success." "Yo' Mr. D. if chu follow me I got yo' payment da rest of chu squad up,so we can go eat." Once at da car Queenie opened da trunk an pulled a duffel bag out dat contained $30,000 fo' all of his hard work of getting everything she needed done on a short notice. "Mr. D. as soon as my son is born I need chu to hook up his trust fund,so he will be set fo' life if anything was to happen to me." Queenie told 'em exactly wut she wanted. "Mr. D. half of my millions will be put aside fo' my youngan inherits. Mr. D. I don't know how much longer I will be 'round,so I need everything to be in order." Neva da less da rest of da family conversated curiously 'bout da things Queenie pulled off an da way she had been talkin' crazy fo' da last month or,so like wouldn't be 'round or somethin'. Prison and death was all their boss talked 'bout. Queenie's pregnancy was like smooth sailin' 'til September 5th at 2am when she went into labor she woke Cortez' wit a squealin' sound dat pierced his ears. "Ooooh, wut da fuck is goin' on? Cortez' I want my moms_shit my water jus' broke." She woke da whole house Chris, Lil' Man, Joc and Jo jumped up an ran into da bedroom. "Yo' call ma and auntie tell 'em its time an 'er water jus' broke." Jo called 'er moms an Chris called Tez. It was like a song da sang in harmony. "Yo' fam' boss water jus' broke its time to fly fam'." "Yo' auntie its time 'er water jus' broke 'bout 5 minutes ago." Cortez' put Queenie in da car an rushed 'er to da hospital wit out waitin' fo' an ambulance. Da family had a seat in da waitin' room while Cortez' was wit 'er in da delivery room fo' an hour. He held Queenie's hand an caressed 'er head as he told 'er; "Come on baby push chu can do it ma." Cortez' was da perfect coach tryin' to help his wife. Queenie gave birth to a 5 ½ pound baby boy an Cortez' a proud daddy cut da cord dat holds 'em an his mothers bond.

Chapter Thirty-Four
"A King Was Born"

Cortez' held lil' Cortez' an welcomed 'em into da world befo' he placed 'em gently in Queenie's arms. "Yo' shawty look at wut we created, he is gonna be very handsome lil' man." Queenie got cocky fo' a minute. "Baby look at who his parents is,see how strong his gens is. Baby I see Miles and Fabs all threw dis lil' man." Mr. and Mrs. Fabs I need to take da baby to da nursery an check 'em ova jus' to make sho' his vitals are okay. Queenie kissed Lil' Cortez' on top of his head an told 'em; "Mommy see chu later an handed 'em off to da nurse. "Oh by da way his name is Cortez' LC Fabs, but chu can put Tez on his crib fo' 'em to be recognized." "Okay Mrs. Fabs we will be movin' chu to room 2 in 'bout 15 minutes den chu can have Lil' Cortez' in da room wit chu. We jus' ask who eva comes in and out of da room put on scrubs an wash their hands dat's jus' to keep 'em germ free. Since chu didn't have any complications wit yo' delivery soon as lil' man 'ere clears which should be tomorrow den chu both can leave da hospital.” “Thank chu.” Queenie and Cortez' said together. Cortez' said; “Baby Imma go out an tell moms and 'em wutsup aiight.” He kissed 'er on da fo' head den da lips tellin' 'er; “Thank chu ma thank chu.” He ran to da waitin' area. “Yo' Imma daddy!” He shouted. Congratulations filled da room. “He weighs 5 ½ pounds 18 inches long he has all of his fingers and toes an da lil' nigga has a head full of hair. Queenie is fine in 'bout 10 minutes she gonna be put in room 2.” “So where is da baby now?” “Dey took 'em to da nursery fo' a check up an long as he good den dey both can go home tomorrow.” Chris asked; “Can we go see Lil' Cortez' an who do he look like chu or boss?” “Queenie say she see Miles and Fabs in 'em, but I want ma and auntie to tell me who dey see.” “Yo' family I don't see 'em.” Chris said. “I see his lil' ass dats cut I see Ueenie throwin' out orders once again huh?” Tez read out loud da name tag. “Lil' Tez I am King.” “Dats wutsup, boss crazy, she be goin' hard, dats on point.” An dey all laughed and joked. “Wutsup cuz how chu feelin'? We see chu already dishin' out demands, givin' lil' nigga his props already.” Queenie said; “Fo' sho' cuz dats my son he a blessin' in aye did chu see how handsome he looks already? Dat lil' nigga gonna be hell on wheels watch wut I tell ya cuz. An da best part is he got 9 niggas to look afta' 'em a granny a great aunt and great uncle family is all he got.” Tez and Cortez' noticed Queenie didn't mention 'er self when she named da people he had to raise 'em, but dey thought better of it to say anything. Tez jus' made a mental note to holla at his cousin later on. A nurse wheeled lil' Tez bed into da room an parked it by Queenie's bed side, so she could reach 'em. “Yo' dey say befo' anyone touches da baby ya gotta wash yo' hands an put on some scrubs.” Liz was da first one to hold 'er new gran baby. “My gran son look at granny's lil' cuttie. Cortez' and Queenie he is beautiful.” Liz exclaimed. “'Em gonna have all da lil' girls wrapped 'round 'em finger yeah 'em is.” She said in baby voices. “Some wut Cortez' son he do have both yo' features, but right now his stronger genes are doe's of da Miles. Don't worry baby our family genes is very potent, but he a baby an all baby's features change daily at da moment he looks like his mommy. But in a coupla hours he can have all yo' features he can have all yo' features son neva know only time will tell.” “Aiight auntie let da nigg look like me.” Tez said jokingly wit his arms out fo' 'er to put lil' Cortez' in 'em. “Aye wutsup lil' man? I'm yo' big cuz__ Tez walked 'round da room, back and forth talkin' to 'em. We family lil' cuz aye he smilin' at me yo'.” Tez smiled wit tears in his eyes as lil' Tez held his smile fo' as long as he had one on his face. Lil' Tez finally opened his eyes fo' Tez to see 'em fo' da first time. Dey were beautiful,but very different an unusual from anything he had eva seen. “Yo' Ueenie have y'all seen his eyes jet?” “Nah maybe a quick second befo' dey took 'em to da nursery.” Queenie responded. Cortez' jumped up an walked ova so he could get a look,but jus' as he got close a nuff to Tez to see lil' Cortez' closed his eyes again. Its like he didn't want anyone else to see his eyes,but Tez. Queenie asked 'er cousin wut did his eyes look like? So he described 'em as bein' a light green yellowish color an dat was da white part of his eyes an da pupils are a cold black. “Yo' Ueenie did chu request fo' da doc to check lil' Tez head out?” “Nah not jet.” “But I did he'll do it tomorrow,but he said most likely nothin' will sho' up 'cus he,so small, but we can have da next test done when he turns 2 years old. Da doc said at dat age his brain will sho' mo' active waves.” Heather stepped up beside Queenie's bed an said; “In da meantime we all jus' pray.” Kissin' 'er niece on da fo' head an strokin' 'er hair_ “Dat lil' Cortez' LC Fabs will grow up jus' fine wit out havin' his mommy head conditions.” As time went on it seem to fly by, lil' Tez was growin' bigger and stronger befo' everyone's eyes. All of da biz'nesses were doin' well Tre' had gotten his licenses to officially open his barbershop which he asked Queenie if he could rename it to say; “PLAYAZ & Lil' PLAYAZ DADS

& TOTS BARBERSHOP" she gave 'er approval an Tre' grand openin' was a smash hit. It was such a success he made ova $20 grand openin' day alone. Tre' couldn't believe it 'em self da clientele dat walk through da doors of his own biz'ness an once he closed up shop he went straight to see his boss.

"Boss can we talk ma?" He asked wit sincere in his voice. "Fo' sho' fam' wutsup?" "Boss Queen" I jus' wanted to let my appreciation be know, 'cus nah mean I feel it takes someone to love and care 'bout someone as much as chu have fo' us ma to do da shit yo' ass do fo' us alone. Yeah I know we all family now, its da way chu came into it boss,an intrigued all of us. Fo' example look at da impact yo' ass made on my bro's life, Cortez' he hasn't changed to much fo' da most part he still 'em,but I do see a softer side mo' dan befo'. When it was jus' us 11 'em and Chuck was our source of livin' dey showed us da way an I love 'em both fo' dat,but when chu came into his life I believe chu,chu boss made our family complete." Tre' shook his head up and down an said;"Yeah its complete now ma it was missin' a puzzle piece an when "Boss Queen" showed up shawty chu fixed dat,an since den dis family has grown." He stop to look at Lil' Cortez' an told Queenie; "Lil' Tez is a very lucky kid to have chu as his mom. Boss I say all dis 'cus if it wasn't fo' chu ma I can honestly say I don't know where I woulda ended up. Nah mean chu gave not jus' me,but all my bro's a chance to make somethin' of ourselves,so we wouldn't have to be on da corner. I mean chu took us from da corners an put us in stash houses makin' mo' money in a day dan I woulda imagined. Ma my weekly doe was mo' dan somebody workin' at Wall Street dat alone was a blessin' wit in itself, den to go an purchase all of us_shit biz'nesses 'cus chu wanted us_." "Chu mean my family." She told 'em. "Yo' family to go legit an no longer be in da streets no one could eva tell me any different dat he didn't put chu in our lives as da beautiful angel chu is boss,so I wanta thank chu ma fo' it all an man ma don't eva leave us boss." Tre' handed Queenie a manila envelope wit nothin', but hunnid dollar bills inside. "Wuts dis Tre?" "Boss Queen" its half of wut I took in from my grand openin'." "I didn't" "Wait boss I know chu didn't ask fo' a dime back in return,but Imma ask chu to keep it 'cus Imma feel better knowin' I was able to give back. I realize it ain't nearly da amount chu dished out,but dis is my way of sayin' thank ya an I love chu to da end ma yo' know its ride and die." Queenie was some wut speechless clearin' 'er throat she asked Tre'; "So how much did yo' ass pull in on yo' first day?" $20 gs ma an dat was jus' hair cuts alone I didn't empty da baller's play pin jet nor my movie area.""I bet chu neva thought in a million dat chu would be sittin' on a cash cow huh?" She asked. "Nah mean not really boss it is great fo' wut it is doe, but its jus' me I could use some help doe mo' money would be made if I had da hands." Queenie replied to his statement. "Hire chu some people den, yo' chu gotta nuff room fo' at least 5 mo' booths an still keep it roomy fam'." "Yeah boss I remember chu tellin' us we can hire who we want,but I don't want any out-siders. I want my people my brothers, dey all busy an seem to have their own shit goin' on ma."

"Listen Tre' Imma call a meetin' Friday an Imma find out who wouldn't mind goin' to school an makin' extra paper to get down dere an help yo' ass rake in some of dat doe, aiight fam'." "Oh yeah boss I talk to auntie she told me dat if I was available she would pay me to keep 'er books straight fo' wut da laundromat pulls in also." "See dats wut I'm talkin' 'bout dats cool fam' hell yo' ass need to holla at moms an see if she needs chu to do da same fo' 'er. Now chu getting da concept of it all. Dats all I want chu niggas to get da mo' yo' asses help each utter da mo' money y'all can make an it all stays in da family." "Fo' sho'." Tre' paused an picked up Lil' Tez to play wit 'em as he asked 'em ain't dat right fam' we gonna keep it between us? Lil' Tez started laughin' wit a wide smile like he understood da words comin' out of Tre's mouth. "Aye boss wutsup wit my lil' niggas birthday he finna be one soon?"

"I haven't talk to Cortez' jet,but I thought 'bout havin' everyone close down da biz'nesses on Tuesday night,so all y'all can be free fo' 'bout 4 days. Since lil' Cortez' will only be turnin' one I'm give 'em his very own mini circus ova in CTC parkin' lot fo' 2 days den Friday mornin' we all head to Chi-Town an give 'em his first pizza party at Chuck E Cheese let 'em run 'round 'cus he likes da bouncy houses. Den on Saturday mornin' which is his actually b-day we can all take 'em to da Bud Billiken Parade afta' da parade we'll have our own lil' cookout in da park an eat sing happy birthday to lil' Tez an have cake and ice cream." "Damn lil' man chu da King fo' 4 days mommy gonna hook chu up nigga. Yo' chu got da best mom in da world fam'." Tre' an da rest of da fellas had been showin' lil' Tez how to give 'em pounds,so he balled up his lil' fist an raised it in da air. "Dats my nigga." Tre' told 'em as he gave 'em back to his mother. Tre' passed word on to his brothers of da money he gave to "Boss Queen" jus' on GP 'cus of wut she had done fo' 'em an he felt dey should step up to da plate an sho' 'er some love also. Only odd thing to Tre' was his brothers had made way mo' dan 'em, do to da fact dey all had ahead start on 'em by a good six months,so Tre' spoke up. "Yo' wit out boss non of us would eva had thought 'bout goin' legit. Why 'cus we dope boys straight from da hood an da streets were all we knew." Tre' looked at Chris an told 'em; I'm surprised at yo' ass bro dis yo' mentor someone chu look up to fam' shawty yo' ass will kill fo' an chu didn't think once to give 'er shit back family." Chris said; "Boss don't want money from us fam'." "Bro dat ain't da point if she want it or not, think 'bout it wit out 'er non of dis woulda been possible. Did chu even stop to think, really think why non of us is in jail or prison right now? 'Cus we done plenty of stupid dumb shit dat shoulda landed us in da pen fo' along time comin'. Its 'cus of ma we all still able to walk 'round dis ma'fucka an do da shit we do an enjoy da shit we do bro. Yo' look when boss first came into our lives an she showed 'er murder game dat night non of us really didn't know wut to expect from dat hell I jus' knew we was all goin' to da pen behind dat bullshit an we didn't even know 'er at da time. Yo' check dis doe dat murder on Tez ex-girl bro yo' ass was first one at boss aid. Correct? Now chu tell me chu didn't think yo' ass wouldn't be locked up fo' along time behind dat shit nigga." "Wuts yo' point fam'?" Chris asked. "Nigga my point is if it wasn't fo' boss yo' ass would still be locked up bro, boss pull out all stops fo' dis circle 'cus we all family. When Ola came in she knew dey were comin' fam' an even doe it was 'er dey wanted y'all know dey was comin' fo' our asses to,but boss stopped all dat its like she made us untouchable an da time she did it wasn't jus' fo' 'er it was fo' us to,so all Imma say is stop bein' selfish family.""Mornin' baby chu want breakfast?" Queenie asked Cortez'. "Nah mean only if I can have yo' ass first." He said as he pulled 'er back ova close to his body." "Oh so yo' ass didn't get a nuff of my juices last night daddy?" Wit a smile Queenie placed 'er hand inside his boxers an stated; "If I didn't know any better I would say yo' ass tryin' to bring a nutter lil' Fabs into da world." "Shawty chu makin' my dick harder ma an I know chu not finna fuck a nigga,so why chu teasin' 'em?" 'Cus its mines nigga an I do wut I please wit 'em." In earshot she whispered in a sexy seductive voice; "Not today will I tease chu daddy." Straddled across his waist already she did a stunt only an acrobat could do leavin' Cortez' amazed. Queenie balanced 'er self on 'er arms bringin' 'er legs up in da air tucked 'er ass passin' his face an easin' 'er love box down on his long hard rod slowly like she was performin' on da uneven bars at da Olympics. Instantly makin' his toes curl. Cortez' squeezed Queenie's ass cheeks an grind like neva befo'. Between his growls and grunts he asked 'er; "Wut if I was tryin' to make a nutter shorty ma?" "Hmmmm, not jus' jet daddy lil' Cortez' ain't even one jet_sssss, ahhhh hold on chu gonna get yo' baby girl fo' its__ ooooh shit." "I can wait ma 'cus I got dis pussy fo' life ma. Oh fuck ma I'm 'bout to come shawtyyyyy." "Fuck nigga wut was all dat 'bout?" Queenie exclaimed wit a smile. "Oh shit ma dats fo' yo' ass teasin' me nah mean. Now lets get dat breakfast." "Lets jump in da shower first_ nah better jet Imma jump in da shower first an chu go get yo' son ready an by time I get out chu can hop in an me and lil' man can go start breakfast." Queenie kissed his lips den walked away,but not befo' he smack dat ass up. "Aiight nigga chu know I like dat freaky shit." Callin' out from da shower she told 'em; "Lil' Tez clothes is already laid out on his dresser dress 'em in dat baby Gucci. I fo' got to take out his kicks he has a new pair of air force ones in a box on da top shelve of his closet." "Yo' ma I got dis I think I can dress my boy." Queenie walked out da bathroom an father and son walked into da bedroom. "Aye dere go mommy ain't she beautiful?" Lil' Cortez' smiled at his parents. "Look at my 2 handsome men." As she walked pass makin' 'er way to da closet to retrieve 'er gear she kissed da top of lil' Cortez' head. "Baby put lil' Tez on da bed an go get in da shower 'cus I need chu and Tez to call up da fellas an get 'em ova 'ere fo' a meetin' dis mornin'." Queenie grabbed jus' a pair red skinny jeans Levi wit a white Levi fitted t-shirt a red Levi vest an a pair of white air force ones. Afta' dat she put on jewelry placed 10 stacks in 'er vest pocket. Da only thing she changed up on 'er routine was puttin' 'er burner in da small of 'er back, but she always kept one in every room 'er and lil' Tez would be in. Outside of da home would be da only time she'd carry nina on 'er. Befo' she left out da bedroom she laid out 'er husbands gear. A pair of Gucci jeans hoodie a Gucci vest an a pair of Timbo's. Dress to impress Cortez' ran down to da kitchen were his family was. Knock, Knock. Tez walked in an asked; "Wutsup family?" He embraced Cortez' said wutup to lil' Tez give me pound. "Wutup Ueenie?" He kissed 'er on da fo' head. "Chu got it smellin' good in 'ere cuz a nigga stomach touchin' his back." "Yo' gonna be done in a minute cuz in da mean time I need y'all to call up da fellas gotta discussion of a few things an we also need to talk 'bout lil' Tez birthday party." Knock, Knock. Chris and Jo walked downstairs da smell of food grabbed their attention. "Yo' I got it ma." Chris yelled out. "Nigga why y'all still sleepin' like yo' asses been palayin' all night long?" Giz'mo asked as he walked towards da smell dat came out of da kitchen. In walks Flex, Stacks, Tre', Joc and Lil' Man an Chris ask; "Where y'all niggas been?" Speakin' to Lil' Man and Joc__ "Bro we had a few cars to knock out dis mornin'. "Yo' boss must be in

da kitchen 'cus we know it ain't Cortez' got shit smellin' fye like dis.” Jo said jokingly. “Aye wutsup boss?” Dey asked at once. “Shit family y'all jus' in time fo' a breakfast meetin' feel me.” “Y'all saved a niiga a lil' finger work, 'cus fam' and I jus' finna call yo' asses up. Wuts goin' on anyway wit y'all asses, why da fuck y'all look suspect fam'?” “Damn nosy ain't chu bro?”Flex replied. “Aye boss can we holla at chu fo' a sec befo' we have da meetin'?” “Wuts good fellas?” She questioned. Giz'mo stepped up an told Queenie; “Ma to make a long story short_he paused as da eight of 'em placed manilla envelopes on da counter top. Ma it was brung to us dat we been selfish an to think 'bout it we are,but neva was it meant to come off like dat at all. “Boss Queen” it'll neva be a nuff to repay fo' wut chu done fo' us ma,but we ask chu please except dis.” Queenie glanced at Tre' leanin' against da sink wit his arms crossed standin' next to Cortez',but of course she knew he had everything to do wit wut was goin' on. “Aiight listen Imma take it,but don't make dis no habit 'cus I don't do wut I do fo' y'all to repay me, now lets sit down and eat. Family let dis meetin' begin. I gotta coupla things to say den I want da feed back. Nah mean Lil' Tez first b-day is next Saturday he gonna be one an wut Cortez' and I have in store fo' 'em is gonna involve each an everyone of chu to close up shop fo' 4 days. Actually Tuesday night dats gonna be da last day y'all work 'til chu reopen on Sunday or Monday. Lil' Cortez' will have his first mini circus in da parkin' lot of CTC fo' 2 days. An on Friday we'll all load up an head to Chicago an take 'em to Chuck E Cheese,so he can have his first pizza party den on Saturday his birthday we all goin' to da Bud Billiken Parade an have a cookout,cake and ice cream in da park.”
Tez said; “Y'all know ain't no family like ours,so lets make dis shit a memorable fo' my godson, lets go sho' up family an sho' out. Lets do it da way we know best feel me.” “Now let me get to da utter matter at hand. I know how well everyone's biz'ness is performin', but its my understandin' dat y'all could all do much better. One of yo' brothers finally got da grasp of my intentions I wanted dis family to

recognize an if y'all took some interest in da utters biz'ness an take up da trade fo' it yo' asses would make way mo' money an it all stays in da family. Feel me? Now dis wut Imma finna do I'm puttin' all yo' asses threw school,so get y'all shit together an pick a trade to take up." Queenie loved 'er crew but sometimes it was a must fo' 'er to stay firm wit 'em an since she was 'bout makin' money she set da rules to stick. "Tre' don't want outsiders workin' in da barbershop,he prefer it be his brothers takin' up dat space he could have made way mo' dan wut he did if he had da hands on openin' day." Chris spoke up an said; "Boss we finna get right on dat ma." "Yo' fam' no disrespect,but lil' nigga I thought yo' ass woulda been da first to take da initiative an put yo' head in some books homeboy when I gave da first demo." Lookin' directly into Chris eyes she told 'em; "I'm not gonna suggest shit to y'all I won't do fo' myself,but family I got mines an Imma make sho' chu get urns. So don't let da way I talk or act give yo' ass da wrong assumption of me 'cus I got mines,an dis ain't 'bout me its 'bout my lil' King 'ere.

Chapter Thirty-Five
"Dere's A Million On 'Er Head,But Who Knows 'Er Son"

I need role models in his life,so take it as a privilege an respect da fact fam' dat Imma look in yo' direction fo' dat 'cus trust and believe if I didn't see da potential in chu cats, non of chu__she paused lookin' at each individual__non of chu an I do mean non of chu would be near my son. We all family yo' an I jus' want fo' each of chu to be smart 'bout wut chu do. Be happy and enjoy da shit chu do while chu do it aiight. Now lets all get dis paper." 'Er meetin' was ova wit an Cortez' helped 'er clean da kitchen up. Together dey washed an put away dishes. While da rest of da family joked 'round an play wit lil' Cortez'. "Come 'ere lil' Tez wut cuz want fo' his birthday huh?" Tez asked,but lil' Tez wasn't really talkin' jet except fo' da usual ma an some baby jib,so of course when Tez ask da question he jus' laughed, giggled and smiled. Dat's when Tez realized his eyes changed da exact same way his mothers eyes would be when she went into 'er trans. Tez thought to 'em self lookin' at da baby dat Queenie had passed on 'er head problems he recognized da signs,so he made a mental note to bring it to Cortez' and Queenie's attention soon. Tez mumbled to lil' Tez; "Damn we got a nutter killa on our hands." Dat's when baby Cortez' smile became big an bright as da sun itself. "Yo' nigga lets head down to moms and aunties house fo' a minute family." Cortez' exclaimed. "Aye cuz is chu lettin' Chaos be part of lil' mans party?" Tez asked. "Why not it's his great uncle an I won't take dat away from my son 'cus it wasn't given to us cuz, feel me. Imma neva deprive 'em of not knowin' family,but lets not get off into dat doe. Come 'ere my baby let me change his pamper, den we can be out to granny's." Queenie changed lil' Cortez' an tucked nina in da small of 'er back. "Y'all ready?" She asked. "Yo' wut chu wanta do walk down da street? Damn baby girl yo' ass feelin' aiight, 'cus my lil' nigga ain't neva wanted to walk no where even if it was jus' up da street cuz." "Nah mean I gotta a shorty now I can't make 'em miss out on bein' a kid by always puttin 'em in da back of a car. So since I got all my niggas 'round why don't y'all sho' my baby how to ride his 4 wheeler. Chris go get it out da garage fo' me fam'." Queenie grabbed a white leather bomber jacket she had made jus' fo' lil' Cortez' an on da front in red letters Da King Ride and Die, on da back was airbrushed My Angels Cortez' LC Fabs wit pictures of Lu and Chuck. "Yo' ma dat shit hot, much love and respect fo' sho'." Queenie held his arms out an told 'em let daddy put dat baby jacket on. "Aiight boss his quad is out front waitin' fo' its King to hop on, damn dat jacket yo' dats hot lil' man." Chris reached fo' lil' Cortez' from his boss. "Come on lil' Tez lets ride to yo' granny's house my lil' nigga." Chris took da baby an kept a close knit on 'em like he was his protector. "Let bro sho' chu how dis shit is done." Chris knew he had no win against Tez wit bein' lil' Cortez' godfather,so instead he played second in line,an he decided to care fo' 'em as his big bro afta' he ran it by Queenie an she seemed to be cool wit it. He did look at Queenie as mom in many ways. Lil' Cortez' sat on his quad like a big boy an Chris guided 'em all da way down da street to their destination Liz and Heathers crib. Takin' 'em off da quad da crew walked into da house. "Yo' ma, auntie where y'all at?" "In da kitchen." "Wutsup ma Tez and Queenie sang in unison's. Queenie kissed both ladies on da fo' head an Tez did da same. Tez asked; "Where Chaos?" "Right 'ere behind chu nephew, wutup wit chu?" Tez gave his uncle dap as Chaos said; "Wutup family?" Speakin' to all da fellas. Den he asked; Queenie wut I can't get no love?" She looked at 'em an gave a nod as to say wutup,but dat's far as it goes wit 'er, but fo' some strange reason Chaos wanted to take it further an tried to take his convo further. "So "Boss Queen" its still like dat huh, afta' all dese years huh chu still won't let it go Ueenie?" Queenie shot 'em a look dat could kill, she had a nonchalant look on 'er face as she snapped. Queenie was pissed off 'cus Chaos opened his mouth to even speak to 'er. "Ma, auntie excuse me fo' wut Imma 'bout to do underneath y'all roof." Tez and Cortez' looked on in awe state 'cus dey knew Queenie was 'bout to go hem in da worst way on Chaos. "Yo' fam' yo' ass ain't shit to me I don't fuck wit chu, nigga dat bridge been burnt wit us. So nigga yo' triflin' ass ain't got shit comin' from ova 'ere. Dude dis shit 'ere real,so when I say I cut chu loose dats dat." Queenie look Chaos square in his eyes an said; "Nigga dat mean I have nothin' to say to yo' bitch ass at all an nigga da only reason chu still breathin' is 'cus of yo' sisters,but yo' ass keep pushin' up on me to talk to yo' lyin' ass an ma'fucka chu gonna come up missin' wit da quickness. Imma bury yo' ass alive." Tez finally stepped in an grabbed Queenie 'round da waist pickin' 'er up an whisked 'er off to a nutter room. "Yo' Ueenie cuz chill out baby girl chu fo' got where chu at? I know how chu feelin' an I know dat dis has been along time comin' ma, but chu disrespectin' da ol' girls ain't cool." She looked at Tez an told 'em; "As long as dat nigga lives 'ere I won't step foot back up in dis bitch. When y'all done 'ere bring my baby home I can call moms and auntie later to tell 'em 'bout lil' Cortez' party." Tez hugged an kissed 'er fo' head, but Queenie pulled away. "Aiight fam' I'm out!" As she walked towards da door an prepared 'er self to neva walk through da door of dat house again Tez spat; "So Ueenie chu jus' gonna walk away an disregard everything I jus' said to yo' ass wit out givin' it a second thought?" Da front door slammed shut as Cortez' walked into da foyer. "Tez wutsup homeboy where's Queenie? He asked. "Yo' cuz piss she didn't like wut I had to say 'bout da situation, cuz ain't gonna neva get ova da lies dis family produced." "Where did she go?" Cortez' questioned. "Yo' all she said was she out an neva will she step foot back in 'ere." Queenie walked back towards 'er home 'er hitter rung,but she didn't answer it. Queenie knew who eva was on da utter end would wanta talk logic in 'er ear an dat wasn't anything she was ready to listen to. As stubborn as she was Queenie knew Tez was da last person she would eva hurt in da world. Family was everything to 'er, but losin' Lu an findin' out dat Chaos was their uncle instead of their cousin an he was Lu father put a even bigger hole through 'er heart. She felt dey neva gave 'er a chance to fully know either one of 'em. Ring,ring,ring,ring! Queenie answered it was da circus planner. "Hello" She let da person on da utter end control da conversation. "Hello Mrs. Fabs, I am callin' in regards of da plans to bring our circus chu requested fo' yo' sons party." Queenie responded; "Yeah an jus' call me Queenie." "Okay Queenie its jus' a few final details I need to make sho' I have correct den I can give chu an actual total I need from chu." Queenie cut in an retorted; "I only deal in cash no checks or credit cards." "Dat's fine Queenie now chu wanted 5 of each animals. I have down 5 miniature horses, 5 miniature pony's, 5 elephants, 5 giraffe's, 5 goats , an 5 black panthers." "No only 1 panther, 1 lion, 1 tiger and 1 monkey." "Okay, Queenie dat completes da animals now we have a train ride an chu still would like da venders to be setup also?" "Yeah dats correct." "Alright we have da hotdog venders dey also provide polishes and grill burgers. We have our rib tips on wheels vender as chu requested fo' da adults an also dere's our cotton candy stand dat has plenty of goody's fo' da children last,but not least dere will be 15 clowns to help da children wit any utter needs and wants." Queenie replied; "Dat sounds perfect." "Now yo' total fo' everything together gives chu a balance of $40,000 dollars an usually a price of such a big order we require half down,but since chu a well known individual yo' word is good a nuff fo' me,so wit dat bein' said I guess we will see chu in a few days." Queenie said; "Thank ya." An da phone went dead,but jus' soon as she hung up 'er hitter rung again. It was Cortez' she thought against answerin', but fingered 'er husband had no clue of how she really felt, an dat it was 'bout high time she filled 'em in completely on 'er entire life,so she answered. "Hello, wutsup baby?" She asked. "Wuts good ma, is chu aiight?" "I'm straight,but I believe its time fo' us to talk 'cus its long ova due.""Aiight when ya wanta make dis happen shawty? We 'bout to go to da house where is chu at baby?" "I'm 'ere at da house,but I need a one on one wit chu,so it can wait 'til later aiight." Cortez' said; "Nah mean we can go out on da town tonight jus' me and chu ma dat way chu can have me all to yo' self. Afta' words we can get a suite an relax word is bond ma we can leave lil' Cortez' wit his godfather fo' da night. So go head pull out yo' best dress ma well it don't have to be a dress, but chu know wut I mean." "Aiight,so I guess I won't cook dinner." "Nah yo' chu ain't gotta cook shit jus' prepare yo' self fo' yo' self wit me." She rambled threw 'er closet,but came up wit nothin' she wanted to wear, so she called Cortez' back up. "Yo' wuts good baby?" "Yo' baby chu and da fellas wanta roll to da underground mall wit me?" He yelled out; "Yo' family Queenie asked if y'all wanta bounce to da mall wit 'er? Yeah baby we on da way to da house jus' let me get lil' Cortez' together." "Aiight jus' leave his quad dere chu can get it later see ya in a minute." When 'er phone rang again she figured it was Cortez' callin' back fo' somethin', so she jus' answered. "Hello" Da person on da utter end sounded like a robotic recordin' dat stated; "Bitch chu are dead 1 million has been placed on yo' head,so I will be to see chu. Oh by da way kiss yo' lil'

King by by bitch." Befo' da caller hung up dey said Boom! Da raw feelin' Queenie had in 'er throat from da caller mentionin' 'er son was unbearable which put 'er in a rage,so tryin' to focus was somethin' she couldn't do. Dis only made 'er furious to da point she started to cry. Queenie paste da floor from da foyer to da door way of da kitchen not rememberin' dat da fellas were on their way to da house. Wit her back turned away from da door playin' da recordin' ova and ova unfortunately 'er mind was blank at dis point talkin' to 'er conscience she was conjurin' up 'er next chess move only thing was she had no idea who da fuck she needed to look fo'. Dis was da upper hand ova Queenie at dis point,but she knew 'er son could be in danger also. When da door opened all Queenie could hear was a beep, beep from da house alarm an wit out thinkin' she swiftly drew 'er nine an open fire towards da front door 'til she emptied da clip. It was a good thing Joc hadn't made it inside wit lil' Cortez' jet 'cus Queenie tried to take off da heads of who eva walk threw da door. "Yo' ma wut da fuck?" Everyone screamed as dey ran back outside to take cover. "Ueenieeee!" Tez yelled its us baby girl hold yo' fire, wut da fuck on yo' mind?" Tez always distilled in his cousin head shoot first ask questions later,but dis he didn't know wut to make of it. Queenie dropped to da floor slidin' down da wall grabbin' 'er head. Cortez' and Tez rushed to 'er side as dey reached 'er dey noticed she was cryin' an gripped in 'er left hand 'er hitter dat was still playin' da recordin' ova and ova, but it was muffled. Tez saw blood drippin' from dat same hand. "Yo' get me a towel she bleedin'." Lil' Cortez' screamed at da top of his lungs an Tez told 'em; "Get yo' son homeboy an calm 'em down so Ueenie won't freak out." "Give me my baby." Queenie whispered. "Nah mean I got 'em ma let Tez see 'bout yo' hand." "Baby girl let da hitter go an tell me wut all dis 'bout. Cuz can chu do dat fo' me?" Chris gave 'em a towel to clean 'er up. "Thanks bro." Tez dried Queenie's face first den told 'er to open 'er hand an let da phone go. She wanted to know was 'er baby okay. "Yeah shawty he fine, but wut were chu thinkin' 'bout?" Cortez' asked his wife as he bent down, so she could see lil' Cortez' was good. She responded; "Savin' da life of my son and maybe my own." "Cuz wut is chu talkin' 'bout?" Queenie finally open 'er hand jus' as da recorded message started ova. Bitch chu dead 1 million has been placed on yo' head,so I will be to see chu by da way kiss yo' lil' King by, by bitch boom! Everyone heard exactly wut Queenie heard now dey knew da cause of 'er reactions. "Yo' take lil' Tez back to auntie an tell 'er wut happened an dat I will call 'er in a hour." Tez was callin' da shots now fo' da moment. "Tre', Flex and Jo stay on point don't leave lil' Tez side fo' shit family, if its a bounty on Ueenie's head he will be a perfect candidate to get at 'er." Tez knew dat lil' Cortez' was Queenie's weakness an to protect 'em she would pull out all stops on dis one. She pulled 'er self together an grabbed a on da go bag fo' lil' Tez an gave it to Flex. "Wuts dis ma?" He asked. "Doe's things my son needs its his jus' go bag." Cortez' told 'em; "Its an emergency bag fo' shit jus' like dis its everything he will need." Flex took a peek in da bag while Queenie hugged and kissed 'er lil' King. "Damn ma yo' ass be on point wit everything huh?" I have to be mo' so now 'cus of lil' Cortez' family wit my life style, its obvious I'm not untouchable an its very clear dat I let my guard down to far an now someone see's my son as a target to get to me. 'Ere take 'em." She handed da baby off to Tre'. "Take my son an guard 'em wit yo' lives." Queenie stated to all in da room as she kissed 'er son on top of his head "Mommy won't rest 'til she finds da ma'fucka who had da balls to even mention 'er lil' Kings name. I love chu lil' Cortez'." Tre' turned to walk out da door leavin' Flex and Jo to pull out their burners to lead da way an surround 'em an da baby. Back at da house Queenie was snappin' as she paste da floor. "Yo' listen y'all know ain't no way I'm runnin' from dis now I'm runnin' towards it. I don't give a damn wut happens to me, but my son is a different story I gave life to dat lil' nigga an I be damn if he's taken from me, I'll die or go down fo' life ova my son fam'." Flex, Tre' and Jo walked into Liz and Heathers home. "Auntie's!" Dey yelled out. Heather and Liz hurried into da room an asked wut was wrong. Tre' handed lil' Cortez' to Liz an Flex started to explain settin' lil' Cortez' bag on da floor as he stated; "Auntie's have a seat. Tonight boss damn near killed us 'cus she received a threat on 'er life an da caller happen to mention lil' Cortez' bein' 'er lil' King." "Wut Liz exclaimed. "I thought Queenie was out da game,so who in da hell wants to kill my baby!" "Auntie please calm down." Tre' stated; "Even doe she out da game she's still a target in da streets an now dat she has someone closer to 'er dan anyone else in da world. People out 'ere knows lil' Tez is 'er weakness,so dats who dey will gun fo' to snuff boss out. Tez gave us word to bring 'em to y'all an fo' us three not to leave his side,so I guess we are da new house guest auntie." Lookin' at da both of 'em. Heather told 'em; "Y'all family,so ain't non of chu guest,so make yo' selves at home." "Heather questioned,so wut do all dis really mean, how is niecy poo doin'?" "Nah mean, auntie she ain't I can tell dis situation has hit 'er hard an from da way she was talkin' dey jus' unleashed da beast boss had,so well concealed since lil' Tez been born. Sorry to say but y'all can expect da ol' Queenie to reappear." Flex responded. "Yo' da basics is boss on a whole utter level an she has no intentions of lettin' dis go__excuse my words auntie but she says she won't rest 'til she finds da ma'fuckas who spoke 'er sons name." Heather asked; "Who knows my nephew's name besides dis family?" "But auntie dats not da half of it dey didn't call 'em by his name at all. Dey called 'em 'er lil' King, now who knows dat besides family?" Jo questioned. Da weekend passed an Queenie still had 'er killas on point non of 'em ever left 'er side, where she went dey went. It was Monday an she had Cortez' and Chris to go get 'er son from 'er moms. "Yo' baby tell da fellas we gotta meetin' in 20 minutes." Cortez' and Chris walked Liz and Heathers house. Knock, knock Cortez' holla as he pushed da front door open. "Yo' ma why y'all doe open?" Liz yelled;"Baby we in da kitchen." Dat's were he found Liz, lil' Cortez', Heather, Jo, Flex and Tre' along wit Chaos talkin'. As he walked in he felt as though dey were bein' a lil' careless wit his sons life. “Why y'all got da door unlocked,so anyone can jus' walk in,while my son and wife lives are hangin' in da ballets right now? 'Cus keepin' 'em both safe is my main priority at dis point.” Directin' his anger towards Tre', Jo and Flex he told 'em; “If y'all suppose to be on guard wit yo' lives fo' my boys den why is da fuckin' doe wide open family?” “Bro chu right ain't no excuse fo' it we shoulda checked da doe afta' Chaos nurse left, but come to think of it Chaos yo' ass wheeled to da doe wit 'er fam',so why didn't chu lock it?” Tre' questioned. “Yo' I apologize ma.” Kissin' 'er an huggin' both of da lady's. “I came to get my lil' man fo' his mama.” Liz put lil' Cortez' coat on 'em an handed 'em off to his daddy. Cortez' looked at Chaos an pointed his finger an stated; “Yo' nigga yo' ass, chu fucked up,I don't know why chu insist on fo' getting who Queenie is an wut she represents,but right now is not da time homeboy. My son is all she liven fo' so nigga killin' chu or a nutter ma'fucka dat she feels a threat to 'em won't be a problem in 'er eyes. Nigga chu pushin'.” Cortez' told da fellas to squad up 'cus dey had a meetin'. “Ma, auntie Imma give a call later to let y'all know wutsup.” Chaos shouted; “Lil' nigga who da fuck chu think chu talkin' to, nigga do chu know who da fuck I am? I'm not some lil' punk ass nigga chu be runnin''round wit.” Chaos pulled a burner from underneath his wheelchair an pointed it at Cortez' while he had his son in his arms. Click,Click,Click was da sound of Cortez' and Queenie's goons puttin' one in da chamber of da nines, 45 glock and .44's. Whoa, no! Were da screams comin' from Heather and Liz. “Hold on family.” Cortez' told his boys. “Chaos wut da fuck is chu doin' dis is family an my grandson yo' nephew is in da room an chu trust to pull a gun?” Liz was distraught by da entire scene, but knew da out come wouldn't be good once 'er daughter got wind of da situation at hand. “Big bad ass Chaos washed up at dat.” “Bro let me put dis nigga out fo' da count fam'.” Chris piss at da stunt Chaos jus' pulled. “Fam' let me flat line dis nigga!” Chris had an uncontrollable itch dat he wanted to scratch badly. Queenie was at da house waitin' on Cortez' to walk through da door wit lil' Cortez' an da rest of their family as she spoke wit Tez on da phone. "Yo' cuz I jus' called a meetin', but I sent yo' yo' homeboy to get lil' Tez fo' me,but ain't non of came back jet. Dey shoulda been 'ere 15 minutes ago feel me." Tez responded; "Chu know how 'em niggas get when dey get wit moms and auntie, jus' hold da line Imma call down dere real quick." Tez snatched his utter hitter from his waist, an called Chris hitter. Chris snatched his phone out his pocket an wit venom in his voice_ "Hello who da fuck is dis?" "Yo' fam' chu better check yo' self cuz. Dis Tez an wuts got yo' ass beefed up?" Chris short talked Tez real fast befo' he hung up. "Fam' Imma 'bout to push dis niggas wig back." "Yo' homeboy where Cortez', I thought yo' ass went to moms crib wit fam'?" "Yeah we 'ere fam'." "So who fuckin' wig yo' ass finna peel back bro?" Tez could hear voice of his mother screamin' no hold on put it down Chaos. Tez heard Queenie on da utter phone yellin' fo' 'em askin wut was up. "Tez wut da fuck is wrong?" "Shawty I don't really got all da details,but grab yo' shit meet me__dead silence sent a light off in Tez head dat Queenie was already headed full speed to their parents home.

Chapter Thirty-Six
"I'm Da Bitch Who Decides His Fate"

All Queenie could think 'bout was 'er son bein' in danger, she had no facts, but wut she did know was Cortez' and Chris had not made it back wit 'er child an dat sent off an alarm. Nina was tucked in 'er back an she loaded 'er Uzi afta' she ran out da house jumpin' off da porch gun in hand. She ran as fast as 'er legs moved 'er to make it to their parents house Tez had to catch up. By time he caught 'er dey were in da front yard. Queenie and Tez ran in not knowin' da situation at hand. Unfortunately Queenie's state of mind didn't allow 'er to give a fuck,all she could see was 'er goons wit guns drawn an she heard 'er son cryin'. Dey made it to da kitchen. "Wut da fuck goin' on in 'ere?" Standin' next to Cortez' Queenie and Tez came in wit their guns pointed in da same direction of da rest. Queenie den noticed Chris had a gun at Chaos temple. "Yo' fam' hold on wut da fuck my nigga?" Liz and Heather stood in a corner by da back door cryin' scared fo' wut was to come. Queenie placed 'er Uzi top of da island counter top an took 'er son from his father an told 'er moms and aunt to take 'em out of da kitchen. "Go to a nutter room, now!" She raised 'er voice out of frustration. Liz and Heather begged an plead wit Queenie not to do anything drastic. "Ma, auntie leave go now." Queenie wasn't tryin' to hear wut dey had to say an once dey left out Queenie questioned how all of dis came 'bout? "Lil' Chris baby why chu at dis nigga head?" An his only response was; "Fam' let me do dis nigga." Queenie observed da room an seen no one sayin' a nuff fo' 'er,so she told 'em; "Look somebody better start talkin' fo' I let it ride my nigga, now wut da fuck happen to have Chris at dis nigga?" Cortez' didn't want to tell Queenie 'cus he knew his wife would go hem an dere would be no way to stop 'er stubborn trigger happy ass. Tre' said; "Boss dis nigga 'ere think he runnin' shit, he didn't lock da front door afta' his nurse left an when bro snapped out on 'em bout lil' Tez he grow some balls an up burner on bro." She snatched up da Uzi an pointed it at Chaos as she had flashbacks of da scene she saw when 'er and Tez entered da house. One vision was 'er husband standin' dere holdin' 'er son in his arms. "Yo' family let me get dis 'ere straight, I walk in chu holdin my son an dis nigga 'ere had a gun pointed at chu wit my shorty puttin' 'em in harms way?" Chris said; "Ma let me do dis nigga." "Nah baby boy dis nigga mines." Queenie replied. Chaos tryin' to hold a firm voice shouted; "Shoot den ma'fucka, shoot me den my life fucked anyway chu took everything from me." Chaos told Queenie look at me it feels like dis wheelchair will be my life from 'ere on out." Chaos raised his gun pointin' at Queenie his ex-boss da hand dat made sho' he ate da same person he woulda killed fo' ova 'er. His niece now 'ere he was pointin' a .45 at 'er. All of dis ran through Queenie's head, not leavin' any room fo' sympathy. In da back of 'er head 'er conscience awakened; "Boss Queen" fuck dat nigga who is he? Yo' ma listen chu took care of dis nigga needs an he returns da love by point a gun at yo' son. Bitch chu better wake up dis nigga don't mean chu or yo' family circle any good. Do dis nigga an put dis memory behind us do his ass." Queenie's conscience showed 'er a bigger picture. Calm as doe nothin' had even happened Queenie placed da Uzi back down on da island an stated; "Clear da room out." "Huh?" Everyone asked curiously. "Chris I said clear da room." No one moved. So in a much sterner voice she said; "Move out now youngan!" Everyone in da kitchen was hesitant,but cleared out as dey were told. As Chaos lowered his burner Queenie pulled nina from behind 'er back shackin' 'er head from side to side. She told Chaos; "Naw bro chu gonna need dat." Chaos raised his gun back up pointin' it at 'er. "Now let me see if I got dis correct, chu wanta now play big bad ass Chaos talkin' shit an get grimy wit da pistol play? Is dat correct uncle Chaos?" She said sarcastic, but befo' Chaos could respond she shot da 45 out of his hand blowin' Chaos trigger finger off. "Auuuuugh, shit chu stupid bitch!" Queenie could hear 'er moms and aunt screamin' 'er name,but she pay no attention. Tez and Cortez' ran back in da kitchen to see wut took place. "No baby girl wut da fuck chu doin' ma?" Tez asked. Queenie hollard; "Get da fuck out leave da house now, an take my baby out of dis house Tez! Take moms and auntie to now!" She yelled as she quickly turned 'er head 'round lookin' in Tez eyes, he noticed da icy black gleam in 'er eyes an felt da coldness in 'er heart. Queenie loaded a nutter hollow point in da chamber of 'er nine an walked ova to Chaos who squirmed in his chair. Getting right up on 'em close and personal she told 'em; "Count yo' blessin's fo' chu still breathin' fam', 'cus I consider yo' ass lucky right now." Chaos pleaded an begged Queenie to call fo' help so he wouldn't bleed to death as he said da lords prayer: "Da lord is my shepherd I shall not want." "Nigga chu prayin', now chu wanta pray! Fo' wut?" She questioned. Queenie let off a nutter shot into Chaos left leg an spoke in third party; "Boss Queen" is 'ere an she has yo' God and Devil all wrapped in one. Ma'fucka "Boss Queen" will sign yo' fate today an every utter day 'til yo' bitch ass__ Chaos told Queenie; "Fuck yo' crazy ass." She broke out into laughter_ "I can except dat bein' called crazy it wouldn't be da first time I heard I gotta problem. But yo' remember dis doe my crazy ass gotta hold on chu nigga,so when I decide da perfect time fo' yo' ass to leave dis earth jus' remember Imma see chu in hell. Imma be dat bitch wit all red on sittin' on dat all black throne dat has a flashin' light above my head dat reads: "Boss Queen" 'cus I definitely wouldn't want yo' ass to miss me." Queenie shot Chaos one last time in his right shoulder. "Auuuuugh!" Queenie den walked out of da kitchen into da den an stared out of da window, while Chaos screamed out fo' help. She waited 30 minutes befo' she called Tez, Flex, and Stacks to come take 'em to da hospital or call da paramedics fo' Chaos. Queenie didn't care wut dey did to 'em or fo' 'em, she didn't even give a fuck 'bout 'em tellin' Ola she was da one who damn near decapitated his ass. "Hello Ueenie." Tez whispered into da phone. "Yo' come get his ass." Queenie walked out da front door wit da Uzi in one hand an nina in da utter as she headed home. She saw images runnin' towards 'er. As dey got up on 'er dey noticed she was covered in blood. "Yo' ma chu hit?" Tez asked. "Yo' Chris take dis shit an take Ueenie to da house." Tez could hear sirens in a distance. Flex and Stacks had made it in da house to only find Chaos slumped ova in his chair. Flex yelled out; "Fam' chu might wanta see dis homeboy." Stacks retorted; "He still alive family she didn't kill 'em." "Fuck!" Tez yelled. "Yo' cuz it wasn't 'er intentions on killin' 'em jus' jet." "Yo' fam' wut chu mean jus' jet?" Flex asked. "Lets talk 'bout it later right now call da medics doe's sirens getting closer." Tez had to think quick: "Yo' we don't know shit we ain't seen shit we jus' came to check on moms and auntie,he was 'ere an dis how we found 'em." "Gotcha family." Queenie and Chris ran into da house where everyone else stood and sat in da dinnin' room waitin' on word of wut happen,but seein' Queenie run in covered in blood da entire room went into panic. "Yo' y'all calm down she fine." Chris stated its not 'er blood. Bro take dese put 'em up. Boss go hit da shower an I need yo' clothes ma." Chris told his boss. Queenie broke da stare she had wit 'er mother an ran upstairs. "Boss take dis wit chu an put yo' clothes in 'ere an drop da bag outside da bathroom doe." Queenie placed all da soil clothes in a garbage bag an jumped in da shower. Within 5 minutes she damn near scrubbed 'er body raw, den she ran back to 'er bedroom an met Cortez' sittin' on da edge of their bed. Queenie had no time fo' talkin' she jumped into an all black Gucci sweat suit wit a pair of red and black air force ones. "Shawty look at me." She turned an looked at a curious Cortez'. "Ma did chu kill 'em?" "Nah I didn't,it wasn't my intentions to kill 'em jet. Imma make his ass suffer 'til I'm ready to send his ass to hell." Cortez' thought no matter how much he talked 'bout da situation at hand, Queenie would neva change 'er ways. Queenie asked Cortez'; "Baby wuts on yo' brain?" He replied; "Queenie I love chu baby, but chu not God, jus' hold on please let me speak. Now chu come in da house covered in blood not hit,but can chu even imagine da pain da shot through my heart ma? Nah mean chu can't 'cus chu neva think 'bout da consequences of wut yo' ass do or da people its gonna hurt." Queenie said; "Hold on my nigga was my feelin's thought 'bout or even considered when I walked into my moms crib to find out dis nigga had a gun pointed at my son? Huh wut happen to my feelin's or how I would feel. Da slip of his finger or da wrong move chu an our son coulda killed y'all den wut Cortez'? Huh baby chu gotta come back fo' dat one?" Cortez' stood to his feet an walked ova to Queenie an put his arms 'round da small of 'er waist givin' 'er a kiss on da fo' head. He said; "I love all of chu everything dat comes wit yo' ass,but chu wild hunnid an I'm not tryin' to see anything happen to chu ma. Me an dat lil' King of urns need chu, feel me." Tez ran upstairs "Yo' y'all decent?" "Yeah bro." Cortez' replied. Tez stood in front of Queenie an questioned; "Baby girl chu good?" "I'm cool cuz I preciate chu an da fella handlin' da mess I created an hopefully chu can except my apology fo' leavin' chu to deal wit dat shit cuz." "Ueenie we family chu my baby girl no matter wut chu do if chu need me Imma always be dere. Only problem I got wit dis is yo' ass left da nigga alive to talk 'bout it ma,so please make me understand why chu would let Chaos live?" She said its simple; "I want 'em to live in my world, dats wut he wants fo' somebody to put 'em out of his misery 'cus his ass is miserable sittin' in dat fuckin' wheelchair. He has no idea if he eva gonna eva get out of it,but fam' dis is my call he don't get a say so on his life he signed his fate ova to me when he pointed a gun at my son." Lookin' from Tez to Cortez' she said; "An since I'm dat bitch da nigga will not flat line 'til I send his ass to hell. Word is bond, now can y'all get me my son?" Tez told Queenie in a jokin' manner; "I don't know wut I'm gonna do wit chu cuz." Queenie smiled an responded; "Love me." Da three went back downstairs to only find out dat Liz and Heather left fo' da hospital to see 'bout their only brother. Chris handed lil' Cortez' to his mommy. "Wutsup mommy's lil' King?" "Yo' family I apologize to y'all fo' puttin' chu in dat position it was pretty fuck'd up fo' me to leave y'all to clean up my mess.""Boss no matter wut we got yo' back. We all family an to be honest Chaos deserved all his ass got." Tre' exclaimed. Queenie said; "Look I still need y'all to close up shop tomorrow evenin' fo' lil' Cortez's event to begin'. It's my lil' mans day an it will be a cold day in hell befo' I go back on my word. Cancelin' his fun I won't do 'cus a number was placed on my head. Don't worry Imma be cautious fo' my son, y'all jus' be on point suited and booted fam'." Everything went as planned out an da miniature circus was a hit an lil' Cortez' enjoyed 'em self an dat made Queenie proud and grateful 'er son wasn't harmed. It seem like da entire East St. Boogie attended,but now dat it was ova dey had to pack up an move on to da next. Next stop would be Chuck E Cheese. So da family retrieved their bags loaded up an headed fo' Chi-Town, everyone was tired do to all da excitement dey had wit lil' Cortez' at his circus,so sleep was long ova due fo' everyone. Queenie purchased double suites fo' da crew. Liz told Queenie to let lil' Cortez' stay wit 'er and Heather fo' da night if it was okay wit 'em. "Cortez' replied; "Ma dats cool take 'em I need sometime wit his mama." "Okay son." Liz chuckled. "Imma bring his bag to da room in a minute." Afta' Liz and Heather walked in their suite da rest walk to their suites. Queenie said; "Yo' I need to make a run up to Chuck E Cheese an pay fo' dis party give me 2 hours an Imma be back." "Baby girl I know yo' ass still got pull out dis ma'fucka,but Ueenie chu also collected an enormous amount of enemies out dis bitch ova da years ma. So if chu gotta go take Chris wit chu an don't have no mishaps." Tez pulled Chris in close an whispered; "Nigga guard 'er wit yo' life fam'." Queenie thought 'bout wut Tez said an she knew every word was true bein' out of da loop an not in touchin' down in Chicago as much when she lived in da city most people felt Queenie had gotten to big headed fo' their kind. Unfortunately da city had grow wit a lot of new faces an era an dere was still one nigga Queenie hadn't taken care of jet. Dis was one of da three niggas who Triple had on his team of flunkies dat was suppose to take 'er out. Neva sweatin' da small things,to be truthful Queenie neva sweated anything. She is a very determined person,so when she sets 'er mind to it she always makes it happen but 'cus,so much had been happenin' ova da years getting money 'er getting locked down, havin' a child and keepin' 'er entourage fed an on point she put da nigga Social on on da back burner an hadn't gave 'em a second thought. Dat was 'til Tez made his statement, 'bout 'er collectin' enemies. "Yo' cuz I'm good dis won't take long,so don't trip nigga we gonna be back, if shit gets thick nigga yo' ass will be da first one we call." "Now lets be out Chris." Chris told Tez I gotta bro." Queenie and Chris jumped in 'er truck an headed down Lincoln Highway to their destination afta' words she back track an headed to da Swamp-O-Rama in Aspine while drivin' she needed to fill 'er lil' protege' in on da nigga Social an 'er next move to take his ass off da map. Now dat his name appeared back in 'er memory bank. She knew Social was an vendetta dat she wouldn't let go again. "Yo' Chris my lil' nigga Tez was correct dese streets gotta lot of ma'fuckas in 'em now mo' dan eva who wanta see me dead. I done a lot of treacherous shit out 'ere fam' an even doe my innocence at dat age gave off as a nonchalant persona I was off da chain wit my hustlin' an murder game. Mo' dan I percent now since lil' Tez has been born,of course I slowed my role a lot since,but I believe its time fo' me to remind dese ma'fuckas who "Boss Queen" is wit dat bein' said I need to bring dat nigga dey call Social to surface." "Boss who da fuck is Social an do Cortez' and Tez know 'bout dis nigga?" "Yo' Cortez' don't less Tez told 'em 'bout dude. Dis went on while Lu was alive befo' we even came to East St. Boogie, so I'm not fo' sho' if he knows or not. Shit I don't think Tez even remembers cus' neither of us knew who dude was,but I put in a call an found out where dis nigga be." "So ma where dis cat at?" Chris questioned. "His last residences know was Cabrini Green projects." "Well Cabrini Green is where I'm at ma. Imma find out dis nigga where 'bouts fo' chu." "Only thing is I neva seen da nigga befo',but I'm pretty sho' he knows how da fuck I look. Afta we leave da swamp we gonna shut ova towards Cabrini an chu can see if chu can get a heads up on how da nigga looks. Den afta' lil' Tez has his day at da parade I will deaden da nigga fam'." "Ma I got chu on all aspects of da word,but of course I do gotta ask if chu don't mind da question?" "Let it out nigga ask wuts on yo' mind fam'." "Do chu got any intentions on lettin' family and 'em in on wuts happenin'? 'Cus I'm all fo' da get down,but I can't afford da consequences of fam' and 'em comin' at me if anything was to go wrong an dey knew I had apart in it an didn't tell 'em wut was up." Queenie looked at Chris an understood wut he said,but it didn't matter 'cus it still would happen wit 'em or wit out 'em. "Look somebody gotta live to tell da story nigga an since I have no intentions on getting killed. No I refuse to put my family in any mo' danger. Fam' dat even includes yo' ass dats why only thing chu will do is find out where dude lives an how da nigga looks fo' me an Imma take it from dere, feel me. Dis one 'ere is mines. Social will die by da hands of "Boss Queen", an word is bond fam'." "Aiight ma its yo' call jus' know Imma be 'ere if chu need me fo' wut eva." She didn't repond 'cus she drove in deep thought. Queenie couldn't get 'er mind off of killin' Social considerin' dere was a million dollar ticket on 'er head. She was not 'bout to knock 'em out of da equation of niggas who could be afta' 'er. Dey pulled up at da Swamp-O-Ram an it was packed most likely 'cus of da biggest parade of Chicago would be startin' up tomorrow. Everyone dat wasn't or claimed to be important would be geared fo' da Bud Billiken Parade. Queenie and Chris parked a block away an walked back up to da buildin'. "Fam' yo' ass suited and booted?" She asked Chris. "Ma chu know I can't leave da house wit out it." Queenie laughed__ "Aiight lil' mini me lets get up in 'ere,so we can get back to da hotel." Once dey paid to enter a few people noticed who she was off da back an yelled wutsup "Boss Queen" dat caught 'er attention an Queenie threw 'er head up as to say wutsup showin' acknowledge of 'er appearance. "Chris lets go ova 'ere to da airbrushin' station,so I can see wutsup." Chris was a freaky ass nigga fo' women who had a nice shape big asses an pretty face. He was all ova it didn't matter to 'em one way or da utter if she had a nigga when he wanted somethin' he would take it an deal wit da consequences of it later. Chris spotted a coupla of females 2 booths down from where 'em and Queenie stood. "Yo' boss I see a coupla pieces Imma holla at right fast." Wit da girls backs turned towards 'em only thing Queenie could see was backs of their heads,so she jus' laughed at Chris an told 'em; "Nigga yo' ass ain't gonna get a nuff huh." "Wutsup beautiful can I get to know ya shawtys a lil' better an maybe one day we can do dis shoppin' thang together sometime." "Hopefully soon den." One of da girls stated. "So chu ova 'ere wit us I take it chu don't have a girl or is she off shoppin' somewhere 'round 'ere why yo' ass ova 'ere tryin' to get in our panties?" "Damn shawty I like chu already,its jus' straight to da facts wit chu huh?" "Well ain't dat wut chu want from us?" "Since we bein' blunt 'bout it yeah it is,but I'm not yo' average ass nigga. I wanta get to know y'all first,so slow ya heels a lil' we definitely get to dat. But to answer yo' question 'bout if I got a women da answer is no. I'm 'ere wit my boss she needed_ bein' cut off by da girl she asked; "She, yo' boss is a female wut type of work do chu do fo' 'er?" Da utter one asked; "Wuts yo' boss name an where y'all from?" Chris told 'em; "We live in East St. Boogie baby,but my boss from yo' city of Chi-Town." Tryin' to put his mack down Chris got a lil' loose at da lips, 'bout Queenie's biz'ness. "So who is she can we meet 'er?"

Chapter Thirty-Seven
"Kill Or Be Killed
Is Dis It Fo' "Boss Queen"

Chris told 'em; "Y'all should know 'er if y'all from Chicago,she go by "Boss Queen"." Da girls yelled out Queenie askin' 'em loud a nuff fo' Queenie to turn an look in his direction. Chris had no idea who he had been talkin' to fo' da last 10 minutes. Dis was da same girl from Navy Pier dat Queenie almost flat lined when she was pregnant wit lil' Cortez'. Next thing he knew his boss up nina an pointed in their direction. "Chris move!" She yelled Chris ducked an both girls pulled out from their purses an rounds were fired from all parties involved. Everyone of da on lookers dropped to da floor an screams filled da warehouse. Pop,pop,Thuf,thuf. "Chris watch out nigga." Queenie dropped da utter bitch afta' she seen 'er tryin' to sneak Chris. Queenie only caught 'er in da shoulder doe. Chris made his way back to where Queenie was afta' dat an Queenie told 'em; "Nigga squad up we gotta raise up fo' our asses end up in 26 an California fam'." "Wut, wuts dat ma?" "Its da fuckin' county jail nigga. If I can get dis bitch outside befo' Ola gets 'ere Imma deaden 'er ass. Look fam' 'ere da keys go get my shit,so we can bounce."She gave 'em da keys,but he refuse to leave 'er. "Ma hell no shawty I'm not leavin' chu in dis ma'fucka by yo' self." "Nigga I preciate da love an concern,but time ain't on our side right now,so nigga move yo' ass go!" She screamed. "Queenie bitch Imma kill chu." She jus' struck a nerve Queenie said out loud to no one. "Yo' shawty Thuf,thuf__dats da only word in yo' vocabulary is it, well unfortunately Imma help yo' ass out wit dat today to da point chu neva have to worry 'bout expandin' it. Thuf,thuf_Pop,pop,pop. Queenie loaded 'er last clip an she knew she had to make it outside wit wut she had. Not bein' da one to run from anything Queenie wanted to get 'er vic outside,so she would have a better chance and shot,so she took off like a jet she coulda been Flo' Jo at dat moment. Three mo' shots were let off by one of da girls she didn't know which one, but as she ducked, jumped ova civilians an pushed people out of da way she heard a bullet wiz pass 'er ear. "God dammit!" Queenie knew at dat point it was time to take 'er enemy out or be took out. She made it outside an seen 'er truck wit Chris standin' dere waitin' on 'er as made it half way to 'em she quickly stopped turned 'round as doe she was in a stand off. Out in da open she waited fo' 'er prey to make it out da door. "Boss wut yo' ass doin?" Ola sirens in da back ground an Chris had no idea which end dey would come from. "Ma Ola comin'." Thuf,thuf,thuf,thuf,thuf 5 shots Queenie had left, droppin' da girl she had hit in da shoulder. Pop! One shot came from Tez ex-girl friend gun befo' Queenie unloaded da rest of 'er clip. She left 1 bullet in da gun an walked up on 'er afta' she fell to da ground an put da last round in shorty's head. Thuf! "Boss lets move ma!" Chris yelled out. Queenie ran an jumped in da passenger seat. "Drive nigga, up 'ere make a right an stop at da first gas station chu get to an we can switch fam'." Queenie put a call in to Tez. "Hello wutsup baby girl where y'all at_Queenie cut Tez questions short. "Fam' we in trouble." She said in a hostility tone. "Yo' fam' switch up 'ere. Yo' cuz listen I jus' murdered yo' ex-girl an 'er friend in front of da entire Swamp-O-Rama. Ain't no way in hell I can come back to da hotel." "Wut!" Tez screamed into da phone. "Nigga I can't go threw dis wit yo' ass now Tez I need chu to open up da stash house fam' now dats where I'm on my way to__ "Yo' boss I see Ola in my view ma." "Fuck! Change da game cuz beat me dere don't meet me dere." Queenie told Chris; "Hold on fam'." An she hit da nitro switch,so she could get ghost from Ola. Bobbin' in and out of traffic Queenie's hitter dropped to da floor not realizin' Tez was still on da line screamin' 'er name. Tez kept his line runnin',so he could try an hear wut was goin' on inside da truck wit Queenie and Chris. "Nigga ammo up its time to squad up Queenie and Chris dan got into some deep shit." Tez turn to look at Cortez'; "Ueenie jus' murdered 2 bitches,lets go we need to beat 'em to da stash house. Flex call Chris hitter an keep his ass on dere. Cortez' call auntie let 'er know wuts happen an fo' 'er and moms to stay put no matter wut." Cortez' called Liz an told 'er wut he knew an dat he would call 'em back soon. Ring. "Hello!" Chris answered. "Lil' bro dis Flex wut da fuck goin' down?" Chris responded "Man shit crazy right now, boss jus' killed 2 bitches in broad day light my nigga an Ola on us. Boss tryin' to shake 'em_Oooooh shit boss got damn ma." Den all Tez and Flex could hear was a big ass crash an screams comin' from 'em. Queenie did every bit of 190 at da time an she did a three 60 to avoid da on comin' Ola car an slammed da tail end into a parked semi. Queenie screamed; "Nigga put on yo' seat belt fam'." Ola started shootin' at da tires on 'er truck. "Get down fam' reach underneath yo' seat family an give me dat." Chris also retrieved his hitter from off da floor. Chris handed his boss da Uzi as he put da hitter to his ear nervous as hell at wut was 'bout to go down he needed to let their people know wut was up. All Chris could hear was da sound of da Uzi Queenie let ride. "Yo' Flex we in a shootout nigga wit Ola." "How far away is y'all?" "Ma where we at?" "Headed towards ninety-fifth six block away from da stash house." Ola ha a road block up blockin' ninety-fifth da street she needed to hit fo' a straight shot to 'er destination. "Yo' fuck me! Fam' its ride and die my nigga." Slowin' down jus' a nuff by takin' 'er foot off da gas paddle as she looked at Chris an said; "I love chu nigga, but ain't no way in da hell I can turn back da hands of time." Queenie knew dat dis was it death or da penitentiary fo' sho'. "Fam' chu a good nigga an right now I wish yo' ass wasn't wit me 'cus I'm goin' threw dis block Ola has up an I doubt if I make it home fam',but chu do gotta choice chu can get out 'ere an give up or yo' ass can stay in da truck an take a chance." "Ma dis look all to much like da scene from da movie Set It Off." She replied; "Well I guess I'm Cleo right now my nigga." Chris reloaded his 4-4 as Queenie added a new clip to 'er Uzi. "Guess its ride and die den boss." Queenie slammed down on da accelerator an tires were heard screechin' from a ten block radius which meant Tez and Cortez' could hear it from da stash house dey jumped in their cars to make da six blocks to where Chris and Queenie were. Non of 'em woulda eva imagined wut dey would see. Queenie once again hit da nitro switch an pointed 'er Uzi out da driver window an Chris did da same thing wit his 4-4. Ola stood their ground an let da gun fire ripe 'til dey noticed Queenie was not stoppin' 'er truck willingly. She dropped 2 officers befo' crashin' through da road block. A big boom was wut everyone heard and saw, when da fellas arrived dey could only see a big ball of fire an clouds of smoke. It was Ola's squad cars blowin' up from da impact,but dey could also see da truck comin' to a slow roll as flames disputed from underneath da hood of it. Miraculously Queenie and Chris were still alive,but Queenie was hit. "Yo' fam' I'm hit homeboy,but we gotta put in some foot work." "Shawty where chu hit?" Queenie replied; "My shoulder and my hip." "Ma can chu make it wit out passin' out?" "Yeah!" Queenie knew as long as 'er adrenaline was at its all time high she would make it. "Nigga run." Queenie yelled as she jumped out da truck. "Stay wit me fo' 2 blocks afta' dat Imma cut off its a straight shoot hit Stony an den yo' ass should know where da house at from dere fam'." Queenie was losin' a lot of blood,but she was determined to make it to da stash house. Figurin' if she clasped or Ola shot 'er down dat 'er family would neva find 'er body 'cus one thing fo' sho' Queenie knew Ola would kill 'er an would not think twice. Chris ran into da crew. "Where da fuck is Queenie bro?" Tez and Cortez' screamed. "She broke off from me 2 blocks away fam'. Yo' she been hit an Ola all ova 'er ass." "Flex pop da trunk, Chris get in da trunk an y'all take his ass back to da house an hit my hitter if Ueenie makes it dere befo' we get back." Tez and Cortez' jumped in Cortez' car an went towards da scene to search fo' Queenie prayin' dat dey reached 'er befo' Ola did. Flex went in da opposite direction headed to da stash house to retrieve Chris from da trunk. Hittin' da corner of Stony Flex pulled in da alley to park in da privacy fence. Dey got out an pop da trunk fo' Chris to get out. Giz'mo said; "Damn bro Ola sound,so close like dey right 'ere." Who would have known Queenie damn near got away,but almost wasn't good a nuff. Ola had Queenie surrounded in front of da house. "Oh shit dats boss in front fam', Flex had jus' hit Tez up. "Bro dey got 'er right 'ere in front of da crib it looks like a ma'fuckin' ambush bro please get 'ere now." Freeze chu got da right to remain silent an anything__Queenie dropped to 'er knees she had lost so much blood she could no longer hold da weight of 'er body. Tez and Cortez' couldn't get threw da barricade so hoppin' out da car dey took off like track stars down da street. Seenin' Queenie fall down put fear in both of their hearts in da worst way. Giz'mo walked from behind da house wit his hands up don't shoot." Screamin' she's been shot. Tez yelled wait wait she needs an ambulance she's been hit." Sir step away from da purp. Tez wit his hands in da air dropped to his knees next to his cousin screamin'; "Call da paramedics fam'." Flex had already called dey were on da way. Cortez' stood on da utter side of his wife while Tez tried to shield his baby girl. "Tez wut is chu thinkin' cuz? Its ova fo' me fam' chu no longer have to put yo' self in harms way fo' me,no mo'. Yo' lil' nigga has put chu through a nuff." Da last words dat came out of Queenie's mouth were; "I love y'all take care of my King." She fell forward an 'er pulse went faint,jus' as da paramedics made it to 'er. Dey put 'er on a gurney an pulled off to U of I hospital.

Dey radio 'er status in as da victim into da trauma center, but it would be only later dey found out dat Queenie was da assassin. "We have looks to be 18 or 19 years old wit 2 gun shot wombs one to left shoulder an one to left hip, pulse is faint an she's lost plenty of blood. We're in route now three blocks to trauma." Dey started a IV on da victim an gave 'er 2cc of Morphine. Ola were already on da scene an da hospital was shut down 'til dey got Queenie to da surgery room. Da crew ran into da hospital wit eyes filled wit tears. "Ma'am dey jus' brung my wife in__he was cut off by da nurse who sat at da nurses station. "I'm sorry sir,but da hospital has instructions from da officers dat yo' wife is under their watch even when she comes outta surgery no one will be able to see 'er. But chu can wait ova dere in dat area,an I will see if I can get some info on 'er an keep chu updated." "Thank ya." Tez said to 'er. "Come on fam' lets go ova 'ere an wait." Joc said; "Bro I called aunties,so Imma go pick 'em up from da hotel." "Preciate it fam' Imma call my moms an talk wit 'em 'til chu get to 'em." Stacks rode wit Joc to help wit lil' Tez. Cortez' was so distraught ova Queenie his heart was in excruciating pain givin' 'em a numb feelin'. Makin' it back from pickin' up Liz and Heather an da baby. Da 2 lady's ran into da hospital only to find everyone cryin' an dey admittedly started cryin' and screamin' all ova. "No,no please don't say its true." Liz thought da worst from all da teary eyes in da room. Giz'mo carried lil' Tez in an stood in a corner tryin' to keep lil' Tez quiet. "Auntie!" Tez hugged an told 'er dat Queenie was in da operatin' room an da nurse jus' went to da back to see if she can find anything out fo' 'em." "Tez wut happen we thought y'all were in yo' suites." "Auntie lets not talk in 'ere lets go outside." Jus' as dey headed out da door da nurse reappeared an gave 'em a lil' info to help ease their pain some. "Excuse me I found out Mrs. Fabs is still in surgery, an da doctor retrieved da bullet from 'er hip,but da bullet shattered a bone,but in time it will mend itself together an da womb to 'er shoulder went clear threw. She lost a lot of blood,so dey tryin' to get 'er stabilize of course she had to have a transfusion. Sirs da utter thing I ova heard da officers talkin' 'bout Mrs. Fabs, dey say she's goin' to da penitentiary behind dis one an she will neva see da light of day again." Dis news made Liz Heather and Cortez' legs buckle at da knees. "Thank chu ma'am." "Its Crystal,an ya welcome, Imma keep y'all posted." Dey all walked outside to da front of da hospital to talk. "Somebody please tell us wuts goin' on,why is my baby on an operatin' table again." Chris spoke up. "Auntie I was wit 'er we went to pay fo' lil' Tez party den we ended up at da Swamp-O-Rama, boss wanted to stop at da airbrushin' booth. I went 2 booths down an hollard at 2 cuties I saw. Boss joked wit me 'bout it. Talkin' wit da females I said who my boss was an da braud screamed out Queenie's name she turned 'round an seen dat it was bro's ex-girl. Auntie I didn't know I knew I seen 'er face befo',but didn't place it. Boss den upped da nine on 'er an it was a shootout in da buildin'. She made me go get da ride afta' I pulled up she ran out an on 'er way to da truck she stopped mid-way turned 'round an jus' started blazin' she unloaded 5 shots droppin' da girls friend den she shot fo' mo' times droppin' Tez ex, but ol' girl was still movin' an dats when boss ran up to 'er an put da last shot in 'er head." Chris started to cry as he tried to finish da story. "Ma den jumped in da truck an told me to drive to da first gas station an she would take ova. Ola closed in on us quick, boss hit da nitro switch an at first I thought we lost 'em,but as we jetted in and out of traffic doin' 190 on da dash Ola was comin' on wit us. Dats when boss did a 360 to go back da utter way an we slammed into a parked semi. Ola must of realized da truck was to fast fo' 'em or somethin' 'cus dey tried to shoot out da tires. Dats when b__boss told me to reach underneath da seat an I handed 'er da Uzi an she swung it out da window behind 'er an let it ride. Dere was no anticipation or hesitation on boss behalf, she den eased up on da accelerator. Boss didn't want me to stay in da truck 'cus she new dat she was finna go threw da barricade Ola had setup fo' 'er. She reloaded, I reloaded an boss told me its ride and die an she hit da nitro an befo' we crash threw da block she killed 2 Ola's an when she told me she had been hit it was time to put in foot work 'cus da truck was on fye." A pause of silence filled da air long a nuff fo' Chris to get da lump out his throat. "Boss I wish she woulda stayed wit me, but I figured she knew wut she was doin' since dis is 'er hometown. But fam' she told me stay on da path I was on an 2 blocks up she cut off an we would meet me at da stash house." Chris cry got louder as he said; "Bro non of dis woulda played out like dis only if I coulda got 'er to stay wit me an we ran in to y'all together." Tez spoke; "Bro we can't dwell on da wut if's, we need to look at da bigger picture 'ere family. Queenie ain't no kid no mo' dis shit 'ere is finna land baby girl in da pen fo' a very long time if not life." "Life!" Liz screamed,so loud it scared lil' Cortez' into a frenzy. Cortez' took his son from Giz'mo an Tez rushed to his aunts side to catch 'er as she fainted."Ma get da doctor out 'ere now." Tez said. Liz was havin' a anxiety attack. Heather ran back out wit a doctor an dey rushed Liz inside to treat 'er fo' hypervenitalatin'. Nurse Crystal came outside an told da family dat Queenie jus' came out of surgery, she was in recovery, an she's stable, so da procedure went good. "Crystal can chu please try to get word fo' us to get back an see 'er befo' Ola takes ova?" She told 'em; "Listen shift change in 30 minutes fo' 'em den 2 utter officers will come on an stand guard, but usually dey take a 15 minute break befo' da next 2 walks through da doors. Once dey leave their post Imma come get three of chu." "Thank chu ma." Afta' she returned to 'er desk Chris asked Tez did he call Mr. D. jet? Which he had already did. "He already on his way fam'." Befo' he could finish Mr. Demontea' walked up. "Mr. D. wutsup my nigga?" Dey all spoke at once. "Mr. Miles wut do we have dis time, hows our girl doin'?" "Well we jus' got word she's fine jus' comin' out of surgery,but dey won't lets go back willingly an check on 'er, but nurse Crystal at da desk been keepin' us posted on da low. She says Ola got custody of Queenie an dey talkin' 'bout 'er goin' down fo' life. Mr. D. Queenie needs chu mo' dan eva now." "Well Tez I need to know exactly wut has taken place an we can go from dere." Chris explained everything dat happened word fo' word again since he was da one wit 'er. "Mr. Miles y'all can see 'er now follow me quickly." Nurse Crystal exclaimed. Tez asked da nurse; "Is it aiight if 'er son went back also?" 'Cus he knew Queenie would be happy to see dat he was aiight. "Yes dats fine as long as chu can keep 'em quiet." Tez, Cortez' and Mr. D. followed 'er to da recovery room. In a whispered she told 'em; "Chu only got 10 minutes." Queenie was groggy from da anesthesia,but was comin' 'round she heard lil' Tez say mama an she opened 'er eyes an a tear ran down 'er cheek. Cortez' leaned in an kissed Queenie on 'er lips den put lil' Cortez' in closer fo' 'er to kiss 'er baby. Tez kissed Queenie on da fo' head an whispered; "Da family out in da waitin' area dey send their love." "We don't have much time,so let me get started. Queenie I heard everything dat happen,so I'm goin' to take dis to court fast as possible,but I need chu to know dis is extreme,so unfortunately chu gonna be sent to da penitentiary. I am goin' to make a phone call an see if I can take yo' case back in front of Judge Webster." Queenie said; "Thank chu Mr. D., but how long befo' dey send me to jail?" "Chu already in custody dey have Ola on guard,so I'm not sho' how long dey givin' chu in da hospital,but as triflin' as Ola can be dey wanta take chu soon as dey get word on chu bein' well a nuff to be moved. Imma talk wit yo' surgeon befo' I leave." "Excuse me Mr. Miles its time." "Baby girl we gotta go kissin' 'er on da fo' head Tez told 'er; "I love chu lil' nigga." Cortez' kissed his wife an let 'er son. "Don't cry shawty jus' let Mr. D. handle it,we love chu." Queenie closed 'er eyes an a nutter tear rolled down 'er face. She visioned da entire scene from earlier an didn't feel anything. Queenie went into deep thought wit 'er conscience.

Chapter Thirty-Eight
"A Killa Has No Remorse"

"It's come to an end huh ma? We didn't expect dis one,so soon huh? A ma'fuckin' volcano opened an we standin' in da pit of it shawty, but now I need yo' ass to remember who da fuck chu is. "Boss Queen" an dis is yo' city an as tragic da situation. Its ma'fuckas in yo' back pocket,so stop all dat punk-ass cryin' an dig down wit in dat pain of urns an bring dat bitch "Boss Queen" to surface." 7am da next mornin' an Ola wasted no time to come an snatch 'er up to wheel 'er off to jail against da doctors orders. Queenie stayed in county jail fo' three months befo' Mr. D. could get 'er in front of a judge. Meanwhile Queenie had to give 'er own self physical therapy since da county wouldn't provide it fo' 'er. A month afta' she started to workout daily a lil' at a time,day by day she regained 'er strength. Da task at hand was hard fo' 'er,but she pulled it off. Da first day she appeared in court Queenie "Boss Queen" walked in wit 'er head held high wit a body to die fo'. Queenie had a slight limp from da bullet womb to da hip,but "Boss Queen" swagg was,so sophisticated no one could tell da limp was dere. Treated like da Queen she carried 'er self as Queenie stood in front of da judge an took 'er time like a champ."Mrs. Fabs I reviewed yo' case an I have no choice,but to send chu to da penitentiary. Mrs. Fabs chu will be sent to a women correctional facility fo' 60 to life. Half da courtroom yelled out in joy an da utter half screamed out wit cries of hurt and heart ache. "Mrs. Fabs do chu have anything to say to da courts?" Judge Webster asked. A nonchalant Queenie nodded 'er head an responded yeah. Queenie turned towards 'er lawyer an said "Thank chu Mr. D." Den she turned back to da judge an he motioned his hand fo' 'er to turn to da courts an make 'er statement. Queenie put on a devilish grin on 'er face an said; "I'm "Boss Queen" fo' all dat don't know I'm dat bitch dat has paid most of yo' bills and fed yo' kids wit no recognition an I have no regrets of wut I did an da time I received 'ere today makes no difference to a bitch of my status.” Da entire courtroom was in shock of wut came outta 'er mouth. Queenie looked at Chris as Ola put da shiny bracelets back on 'er an said; “I am boss “Boss Queen” fo' life ride and die.”

"THROWIN' BRICKS AT THE PENITENTIARY"

This book is wrote in slang or country grammar an Ebonics, so for those who may not know how to speak it or if you would like to know the words meaning when you read this book. I have made a list out for you so will enjoy this novel.

1.her-('er)
2.here-('ere)
3.they-(dey)
4.what-(wut)
5.that-(dat)
6.the-(da)
7.though-(doe)also goes for door
8.over-(ova)
9.you-(chu)
10.for-(fo')
11.them-('em)also goes for him
12.your-(yo')(urn)
13.never-(neva)
14.then-(den)
15.yes-(yeah)
16.alright-(aiight)
17.those-(dose)
18.enough-(a nuff)
19.just-(jus')
20.around-('round)
21.about-('bout)
22.yet-(jet)
23.these-(dese)
24.other-(utter)
25.there-(dere)
26.cousin-(cuz)
27.family-(fam')
28.after-(afta')
29.than-(dan)
30.because-('cus)
31.more-(mo')

"THROWIN' BRICKS AT THE PENITENTIARY"

Acknowledgments

First of all I would like to thank my Lord and Savor Jesus Christ. My achievements wouldn't be possible without him. Many things have happen in my life that no one will ever understand except the man upstairs, but now that I have done it all and seen it all I know what I came here to do. An with him I can see it threw. An to all my love ones that has been there, stood behind me to make this passion come true. I want to thank you all be blessed because I'm me an I'm gonna stay true.

Thanks,
Que

Coming Soon

"THROWIN' BRICKS N THE PENITENTIARY" PART 2

Made in the USA
Columbia, SC
31 January 2021

32072625R00185